"Thief! She killed him!"

Kehrsyn turned and fled blindly as the false witness broke into another fit of coughing.

She ran down the twisting back alleys, dodging barrels of refuse and ducking under laundry lines, puffs of steamy breath peeling from the sides of her panicked face. When she'd been pursued as a child, she'd used her small size, fast feet, and knowledge of the terrain to evade pursuit, but she had none of that left to her. She was an adult, somewhat the weaker for chronic hunger, and had only been in Messemprar a few months. Worst of all, she was outnumbered far worse than she'd ever been as a kid; an entire city's worth of guards and deputized mercenaries had become her foes.

Her only hope was that they hadn't seen her face.

**From the mean streets of Faerûn.
From the edge of civilized society.
From the darkest shadows.**

The Rogues

FORGOTTEN REALMS

THE
ALABASTER
STAFF

EDWARD
BOLME

The Rogues

THE ALABASTER STAFF

©2003 Wizards of the Coast, Inc.

Distributed in the United States by Holtzbrinck Publishing. Distributed in Canada by Fenn Ltd.

Distributed to the hobby, toy, and comic trade in the United States and Canada by regional distributors.

Distributed worldwide by Wizards of the Coast, Inc. and regional distributors.

Printed in the U.S.A.

Cover art by Mark Zug
Map by Dennis Kauth
First Printing: July 2003
Library of Congress Catalog Card Number: 2002114367

9 8 7 6 5 4 3 2

US ISBN: 0-7869-2962-6
UK ISBN: 0-7869-2963-4
620-17885-001-EN

U.S., CANADA,
ASIA, PACIFIC, & LATIN AMERICA
Wizards of the Coast, Inc.
P.O. Box 707
Renton, WA 98057-0707
+1-800-324-6496

EUROPEAN HEADQUARTERS
Wizards of the Coast, Belgium
T Hosfveld 6d
1702 Groot-Bijgaarden
Belgium
+322 467 3360

Visit our web site at www.wizards.com

DEDICATION

For the dedicated volunteers of the International Alliance of Guardian Angels, Inc. I gave them two and a half years and my front teeth. What they gave me was priceless.

ACKNOWLEDGMENTS

Thanks and applause go to: Peter Archer for giving me a new challenge; Phil Athans for telling me it wasn't good enough; Sean K Reynolds for being a bottomless pit of resources; Heather Easterling for tutoring me in High Untheric; Glenn Oliver and Sharon Blackford for looking things over; Jessica Kristine for being such an amazing perfectionist; Dad for raising me right; and Mom for removing my boundaries.

WINGS REACH

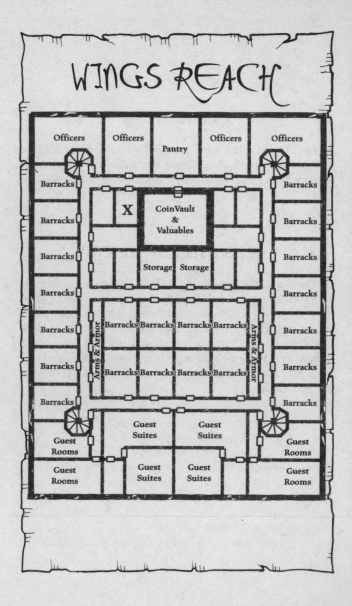

PROLOGUE

THE TIME OF TROUBLES

Zimrilim felt his heart thudding in his chest, beating out what might prove to be the last moments of his life. All his experience, his tenure as a war priest, his pogroms against heretics, his repression of the other churches of the Untheri pantheon, his officiating at the execution of hundreds if not thousands of citizens, his aggressive climb to power in one of the most ruthless religious organizations known, his entire life in a society built upon suffering and hardship, all of that had still left him woefully unprepared for what was happening in this remote field.

They faced a goddess.

Tiamat herself, the Dragon Queen, stood across the field from them, her five scaled heads weaving in a hypnotic serpentine pattern. There was no superlative that surpassed Tiamat's lusty, greedy evil. There was no greater threat to the god-king whom Zimrilim served.

It was true that they had a god on their side, as

well: Gilgeam, Master of Wars; Father of Victory; God of the Sky and the Cities; Supreme Ruler of Unther, Chessenta, Threskel, Chondath, Turmish, the Shaar, and Yuirwood; who had ruled from his throne in Unther with an iron fist for over two thousand years.

The god-king stood tall and proud in the center of their battle line, with not a trace of fear in his handsome face. His golden hair and beard glowed in the sunlight, and for armor he wore only a skirt of bronze scales, each as large and as thick as Zimrilim's hand. Secured by a wide belt that reached up to his ribs, the skirt protected his most vital assets, and left his awe-inspiring physique exposed to enthrall his followers and intimidate his enemies.

It was hard for Zimrilim to imagine a finer physical specimen than Gilgeam. His shoulders were so broad that a grown woman could sit on each comfortably (and, in fact, they often did so at his official debaucheries). His arms had muscles the size of watermelons, with sinews as strong as steel. In his hands he held a great war mace, with a long handle as thick as Zimrilim's arm and topped with a spiked ball of solid bronze that weighed more than Zimrilim could lift.

Gilgeam always kept his body oiled, so that the sun's reflection might better contrast the shadowed crevasses of his chiseled musculature.

The god-king's forces stood arrayed at his direct orders. Nearest him were his high priests, of which Zimrilim was the senior member. Gilgeam's bodyguard, a dozen phalanxes of handpicked troops, surrounded them. A legion of loyal troops protected each flank, their morale bolstered by the petty clergy that moved among them, incanting blessings and prayers. The sycophants, servants, and other non-combatants huddled to the rear, bleating their supplications like sheep, helpless to avoid whatever doom befell Gilgeam's forces.

Under ordinary circumstances, the sight of Gilgeam's

force would send the enemy army into flight . . . but these soldiers had not only refused to flee, they had deliberately sought out the retinue, ambushed the procession as Gilgeam toured his realm.

And while Gilgeam was tall, he was nowhere near as towering as the draconic monster that had challenged him.

Legends said that Tiamat's five heads could spew forth death, each in a different form. Fire, lightning, acid . . . with such a mighty arsenal, Zimrilim knew that mere mortals such as him would not last long in battle with her. They would do their part, of course, fighting with each other in an attempt to sweep away the worship and adoration that supported the two deities, but in the end the outcome would be decided between the two immortals.

The sun reflected off the sweat that beaded Zimrilim's shaved scalp. He wiped his hand across his forehead, smearing the three rings of blue that adorned the front of his brow. The rings were a traditional symbol that identified him as a member of the priesthood and a user of great magic—and a user of magic he would remain, so long as Gilgeam lived. Just as Zimrilim's worship supported Gilgeam, so did Gilgeam's divinity empower Zimrilim's supernatural abilities.

The priest looked across at Tiamat's forces, just beginning their advance. Arrows flew from Gilgeam's troops, striking the first casualties of the day.

He was glad that he was not a soldier, fighting for three meals and a copper a day. They did not comprehend the grave import of the day. He knew that somewhere among the enemy forces was a high priest like himself, and that, like him, the other knew that doom would crush the one or the other. By the end of the day, one of them would be broken, his god dead, his power stripped. At worst he would be dead with no deity to lead him to the afterlife; at best he would survive to flee into hiding and assume a new identity to escape the wrath of the victor's people.

The yoke of destiny weighed on Zimrilim's shoulders. As with all his people, it was a burden he bore gladly, and he knew that whichever side better bore the burden would, in the end, prove victorious.

"There," rumbled Tukulti, the high priest of the City of Firetrees. He gestured with one arm. "I see Furifax. Gilgeam grant that I might crush his skull."

Zimrilim looked, and he saw the banner of the famous outlaw on the other side of the field, and next to it a tall elfin figure mounted astride a swift horse. As they had suspected, then, Tiamat had an alliance with Furifax, at least temporarily. Doubtless Furifax had used his woodsman's skills to lead the Tiamatan forces to the battlefield and arranged to surprise Gilgeam as he journeyed to visit the City of Shussel, where Ekur the Cruel ruled as high priest.

Tiamat's forces closed. Though waiting to receive the charge was agonizing, the melee started all too soon. Zimrilim called down the power of Gilgeam upon his foes, channeling the god-king's divine might through his own body. Tiamat unleashed her terrible weapons upon the assembled troops, felling friend and foe alike. With a mighty roar, Gilgeam leaped to the attack, his mace reaping death as easily as a farmer's sickle hews grain. Blood and limbs, the chaff of battle, flew around wherever the god-king strode.

The noise was unbelievable. Thousands of soldiers pounded upon each other. The clash of bronze, steel, wood, and flesh resounded again and again. The press of the melee threatened to crush Zimrilim. Warriors on both sides pushed forward with their shields, churning the ground, attempting to break the enemy line.

The grunts and screams of the soldiers, the smell of sweat, blood, fear, and death, the gravity of the battle, the chaos at all hands, and the threat of imminent harm all turned each soldier's grand battle into a personal struggle for survival where the horizon stood no more than fifty feet in any direction. Arrows rained indiscriminately. Lightning struck from the cloudless sky, and great gouts of flame erupted from spellcasters' fingers. In the midst of it all, Tiamat towered over the grand melee, her massive heads protecting her great flanks while also trying to strike down her immortal foe.

Zimrilim and Tukulti worked together to keep Tiamat's flank exposed, using their great magic to smite those who sought to protect their vile draconic goddess. Brave Untherite soldiers charged into the gaps rent by the priests' spells and, as Zimrilim and Tukulti prayed for their strength and prowess, tried to pierce the Dragon Queen's hide with spear and sword.

Zimrilim saw one of the sergeants thrust his spear deep into Tiamat's side, then bury it almost entirely in her flesh with another strong heave. Zimrilim cast a glance toward the god-king and saw the golden man break the jaw of one of Tiamat's heads with a fell stroke of his great mace. Zimrilim's lip curled in anticipation of victory; the great beast was faltering!

Just then, Zimrilim heard a thundering noise break into his own private war. He looked up and saw a group of chariots bearing down on their position, intent on striking down the high priests.

"Tukulti!" he cried, and the storm broke upon them.

A long lance wielded by a soldier in the lead chariot impaled Tukulti through the chest, slaying him in an instant. The soldier let the spear drag along the ground behind him until Tukulti's limp body tumbled off.

Zimrilim dodged the spear presented by the second chariot, but the chest of the horse struck him and knocked him senseless. He was dragged by the horses' harness, until he, too, fell off, rolling along the ground to a painful stop.

The high priest's hip ached, and he could feel that several ribs had broken. He assumed he had internal injuries, as well, a presumption proven when he coughed and a fine spray of blood patterned his fist.

Another chariot passed, rolling across his ankle and breaking it. Desperate, he grabbed a shield, and, ignoring the body to which it was still attached, pulled it over his head and chest for protection. He heard a hoof strike the bronze, then was crushed again as a wheel rolled across the shield's boss, but after that the thunder passed, and he dared peer out to see how events had transpired.

As he was not in the heat of the battle, he could take time to scan the whole field from beneath the protection of the dented shield. Great carnage had been wrought, and past the scattered remaining pockets of melee he could see, in the distance, the banners of the Shussel legions approaching quickly. Ekur had indeed received the summons from his god and had sent help.

Heartened, Zimrilim turned the other way to see how his divine leader fared.

Neither of the gods looked healthy. Tiamat bled from over a dozen wounds on her flank, two of her heads were held away from the melee, and a third seemed to be unconscious on the ground. Her tail lashed angrily, keeping away any others who might try to spear her but also striking down anyone who strayed too close while protecting her. Gilgeam staggered with exhaustion. His beautiful golden hair had been scorched in places, and his skin showed raw where acid, flame, and searing cold had eaten it away. The haft of his mace had been splintered, and he wielded the item one-handed, the other arm held close to his chest. Zimrilim could not tell if Gilgeam nursed a broken arm or several fractured ribs . . . perhaps both.

Tiamat reared up her right foreleg, preparing to smash her enemy flat, while baiting Gilgeam with her two remaining heads. Gilgeam charged forward, swinging his mace in a circle around his head to strike a devastating blow at the breastbone of the Dragon Queen, left exposed by her maneuver . . . and he fell right into her trap. With an agility that seemed impossible for a beast of her size, she hopped up with her left foreleg, and, with a swipe backed by her massive weight, smote Gilgeam on his fully exposed side. The crack of breaking bones resounded across the battlefield, and Gilgeam pinwheeled through the air. He landed on his shoulders with a crunch a few yards away from Zimrilim, tumbled end over end, and stopped as his head struck Zimrilim's shield with a clang. Tiamat thundered to earth as well, her heads studying her foe.

In the stunned silence that followed that crucial moment, Zimrilim heard the last breath rattle its way out of Gilgeam's divine breast.

Tiamat turned and roared her defiance at Ekur's approaching forces, then lurched her way back onto her feet. Using two of her heads to carry the unconscious head by the scruff, she retreated from the field, limping. She managed to get airborne before she reached the edge of the forest, her flight as ungainly as that of an aged albatross.

As the sounds of battle ceased, Zimrilim let his head fall back into the mud, coughed once, and waited as waves of despair washed over him until blessed darkness closed his eyes.

Fifteen years later . . .

CHAPTER ONE

In times of war, the gates of Messemprar closed each evening at sundown and did not open again until a sliver of the sun could be seen rising above the waves of the Alamber Sea. The guards strictly observed the rule in accordance with the city's extensive laws—a compilation of regulations, fiat, common sense, and bureaucratic whimsy all carefully inscribed in a huge aggregation of conflicting scrolls dutifully assembled and catalogued throughout the city's three-thousand, four-hundred-year history. Clever administrators occasionally "lost" a scroll filled with particularly troublesome requirements, but the bulk of the ancient papyrus still weighed upon the city's populace like a well-worn yoke, providing direction and security, if not freedom.

Outside the city, however, those time-honored directives offered little consolation, especially in mid-winter. A large crowd of pitiful refugees huddled in the lee of the city walls, poorly sheltered from the cold, moist easterly wind that blew in from the sea. It was bad enough that the sun was nearing the winter solstice and thus rose nearly as late as it ever did during the year, but, even worse, slate-colored clouds covered the midwinter sky. When the city guard could not see the sun rise to the east, they delayed opening the gate, just to ensure that the sun god Horus-Re had indeed ascended.

The refugees huddled like helpless sheep, an analogy that occurred to the guards who paced atop the walls, furled in heavy cloaks. Confident in the refugees' chill misery, they drew their chins deep within the folds of their cloaks, and, their minds turned to their own discomfort, they did not notice that one of the refugees, impatient for the gates to announce the dawn, stealthily climbed the city walls.

His name was Jaldi. He was small, but his clean and experienced movements showed that he'd put several rigorous adolescent years behind him. He scaled the wall easily, as the ancient stone offered many good holds for his strong, thin fingers. He made no more noise than a spider and climbed as rapidly as one, as well. Dressed in drab, ragged clothing and hidden in a shadowed angle of the weather-stained wall, he was nearly invisible.

The chill wind cut through his scant clothing, but Jaldi preferred to endure an extra bit of cold over sitting any longer in that rank and foul-mouthed crowd, waiting for the chance to enter Messemprar legally. There was also the simple fact that he had no coin to pay the entry fee and thus would have to try to dodge behind the gate guards yet again. Better to dodge them on his terms, atop a darkened wall, than on theirs, at a narrow and crowded gate.

As he neared the top of the wall, the salt-smelling wind blew unfettered by trees or refugees, and it pierced the small holes in his jersey like a spear, turning the sheen of his sweat into painful patches of cold. As he had no fat on his lithe body, he was forced to use his tongue to keep his teeth from chattering, though, thankfully, his hands remained sure as he scaled the precipice.

Jaldi's fingers probed the gap at the base of the topmost stones of the wall, looking for secure purchases. A bronze climbing spike, pounded into the crack between two stones centuries ago by Chessentan mercenaries, offered its pitted surface as a handhold, but, like most citizens of Unther, Jaldi felt safer relying on venerable Untheri stone. He found a cleft, brushed away the moss that had accumulated there, and pulled his head close to the top of the wall. He held the position for no little time, rolling his eyes in juvenile impatience as time seemed to slow to a stop. Soon he saw the tip of a spear, barely visible over the rampart, slowly working its way toward his position like an inverted pendulum. He ducked his head.

The wind interfered with his hearing, so he pressed one ear to the cold stonework. Through the stone he heard the slow step of a miserable guard walking the monotonous pace of the exhausted soldier. As the noise passed his position, he hazarded a quick glance over the parapet. The guard indeed had passed, head down, shuffling along the wall.

Jaldi pulled himself up and rolled over the battlement, dropping quietly on the inside of the waist-high stonework that gave cover to the guards on the wall. Jaldi glanced left. The guard that had just passed continued pacing his post. Glancing right, he saw the next guard, a long arrow's shot away, just turning and starting to hobble his frigid way back toward Jaldi's position, dark against the lightening sky.

Jaldi scuttled crabwise to the inner side of the wall and glanced down. The interior edge of the wall's walkway dropped into the cramped, labyrinthine streets of Messemprar. The lack of any kind of barrier or crenellations on the interior side made wall duty rather more dangerous for the guards when a storm rose, but it certainly made life easier for a roguish young interloper seeking free entry.

He swung his legs over the wall, then flipped over to his stomach and slid down to his ribs, holding himself steady by propping himself up on his elbows. His feet searched the interior stonework for a foothold, rooting around the way a dog's nose roots through a pile of rubbish. He glanced right and saw that the receding guard was still oblivious.

Jaldi's feet continued to scrabble, finding no crevices worthy of the name. He looked over his shoulder at the more distant guard to his left. As he watched, he saw the guard pause, peer forward, and straighten in surprise. If the guard yelled something, the wind caught it before it reached Jaldi's ears, but the guard's gesture was unmistakable. Jaldi had been seen.

Glancing down, he saw a straw-thatched roof below him, some meager house built right up against the city's walls. With a quick prayer to any available god that might look after petty rascals like himself, Jaldi let go his perch. As he fell, he pushed off from the wall, both to distance himself from the cold stone and to try to align his body to land as flat as possible against the sloping roof and absorb the impact of his fall.

Jaldi landed awkwardly on the roof, jarring his head and feeling a pain shoot through his lung. He heard a crack and hoped that it was a thatching strut and not one of his ribs. He slid off the roof and dropped onto the street.

He landed on his feet on the rough and stony ground. With a quick glance up, he saw that neither of the two closest guards could see him at the moment. As quick as a monkey, he scuttled back up the side of the house, in the corner where it met the great stone wall, and sequestered himself among the eaves, wriggling slowly and patiently into the insulating straw thatch until he was well concealed.

He made himself as comfortable as his unusual situation

would allow and hoped the grumbling of his stomach would not give him away before the guards tired of searching for one lone urchin.

❂

By midmorning, the city streets and markets were filled with activity. Jaldi padded through the edges of the crowd, his fast, youthful reflexes directing him through the jostling throngs like a fish through a hard current. He could feel the movements of the crowd. His years spent as an urchin had taught him to sense the mood of the people and therewith the source and probable cause of any rippling disturbance. Sometimes it was danger, as when the Mulhorandi army first marched across the River of Swords and attacked his village, but occasionally it was entertainment, as when some criminal was dragged forth and pilloried to the amusement of the public.

Usually, though, the mood of the crowd warned him when a whip of constables was approaching, looking for little thieves like him . . . and receiving that warning had often kept him in possession of his hands. Untheric justice was as creative as it was cruel and thus served Jaldi both as a diversion and as a goad to excellence, for he determined that he would never be caught at his work. In his few years, he had seen tortures the like of which were unknown outside the Old Empires, punishments that the public and accused alike not only bore without comment, but prided themselves upon withstanding with great solemnity. It was the firm belief of all Untherites that the mark of a high culture was to promote at once high arts and ruthless punishment, and to appreciate both with equal aplomb.

In that hour, however, the mood of the crowd spoke of hope. And since the Mulhorandi invasion a year and a half ago, the hope of the crowd meant one thing: food.

Jaldi vividly remembered seeing the Green Lands get

churned into mud by the armies of Mulhorand and Unther during the opening months of the campaign, when he had been pressed into service as a camp slave for his people's army. His left triceps still bore the scar of the slave branding. When the Mulhorandi army emerged victorious, Unther lost not only its field army, but also the crops that were meant to feed the majority of its populace.

The enemy forces had besieged and taken Unthalass, capitol of Unther, during which time Jaldi had made his escape from military duties. Since then, the Mulhorandi had driven a swarm of refugees before them. He, like many others, had fled north, pursued by the invaders until the River of Metals and Messemprar itself were all that stood between Mulhorand and the complete conquest of Unther.

Thus Messemprar was the last refuge of the Untheri, a city bloated to thrice its natural size by the influx of fearful peasants, wounded soldiers, and desperate officials. The city's stocks of food had run out quickly, causing everyone to feel the pangs of hunger. The raw, gnawing feeling of empty stomachs turned society's solid foundations into greasy, treacherous slopes, and he had seen just how fast the most noble of people could fall to barbarism over a scrap of food. The hands of justice were swift these days, swift and brutal, lest defiance breed upon defiance, and all order be lost.

These were interesting days for the young thief. Everyone was suspect, for a change, for hunger made a thief out of even the wealthiest noble, yet whereas before he might have faced a flogging for his petty theft, in these hard days he would surely be killed for stealing food.

He glided through the crowd toward the docks, where his instinct told him the source of the crowd's hope could be found. Most likely a merchant ship had slipped past the Mulhorandi navy and arrived with a cargo of precious foodstuffs. Though such journeys risked annihilation by the Mulhorandi, the cargo sold for exorbitant prices, purchased with Untheric iron, cloth goods, slaves, and priceless antique art. It was a seller's market for food.

Good living for a thief . . . if he could survive it.

A throng milled at the quay that jutted out into the Alamber Sea, where a deep-drafted merchant vessel had moored just inside the breakwater at the Long Wharf, flying a proud black pennant emblazoned with a gold Z. Stevedores, stripped to the waist but still wearing their heavy winter breeches and boots, lumbered up and down the ship's gangway, unloading the vast cargo. The city guard had turned out in force and kept the pressing throng back, while merchants and nobles pushed forward in bids to do business with the captain. Shouts, oaths, laughter, the jingle of coin, and the thump of heavy crates and barrels being dumped on the dock filled the area with a great din.

The crowd pressed, and Jaldi saw one of the guards waving his khopesh, a vicious sword curved inward the better to cleave naked limbs. The young thief smiled. The greater the tension between the guards and the mob, the lesser the attention for a larcenous rat like him.

He slid past the rear of the crowd, edging his way farther out on the dock. When it became impossible to continue, he lowered himself beneath the dock, using the gaps between the ill-fitted planks for finger holds, and continued toward the ship. His feet dragged in the icy seawater, and those above occasionally trod upon his fingertips, but he was Untherite; such trials were the bread and water of his people.

He worked his way around the edge of the dock until he was behind—and beneath—the unloaded cargo. Peering between the gaps in the planks, he located a site already piled high with crates, sacks, and barrels, and therefore concealed from the view of the guards and stevedores. He crawled back on top of the dock and pulled a small knife from his belt. With a few moments' work he pried open the lid of a barrel filled with cured meats. Stuffing his soiled jersey as much as he could without disrupting his scrawny appearance, he replaced the pried lid and disappeared once more beneath the wooden dock.

Two more bruised fingertips and a pair of frigid feet later, he was back on land, hiding in an alleyway and breaking his fast in as royal a fashion as he could imagine . . . but his thoughts kept wandering to the Jackal's Courtyard and what awaited him at noontime.

❂

By midday, a chill drizzle washed over the streets of Messemprar, brushed around by the remnants of the morning's east wind and filling the streets with the smell of winter. At the moment, Kehrsyn was warm enough. She wore a faded green long slit skirt hemmed with gold over white leggings that tucked into her nearly knee-high brown leather boots. Her heavy violet blouse was laced with a leather cord from her sternum to her throat and a bright gold sash bound it around her waist. Her hands were bare. Over everything, she wore a brown cloak with a wide hood. The quilted pattern of the inside made it look almost like a cobra's hood when pulled up, an image she felt gave her some protection. The merchant had promised the cloak was waterproof. Unlike the merchant's word, the cloak was better than nothing.

She paused under an overhang before entering the square, surveying the crowd with auburn eyes. Brisk trading took place all around, precious food changed hands, along with coins and goods. The crowd was busy, but it was in a good mood. All Kehrsyn had to do was get people's attention. Given that she'd been performing in the same spot in the Jackal's Courtyard for a tenday, she hoped it wouldn't be too tough.

She didn't know how the Jackal's Courtyard got its name. She'd heard a jackal once stood guard over the area, though she wasn't sure if that was a literal truth or if the large, shivered pole in the center of the square had once been surmounted by the graven image of a beast-headed god of the ancient Mulan, progenitors of Unther and Mulhorand alike.

She pushed back her hood, pulled the collar of her cloak more closely around her neck, and stepped out into the drizzle. It would have been more comfortable to wear the hood up, but it was harder to dazzle a crowd when the people couldn't see your face. A smile, a wink, and an air of nonchalance were all essential to her performance.

She strode over to the great, decapitated pillar and set her small shoulder bag of props down at its base. She pulled out a small box and opened its lid, providing those of generous heart a place to gift her with a few coppers or, should she manage to charm one of the haughty nobility, a whole silver. Her rapier she kept at her side; the city was at war, overcrowded, and hungry, so it seemed only prudent.

She looked again at the crowd. A number of people were looking at her, perhaps knowing what was to come, perhaps curious as to what the slim young woman was setting up in the center of the plaza. Here stood a small child whose tongue dabbed at the bottom of her nose, there watched a young boy trying to evade her eyes, and over there stood a cluster of guards and soldiers, no doubt speaking of her in salacious phrases.

Feigning obliviousness to the eyes upon her, she reached up and untied her brown ponytail, hair so dark it was almost black. She fluffed her locks around her shoulders, knowing that the motion of her long hair—her mane, some called it—would draw attention. And lo! when she drew her hands out, she held a bouquet of flowers, which she brought to her nose and smelled daintily.

She paused, savoring the scent, then glanced up beneath her eyebrows and saw that she indeed had the full attention of the soldiers, two of whom had their mouths wide open in surprise.

The little girl with the darting tongue toddled over to her, unsteady on the rain-slicked cobbles.

"How do do it?" she asked, her tongue still bobbing.

Kehrsyn smiled and kneeled down, her cloak crumpling against the ground, and she asked, "Would you like to smell them?"

The girl put her face into the parchment flowers and sniffed at the perfume fragrance.

" 'Mell good," the girl proclaimed.

"Hey," said Kehrsyn, "you have a jewel in your ear. Did you know that?"

The girl furrowed her brows and tugged uncertainly at one ear as her tongue once more wiped her upper lip clean.

"Not that one," teased Kehrsyn. "This one."

So saying, she reached out with her hand, gently caressed the curve of the girl's ear, and produced a small, polished stone with the hue and grain of well-varnished wood.

The girl squealed, "Momma! Momma, lookit my ear! Lookit she saw my ear!"

She ran back over to her mother, holding her "jewel" aloft, stumbling on the cobbles in her glee but never quite falling. The mother turned on the child with a look of weary frustration but softened as the child's exuberance overflowed. The child pointed back at Kehrsyn, and the woman favored Kehrsyn with a knowing look. Taking the girl by the hand, the mother put her worn purse back into her sash and strode away.

Kehrsyn sighed and stood up again, her slender hand reaching for the hidden fold in her sash and palming another stone from the score she carried there for just that purpose. It felt good to bring some small joy to a little soul in the midst of the cold, hungry winter. She didn't want anyone to experience the same grim childhood she'd had.

Let the adults worry about the enemy that stalked the lands across the river; children needed to have their fun. So long as Kehrsyn could keep the war from stealing their innocence, she would.

She just wished it was a little easier to get their parents to show a little charity.

Despite her mother's miserly demeanor, the little girl had attracted Kehrsyn some attention, just as she'd hoped. The beginnings of an audience were forming, most notable of whom were the soldiers, who walked up to her directly.

"Olaré!" said one in greeting. "So you're a sorceress, huh?"

One of his mates, jealous that the other had spoken first, punched him roughly on the arm and said, "Of course not, half-wit. Where's the aura? You ever seen a magician without a glow about her spells?"

"Actually, yes," said a third, a seasoned veteran and clearly the senior of the rowdy group. "It's rare, but it's not unknown. Why, back in Chessenta, in, uh, fifty-four I think it was, I—"

"Come on, Sergeant," said the first, "we hear your stories all night in the bunkhouse. I'd rather hear this maiden's voice right now." A murmur of general agreement settled the issue. "So, young one," he continued, addressing Kehrsyn directly, "are you a sorceress?"

Kehrsyn chuckled and answered, "Of course not."

"I think she is," commented another soldier with a smile. "She's already charmed me."

Kehrsyn flushed with embarrassment.

"So if you're not a sorceress," asked the first, "how can you do all that stuff without magic?"

"It's easier without magic," she said, then she leaned forward toward the soldier. "It's easy to make jewels appear," she said in a stage whisper, "when guys like you don't groom yourselves properly."

With that, she tapped at his nose, striking it so that a

polished stone appeared to fly from his nostril, knocked loose by the flick of her finger.

The soldier stepped back, too startled to know whether or not to be affronted. His comrades laughed uproariously and showered him with a variety of new nicknames, from Gemfinger to Noseminer to Rocksnot.

The officer stepped forward, heedless that an audience had gathered.

"You're a gambler, aren't you?" he asked in a gravelly voice.

"No, I—I don't have any coin," said Kehrsyn. "Not even a wedge."

"A likely story."

"It's true," protested Kehrsyn. She turned to the sparse crowd around her. "But if one of you wants to loan me a coin," she said loudly, "I'll pay you back double."

A half dozen coppers presented themselves, but she picked the lone silver egora offered by a merchant's hand and favored the worthy with a wink and a bright, wide smile.

"All right," she said to the sergeant. "You see this egora, right? This side is crowns, and this side is verses. Crowns, verses. I'll bet you this egora against one of your own. Done?"

The sergeant nodded assent.

Kehrsyn suppressed a smile and said, "Are you ready? Watch closely." She held out her right hand and placed the coin on it. "There, it's showing crowns, right? Crown side up, got it? Now watch closely."

She held her left hand out next to her right, palm down. With a flick as fast as an arrow, she flipped her right hand down on top of her left, concealing the coin against the back of her left hand.

"Now, Sergeant," she said, "tell me which side is up: crowns or verses."

The sergeant snorted, "Verses, of course."

Kehrsyn faked a heavy sigh and lifted her hand.

"Sergeant," she said, "you weren't paying attention."

The crowd gasped; the coin showed crowns. The sergeant blinked a few times and did nothing until the elbowing of his troops prompted him to give Kehrsyn a silver egora.

"All right, let's try it again, shall we?" said Kehrsyn.

The sergeant nodded.

"Look," she said, "we'll try it a different way. I'll put verses side up this time. Got it? Verses up. Remember that. Ready? Verses up." Again she flipped her hand over with the speed of a falcon. "For a silver, Sergeant, which side is up?"

"It was verses up," mumbled the sergeant to himself, ensuring he had been paying full attention and remembering the chain of events properly, "and you flipped your hand over, so now it has to be crowns. Crowns up," he said.

"Sergeant, I'm trying to help. I gave you the answer, you know. I said, 'Verses up.' Three times I did."

When she lifted her hand, the coin indeed showed verses. The crowd cheered, most especially the soldiers. The sergeant handed over another egora.

Urged by those around, the sergeant agreed to a third guess. Kehrsyn placed crowns up once more and flipped her hand, but before the sergeant could say anything, the soldier known as Noseminer stepped up.

"I'll make the guess this time, wench," he said, "and I'll wager three egorae against all three of yours!"

Kehrsyn paused and glanced around, her face paling.

"Uh . . . but the sergeant . . ." she stammered.

"I'm onto your trick," Noseminer proclaimed. He clamped his hands on hers, ensuring that she couldn't manipulate the coin. "The guess is mine. Don't back out!"

Kehrsyn recovered some of her composure and said, "You—you don't have three silvers on you to wager, so I decline."

Ordering one of his fellows to keep a tight hold on Kehrsyn's hands, Noseminer emptied his purse and indeed found he had only one egora's worth of copper on him. So, while carefully watching to ensure she held her hands perfectly still, he quickly borrowed two others from his peers.

"There you are," he proclaimed. "Three silvers, even if two are in copper. Now show the coin!"

"Your guess?" asked Kehrsyn.

"Crowns!" barked the soldier.

"You're sure you won't change your mind?"

"Quit trying to flummox me and show the coin!"

Kehrsyn lifted her hand. The egora very plainly showed verses. The audience erupted in laughter and applause. In the midst of the noise, the soldier stared at her in shock and anger.

"The trick," she told him, "is knowing when to stop."

But before she could scoop the coins from his hand, Noseminer clenched his fist and stormed off, followed by the jeers of the gathered crowd. The rest of the soldiers ambled off as well, chuckling to themselves.

Despite having been shortchanged, Kehrsyn still had a profit to show for her efforts. She paid the merchant back two silvers as she had promised, and received an ovation for her honesty. But, in the end, applause was all that the crowd was willing to part with.

She performed prestidigitation and sleight of hand through the early afternoon, to an ever-changing crowd that watched with enough interest to withstand the drizzle, if only for a short while. Finally, however, the ongoing drizzle chilled her thoroughly, and her hands began to shiver. She had to stop. She looked into her little box, open at her feet. Save a thin film of water, it was empty. She had nothing to show for her efforts but a single silver egora and the fading memories of a score or more of bright, young faces. One silver for a young woman with nothing to eat and no place to stay. . . .

She hoped the children's happy memories of her would last longer than her pittance.

CHAPTER TWO

Kehrsyn had stopped her performance, but the shopping in the plaza showed no sign of winding down, despite the cold rain. The initial crowds drawn by the arrival of a new shipment of food were thinner, but still persistent in the face of prices that had doubled, then doubled again. Chilled guards scowled over the newly arrived edibles, while the city watch occasionally roughed someone up.

Probably just trying to keep warm, thought Kehrsyn.

She gathered her gear and pulled her hood over her rain-dampened hair. Kneeling, she tipped the water out of her small box and closed the lid, put it back into her bag, and slung the bag's strap across her shoulder. As she rose, she saw a scrawny youth standing nearby. Kehrsyn recognized him. He'd been hanging around the fringe of the crowd, trying to pretend he hadn't been watching her. He met her eyes, then dropped his gaze, then tried to look at her again but more or less failed and stared in the general vicinity of her neck.

"Yes?" she said.

"You're real good, Miss," he mumbled. He reached out one hand to her, hiding his face behind his shoulder. He held a large, ripe golden pear in his grip. "Um . . . here."

She took the offering with both hands and smiled.

"Thank you," she said. "Thank you very much. What's your name?"

"Jaldi," said the lad, with a self-conscious smile. He paused, then blurted, "You're real pretty, too." Then he turned and ran away.

Kehrsyn waved at his rapidly retreating back, but he didn't look behind him before he left her sight. She took a big, contented bite of the pear, staring vacantly in the direction the boy had gone.

The delight engendered by his awkward compliment faded and was replaced by a cool dread. The boy's admiration had put her in mind of the sole other member of the audience who'd watched her entire performance: a harsh-looking man with swarthy features and a dark green cloak. At first, she had taken him for one of the army, so military was his bearing. He had situated himself here and there around the plaza, never obvious, always where the view was best, leaning against a wall or wagon, arms folded across his chest, eyes narrowed, running his thumb back and forth over his lower lip.

She turned, chewing her lunch, and skimmed the courtyard. There, to her right. The same man was still watching her, over by the horse trough next to the black-smith's. While Kehrsyn liked admirers as much as any-one, there was something in the man's stance that was far too businesslike for her tastes, as if he looked on her as an adversary and not a potential flirtation.

Kehrsyn casually walked out of the courtyard. She paused to inspect a blade offered by an arms merchant (weapons were priced almost as exorbitantly as food) and, turning the polished bronze weapon in her hand to reflect the Jackal's Courtyard behind her, caught a glimpse of the dark man moving parallel to her on the other side of the plaza. He was shadowing her, to her left and rear.

The merchant stooped under his table, and Kehrsyn's hand strayed to her sash, but she remembered her vow and forced herself to return the blade with a "thank you" and a dazzling smile. She continued on her way to a street leading off the plaza. Once out of the man's view, she increased her speed and turned into an angled street on her right, quickly enough that he—whoever he was— could not have seen her.

Just to be safe, she picked up her speed even more, then ducked into a narrow alley that opened to her left, keeping her free hand on her rapier to keep it from bouncing around. She wasn't certain where the alley led, but, whoever it did, she was certain that she had evaded the stranger.

Though the alley protected her from the chill breeze, the rain and the cold remained, enhanced somewhat by the foul smells of rotting refuse. For once, Kehrsyn found a reason to thank the cold weather. In the summers, alleys stank something foul. Her breath steamed around her limp hair as she moved down the alleyway, looking for an outlet to another avenue. Navigating by instinct, she moved through the narrow, winding gap, passing a few branches before coming to a dead end. She paused and stared blankly at the wall in front of her, concealed as high as her waist by a pile of decomposing garbage. She pulled a lock of wet hair out of her face and retraced her steps, but just as she arrived at the first juncture, she saw her way blocked by an armed man.

She was relieved to see that it wasn't the same man from the plaza . . . and, for just a moment, she also felt a slight pang of disappointment.

He was short, shorter than she. The steam curling from his sneering lip combined with his powerful build to give the impression of a bull or a fighting dog. A thick cloak covered his head and shoulders, and a black tabard with some sort of gold emblem draped off his wide chest, the hem shedding droplets that splashed in the dirty puddles at his feet. A shield hung across his back. He straightened as he saw Kehrsyn approach, and her ears picked up the grate of steel on steel. He's wearing mail beneath his cloak, Kehrsyn thought, splint or scale.

"Olaré," she said, for lack of anything better, and took another bite of her pear. "So, um, what kind of uniform is that? That's no soldier's outfit that I know. And you don't have that medallion the Northern Wizards' people wear. Are you a mercenary? Or some kind of deputized . . . "

Kehrsyn's words trailed off as the burly man drew a long sword from a well-crafted scabbard. He swung it at his side in a lazy figure eight and stepped toward her.

Kehrsyn jumped to an unwanted conclusion.

"I'll scream," she said.

"Go ahead," said the man in a surprisingly high-pitched voice with a noticeable northwestern accent. "If the local pikegrabbers get here, I don't gotta trot you all the way over to the damn barracks to get my bounty."

Kehrsyn furrowed her brow.

"Don't try to act so damn innocent, pretty little thief," he said, sounding more like a juvenile than the veteran he clearly was. "You stole that pear, and there's a bounty on freeloaders like you."

Kehrsyn's eyes widened as she stared at the half-eaten piece of fruit in her hand.

"I did no such thing!" she blurted.

She began edging backward, down the dead-end alley.

"Of course not," replied the man, " 'cuz I hear that in this city, if you steal food, they don't chop your hand, they chop your damn neck."

"I didn't steal it!" said Kehrsyn, knowing how thin her protests must sound. "It was a gift! This boy, he liked—" She halted her tongue before she said, "he liked my performance," knowing full well it would be taken the wrong way. "He liked me . . ." she continued, even more flustered.

"Uh-huh," said the man, swinging the blade unconsciously in his right hand. "We dock here only this damn morning, and soon as we get them pears out, someone steals a whole damn bunch. You leave the market, eating a damn pear. I follow, and you walk faster. When I get close, you run and duck into this damn alley, and now you say you din't do nothin'. Well too damn bad for you." Then, looking her over, he added, "Though you maybe could work a deal. The others would like the looks of you, all nice and thin like that. The Zhentarim can be . . . merciful. At times."

"I—I didn't s-steal it," stammered Kehrsyn as she continued her slow retreat. Her stomach tightened in knots. "Ask the people at the square. I was performing."

"Quit your damn bleating."

He reached for her with his free hand, but Kehrsyn hopped lightly backward. Glancing at his extended arm, she saw that he indeed wore splint mail. He stepped forward. She dropped her pear and drew her rapier, holding it defensively in front of her with her left hand. As she'd hoped, that caused him to pause briefly. He lowered himself as if to spring.

The man studied her, negligently describing easy, lethal arcs with his sword beside him. For a moment, as he examined her stance, he wore the ruthless face of a tiger, then a cruel smile pulled up one corner of his mouth.

He saw the point of Kehrsyn's rapier trembling ever so slightly. The rain dripped. The fearful trembling grew. His smile widened, as did Kehrsyn's eyes.

The man straightened up again, nodding in smug disdain.

"So pussycat thinks she's got a claw, huh?" he mocked. "Here's what I think of that!"

He swung his sword crosswise and slapped the blade from her hand with a flagrant, sweeping backhand blow, sending it clattering against the stone wall of the alley. As he did so, Kehrsyn was already thrusting with a dagger in her right hand—her good hand—the blade held vertically the better to slip between the strips of metal splints. Too late the man saw that he had fallen for her bait—believed her trembling, fearful feint—and left his body wide open for a counterattack. The long stiletto struck the man at the top of the thigh, just where his leg joined his abdomen, cutting tendons and lancing innards.

Though he yet felt no pain, instinctively the man was already doubling over to protect his groin. He tried to strike Kehrsyn with his return stroke, but she nimbly dodged the blow and countered by tracing a gash across one eyebrow.

The man's traumatized hip gave way and he crumpled to his knees. He glared at her, but the blood welling up from his cut brow started to sting his eye. Just as he winced, Kehrsyn stepped forward and kicked him as hard as she could on the chin, sending the man backward. He flopped on the pavement, his lower legs doubled back underneath him.

He groaned as Kehrsyn gingerly cleaned her dagger on his trousers. She sheathed the blade in its hidden pouch on the bottom of her bag, then recovered her pear and her rapier, which was, thankfully, undamaged.

Glancing back, she saw that the man, despite his injuries and his irritated eyes, had pulled a small vial of bright blue liquid from his sword belt with a trembling hand and was moving it toward his lips.

In an instant the point of her rapier planted itself just behind the wounded man's ear.

"A healing potion? No, you don't . . . not yet," she said. "You can drink it when I'm safely away, so why don't you just put it back for now, hmm?"

He obeyed, if feebly, slipping the potion back into its hidden resting place, and Kehrsyn breathed easier that she'd not had to follow through on her implied threat.

Kehrsyn stepped around him, flicking her rapier's point to his throat.

"Oh, and while we're at it. . . ." she added.

She squatted beside him, taking care not to dirty her knees with the alley mud. She placed her half-eaten pear on her lap and patted the man down until she felt his coin purse tucked behind his belt.

"In Unther, we don't like foreigners trying to arrest innocent people. There's a fine of, um . . ." She yanked his coin purse off his belt, though it took two or three tries before the thin leather thongs snapped. "Three coppers? You pathetic *pah!*"

Kehrsyn looked at the three small coins. Given the day's events, she really needed them. She clenched and unclenched her fist and bit her lip, but she threw them down the alley.

She picked her pear back up and stood.

"You count to fifty before you try drinking that potion in your belt, you hear me?" she said, redirected anger adding force to her words. "And don't you go looking for those coppers. Understand?"

He nodded.

Kehrsyn took two incautious steps, paused for two breaths, then took two more steps, all to give the man the illusion that he'd hear her when she left.

She intended to glide silently away, but just as she was about to leave the hapless merchant's guard, she heard the sound of clapping.

CHAPTER THREE

Startled by the sudden applause (even if it only issued from a single pair of hands), Kehrsyn jumped forward, spinning with remarkable grace, and drew her rapier again, swinging it from side to side. The whispering sound of the blade slicing the air did nothing to dissipate the loud, arrogant clapping.

The ovation made up in wet loudness what it lacked in quantity of hands, and the narrow, angled alley echoed the sound all around the startled young woman. Glancing around, Kehrsyn saw the alley was empty of anyone other than the wounded soldier and herself, but as her heart slowed to a more reasonable speed, she finally figured out the situation.

She hazarded a look up. Despite the overcast, the sky shone brighter than the narrow alley, especially since the winter sun was edging toward the horizon, leaving the alley in relative shade. Kehrsyn shielded her eyes from the diffused light and the drizzling rain with the hand holding her pear.

There, above her, the silhouette of someone's torso peered over the roof, elbows moving in rhythm with the clapping sound. Just as she spotted her audience, the person stopped clapping and leaned out over the edge of the roof.

"Ooh, that was slick, hon," said a hoarse, dusky female voice. It had a nasal tinge, as if the speaker was thoroughly congested. "You dropped that pasty-face like a poleaxed heifer."

Kehrsyn narrowed her eyes, trying to get any better idea of what the interloper looked like, but all she could see was the black of the silhouette.

" 'Bout as strong as a piece of moldy bread, I'd say, but you got the dance down right. Yessirree." She paused to cough and clear her throat.

"What do you mean?" asked Kehrsyn, stalling, trying to find a better angle to look at her. Had the sun been out, Kehrsyn might have been able to settle herself into a shadow to eclipse some of the brightness, but the clouds evenly scattered the light that bled through.

"I mean I wouldn't bet a half-eaten herring on you to wrestle a wolf pup three falls of five, but you got the eyes of a hawk and the strike of a viper." She paused to clear her throat, hawked up something vile from her lungs, and spat down the alley to Kehrsyn's left. "Yessirree, I don't think a black hare could slip past you at midnight under a new moon."

"Well, thank you," said Kehrsyn as she started to back away.

"Oh, don't be scootin' off now, hon. No, that wouldn't be the best snap of your nut today. We need someone the likes of you."

Kehrsyn paused. The guard, one hand pressed against his bleeding leg, started to try to pull himself back up into a sitting position.

"What do you mean?" asked Kehrsyn, only partially

focused on the conversation. Most of her mind was filled with watching the guard she'd had to discommode, while also unobtrusively searching for the best escape.

"Heard that question already, missy, so let me put it to you simply. We've been watching you back there in the plaza. You got real good hands. Long, slim, and agile. Your body's about the same way, for that matter. And you can use them like nobody's business, too. Your hands, that is. You make stuff appear and disappear like you were a regular fire-slinging scroll-thumper. And I should know."

The woman's silhouette leaned precariously over the edge of the rooftop. Just as Kehrsyn was sure she'd fall, the woman began to crawl headfirst down the side of the building, using her hands and bare feet. As she descended, Kehrsyn could see ghostly wisps of blue energy curling away from her extremities and rapidly fading to nothing in the steady rain.

"You're a magician," said Kehrsyn.

The woman paused in her descent and said, "Well, maybe I gave you too many chops for smarts, but we can work around that. Yes, some of the time I'm a sorceress, if you must know."

Working her hands to the sides, the stranger levered her torso up until she sat on her heels. It looked much like she was kneeling on the floor—except that her feet were flat against a wet, vertical wall ten feet in the air. She pulled at her collar and tried to clear her throat, but to no particular avail.

Since the sorceress had come closer, removing herself from the backlighting of the clouds, Kehrsyn could see her more clearly. She had a squarish face, tanned, with Untheri features and the leathery wrinkles of too many seasons in the sun. Her red-rimmed eyes drooped at the outside corners, and her nose was very small. She wore several layers of nondescript traveling clothes, mostly in sun-faded browns and grays. Kehrsyn noted that the layers and loose, wrapped cut to her clothes gave her a number of great places to conceal small items. She looked a few pounds toward the heavy side, but the clothes made it impossible to tell if the extra weight was muscle or fat. Finally, Kehrsyn noticed that, while her hands and feet were bare, she had soft leather boots with thick stockings tucked carefully into her belt. It seemed only reasonable that she wouldn't habitually go barefoot in that kind of weather.

The woman sat on her heels, elbows resting easily on her lap and hands dangling between her knees. Her left thumb fiddled with a bright silver ring she wore on her left middle finger. She cocked her head to the right and studied Kehrsyn, eyes roving carefully over her body from feet to hair. The sorceress spent a fair amount of time looking right at Kehrsyn's eyes, but Kehrsyn steadfastly refused to drop her gaze. For the rest, Kehrsyn chose not to move. It was best not to upset a magician too much until one had a better idea of how capable her magic was. Novice magicians could cause someone a bit of trouble; an experienced one could leave her victim as a pile of ash in the blink of an eye.

While the two women appraised each other, the wounded man at Kehrsyn's feet managed to push himself up into a sitting position and lean against one wall. The shield on his back grated on the rough, gritty stone. With a sigh that was one part pleasure and one part pain, he set his legs straight out in front of him and put pressure on his wound with his balled-up fist. With his other hand, he tried unsuccessfully to wipe the blood from his wincing eyes, then he began to pull his healing potion from his belt.

The mysterious woman gestured to the man with a casual motion of her thumb. Without taking her eyes off the mage, Kehrsyn flicked her rapier to her right and tapped the man's cuirass twice, just as he drew forth the vial.

He sagged, and gasped, "Oh, damn. I thought you two had left."

The woman flipped her hands over, revealing her blue-haloed palms as if doing so might convince Kehrsyn of her sincerity.

"All right," the sorceress said, wheezing, "let me sing your dance for you. There's something in this town that we need, and your talents can get it for us."

"We?" said Kehrsyn, her eyes narrowing.

The woman pursed her lips. and replied, "Why, the guild, if you must know." She cocked her head to the other side.

"The guild? Which guild?"

The woman shook her head in disbelief. "Why, what guild do you think, hon?" she asked.

"I—I don't know," stammered Kehrsyn.

The woman snorted, "The thieves' guild, of course."

She pulled a small, soiled kerchief from an inner pocket and blew her nose.

"But there's no thieves' guild in Messemprar," objected Kehrsyn. "They wouldn't dare make one."

"If only your mind were as nimble as your vixen hands, hon," said the sorceress with a rattling sigh of exasperation. She returned the kerchief and clasped her hands together. "You got to keep up with the times, especially here. The Northern Wizards don't have the control everyone thinks they do. The ex-Gilgeamite priests don't have the control they wish they had. And no one trusts the church of Tiamat, or the army, or the Banites, or—or the followers of Furifax, or anyone. So when the Mulhorandi army starts looking like a good option, well, that's when there's cracks large enough for a guild to move in, and with this many people packed into the streets, we got ourselves a good set of targets."

"Move in?" asked Kehrsyn

"Yeah, we've been operating elsewhere for a while, so it's nice to be home again."

Kehrsyn paused and considered what she knew. If the sorceress was powerful, she could have laid a geas upon her to do whatsoever work she had in mind. If, as the sorceress had implied, the guild was new in town, its members might not know their way around too well.

Kehrsyn studied the gloating eyes of the sorceress for another breath and said, "Well, welcome back to Messemprar. Sorry to disappoint you, but I don't steal. Olaré." She tapped the guard on the shoulder with her rapier to get his attention and added, "I'm leaving now, but you're still not alone. Good luck."

So saying, she started to back away. The sorceress cleared her throat again, snuffled, and spat.

"Don't do something you might regret, hon," she said, waggling her fingers.

"Life is full of regrets," said Kehrsyn, "and mine has been full of threats far more intimidating than yours."

"Why, I'm not threatening you, hon," said the woman, as more wisps of bluish energy coalesced around her hands. "I'm offering you protection. Assistance. Help, you know."

"Help? Sounds to me like you're trying to bully me into doing your dirty work. Pretend I'm in danger, then offer me an imaginary way out."

"Imaginary? Far from it. Seems a fair trade to me: you do us a favor and we help you avoid your due punishment for killing this here guard," said the woman, rubbing her nose with the back of her hand.

"What?" asked Kehrsyn. "What are you talking about?"

"I tell ya, hon," said the woman, a catch in her throat adding gravel to her tone, "you got to keep up with the times. If you don't keep up, it'll do you in." She paused to hack a few times, then spit a large wad at the ground at the guard's feet. "That there guard, he's a member of the Zhentarim. You heard him say that, didn't you? Or weren't you paying attention? Anyway, those Zhents, they look after their own. They don't take kindly to sleek little thieves like you killing one of them."

"But I didn't," said Kehrsyn.

"Your nut might be a little slow, but your eyes are fast enough," the sorceress said, pointing her finger at Kehrsyn's bag.

Kehrsyn looked down just in time to see her dagger slide from its hiding place, a slight blue aura shining around it. She gasped in surprise and started to reach for it, but as it flew away she stayed her hand, lest she slice her own fingers off trying to grab the wicked blade. Kehrsyn glanced up at the sorceress, who was gazing at the guard with a cold, passive stare. The woman swept her finger with an efficient gesture. Kehrsyn looked back down just in time to see the dagger plunge itself into the guard's throat, lodging just between the collarbones. The mortally wounded guard coughed in pain and surprise. Even as he reached for his throat, the dagger flew back to the sorceress's hands. She caught it by the pommel and held the blade down. Blood dripped into the alley, where it feathered itself apart in the cold puddles.

Gurgling and choking, blood welling from his neck, the guard tried to unseal his healing potion with his right hand. The left he kept pressed to his leg, until his cold, desperate fingers fumbled the precious blue vial. Feeling the vial slip from his fingers, he scrabbled for it with both hands, letting more blood flow from his leg wound.

Kehrsyn glanced once more at the sorceress, who watched the proceedings with a thin, lopsided smirk. Kehrsyn dropped her rapier with a clatter and dived for the elusive vial.

"Got it!" she said as she broke the seal.

Holding the back of the guard's head with one hand, she pressed the healing potion to his lip, but as she did so, he coughed up the blood that was trickling into his lungs, spraying the precious liquid and spattering Kehrsyn's face and hands with crimson and cobalt.

She flinched, pulled back, and wiped her eyes. She opened them again and saw the guard slump to the side, the shield on his back grinding slowly along the stone wall. He hacked and gasped, his face twisting in agony and going pale with shock. His breathing, what there was of it, was forced and noisy.

Trembling, Kehrsyn tried to force the remaining fluid into his throat, but he flailed his arms, desperately clawing for air. She was able to get the vial to his mouth as his movements faded, but the blue liquid pooled in his cheek and dribbled out onto the grimy alley floor. A moment more, and Kehrsyn heard his dying breath rattle its burbling way out of his lungs, giving up its last shred of warmth to the cold winter's air.

"Great gods!" gasped Kehrsyn, appalled at the turn of events. She glared at the sorceress on the wall. "You—you killed him!"

The woman had pulled her kerchief back out with her free hand and was rigorously trying to clean her nose some more.

"No, hon," she said as she explored her nostril, still gently dangling the dagger between the fingers of her other hand, "*you* killed him. You took him down. You stopped him from drinking his healing potion. Your dagger slit his throat. Your face wears his blood. Any divination spell will show all that. If the Zhents here don't have a wizard at their immediate disposal—" she shrugged, helpless, and returned the kerchief to its hiding place—"why, I'm sure they can locate a freelance mage somewhere around here."

She paused to clear her throat, then coughed a few times to get something clear of her lungs.

"But I tell you what, hon," the sorceress added with a conspiratorial wink, once she'd gotten control of her cough again, "we of the guild got to stick together against the cold, cruel world." She gestured vaguely around, at once taking in the vast city that surrounded them as well as the chill, gray weather. "I can personally guarantee you that no one will hear of this, no one will find your dagger, and no diviner will offer their services to the Zhentarim. All you have to do is provide us with what we need."

Kehrsyn looked at the blood and liquid on her hands, and, cringing, used the dead man's cloak to clean them and her face. When she was done, she picked up her rapier and looked up at the sorceress again.

"Why don't you just get it yourself?" she asked. "You can walk on walls and stuff. I can't do that."

"It don't work quite like that, hon," the woman replied with a grimace. "I use magic to augment my skills, but, you see, magic is not the best tool for slipping into a manse." She waggled her fingers, sending the blue strands of energy spiraling around. "Little lights, little flashes, little noises of spells or incantations, they all attract attention, and good merchants have wards and other traps to snare those who try to magic their way into a valuable area. No, far better to go tippy-toe like a little mouse, all small and quiet and twitchy whiskers. And that, hon, is something I wager you're darned good at. So confident, in fact, that I'm choosing you for the task."

Since the sorceress had shown spells—wall-walking and a little telekinesis—Kehrsyn was growing bolder. Not only was the woman staying out of easy reach, but Kehrsyn knew that the spells she'd used were little more than minor cantrips. She'd seen magic—real magic—several times in her life, and the sorceress's offerings were a far cry from those spells. She believed she could parry or dodge whatever telekinetic assault the woman might launch with her dagger, and the studded leather vest Kehrsyn wore beneath her blouse offered her vitals some protection.

She paused as if considering, and studied the woman some more, letting time pass. The sorceress was clearly suffering from some kind of contagious catarrh or grippe. Kehrsyn sucked in her lips and nodded, as if she was indeed deciding to go along with the woman's demands.

She waited until the sorceress cleared her throat again—Kehrsyn well knew how the grippe sapped people's willpower—and coughed to see how suggestible the woman might be.

Very, as it turned out.

No sooner had Kehrsyn cleared her throat than the woman stretched her neck and tried to clear hers. Kehrsyn put the pear to her mouth as if to take a bite and forced a sudden cough around the fruit. That brought a coughing fit upon the unhealthy woman as well. Kehrsyn watched for just a moment while the rasping cough gathered momentum, and just as the woman's eyes started to close with the force of her hacking, Kehrsyn made her move. Pear held in her teeth, Kehrsyn leaped forward, jumped up the wall with one boot clawing for just a bit of traction and stability, and neatly flicked her rapier at the woman's hand. The tip of her rapier caught her dagger just below the hilt and spun it out of the sorceress's helpless fingers. Deftly Kehrsyn caught the dagger by the handle as she landed on the uneven alleyway ground.

"You w—*cough!*" spluttered the woman, pointing with her newly emptied hand while the other futilely clawed at her collar.

Kehrsyn sheathed her rapier and took the pear from her teeth.

"The only protection I need," said Kehrsyn, "is for you to cover your mouth, so I don't catch my death."

She slung the blood from her dagger, sheathed it, and withdrew.

Kehrsyn hazarded one last glance over her shoulder before she turned a corner in the alleyway to leave the sight of the coughing woman. She caught a glimpse of the woman making mystical passes with her hand once more. Blue motes sparkled around her fingers, and something small and shiny zipped through the air to the woman's hand. Kehrsyn had just an instant to wonder what it might be.

The woman moved her hand to her mouth, and a high-pitched two-tone whistle filled the alley. Kehrsyn recognized it instantly: a constabulary whistle. One long, shrill blow was the signal for riot or assault upon a guard.

The response was immediate. Like feral dogs echoing the baying of the pack, other whistles began calling in the surrounding streets. Kehrsyn staggered, frozen by the abrupt flare of mortal fear, the return of the all-too-familiar feeling of being human prey.

The sorceress fixed Kehrsyn with a look of disgust as she slung the whistle back at the guard's corpse.

"Guess we'll see how good you really are now, won't we, hon?" she called out. Then, at the top of her lungs, she screamed and yelled, "*Thief!* She killed him!"

Kehrsyn turned and fled as the false witness broke into another fit of coughing. She ran down the twisting back alleys, dodging barrels of refuse and ducking under laundry lines, puffs of steamy breath peeling from the sides of her panicked face. When she'd been pursued as a child, she'd used her small size, fast feet, and knowledge of the terrain to evade pursuit, but she had none of these left to her. She was an adult, somewhat the weaker for chronic hunger, and had only been in Messemprar a few months. Worst of all, she was outnumbered far worse than she'd ever been as a kid. An entire city's worth of guards and deputized mercenaries had become her foes. Her only hope was that they couldn't identify her.

CHAPTER FOUR

Kehrsyn ran down the haphazard scattering of alleyways, trying to find a way out into the main city
streets. The whistles petered out, but she knew
they'd sound again if she were spotted. In the
meantime, she was certain the sorceress had given
the city watch a good description and that the information would leap like sparks from guard to guard.

The thought struck her that carrying a half-
eaten pear in her hand was not a wise idea. She
almost tossed it away, but her gnawing stomach
overcame her fear, so instead she slipped it in
into the rear portion of her sash, where her cloak
concealed it. The meager camouflage wouldn't
pass a close inspection, but she hoped to avoid
that possibility.

With her left hand she held her bag against her
body, while her right gripped the hem of her cloak
and wrapped it around her rapier's scabbard,
both securing the blade and thinly concealing its
deadly purpose.

Kehrsyn slowed to a jog. Moving adroitly through three thousand years' worth of urban growth proved more than she could handle. She didn't want to run pell-mell into a dead end, or worse, a whip of city constables, but though she slowed her feet, Kehrsyn's heart continued to race. She had never exited the Jackal's Courtyard in that direction before, and she knew neither where she was nor where she should go. On top of that, she wasn't sure whom she should fear more, the Messemprar constabulary, who would obey the law, harsh as it was; or the Zhentarim, of whom the sorceress had spoken in such dark tones. It didn't help that Kehrsyn knew next to nothing about the Zhentarim, and thus her fears had fertile fields in which to grow in the darker recesses of her mind.

The whistles started up again, piping out a rhythm that sent a message to other guards within earshot, followed by the clank and thump of armor and hobnailed boots. The dreadful sound came washing down the alley like a flash flood in a sandstone gully. The guards had come across the sorceress, and with her the guard's dead body. Kehrsyn feared that the mage might have brutalized the body before the guards arrived, making Kehrsyn seem all the more ghoulish.

Casting around for any hope as she trotted along, Kehrsyn found an alley branching away, one that had a wide gutter running down the center, a sluice for rain and sewage. It was a time-honored system for large cities in Unther; thus Kehrsyn surmised that the alley, in some distant past, had been a major thoroughfare, even though at present it was as choked with waste as a fat and aging noble. She took it, hoping it would lead to a main avenue. Even if she didn't recognize the street at the outlet, any major thoroughfare was better than being trapped like a rat in the narrow passages.

Despite its grandiose heritage, little more was left of the humble alleyway than a twisted, narrow warren. Though still somewhat broad in places, it writhed for most of its length among an indiscriminate collection of construction. The homes, huts, and houses jostled each other for living space, crowding into and sometimes completely over the alleyway. Kehrsyn was forced to slow to a fast walk to navigate it. The sound of coarse voices echoed down the alley, so garbled into a mash of random syllables by the irregular architecture that Kehrsyn couldn't even tell if they were speaking Untheric or a foreign language. The incomprehensible noise reminded Kehrsyn of those unhappy moments of her childhood that returned in her nightmares to that day, of hiding in the underbrush while adults hunted for her, speaking angry words at times too complex for her uneducated mind, but the intent of which was all too clear.

The twisting alley, bitter cold, and nightmarish voices threatened to overwhelm Kehrsyn's self-control, but then she saw, quite literally, a ray of hope. Filtered sunlight splashed the walls of the alley ahead of her—an egress into the main city streets. She turned the corner and stumbled into the open street, smiling in spite of her misgivings and feeling as if she could breathe once again. All she had to do was blend into the crowd, walk calmly near a group of people as if she were one of them, find a place far away from the Jackal's Courtyard to hole up for a watch or two, and make sure she spent her single coin slowly, while giving the impression she had a far heavier purse to her name.

No problem. Acting was one of her strong points, and had been since the days she called it "playing pretend."

She blinked a few times. Despite the ongoing drizzle, the broad avenue was far brighter than the tight passageway behind her. Several varied groups and solitary people sulked along, hunkered against the weather. Scanning quickly, she saw no constables or soldiers, nor any of the black-tabarded Zhents, but off to her right she saw the green-cloaked man who'd first shadowed her as she'd left the Jackal's Courtyard. He turned toward her in recognition and stepped in her direction. She noticed that he moved with strength and confidence, as well as a definite clarity of purpose.

Her mind raced. Was he with the sorceress, a scout for the thieves' guild? Was he a slaver looking to corral a few coins for her hide? Or were his motives purely selfish and prurient? Though she feared each of these, she found the first to be both the most likely and the most frightening.

In any event, her choice was clear. Feigning not to have noticed him, she turned to her left and moved away, angling for the far side of the street. A side street branched off to the right up ahead, and if things became urgent she could see an alleyway nearer to her. She hoped she wouldn't need it . . . but even as she thought that, she heard someone's footsteps break into a jog. She drew a wayward strand of hair from her face and pulled it behind her ear, using the motion to conceal a peripheral glance over her shoulder. The grim stranger was closing in, his cloak billowing like the wings of a crow.

She ran for the alley.

"You!" the man called after her.

Just then, a whip of city constables emerged from another alley entrance on the left-hand side of the street. The man's cry and Kehrsyn's rapid motion attracted their attention, and the shrill duotone of the whistles pierced the air again.

Kehrsyn ducked into the alley and ran as fast as the irregular architecture would let her. Behind her she heard the pounding of heavy feet and the staccato cry of the guards' strident whistles signaling that they had her track. She heard a loud, tumbling crunch and the vehement curses of a half dozen men. She cast a quick glance over her shoulder as she rounded a corner, and saw the unknown guild scout crumpled on the dirt with three guards fallen atop him, a mess of bodies, shields, helmets, and khopesh blades scattered in chaos. As the four men tried to regain their feet, the other guards tried to pick their way over the pile of struggling soldiery, giving Kehrsyn precious moments of time.

As with the maze she'd just negotiated, the alley twined between a variety of hovels and buildings, built by those willing to sacrifice freedom and space for the heavy security of living within Messemprar's ancient, massive walls. She came across one intersection, then, a short distance afterward, another. At each of them, she attempted to take the least inviting passage. In that way she hoped to lose her pursuers. Her hope began to grow. With even one more intersection, the guards would have to start leaving branches to go unsearched.

Her evasive strategy betrayed her when the alley branch she'd chosen slithered around an amateur wooden structure and dead-ended in a tall mud-brick wall. There was a heavy wooden door, but it had neither an external latch nor even a viewing slit by which she might hope to plead admittance.

She retreated back the way she'd come, hoping she hadn't lost too much time. She slowed as she reached the place where the branch spurred off the alley. She listened intently, opening her mouth to improve her hearing. Footsteps approached.

"I think we've lost her," said one voice, a youngster by the sound of it.

"I don't care," replied a second, less cultured voice. "We're gonna keep looking."

"Whatever," said the first.

"Hey, Pupface, don't forget the Zhentarim said they'd match the bounty on her head. We stand to earn mint-weight, especially if we find her before Chariq gets back from searching that other spur."

"You think she'd be dumb enough to go into a blind alley?" asked the youth.

"Dumb enough to kill a Zhent," said the older man with a grim chuckle. "And if dumb buys my grog and wenches, then she's dumb enough for me."

"Absolutely."

Kehrsyn realized that fear and curiosity had rooted her to the spot like a hare transfixed by a cobra. The guards drew close, close enough that if she tried to move away quietly, they'd probably see her; but if she moved away quickly, they'd hear her. Either way, they'd pursue . . . but standing there thinking about it made each option less likely to succeed. Kehrsyn turned and ran hard back toward the dead end, counting on surprise to give her enough of a lead.

With a foul oath, the two guards gave chase, their armor clanking in the narrow confines of the alley. Kehrsyn ran to the end, and just as she turned the last corner, she started scrambling up the wooden structure. It wasn't easy. The planks were vertical, not horizontal, and slick with rain, but the few haphazard supporting members that angled across the wall gave enough of a foothold to help her ascend.

She heard the guards turn the corner beneath her. Her sudden disappearance flustered them for a mere moment, but enough precious time for her to reach up and hook her fingers over a windowsill above her head. She prayed the sill was sturdy enough to support her weight and she pulled herself up as quickly as she could. The sill made a slight cracking sound, and Kehrsyn hoped it was simply the wood settling under her weight. She scrabbled with her feet to get any amount of elevation she could.

"Up there!" shouted the younger guard.

"Get 'er, curse you!" growled the elder.

The fear of getting her foot cut off by a khopesh renewed her strength, and she pulled herself up farther.

"Curse it! Jump, Pupface, she's gettin' away!"

Kehrsyn kept her ears tuned as she climbed. When she heard Pupface grunt with exertion, she raised her heels.

She heard the silky whisper of a blade slicing the air and felt a tug as the sharpened tip of the khopesh sliced her leather boot midway up her right shin.

She put the windowsill to good use and scrambled farther up, out of reach of the guards.

"Get up after her!" shouted the elder guard, striking the younger a cuff across the helmet that resounded in the narrow alley. "Now, or I'll throw you up there myself!"

Kehrsyn scrambled up onto a de facto balcony atop the second story of the structure. Pulling her cloak across her face, she peered back down at the two guards. The younger one was beginning a tentative and fearful climb after her. He probed the wall with his hands, trying to discover handholds that were more secure than the ones that Kehrsyn had used. Kehrsyn had to smile. There were no good holds to be offered by rough-hewn, poorly assembled, thinly cut, rain-slicked wood.

She waited until the guard looked up again, then said, "I have a large rock up here that I could drop on you, and it's a long fall back to the ground. If you give up now, your head and back will stay in one piece."

The guard nodded almost imperceptibly and began scanning the wall for a safe way back down.

The elder guard thrust the tip of his khopesh under the younger guard's armored skirt and growled, "It takes more than a few bones to make a man, Pupface."

Kehrsyn saw the younger guard grow rigid, his face twitching in a rictus of fear and pain. His breathing grew in speed and volume. He looked back at Kehrsyn and his eyes narrowed in pleading desperation. He began to climb again.

Kehrsyn wondered if he was deliberately trying to climb slowly enough to give her a chance to escape before she'd have to drop a rock on him. Not that she had one, but bluffs were the most effective when they played right into someone's fears.

"Well, then," she said, "I'll just wait until you're almost up to drop it on you. I can wait." She waved at the elder guard. "Will you be next, or does your protégé have more manliness than you?"

"You may act brave, you murdering thief," he spat, "but we'll see what happens when we catch you."

"Yeah, you're plenty brave to force someone to climb something when you haven't got the guts to do it yourself. I'll bet when you were in his position, you just climbed back down and let them cut yours right off, am I right?"

"You little—*arrrggh!*" bellowed the elder guard. "Come on, Pupface, she's only got one rock up there!"

As Kehrsyn had hoped, the elder guard started to climb also.

With the two guards climbing after her, Kehrsyn's confidence grew again. She had feared that they would circumvent her escape if she fled across the rooftops, but she'd managed to coax them into taking the hard route: difficult climbs and long jumps in armor. Kehrsyn saw that there was one more story to both the wooden structure and the much older stone building against which it leaned. She climbed up the wooden wall and clambered onto the roof of the stone building.

It was one of the huge, ancient structures of Messemprar, one that had, millennia ago, been someone's palatial home. Since it was in the poorer section of town, Kehrsyn surmised that it had likely been subdivided again and again, and served to house a wide variety of families and businesses. She saw empty clotheslines and rubbish scattered over the large, flat roof, along with a large fire pit and several trapdoors that led into the monolithic building. Not that that was any help. Those who lived in that part of town would be plenty happy to turn in a fugitive for a reward. For that matter, in these dark days, *anyone* in town would. Rewards meant gold, and gold meant food.

Kehrsyn moved across the rooftop, scouting out the

perimeter of the roof. Two sides fronted on large thoroughfares, ancient streets wide enough for eight chariots to ride abreast. The third side looked dangerous, a long jump reliant on the undependable footing of recent construction. The fourth side looked like it had a reasonable jump, one that was only foolhardy as opposed to downright suicidal. She located a likely landing spot, then stepped back to get a good running jump. Behind her, she heard the cursing of the older guard rising from the alley like a stench, followed by a triumphant cry from the one called Pupface.

Kehrsyn untied her scabbard from her belt and pulled her bag's strap from her shoulder. She took a deep breath, steeled her mind to her task, then began to run. Her ears heard Pupface call out for her to stop, but her mind paid no heed. She leaped from the rooftop across the narrow side street, holding her arms out to the side and pinwheeling them once for stability. Time seemed to dilate for her, and she could feel each drop of chill rain brushing her skin as she arced between the buildings. Each ripple of cloth reminded her that she had a long fall beneath her.

For as slow as time seemed to move, the opposite rooftop closed in quickly. Kehrsyn let go of her bag and scabbard and pulled her hands back close. She tried to tuck her legs in, but her feet hit the edge of the roof just below her ankles, and she sprawled painfully on the uneven split-log roof, flopping once over one shoulder with her momentum. She felt like she couldn't breathe, felt like she was going to throw up. Mouth hanging open, she looked around and located her sword and bag, both of which appeared to have landed in better shape than she had. As she picked them up, she heard the guards' telltale whistle again.

Looking back, she saw Pupface running across the rooftop toward her, frantically blowing a signal. He reached the edge of the rooftop and looked down.

"You!" he yelled, pointing with his khopesh. "Hey! Zhentilars! She's up there! Don't let her get away!"

Kehrsyn saw a squad of Zhent guards in the street, staring up at her, eight or more in number. One issued a string of orders, and the pack fanned out to seal off the building, moving swiftly like a pack of wolves.

Several other people stood nearby, also looking up at Kehrsyn, but one woman in particular caught the fugitive's eye. The woman waved cheerily.

"Olaré, hon," she said, fiddling with her ring.

Kehrsyn turned and fled across the rooftop, heart pounding.

Kehrsyn knew she couldn't stay on the rooftop. The longer she did, the more time the Zhentarim and the guards had to seal off the building. Her only hope was to get off the rooftop as soon as possible and lose the pursuit in the streets below. She ran straight across the center of the jumbled collection of rooftops, looking for the telltale gap of an alleyway spur.

She found one, and, knowing that she had not the leisure to find a better, she looked for the quickest way down. No decent choices offered themselves. She hopped down to a lower roof. Before she could think about it too much, she hopped the rest of the way to the uneven alley floor.

Kehrsyn hit hard, trying to tumble to ease the impact, but she felt a ripping, popping sensation tear through her right leg and ankle. She felt no pain, but her foot felt loose, almost unhinged. She pushed herself up, keeping her right foot off the ground, and shifted herself to a sitting position. She scrunched up her eyes and brought her ankle around to take a look at it. A limp foot, dangling from her shin like a dead fish, was what she expected to see. Instead, she saw her boot flayed open, laces burst asunder from ankle to knee. A bright scar of cut leather ran from the outside of her ankle upward, then reappeared near the inside of the top.

It struck Kehrsyn what had happened: Pupface's khopesh

had grazed her leather boot, slicing along the laces, cutting into them, but not quite all the way through. The added stress of her last jump had burst them. The surprise and relief was so great that a giggle bubbled up from her throat.

She heard a sudden scuffing step up the alley, then silence. Kehrsyn's cold fear returned. She froze, trapped in the dead end of a narrow alley. She opened her mouth to aid her hearing—could she hear someone coming closer? It was hard to tell . . . until she heard the splash of a puddle being disturbed. She quietly picked up her rapier and bag and tried to scoot into an inset doorway to hide. As quiet as her movements were, she heard the footsteps pause.

For untold pounding heartbeats, she dared not move, dared not even to breathe lest the mist of her breath give her away.

The footsteps turned and scooted away. Kehrsyn held her breath until she heard them no longer, then let the air out in a heart-pounding, trembling heave. She tried to breathe deeply and quietly in hopes of stilling her heart and frazzled nerves. Whichever guard or bounty hunter that had been, her hunters were still out there, so she couldn't leave just yet. Instead, she pulled out the longest scrap of leather thong she had left in her boot and used it to tie her boot tight across the ankle and again across the top. It was serviceable, if uncomfortable.

She hid for a while longer, then began to creep out, wondering if she could make an escape. She found that the alley she'd jumped into was a short branch off a minor paved street. Not good. She inched closer to the mouth of the alley, listening intently.

She heard boots pacing slowly along and voices quietly speaking a foreign tongue. She quickly moved back down the narrow passage to her scant hiding place, but as she pulled her rapier in beside her, the tip of her scabbard scraped on the stone doorframe.

She heard the voices pause. They spoke again, some sort of interrogative. She heard the whispering sound of steel being drawn, then the scuff of feet moving into the alley.

Kehrsyn pulled a tiny mirror from a secret pocket at her waist and used it to peer around the side of the doorway. Two black-tabarded swordsmen moved slowly down the alley, peering into windows, doorways, and barrels, as well as scanning the walls and ledges above them.

There was no way out. Kehrsyn hadn't a clue what to do. She fingered her rapier . . . If I'm going to suffer for killing one of these bullies, she thought, I might as well actually do it. Deep inside, however, she wasn't certain she could.

She watched them draw closer and saw that they were too cautious for her to be able to ambush one of them. Just as that realization crossed her mind, she saw something move at the open end of the alley. The guards turned just in time to see a cloaked figure vanish from sight behind them. They looked at each other, startled and confused, then somewhere nearby the keening cry of the guards' whistle started again. The two sprinted from the alley to pursue, blowing their whistles in response.

Kehrsyn sagged against the wall and let herself drop to the ground. She didn't care that the cold rain soaked its way through the seat of her skirt and into her leggings. Kehrsyn could hear the guards' whistles moving farther and farther away through the city. She didn't know who or what those Zhents had chased, but in all likelihood it had saved her virtue and her life. Not knowing what else to do, she reached around, found her pear still in her sash, and took it out. For some reason, it no longer looked appetizing, so she let her hand droop over her knee.

She hung her head and let silent tears of relief trickle off her nose and join the cold rain that slicked the grimy street.

CHAPTER FIVE

Ruzzara stalked the rooftops, cursing the luck that had her chasing a reluctant recruit through near-freezing rain. The throbbing chill in her feet had not abated when she'd put her boots back on. In fact, the dampness of her feet had balled up the lint in her stockings, making them even less comfortable.

Her feet slid out from under her on the slanting rooftop, dropping her hard onto her left hip. Despite the fact that her legs slid most of the way off the rooftop, dangling over empty space, she appeared merely inconvenienced. She stood back up, muttering an inventive string of rural invectives and rubbing her hip.

Ruzzara had seen the confusion in Hooper's Alley, seen how a premature whistle had sent the city guard, the deputized brute squad, and a hopeful bounty hunter all running in the wrong direction, chasing their own alarm like a stampede of maddened bulls.

She wasn't sure how the young lass had done it, but it was very clever. In fact, Ruzzara hadn't expected the young girl to do that well at all. She'd thought the guards would have long since taken care of the "murdering thief," forever concealing Ruzzara's role in the killing. Instead, she searched in the rain, trying to find the thief again.

Ruzzara wasn't sure where the thief had holed up, but she figured circumnavigating the block on the rooftops would flush her out eventually. Ruzzara peered down into the alleys as she sauntered along, looking for motion or likely hiding places. She hoped she'd be able to find the vagrant, whose fear of Ruzzara's power made her a useful tool and whose evident skill made her an effective weapon.

She found her, sitting on a stoop. Ruzzara smiled with relief, then her face darkened into a frown. The young lady was down on the ground, while Ruzzara was on top of the roof, three stories above.

She contemplated using her magic to spider climb down the wall, but her digits were only just starting to tingle with returning sensation. She had no desire to pull off her gloves and boots and press her numb hands and feet to the cold, wet stones yet again.

She had a better idea, more comfortable . . . and more dramatic, besides. She had long before purchased a ring— a magical circle of silver—that protected her from dangerous falls by floating her slowly to earth. She'd bought it for protection, a magical safety net, but it occurred to her to use it aggressively. She rocked it back and forth on her middle finger with her thumb. It was an unconscious habit. So much wealth tied up in one little object made her check its presence almost continually.

Ruzzara moved as quietly as possible along the rooftop until she was opposite the young thief who cried quietly in the alley. Fidgeting with the ring to reassure herself, she crouched down and let herself lean forward. As she felt herself start to fall, she pushed off the rooftop gently, quietly. Just as her heart started to thrill with instinctive panic, her senses realized that she wasn't accelerating; she was descending at the speed of a brisk walk. It was an unnerving sensation.

As she drifted downward, Ruzzara pinwheeled her arms once to right herself, then put her hands on her hips and assumed a cocky and arrogant stance. She landed with a light sound of crunching dirt not three feet in front of her quarry.

The young woman jerked her head up in fear, staring wide-eyed at the sorceress through a veil of haggard, damp hair. She gasped in recognition, and her mouth flapped in silent amazement.

"Well, at least I know you can stay silent," said Ruzzara. The young woman glanced down the alley and back at her "Oh, come on, hon, don't look so shocked," added Ruzzara. "You think the guild lets anyone in if they can't sneak around?"

The young woman held up her hands placatingly, one hand spread wide and the other still ridiculously clutching her half-eaten pear. When the thief noticed that she still held the pear, she quickly hid that hand behind her.

She stammered a few faltering words, saying, "Please, I—please don't—I mean, I'll . . . just don't call the guards, please . . . ?"

"Give it a rest, will ya, hon?" said Ruzzara. "You think I want to call them guards back here to barge in on our little private time? No thanks. You know, you got a friend out there, hon, I'd say you do."

"A friend?"

"I saw what happened. You done good, hon, moved like a regular alley cat, but I'd say Mask, God of Thieves, has a soft spot in his larcenous heart for little ol' you."

"What do you mean?"

"I sure wish I knew how you done did it, hon, I really do. I swear you were stewed like a rabbit, when all of a sudden you got the whole gaggle of guards galloping off in the whole wrong direction. Showed up just a bit too late to see your trick, but that was slick, hon, real slick."

The young woman's lip trembled. "I—I don't know what to say," she said.

"Well, I'd say you passed the test, hon," Ruzzara said with a smile. "You kept your head in a tough situation, moved nimbly and quickly, and managed to evade a fine ol' dragnet of constables and Zhents alike." She pulled the dead guard's whistle from a pocket. "So are you gonna do our job for us, or shall I give this a little toot?"

"Please!" said the fugitive in a panic. She sagged visibly. "No, please don't. I'll . . . I'll do it."

"Aw, now don't look so sad, hon," Ruzzara continued. "Life is full of adventure, and every adventure begins with a single step!"

"I have found more often that what the bards call an 'adventure' begins with a single mistake."

"Wow, hon, your outlook is as bleak as an eighty-year-old prostitute."

"It's not bleak," said the young woman. "It's realistic. The trick is knowing when to stop so you don't make that mistake."

"Whatever you say," said Ruzzara. She paused and raised one eyebrow. "Are you trying to sneak your hand to that dagger you keep under your bag, hon? My associates wouldn't take that very well," she added, waving a hand vaguely in the direction of the street, or maybe the rooftops.

"Uh . . . no," said the young woman, avoiding Ruzzara's eyes.

"Excellent!" said Ruzzara, though her eyes were as cold as steel. "I'd hate to think you looked at me as a mistake to be unmade." She studied her quarry and smiled. That was the best time to interrogate, when the last shred of hope had been taken away. "What's your name, hon?"

"Kehrsyn."

"Well, olaré, Kehrsyn. So where do you live?"

"I . . . don't really have a . . . a place to stay. Anymore."
Kehrsyn's voice was very soft.

"Well, Kehrsyn, I'd say maybe your luck is changing,"
said Ruzzara. Once someone had no hope, it was best to be
the first one who offered it.

Kehrsyn looked up, and Ruzzara saw a desperate sparkle
return to the waif's eyes. Kehrsyn stood, ending up a little
taller than Ruzzara, which annoyed her. It was harder to be
intimidating when looking up.

"You mean I can sleep in the guild house?" asked
Kehrsyn, with just a shade of fear and hope.

Ruzzara laughed. She liked the hint of desperation in
Kehrsyn's voice. It was best to cultivate that by keeping the
ray of hope to a glimmer.

"Aren't you getting ahead of the horse there, hon? We
gotta talk about the assignment."

"Right," said Kehrsyn, and Ruzzara was pleased to see
that she was focusing her attention so she'd remember
what she was about to be told.

Ruzzara turned so that she faced Kehrsyn squarely. She
folded her arms to add gravity to her words.

"This merchant has somehow laid his grubby paws on
an important item of great magical power," she began.

"You want me to steal a magic item," interrupted Kehrsyn,
her lower eyelids trembling.

"No hook in your blade, is there? That's right. It's apparently pretty potent. Some daredevil grave robber done said
that he dug up this magic staff while under hire from this
here merchant. It must be right important if a merchant
sends folks after it while the city is under siege, don't you
think? We think we can use that staff to protect our city
against the pharaoh's army, or mayhap even drive them
back."

"Drive them back?" asked Kehrsyn. "What does it do?"

"That's not your concern," said Ruzzara. "Leave that to those what can handle it. You just need to know what it looks like. It's a wand one span shy of a cubit, the color of dried bone, and carved all over with those pictoglyph thingies. And there's a wavy band of bronze all wrapped 'round the top, with a big piece of black amber in the top. We think this here merchant intends to sell it to the Zhentarim. They'll take it up away to the north, for their own plans. Needless to say, that makes us as mad as a constipated goat, selling out our whole darn future for a few lousy shekae."

"Sounds to me like it must be worth a mountain of gold," said Kehrsyn.

"That's beside the point, hon," groaned Ruzzara. "Keep the big picture here. We're talking saving Unther's collective hide from the Mulhorandi army."

"Right. Almost a cubit long, you say?" repeated Kehrsyn, measuring the length against her arm. "So where is it?"

"Do you know where the Plaza of the Northern Wizards is?"

"No."

"It used to be called Gilgeam's Altar. Where he used to hold executions."

"Oh, yeah, that place."

"Great. Go down Port Street. At the next corner, on the left, you'll see a large building called Wing's Reach. It's in there.

"This ought to help," she added, pulling a piece of parchment from inside her jerkin.

Kehrsyn unrolled it, trembling. "It's a map," she said.

"I knew you were a smart one, hon. You know how to read that?"

"Yes. Yes, I do. It's . . . rather detailed."

"Yeah, we found the floor plan in the city archives," lied Ruzzara. "That map's as accurate as an elven archer. It's got the location of that staff thing all marked on there. That should be all you need."

"Gilgeam's Altar, Port Street, Wing's Reach," Kehrsyn echoed. "What do I do when I get it?"

"Go to the Mage Bazaar and look for a Red Wizard named Eileph. He knows what to do."

"Won't he keep it?" asked Kehrsyn.

"Boy, you just don't trust anyone, do you, hon?"

"I haven't ever gotten much reason to."

"Well, to answer your question," said Ruzzara, "no, he won't keep it. We gave Eileph a nice retainer."

Kehrsyn nodded and thought for a bit.

"So, the guild house?" she asked .

Ruzzara chuckled, reached out with her right hand, and gripped the back of Kehrsyn's left arm, guiding her out of the alley.

"You gotta remember, hon," she said, "that only guild members sleep in the guild house. To become a member, not only do you have to prove yourself, but we gotta know you're quiet as a crocodile."

"I won't talk," said Kehrsyn. "I promise."

Ruzzara laughed again, shaking her head. "Hon, right now, you're just a contractor. And we never take a contract without security."

So saying, she shaped her fingers into a curious pattern and pressed them very hard into Kehrsyn's arms. With a single command word, she blasted raw magical energy out of her fingertips. They flared, burning through Kehrsyn's sleeve and searing her flesh beneath. Ruzzara pulled her hand back, before Kehrsyn's traumatized skin might have a chance to stick to her fingers.

Kehrsyn cried out and pulled away.

"That's our slave mark, hon," said Ruzzara. "Our brand. You belong to us now. You mess up, any one of us can kill you in broad daylight as you do your little thing in the Jackal's Courtyard. No one will raise an eyebrow, because you're nothing but a slave."

"I am not a slave!" protested Kehrsyn, pinching the very

top of her branded arm in an attempt to strangle the pain.

"Oh, you know that, hon, and we know that, but no one else knows that. Hey, you're just a homeless street urchin, right? So just be sure to keep that little ol' brand covered up, and no one will be the wiser."

"I'll tell them I'm freeborn!" snarled Kehrsyn, eyes narrowed.

Ruzzara could tell she was just barely holding on.

"It'll be hard to tell anyone anything when you're dead."

Kehrsyn stopped in her tracks, trembling.

Ruzzara smiled disarmingly and said, "Hey, that'll only happen if you double-cross us. If you do well, why, the future will open wide just for you . . . nice bed, fancy food, friends who look after you, gold . . ." Ruzzara paused to let her words sink in. "Ta-ta, hon," she said as she walked away. "You have two days. Don't be late. It'd be a shame to ruin a work of art like you."

She walked away, whistling. She passed along the word about the new recruit to the one person who needed to know, then wandered back to rejoin her group. By the time she'd drawn a chair up by the fire, kicked off her boots and socks, and finished her first glass of liqueur, all thoughts of Kehrsyn's plight were gone from her mind.

CHAPTER SIX

Kehrsyn aimlessly walked the streets of Messemprar for the remaining daylight hours. Her partially eaten pear sat in her left hand unnoticed, almost forgotten, its raw surfaces slowly turning brown. Her right hand clutched her left biceps just opposite the throbbing brand. She couldn't see the burn well and dared not touch it, but the unrelenting sensation of heat, the blisters that surrounded the area, and the bitter odor all told her she'd been injured fairly seriously. Tears of fear, rage, shame, and pain quivered at the corners of her eyes, but she refused to let them fall. She was an Untheri; she would persevere. Somehow she would prosper just as her nation had persevered and occasionally prospered under the tyranny of the god-king Gilgeam.

Even worse than the pain of the burn were the knot in her stomach, and the anguish, nausea, and hopelessness it brought to her. She wanted to curl up but wouldn't. She needed to eat but couldn't.

All the darkest times of her childhood were falling back in upon her soul, wiping away what self-respect she'd had, like a thunderhead blotting out a young spring sky. What little hope she had was offered by a den of thieves . . . hardly the most auspicious bearers of gifts.

Her pride urged her to find a way not to let the ugly wall-walking sorceress get the better of her (though, in fact, she already had), but without knowing the guild's reach she could find no sure solution. She'd been placed into a position in which she had no choice. She'd always told herself before that there was hope, yet she could see none left.

She tried not to think about the fact that she could have chosen death instead. She failed, of course, and when she thought about it she tried to tell herself that it wasn't fair that she should die for being a murderer's scapegoat.

None of it stuck. The guilt of her capitulation had torn the scab off of her memories—the days of her youth that she hated—and the pain and self-recrimination welled up from the wound once again. She wondered whether, even without the threat of arrest, she would have done their bidding just to earn a good meal, a dry bed, a bit of security and a hope of belonging . . . somewhere.

The salt in her wound was that someone else would profit from her theft, from her abandonment of her principles. Profit financially, of course, but it was also clear that the sorceress enjoyed exerting power over people like Kehrsyn. She was probably gloating about how she'd directed Kehrsyn like a trained dog.

Kehrsyn tried to focus her turbulent emotions and turn them against the sorceress. If she could, it would give her motivation and drive, perhaps even help her to figure out some way to get back at that false-friendly wench with the supercilious smirk.

But, the guilty portions of her mind said, does a thieving little wretch like me deserve vengeance?

A horn blew somewhere in town, followed by another, and others. The sound snapped Kehrsyn's mind back to the present. The city guard was sounding the curfew. Soon pairs, trios, and full whips of constables would sweep the streets, ensuring that the refugees were ejected from the city before the gates closed. During a war, only those who owned homes or paid rent were allowed to remain within Messemprar's walls after nightfall. With the Mulhorandi army looming to the south, those who had space to let, even a spare corner of a common room, were making mintweight from those fearful enough to pay for it.

Kehrsyn counted her coins. It didn't take long. One silver. One copper left over from the day before.

Even if she found someone with space to let, it was not nearly enough. She put them back into her bag, along with her pear.

She sighed. Without a tent, or even any friendly faces among the refugees, she didn't relish the thought of spending the night outside. Not in this weather. Even if she could find that kid Jaldi, well, he didn't look any better off than she was.

She'd evaded the city guard before, and she could do it again. At least the rain was abating to a light sprinkle.

Kehrsyn realized she had only the vaguest of notions where she was. She'd been wandering in Messemprar's limitless alleyways to keep herself out of the public eye. With the curfew, her isolation worked against her. She knew from experience that the guard always swept the alleys clear each dusk. They were very methodical, starting at the point farthest from the main gate and sweeping the entire city like beaters on a royal hunt.

She moved quickly along the alley, half-guessing her way until she found a side street. There she was able to get rough bearings. She could see the masts of sailing ships peeking over the rooftops off to her left, so she was somewhere near the wharves. Turning toward the city center, she walked casually along, blending in with the thin crowd of people moving for their homes or the city gates.

She reached a main thoroughfare, one that moved parallel to the main gate. Looking both ways, she moved away from the docks, as that direction seemed to have heavier traffic. She moved confidently along with the flow, her easy stride signaling that she belonged within the city walls. Her eyes scanned the crowd, looking for a suitable group of people to blend in with.

Most of the people in the streets were moving sullenly toward the main gate, their paths crossing the road Kehrsyn walked. Kehrsyn tucked her bag under her cloak and watched the people moving parallel to her. Ahead she noticed a large group of people, almost a dozen, moving along in a loose procession. Though it was clear that they were a group, they wore no visible insignia and walked in a cluster instead of a formation. They moved with quiet deliberation through the wide avenue, and Kehrsyn followed them, gradually narrowing her distance until she was not close enough to warrant their attention, yet close enough that she might be considered the group's laggard. She matched their walk.

Once, one of the rearmost people turned and looked over his shoulder. As Kehrsyn saw him pull back his hood, she angled her path and concealed her face with a mock sneeze and sniffle. She continued on her divergent path for a block, then fell back in behind the group.

Up ahead, she saw a cordon of guards stretched loosely across an intersection, awaiting their comrades who were purging the alleys of vagrants. Kehrsyn drew a deep breath to calm herself, even though there was nothing particular to fear about being caught—at worst, she'd be embarrassed and thrown out of the city.

The group she was following didn't even slow as they approached the soldiers. Kehrsyn saw the guards part for the entourage.

One, clearly an officer, touched a finger to his eyebrow and said, "Olaré, Blessed Madame."

Kehrsyn saw the various people in the small procession nod to the guards in acknowledgment, through the woman leading the party did not appear to acknowledge the troopers at all.

The group moved through the cordon without breaking stride. Nodding like the others, Kehrsyn allowed herself to be pulled along in their wake. From the corner of her eye, she saw one of the guards counting the people in the group as they passed. She held her breath as they moved past. Though no one moved to stop the group, she heard the soldier call for the sergeant's attention once they had passed through.

Kehrsyn's heart quickened. She knew her presence had raised suspicions. The procession might well be a nightly affair, and the guard's attention was drawn by an incongruous number. She was of a mind to curse her luck—how was she to know she'd joined in with the entourage of some sort of dignitary?—but as she had not yet been kicked out of the city, were she to curse her luck, the gods just might change it for her.

She could only assume that one or more of the city guards were watching the group. She certainly couldn't draw attention to herself with a suspicious glance backward, so her only hope was to play her interloper's role to the hilt and hope that it held up until the procession was out of sight of the whip.

Much to Kehrsyn's consternation, the assemblage kept pacing up the exact center of the broad street. She had no opportunity to slip away into a side street and vanish into the darkness. She hoped that none of the others would turn and notice her, question her presence, draw unwanted attention . . .

She also began to wonder where they were going. "Blessed Madame" was a title reserved for priestesses, so

the woman heading the group was someone of importance . . . but from which temple? The temple of Gilgeam
was as dead as its deity, populated only by a desperate,
powerless few. The other deities of the Untheri pantheon,
such as they were, had their temples in a different part of
town, an old section filled with monolithic ziggurats built
some three millennia past. She might be a priestess of
Mystra or Ishtar, the deities worshiped by the Northern
Wizards, but if so, Kehrsyn reckoned that she would head
for the city center, where the heart of the de facto government was. What did that leave? Possibly Tempus. He
was popular with the Chessentan mercenaries, common
enough during time of war. She remembered that the
church of Bane had been growing since the death of
Gilgeam, and though she did not like Gilgeamites, she
had grown up with them in power. She knew them. The
Banites—they were rumored to follow the worst of all
deities.

Still the group kept to the center of the street, walking
straight away from the guards' dragnet. While Kehrsyn
tried to figure out from which church the people hailed,
she remained alert for the sound of approaching footsteps,
guards come to question the priestess about her new follower.

None came.

Just as Kehrsyn was thinking she would soon be far
enough away to escape the guards' notice, the group
turned to the right.

Kehrsyn was caught by surprise, and her foot slid on the
cobbles as she tried to turn, to stay with the others. Thankfully, she was to the left and rear of the group, else her
stumble might have attracted the attention of one of the
other members. She glanced up at the front of the building
the group was heading toward.

It was a solid stone building, fronting the street. Two
broad stone steps led up to a large, wooden door. It had no

alcove, gave no cover to someone trying to evade the notice of the guards. Atop the doorway, she saw the sign of the five-headed dragon.

Kehrsyn's heart stopped in her chest, clutching her breath and refusing to let it leave.

The Five-Headed Dragon. Tiamat. The Chromatic Goddess. The Queen of the Dragons (or "Queen of the Evil Dragons" when her worshipers were not around).

But, above all, the Slayer of Gilgeam.

Tiamat's followers were reputed to be among the most ruthless people in Faerûn. They sought to emulate dragonkind, and compensated for their lack of draconic anatomy with an excess of viciousness.

Kehrsyn glanced back to the guards as casually as possible and saw that one of them was indeed still watching the group like an owl as they entered the front door of their small temple. Nothing for it, then. She had to enter; otherwise, the guards would be onto her. It was worth the risk. All she had to do was hide inside just long enough that the guards wouldn't be looking when she left the temple. Or maybe she could slide away undetected and leave by a side route.

She took a deep breath and stepped in just behind the rearmost of the believers, finding herself in a narthex that opened into a large common room. The others pulled off their winter cloaks and hung them on ornate wooden pegs carved in the shape of dragons' heads. Kehrsyn tried to slow down to give the others plenty of time to leave her unattended, but one of the other worshipers, muttering curses against the bitter cold, ushered her in so he could close the door behind her.

Of course, she couldn't resist, lest her reticence draw attention, so she found herself thrust in the midst of the group, all happily divesting themselves of their garb and heading into the next room for the roaring fire that burned in a fire pit surrounded by gigantic dragons' fangs.

"Sheesh," said the man behind her, "you need a new cloak. Here, lemme get that."

Kehrsyn felt his hands starting to pull her cloak off, pulling away the veil of her anonymity. Powerless, Kehrsyn tried to steel herself. Much as she didn't want to be ejected from the walls of Messemprar again, she readied herself to lunge out the front door. It was closed by a modern lever. She could flip the latch and hit the door at full speed.

The concealing darkness of her cloak pulled away from her head and shoulders, spilling light over her dank hair and hesitant eyes. The man stepped past her with her cloak and hung it on a peg, wiping the condensation from his beard with his hand.

Near the fire, one of the other worshipers, who was just sitting down, shot back to his feet, pointing aggressively at Kehrsyn.

"Who are you?" he bellowed.

"Look out!"

"She's got a sword!"

"Horat, watch it!"

The pace of events was far too quick for a scared, tired, wounded, hungry, cold young woman, and within a few heartbeats Kehrsyn found herself with her back to the door, one hand on the latch, surrounded by several fierce-looking men and women. Someone had a strong grip on her collar. Another had a long dagger held up menacingly. Harsh words washed over her like a wave.

"What are you doing here?"

"Just kill her!"

"Who are you? Speak!"

"Who sent you?"

"Shut up!"

"Search her!"

The press of bodies caused her left triceps to flare in pain as it was pressed between her body and the door.

Behind her back, Kehrsyn's left hand tightened on the latch, ready to shove it down and spill into the street. She prayed for a distraction, just one instant, and she'd make a break for it. The moment came, rather quickly.

"Quiet!" a woman's imperious voice rang in the building like a bell. It was a voice that was used to authority and a throat that was used to being loud.

The argument immediately ceased, and the people parted for the priestess to approach. It was the break Kehrsyn had been hoping for, but something in the priestess's voice impelled Kehrsyn to be still as well.

The woman was tall, with a broad build that spoke of physical strength and a jowly neck that spoke of rich foods. She wore a lush, blood-red robe embroidered in emerald, sapphire, sable, and ermine. The robe hid all but the more massive features of her body. In a few years, Kehrsyn surmised, it might hide nothing at all.

The matronly woman moved in, standing very close. Her face bore a nasty, puckered scar, shaped like a five-pointed star. It reached from chin to forehead and almost ear to ear. Her looming shadow seemed to cover Kehrsyn like the scar covered her face, and she glared down with rich blue eyes that, though fierce at the moment, seemed fundamentally warm, not cold.

"What are you doing here?" she asked. Her tone left no room for any other option than a direct answer.

"I was curious about joining your church," said Kehrsyn.

The woman leaned closer. Either that, or she grew by another two inches.

"Are you lying to me?" she demanded.

Kehrsyn considered her options, not moving save only to blink. "Yes," she said.

The woman leaned back, regarding Kehrsyn anew, and said, "I'm glad to see that you've stopped."

Kehrsyn, not knowing what else to do, waited.

"Why are you afraid of us?" the woman asked.

"What do you mean?" asked Kehrsyn, who was certain she didn't want to try another brave lie.

"I can see it in your eyes. You fear us. Yet Tiamat slew Gilgeam."

"And Gilgeam's death brought on this war. So because of Tiamat, we're all crowded in here hoping not to be overrun before we starve to death."

"An unfortunate and unforeseen consequence," said the priestess. "Tiamat was the only deity who cared for Unther. She ended this land's oppression."

"Unther did fine under Gilgeam for thousands of years. Oppression hardens us. A weaker people would buckle under the strains we rejoice in."

"You learned that from your mother, or your priest," observed the matron.

"Kind of both," Kehrsyn answered.

The priestess thought more, and said, in a very professorial tone, "If Unther thrives under oppression, then you should not fear power. Why, then, do you fear us?"

"Gilgeam protected us," said Kehrsyn, "and we gladly bore his yoke. Your religion worships the Queen of Dragons. You hold dragons in awe. You want to be just like them, and yet dragons protect nothing but their own hoard, killing anything that's a threat. So of course I fear you. Why wouldn't I, when your people greet me with blades?"

So saying, she silently opened the latch of the door behind her, ready to tumble out in the street screaming for help.

The priestess stood silently for a moment, then clucked her tongue.

"You are a very brave young woman," she said.

"Not really," Kehrsyn admitted. "I just try to hide my fear." She didn't add that she also always tried to have a back-up plan handy.

The priestess nodded and said, "Hiding your fear *is* bravery." She took a deep breath and rocked on her heels.

"I think I like you. You rather remind me of me when I was younger.

"At least," she added with a wry smile, "you remind me of how I prefer to think of myself when I was your age.

"You may go. If any of my people cause you any grief, tell them that you have the sufferance of Tiglath. That should spare you any trouble not of your own devising."

She waved her hand at the door, nodded ever so slightly, turned, and walked away.

"Thank you," said Kehrsyn to the priestess's departing back.

The others stood back and let Kehrsyn fetch her cloak and leave.

She opened the door and peered around to look for the cordon of guards. Though the rain had petered out, the streets were growing dark. She saw the torches of the guards some blocks away and felt safe to exit. She shut the door behind her and stepped down the stairs, clutching her left arm just below the shoulder in an attempt to throttle the throbbing pain.

Messemprar after nightfall was a far quieter place. Though there was no official curfew, the populace stayed indoors anyway. The weather was miserable, the over-crowded conditions taxed the soul, and the chronic hunger and the fear of war left little gaiety in the hearts of its residents. Even if people were in the mood to celebrate, there was nothing to do it with. The taverns carefully rationed out their overpriced ales, and often they ran dry and had to wait until a new ship entered port. People were in no mood to pay coin to musicians and other entertainers, whom, with the war, found themselves cast as "beggars" or "vagabonds" or "unproductive oafs." Entertainers, like, say, Kehrsyn.

Folks were also concerned about the possibility of being unjustly rousted and cast out of the city after dark, but Kehrsyn had not seen that happen. Once the city's main gate was closed for the evening, the guards didn't want to open it back up.

That left Kehrsyn free to wander the streets of a city filled with closed doors, shuttered windows, and fires sequestered behind mud-brick walls.

Ordinarily, she scouted out potential places to spend the night beforehand. The fact that she almost always ended up getting rousted outside didn't matter; she liked being prepared. That night, however, she hadn't had the chance to, or, more accurately, had squandered it by feeling sorry for herself. She heaved a weary sigh and circumnavigated the Tiamatan temple. If she had the sufferance of Tiglath, she fully intended to use it.

Toward the back, she found a reasonable place, a side door with a couple of wooden steps leading up to it. The small stair step was of utilitarian design, with open sides and close-fit planking. There was enough room underneath for a destitute young woman to crawl in and at the least have a roof of sorts over her head. Kehrsyn spent a few moments trying to gather whatever detritus might be around to provide protection against the wind, then settled in for the night.

She paused and prayed to whatever god might hear her, not that she really expected any of them to pay attention to a miserable little creature like her. Then she tried to find a way to lie down that was comfortable in the limited space beneath the stair and yet wouldn't irritate her burned left arm. Finally she found a reasonable compromise, laid her head on her lumpy bag, and tried to relax.

It was in that moment of quiet that she heard the sniffling.

It was a persistent, weak, whining sniffle, the moan of a small voice that knows no hope. Kehrsyn sagged as she heard the sound. It was one she was all too familiar with, having made it far too many times herself in her childhood. She pushed herself back out of her makeshift den, turned her head to one side and the other, and began to move down one of the side streets.

Three quarters of a block away, she found a man holding his young girl, wedged between a slop barrel and a wagon. Even in the gathering dark, Kehrsyn could clearly see that they were hungry, haggard, and cold. The little girl cried in a quiet monotone of misery punctuated by wet snuffles, a droning, hopeless lullaby of despair. How they'd remained in the streets Kehrsyn didn't know. Perhaps a guard had actually taken pity on them.

Kehrsyn sucked in her lips and sighed. Setting her jaw, she pulled out her half-eaten pear and gave it to the man. His hand trembled as he accepted it. He gave it to his daughter, taking none for himself. Kehrsyn started to step away, then stopped. She pulled out her two coins, separated the copper, and was about to hand it over as well, then she paused.

She stared at the man, only partially aware of his hopeful look, barely registering that the empty cry of the young girl had been replaced by the sound of crunching fruit. Finally Kehrsyn shook her head, slung the silver to the ground at the man's feet, and stomped off, frustration, compassion, guilt, charity, hunger, and pity all warring in her heart.

The heavy strike of her footsteps drowned out the man's hoarse blessings.

❂

Two reptilian eyes the color of emerald watched the cloaked figure stomp back down the deserted street. The tiny dragon wyrmling scuttled along the four-inch ledge that demarked the second story of the building, keeping pace with the strange human.

The wyrmling's sharp eyes saw the tears run down her face, saw the chin that quivered despite its defiant, proud set. Around the corner, it craned its serpentine neck to watch as the slender human crawled back under the stairs like a fox into a den.

These were all very interesting things, for it knew the smell of food, knew the glitter of precious metals, and knew that its mistress would want to know that someone was lairing under her stoop.

Spreading its fragile wings, the wyrmling took off with a faint flutter. It circled up, then landed on the windowsill of its mistress. It tapped the window with its beaklike muzzle.

Tiglath opened the window, picked up the wyrmling, and set it on her shoulders.

The wyrmling placed its muzzle next to her ear and began to speak.

CHAPTER SEVEN

Kehrsyn rose with the sun, though not enthusiastically.

Her teeth chattered with the cold until she found somewhere to spend her sole copper for a bowl of weak but warm broth for breakfast. She also managed to scrounge a new leather lacing for her boot in payment for using minor feats of legerdemain to distract the tanner's young children from their fight.

At some point during the night, the misty rain had turned to snow, and it continued to fall in occasional dustings throughout the morning. The heavy pedestrian traffic ground the snow down, transforming the pristine white glaze into mushy gray-brown clumps of slush that clung to boots and leached their icy water through the seams into people's stockings.

Kehrsyn considered what to do about her arm. Should I sell my rapier for a spell of healing? she wondered. If I did, I would be healed but almost defenseless . . . and I've endured—in fact, I am enduring—worse than a bad burn.

Speaking of which, she thought, maybe I'd best get this over with.

The guild thief, who never had mentioned her own name, had told her to give the wand to a Red Wizard named Eileph. Kehrsyn decided to go meet him.

She sought out the Mage Bazaar, a large, open square filled with towering tents in rich and gaudy colors and inundated with strange odors that at once tantalized and repelled. Kehrsyn walked past small booths selling powdered jade, past wagons with assorted alchemical glassware, and past a tent filled with "sacrificial and companionable animals of the finest qualities, carefully bred in every size and color, guaranteed docile, healthy, and free of infestations."

The Red Wizards' pavilion was not hard to find. It was a cluster of tents encircled by a high curtain of velvet, all centered around a soaring flagpole topped by a vivid red banner that hung beneath its dusting of white. At the entrance stood a huge warrior. Kehrsyn looked him over. He had heavy black armor, a shaved head covered with tattoos, and a greatsword as tall as she was. The unsheathed sword rested on its tip (carefully placed on a tiny wooden stand to preserve its point), and the warrior rested both of his hands on its pommel.

She walked over with an air of confidence that smothered her nervousness and asked the guard where she might find the Red Wizard named Eileph.

"You'll find him right over there, young lady," the warrior answered with a respectful tone. He gestured to one of the tents and added, "Have a nice day."

Kehrsyn stepped over, tentatively pulled back the heavy tent flap, and said, "Hello?"

"Come in, come in, what can I do for you?" said a grating, gravelly voice.

Kehrsyn stepped in and stopped in her tracks, stifling a

gasp. A misshapen lump of a wizard lurched toward her on uneven legs. At first she thought him to be a dwarf, but he was too thin, too frail . . . and, in spite of his bungled heritage, too human. While not a hunchback per se, he had a definite hunched posture, most likely due to a life spent studying musty tomes in dim light. By the numerous candles in the tent, Kehrsyn could see that one of his eyes was missing, the lids sewn together over the empty gap. His uneven nose had a septum that deviated to the side, missing alignment with the center of his mouth by a wide margin. Perhaps some of the distortion was due to a rippled burn scar that covered one cheek. He had bushy eyebrows with long, scraggly hairs, juxtaposed against a thin smattering of long, limp hair on his bulging, liver-spotted pate.

All that Kehrsyn apprehended in the passing of a single heartbeat. She saw as well a change in the wizard's expression from one of cheerful if avaricious hospitality to a glowering and weary disgust.

"I—I'm sorry," stammered Kehrsyn, recovering her composure.

She was impressed with the amount of bilious contempt Eileph was able to channel through his single eye.

"Don't even bother trying to be sorry for me," he said.

"No, I mean I'm sorry for my reaction," interrupted Kehrsyn, meeting his gaze. "It was rude of me."

Eileph raised one eyebrow—the one over the empty socket, a rather disconcerting gesture in itself—and considered Kehrsyn's words.

"Yes, it was," he said. "But in all my years in Messemprar, you're the first to accept your failure, instead of hiding it behind insolence or superciliousness. Therefore, you're forgiven."

"Did it hurt?" asked Kehrsyn, peering more closely at Eileph's face.

"Did what hurt?" he countered.

"That . . . burn on your face."

Eileph raised one hand to his cheek and said, "That was a wee mishap I had while trying to distill a potent acid. Yes, it hurt. There's nothing quite like feeling acid eat away your eye."

"How did you deal with the pain?" Kehrsyn asked.

Eileph looked at her with affronted dignity and replied, "I am Thayan."

Kehrsyn smiled. "Right," she said, finding in that simple truth the key to her own pride. She was an Untheri, and she could deal with a burned arm, even rejoice in her endurance.

"Enough of my face, young lady," said he with a wave of his tattooed hand. "Maker knows I've seen enough of it myself. You came here for business. Your name is . . . ?"

"Kehrsyn."

"Yes, of course. I was told to expect you, but I did not expect you so soon. Do you have it?"

"No . . . no, not yet," she said.

"I see," said Eileph. "Are you seeking some additional . . . supplies? I have quite a range of items both alchemical and—"

"No, I don't have any . . . I don't have a need for any, uh, new items. I was more just dropping by to, you know, see who I was dealing with." Kehrsyn hesitated. "Um . . . can you, you know, cast a healing spell or something?"

"Hmph," grunted the wizard. "I would think that someone going after a high-stakes target like yours would have healing enough of her own."

Kehrsyn shrugged.

Eileph shook his head and said, "Healing is not my specialty, young lady. Besides, pursuant to the war, Thay has made an agreement with Unther that we shall sell healing potions only to the military."

Kehrsyn sagged onto a stool and stared at the ground.

"I couldn't afford a potion, anyway," she said. "I just wanted a little spell."

Eileph studied her for just a moment, then said, "I have a proposition for you."

Kehrsyn looked up, bleak hope in her eyes.

"You're going into a very interesting place," the Red Wizard continued. "You may find some other magical trinkets around. I will purchase the right of first refusal on them. I will give you ten silvers now, as a deposit. If you find anything interesting, you sell it to me at full market price. Deal?"

Eileph spat on his hand and held it out.

"Deal," said Kehrsyn, spitting on her palm and shaking his hand.

Eileph's grip was weak, which, considering how weak her own grip was, Kehrsyn found discomforting.

"Done and done," said Eileph, counting out the coins and pressing them warmly into Kehrsyn's hands. "Was there anything else you needed, young lady?"

Kehrsyn clutched the coins tightly, counted them again, then slid them into a pouch inside her sash.

"Well, no," she said, "not yet, but there's . . ."

"Yes, of course, there's that other business," said Eileph. "Come take a look."

He kneeled down and picked up a large, leather portfolio. He placed it on a side table and opened it up, pulling out a few sheets of fine paper.

"I've been doing a little divination," the wizard cackled, "to help me with my part of the work. Strictly subtle spells, I assure you, nothing that would raise an eyebrow. I must say, I'm looking forward to seeing this beauty in real life."

He laid the pages on the low table in the center of the tent. Exquisite graphite drawings covered the sheets, meticulous studies that showed the details of the carvings in the wand, which lay in a lined box. Kehrsyn studied the drawings carefully. The sorceress's description had left her with a far different impression of the item. She'd expected a sturdy, weatherworn item, but if these diagrams were a good depiction—and, based on the skill with which they were drawn, Kehrsyn felt certain they were—the wand was in excellent shape.

"Judging by its aura," Eileph said, "it might be a necromancer's staff, but it has a unique style I've not seen before."

Kehrsyn pulled back. Eileph's breath was offensive with the smell of untended hygiene.

"Necromancer's staff?" she asked. "You mean, like death magic?"

"Yep. But it's so small, I just have to wonder. . . ."

"By the way," he added, "the information you people had was perfectly accurate. Good thing, otherwise I have no idea how long it would have taken me to find it. Look for a badly weathered wooden case."

"Hey, thanks. That'll help. More than you know."

"When do you think you might be pursuing this activity?"

"Probably tonight," Kehrsyn said. "Get it over with."

"It seems you folks are a bit disorganized. Be careful . . . I'd hate to see anything happen to you, young lady. It's a rare day that someone surprises me."

"Thanks," said Kehrsyn, dropping her eyes.

"Hmph," said Eileph. He drummed his fingers. "I won't be here after dark. It gets too cold. No one comes, anyway. So ask for me at the Thayan enclave. You know where that is, right?"

Kehrsyn nodded.

"Right. I'll ensure the guards know to expect you, young lady."

"Great." Kehrsyn took a deep breath, then let it back out. "See you tonight," she said.

"Eh? Oh, right. Be careful."

"It's too late for that," she said with a wan smile.

She rose and exited the tent, leaving the heavy velvet flap swinging in her wake.

◉

At noon, Kehrsyn tried to perform in the Jackal's Courtyard, but her mind was distracted, her heart burdened, and her left arm stiff and painful. She gave up early, packed up her stuff, and left.

As she exited, she happened upon the sorceress passing in the other direction. The callous woman gave Kehrsyn a meaningful look, never breaking stride.

Kehrsyn scooped up a particularly dirty pile of slush and prepared to hurl it at the insolent woman, but paused.

Nah, she thought, best to wait until after I've done their dirty work.

She let the slushy mess drop back to the cobbles, and moved through town toward the Imperial Quarter. There the original inhabitants of Messemprar had built the government center and the massive temple of Gilgeam. The government center was still in use, and the temple had been converted to a barracks for foreign mercenaries. She entered Gilgeam's Altar, renamed the Plaza of the Northern Wizards, and poked around for Port Street.

Moving slowly down Port, she studied the various signs and sigils on the buildings. Some hung from poles, while others were rendered in peeling paint directly onto the stone or wood of the walls. Up ahead, she saw a well-crafted sign of carved wood, suspended from an arm of green brass. It had a large, well-rendered wing on it, spread wide as if flying, painted in blacks and blues. She drew closer and saw two glyphs, one painted on each side of the door, ancient pictograms representing an abbreviation for Wing's Reach. A sign on the door read, "Purveyors of fine goods, antiques, exotics, and curios."

She casually circled the building. It was an older edifice, solidly built and impeccably maintained. Ornamental carvings of gods, animals, and other more abstract items encrusted the building's circumference, delineating the separation between its three floors. No hint of moss or accumulated dirt could be found in the seams of the smooth stonework. Heavy shutters covered the various windows, and looked like they would do well at keeping the chill at bay. When left open on a summer's day they'd surely admit a nice, cool ocean breeze through the place.

Smoke issued from at least one chimney. According to Kehrsyn's map, there were two main fire pits, one in the kitchen and one in the main hall. Other fireplaces could be found in the best living quarters on the third floor. There were four staircases, situated more or less in the corners of the building. Doors opened onto Port Street, Angle Street, and an alley behind the building, and a generous supply of wide windows adorned the upper floors.

With the weather, the only portals to the building likely to be open were the front door and the chimneys. Just to see, though, Kehrsyn tried the rear door, which she assumed was the servants' entry. The bolt had been thrown, and it was secured with a dwarven bronze lock, which was an obstacle Kehrsyn was not certain she could overcome.

That left the front door and the chimney.

Either way, she thought with concern, I'll be dropping right into the fire.

She was confident in her ability to move quietly and to use the natural camouflage of light and shadow. Those were tricks that had kept her alive since childhood. She trusted in her natural dexterity, her lightness of touch, and her ability to prevent collateral noises when pilfering. She was concerned, however, with her ability to get doors opened, especially if they were locked or ensorcelled.

The fear of becoming enchanted, blasted, or turned to stone gave Kehrsyn pause. Magic that might disfigure or cripple her made the score not worth the risk . . . until she reminded herself that the alternative was to be turned in for the murder of a Zhent guard. She drew in a deep breath between her teeth, tried to evict such thoughts from her mind, and steeled herself for the task at hand.

She studied the building from a safe vantage point down the street. She pulled out the map and pored over it, correlating the exterior features with the interior layout. She marked the streets and nearby doors and side streets, as well as the various items in the alley—items that might be obstacles or cover.

Then she ran through a variety of potential scenarios for breaking in and navigating the building. Many did not seem feasible, and the rest required moving through areas that were, in all probability, occupied by the inhabitants. She tapped her teeth with her fingernail as she thought through the possibilities and outcomes, then tried to divine ways to defeat the various weak points of her plans. For once, she was happy for the nightly dragnets that sought to evict her from the city. They had given her much practice in developing strategies, foreseeing complications, and preparing fallback plans.

The cold slowly crept through her cloak and clothing as she sat inactive, but she didn't notice until the map started trembling with her shivers. She got up, put away her map, picked up her bag, and began walking briskly away, looking to warm herself with exertion.

As she walked past the corner of Wing's Reach, she failed to notice the sorceress watching her from a nearby rooftop.

❦

Kehrsyn purchased a light dinner, but the butterflies in her stomach kept her from eating it all. The night weighed on her mind with everything that could go wrong, and the worry seemed to make her burned left arm throb all the more.

Dusk was beginning to fall, so Kehrsyn pushed her

plate away and left the small, crowded dining room of the resting house. As she stepped into the street, she saw that the snow had grown from occasional flurries to a continuous, if light, fall.

That was the first thing that could go wrong. The more snow that fell by the time she made her getaway, the easier it would be to track her. Kehrsyn would have to strike earlier than she wanted to.

She maneuvered to a wide thoroughfare and looked for the cordon of soldiers. Seeing them approaching, herding a variety of vagrants before them, she took her pouch of coins into her hand, loosened the drawstring, and waited until she saw a sizeable cluster of people moving up the street. A pair of families and assorted pairs and trios, all moved in a dispersed group for their respective homes. Kehrsyn strode out into the street, pacing her step so that she would be at their head.

As she approached the soldiers, she nodded in greeting and began to stride past as if it were the most natural thing in the world. As she tried to slide through their ranks, one soldier reached out and grabbed her right arm, just below the elbow. As he did that, she jerked her hand against his grip and spilled her purse of coins. The silvers and coppers scattered across the cobbles.

As expected, some of the other people—all the refugees and even a few of those with homes—made a quick move to try to retrieve some of the coins, causing the soldiers to turn their attention to them. Kehrsyn berated the soldier who'd "made" her spill her valuables, then quickly recovered as many of her coins as possible, pointing to various stray coins for other soldiers to recover.

Naturally, those who were about to be evicted from the city tried to use the confusion to work their way back through the cordon and hide away. Though the soldiers were too alert to let that happen, the activity kept them distracted. In the general chaos that followed her accident, Kehrsyn concealed herself behind a loud tirade against "careless city constables," an accusation the volume, content, and speaker of which the soldiers were only too happy to ignore.

Seeing that her words fell on deaf ears, she turned on her heel and stomped away. Thus she made her way deeper into the city, unchallenged by those assigned to turn her out.

Once safely out of sight, she counted her coins. She'd lost a silver and three coppers. It would have been more, but her swift and delicate fingers had snitched several pieces back from the open purse of a wealthy resident who'd been helping himself to her spilled coins. As punishment, she'd also slipped one of his gold coins to a particularly needy-looking refugee.

She started to make her way back to Wing's Reach. There were advantages to making her move soon, she reflected. For one, the city guard would still be tied up primarily with ejecting the refugees from the city and therefore be less available to pursue a thief, were they to spot her. The snow was, of course, a second factor, and the chance that Wing's Reach might lock up for the night was a third.

But most of all, and reason enough unto itself, it got the tasteless act done with. She wasn't sure whether she'd deal with post-theft guilt better than she dealt with pre-theft trepidation, but she'd had enough dread for one day and was willing to try guilt, if only for variety.

She approached Wing's Reach from the rear, diverting through the alley to drag a bale of hay from the stables across the street to rest against one wall, just beneath a pair of windows, one window on the second floor and one on the third. She pulled her dagger from its hiding place beneath the bag and tied its scabbard to the back of her left forearm with the scraps left over from her cut bootlaces. That done, she pulled a ball of twine from her bag, then concealed her bag against the wall under the hay.

With great reluctance, she untied her rapier and scabbard. She placed them in a large urn half full of rain. The thin ice covering cracked as she shoved the wooden scabbard through. She hated to treat her scabbard like that, but it would either soak in the ice for only a very short time or else she wouldn't have need of it again.

She moved around to the front doors, which were as old-fashioned as the building was aged. Inertia alone held them closed, and the only way to latch them was with a large, heavy timber. She paused, breathing deeply and rapidly until she was on the verge of hyperventilating. Aside from being a part of her disguise, the slight fuzz it gave her brain helped quash her fears and reluctance.

She burst in the front door without knocking. As expected, she entered into a large foyer with a nicely tiled floor and smooth, white walls covered with traditional, stylized Untheric murals. To Kehrsyn's left, a single lamp hung from a chain dangling from the rafter. Two guards sat at a small table beneath it, wrapped in their cloaks and playing at a game of sava. Kehrsyn's sudden and loud appearance startled them. One tipped over the table—*sava* pieces, coins, wine, and all—as he burst to his feet and jumped back. The other displayed more presence of mind but less grace as he seized his khopesh, tripped over his cloak, and fell to his knees.

"What do you think you're doing?" bellowed the guard on the floor, while the other tried to cover for his surprise by grabbing his weapon as well.

Kehrsyn labored with her lungs, noticing that, even inside the foyer, she could see the vapors of her breath in the air.

"Copper . . . " she panted, "copper for a message, sir?"

"Message for whom?" the guard asked, getting back to his feet.

"Anyone, sir," Kehrsyn panted, "but time is passing."

The two guards looked at each other.

"I'll get Ahegi," said one, and the other nodded.

Kehrsyn paced around the room, trying to regain her breath. At one end she staggered slightly, putting out one hand to steady herself and deftly unlatching the simple clasp that held the shutters closed. Hands on hips, she then moved across to the other corner of the room, cast open the shutters very deliberately, leaned out, and took a few deep breaths of the cold outside air.

"Close that up!" the guard grumbled. "It's cold enough already sitting in here. We don't need snow on top of it."

"Sorry," mumbled Kehrsyn, still breathing deeply.

She closed the shutters and pretended to latch them back shut. She heard footsteps returning to the entry hall, so she walked back over to the guards' table and pulled her hair out of her face.

The second guard escorted a tall, powerful, harsh-looking man. Though he was strongly built, his physique had suffered badly for age and privilege. His head was shaved, and two concentric blue circles adorned his forehead, a traditional Untheric mannerism that signified that he was an educated nobleman versed in magic. The presence of a third ring would indicate that the wearer was a priest, but since the death of Gilgeam, the third ring was almost never seen. Gilgeamite priests had abandoned its use to avoid vengeance, and priests of other religions thought it prudent to follow the example.

The second guard pointed brusquely to Kehrsyn and said, "That is she, Lord Ahegi."

The nobleman approached. Seeing his face, Kehrsyn had a flash of nausea, so she dropped her eyes to protect her expression from betraying her discomfort.

"You wished to see me?" he asked in a thin voice that sounded like it had been scoured by the sands for a hundred years.

"I wished to see someone, sir," she said. "Copper for a message?"

"The message first," Ahegi said.

"Sir, a new ship is just about to dock, sir. They're piloting it in with longboats and lanterns. They say there might be food, sir, and who knows what all else. Thought you might like to know, maybe greet it at the dock."

Ahegi pushed out his lower lip, nodded, pulled out a copper, and tossed it to Kehrsyn.

"Thank you, sir," she said and turned to leave.

"Wait," said Ahegi, and Kehrsyn was surprised at the commanding power his reedy voice had. She froze in her tracks, her back crawling. "Which dock is this ship using?"

Kehrsyn turned, glanced once at Ahegi, and looked back down at her feet.

"That'll be another copper," she said. "Sir. . . ."

She heard Ahegi inhale sharply, and in her peripheral vision she saw him rise up in anger and raise a hand to strike. She flinched away, and he stopped, his raised arm quivering.

"Very well," he said through gritted teeth.

He tossed another copper. It landed on the floor, by the door.

"They said they'd take it to the Long Wharf, sir," Kehrsyn lied. "It's a large ship, you see, but maybe you can buy out the whole shipment before anyone else shows up, right?"

"Begone," he said.

Kehrsyn was only too happy to obey. She wanted to be away from his abraded voice.

Knowing I'll be stealing from *him*, she thought, certainly makes my next task more palatable.

CHAPTER EIGHT

His hooded cloak furled around him to ward off
the chill, Demok moved through the streets of
Messemprar. Ahegi's bodyguard led the way,
scanning the streets for danger, though few
people were even out, let alone lurking around in
such freezing weather. Ahegi followed, along
with a smattering of aides, including one who
carried a locked strongbox loaded with pieces of
gold and platinum, some tradeweight pearls,
and, hidden beneath a false bottom, a silver
necklace studded with diamonds that looked
more valuable than it actually was. Ahegi was
fond of cheating greedy merchant captains.

Demok was one of three whose duty was to
guard the bearer of the strongbox. He smiled in
the dark. Receiving sensitive assignments like
this proved that those of Wing's Reach had not yet
discerned his true allegiance.

The thin layer of snow crunched underfoot as
the group made its way to the docks. Freed from

the impact of thousands of feet, the day's slushy remains were hardening into piles of ice at the sides of the street, beneath a pristine dusting of white.

Demok scowled. The Long Wharf was the easternmost dock, the farthest from Wing's Reach. It stood squarely in the mouth of the River of Metals, washed alternately by seawater and fresh water in the ever-shifting tide. Off-loading the cargo on a slippery, icy wharf would be a hazardous task. Doing so at night would be foolhardy. Even sanding the dock might not avail, with the constant snowfall.

Demok trotted forward until he was even with Ahegi's bodyguard. He scanned the street ahead with his keen, experienced eye. They were moving by the most direct route to the docks, down the grand, wide Avenue of the Gods. A short while ago, some messenger had run from the docks to Wing's Reach, bringing news. A person running at full speed would leave tracks in the snow, perhaps occasionally even wide, scudding marks as she lost balance on the cold, wet flagstones. Yet there were no such tracks.

If enough time had passed, they might have been snowed over. He called for the group to halt. They did, though Ahegi and the others were noticeably perturbed. Demok was, after all, delaying their chance at getting first crack at a new shipment of food.

Demok checked the avenue from one side to the other. He saw nothing, aside from a plodding pair of tracks belonging to a man with a limp and his poorly shod mule. Based on the snowfall in the footprints, they had passed maybe half an hour before. There was no sign of a fast-moving messenger, and even had that messenger taken another route, why would there be only one messenger, and why would said messenger head to Wing's Reach?

Demok waved the group on, then turned back. He'd be most interested to see what sort of tracks had been laid in front of their door. He didn't think he'd like what he'd find.

Hiding in the shadows in a nearby alley, Kehrsyn watched the group of hopeful merchants leave Wing's Reach. Ahegi loomed half a head taller than the others. Once more, Kehrsyn's heart trembled at Ahegi's appearance. She tried to write it off to his authoritarian demeanor. She'd had a lot of bad experiences with those in power throughout her life, and Ahegi comported himself like another budding tyrant with his imposing size, chiseled bald head, and scowl.

Once the group had turned the corner and left her view, Kehrsyn wriggled out of her slit skirt. She would need all the flexibility her leggings would allow. She didn't want to leave the skirt lying around, so instead she put it around her neck like a cowl. She stole back across the street, pulled out her length of twine, and tied one end to one of the shutters near the guards' table. Moving across the front door toward the far corner of the building, she trailed the twine behind her.

She paused in frustration. The twine was a bit short. It didn't come nearly as close to the other window as she'd hoped. She sighed, exhaling slowly, building her resolve. Nothing for it but to try. The longer she tarried, the more likely her ruse might be discovered. She set the twine down, trotted to her target window, and pried it open with her fingers, just enough to ease her work. She moved back to the twine, then pulled off her boots and tucked them into her sash. The cold, wet snow leaked through her socks, but she bore the discomfort; she didn't want to risk having the hard soles of her boots make noises where her woolen-clad feet wouldn't.

She gave a tug on the twine. The shutter didn't budge. Since the twine was almost exactly in line with its hinge, the shutter was very resistant to being moved. She had to tug hard enough to overcome its inertia but not so hard that it would bang open unnaturally. She held her arm out to her side and tugged again. Nothing. She sneered with annoyance, looked both ways to ensure the street remained empty, then took a few steps out into the street and whipped the twine to the side, sending a wave along its length.

Success! The shutter creaked open. Kehrsyn slid back to the walls of the building, tugged the shutter just a little wider, then dropped the string and scooted over to the other window on the opposite side of the front room. She pried the shutter open just a bit—the shutter that hinged away from the guards, so they would not see a telltale gap—and listened.

"Gilgeam's gizzard, it's a cold night," one of the guards groused. "Pony up. It's my roll."

"Hey, no wonder it's so crapping cold in here," the other said. "That stupid idiot girl left the window unlatched. Go grab that, would you?"

"Fine, just keep your hands where I can see them."

"What, you don't trust me?"

The other snorted.

Knowing their attention was on each other and the open window, Kehrsyn pried the shutter fully open and pulled herself up. She carefully let herself down inside, crouching in the shadows in the far corner of the foyer, and closed the shutter without latching it.

She watched as the guard came back from the window, sat down, and resumed the game with his compatriot. Once they were engrossed in the game again, she moved quietly over to the stairwell at the corner of the foyer, keeping low and quiet, letting her cloak conceal her lithe limbs.

The wooden spiraling stairs offered little cover, but fortunately they were not lit, either. If worse came to worst, Kehrsyn knew she could climb over the railing for evasion or escape. She wrung out her socks beneath the stairs, then ascended, carefully walking on her toes along the inner edge of the spiral, for it was less likely to creak. She also knew that most people walked toward the outside, and therefore would be less likely to notice (or worse yet, slip on) the small stains of water her damp socks left behind.

She knew from the map that hallways circled the second and third floors, bisected in the center like a squared-off figure eight. The outer rooms were generally sleeping quarters, while the storerooms sat in the center. The stairwell came up at one corner of the hallway, and the room she wanted to reach was on the second floor, down the long hall and around the far side.

When she reached the second floor, she peered out of the stairwell and down the hallway. She winced in frustration. A guard waited at the center of the longer hall, at its intersection with the cross-connector. He leaned against the wall staring in her direction. An oil-lamp sconce lit the immediate area. Though his stance said he was not alert, she knew she could not sneak up on him. Presumably a second guard stood watch beneath a second lamp across the building, where the two could see each other. That ensured that any thieves would have to surprise and kill both simultaneously to be free to walk the halls.

Kehrsyn crept out of the stairwell, slithering low like a mongoose until she was safe in the short hall. She stalked silently to the other end to peer at the other guard. He paced back and forth, slapping his thigh with one hand and trailing the other along the wall. He only took a few disinterested paces in each direction, but Kehrsyn figured that would be enough.

She waited until he turned his back on her, then she glided quickly forward as far as she dared, to one of the doors. She lay down on the floor, tight against the wall, positioning herself just before the guard turned back. The skin on her burned arm protested being stretched and pressed, but Kehrsyn just gritted her teeth. She bowed her head so that her dark hair would conceal her face, trusting her cloak to hide her body.

She counted the guard's steps as he walked back up the hall, then heard the telltale grind of his feet as he turned.

As he started back down the hall, Kehrsyn rose and scooted forward, walking low, but taking large steps timed to land with the guard's heavy tread. She stopped at the last door before the intersection, the last door safe from the view of the guard opposite. She knew the room was most likely someone's quarters. No light came from beneath the door. It was early enough that she doubted anyone would be in. If they were awake, they'd likely be gathered around the fire in the main hall. She tried the handle, and found that it was unlocked. She gently opened the door, scooted in, and quietly closed the door behind her.

She paused, listening for any sound within the room. It was quiet.

She stood, pressed her ear to the door, and waited until the guard had approached, turned, then headed away once more.

Kehrsyn could make out the outlines of windows, so she crossed the room on her knees, hands out, legs moving in short, gentle steps. After finding her way across the black interior to one of the windows, she unlatched it by touch and peered out. The ornamental carvings made a ledge of sorts—not one she'd use if she had a choice, for the carvings were irregular and covered with snow—but suitable enough to her task.

"Well," she muttered, "at least the snow will help hide me from people on the street."

Slipping outside, she balanced on the balls of her feet on the carved head of an ox. Stabilizing herself by gripping the windowsill, she reached out with her other hand to look for a handhold. None were to be found.

"I must be crazy," she murmured as she advanced along the wall, her hold on the windowsill getting less secure as she moved.

As she feared, the well crafted stone exterior offered no further handholds.

She had to release her hold on the window when her reaching hand was still well shy of the next window, which looked a mile distant. Breathing shallowly, spread-eagled against the cold stone wall and carefully brushing snow away with her stocking-clad feet, she inched her way forward. She thanked the gods that she had decent leg and foot strength, even if her arm strength was lacking. A childhood spent running from adults continued to serve her well.

Her hand reached the weatherworn edge of the next window, and she grabbed on. She couldn't enter that window, for the room opened into the halls' intersection, right next to the lamp and in full view of both guards. Instead, she gritted her teeth and continued moving on the protruding carvings to the next window once more committing her safety to her balance and the strength of her feet. She wondered if Gilgeam's head was among those she stepped on. The very thought filled her with a sort of vengeful glee. The god-king had caused her a lot of pain, first by his presence, and since, with the war and all, by his absence.

At the second window, she took a moment to regain her breath and let her heart calm itself. No light bled through the shutter slats, so she pulled her dagger and worked it between the shutters, lifting the latch inside. When she felt it give way, she muttered a quick, small prayer of thanks to whichever god was looking after her that the latch was of the same make as the others in the building. She listened for noises and heard none. With a quiet sigh of profound relief, she pulled herself safely inside the room. Since her socks had picked up more snow seepage, she rung them out through the window into the alley below.

She left the shutter open, just in case she had to make a quick departure, and crossed over to the door. It was just slightly ajar, and she could see it clearly by the crack of lamplight that wedged its way into the room. Standing well back, she peered out through the gap. The guard passed, and Kehrsyn stepped closer. She heard him slapping his thigh and whistling, heard him pivot, and heard him approach again. Just as she saw him pass the door, she teased it open, slipped out, and pulled it most of the way closed in one fluid motion, then dashed for the far corner of the hallway, again pacing her steps to match the guard's.

She turned the far corner just as she heard the guard reverse his pace. She thanked her stocking feet; she could never have moved that distance silently while wearing her boots. Even bare feet would have made a telltale *pat-pat* sound. She only hoped she'd wrung her socks out well enough, or that, if she hadn't, the guard would not notice her small, wet footprints.

She felt more safe. She was past the guards at the front door as well as the guards posted to watch the valuables. Any security she'd discover from that point forward would be traps, locks, or someone who happened by. Still, she wasn't going to put her boots on until just before her escape. Out of sight, silence was her greatest ally.

She pulled a match from her vest and struck it, using her body to shield its faint glow from the guards in the hall. She moved to the door to the room that had been marked on her map. It was a plain wooden door with a sign saying "Expeditionary Supplies." Just down the hall, Kehrsyn glimpsed the glint of a metal chain and padlock securing the next door. She smiled. On her map, the door was labeled "Treasure Room," and with a big lock announcing the presence of valuables just down the hall, why would anyone raid a simple door marked "Expeditionary Supplies"?

Hiding in the playground, Kehrsyn called it. It was a trick she had learned as a kid: If you look ordinary, no one sees you. When she'd been spotted stealing and had gotten a decent lead on her pursuit, she escaped her pursuers by joining a group of kids in their play. Those chasing her raced right past, searching for a frightened, fleeing little girl, not a happy girl with a big smile playing at crack-the-whip.

Kehrsyn, however, knew the ploy as well as those of Wing's Reach. She tested the door to the expeditionary supplies and found that, true to the disguise, it wasn't even locked. That had been her biggest fear, for she wasn't confident in her lockpicking skills.

She stepped in and closed the door behind her. A lamp hung from one wall, so she lit it and trimmed the wick to a mere glimmer. She looked around the room, searching for the necromantic wand. A badly weathered wooden case, Eileph had said. She poked behind sausages, wax-covered rounds of cheese, cooking tools, and coils of rope, until she found a plain, battered wooden box shoved to the rear of a bottom shelf and labeled "orc bitter tea." It looked like it was the same size as the open box illustrated in Eileph's drawings.

Rather than pull the box out, Kehrsyn decided to play it safe. She cleared the other items away from it, pulled her skirt-cowl up to cover her nose and mouth, and undid the latch with her dagger. A quartet of long needles, curved like cobra fangs, lanced out of their hidden recesses, scything through the air where Kehrsyn's hand would have been, had she been careless.

She pursed her lips. Clearly, that was where the disguise ended. Opening the box could be even more dangerous. She found a small bolt of cloth tucked next to the cooking supplies. She leaned the cloth against the box as a sort of shield, then reached the dagger around to the side and pried the lid open.

She heard a crack, a spatter, and a hiss. Acrid smoke wisped from the back side of the cloth. Kehrsyn pulled the cloth away, and saw some pungent liquid eating into the fabric. She shoved the cloth aside, held the lid of the box open with one hand, and used the dagger to pry the precious wand up from its crushed velvet bed. A razor sliced up from the side of the box, cutting right where her wrist would have been and nicking its own blade as it impacted her dagger.

Once she'd scooted the tail end of the staff out of the box, she cut herself a square of the cloth to protect her hand as she picked the treasure up.

"There now," she whispered. "That wasn't so bad, was it?"

Demok moved at a steady trot through the city, an easy run that he could maintain for hours, with a short, balanced stride perfect for crossing treacherous terrain. The closer he got to Wing's Reach, the more concerned he became about the lack of a trail left by the so-called messenger.

When he reached the building, the first thing he did was check the perimeter. Though the footprints on the steps had been smeared almost entirely out by the passing of Ahegi's entourage, he could still see the young woman's tracks beneath the new dusting of snow. When she'd come to deliver the message, she'd walked at an easy pace from the alley.

He noticed the twine tied to the shutter and followed its trail to spy a second set of tracks on the other side of the door. Though they were of stocking feet, he could tell they were the same size and weight as those of the boots. He followed them to the farthest window of the foyer. The shutter was closed, but it opened easily. The snow on the sill was crushed, showing that someone had indeed entered the building there. He stuck his head in the window and glared over at the two guards. They were gambling with sava, the incompetent buffoons.

He flipped the other shutter open and jumped through, one arm on the windowsill for balance.

"On your feet!" he barked.

The two guards shot out of their chairs, fumbling for their weapons, shocked to see Demok back in the room, reappearing as if he'd been a ghost.

"That messenger is a thief," he growled. He stalked over to them, but his eyes roamed the room and its exits. "She snuck back in. *You*"—he spat the word—"let her pass! You, grab your khopesh, stand against those doors, and kill anyone you don't recognize. If she gets you, make noise before you die.

"You," he ordered the other guard, "grab everyone in the main hall. Get lanterns, and post two at the foot of each stairwell. Bring the rest here and follow. Quietly.

"*Move!*" he barked, and the two leaped to obey.

Gritting his teeth against the mulish incompetence of the hirelings, Demok moved over to the stairwell nearest the open window. A careful look showed the slight glimmer of light reflecting off tiny beads of water and casting small shapes on the polished wooden staircase. He climbed, drawing a short sword with his left hand and transferring it to his right. While he generally preferred the long sword, the thrusting action of a short sword was better suited to the narrow confines of a building.

At the top of the stairs, he spied the guard standing at the intersection. He snapped his fingers once, then twice, getting the guard's attention. The guard peered toward the stairwell. Demok displayed his short sword. The guard nodded, drew his khopesh, and began scanning the halls. He also waved his free arm to pass the message to his companion across the hall.

Demok's keen ears heard the other guard stop pacing. He shook his head. Any thief worth her title would hear the change in the guard's habit and know an alarm had been raised.

Demok leaned down and studied the floor from a low vantage. He could see no marks of any water down the hall leading to the nearest guard. He moved down the short hall and lay down at the far corner to study the opposite long hall, and, visible in the lamplight, saw more damp footprints down one side. He slid to the door where they ended, paused, then lunged into the room.

It was empty.

He crossed to the window and opened the shutters, noting that they were not latched. He stuck his head out, looking up, down, right, and left. He saw that the shutters two rooms down were thrown wide open. He glanced at the narrow footholds offered by the ornamental carvings and whistled a low, appreciative salute to the thief's daring.

He dashed back to the hall, turned, and moved past the concerned guard. He saw the next door slightly ajar and just a trace of water against the wall. He gestured the guard to take the lamp and follow him. Below, he faintly heard the guards grabbing their lamps and weapons, and winced at their incidental noises. His sword held defensively in front of him, he stalked down the hallway toward the corner.

Just as he reached the corner, he saw the thief running toward him, clutching something in one hand. Her eyes widened as she saw him, and he was likewise startled by the sudden encounter. His surprise slowed his reactions for the blink of an eye, but then he reached out to grab her collar.

Naturally she tried to stop, but Demok knew she was too close, her momentum too fast. His wide, powerful left hand reached for her clothes and gripped the material . . . and he was left holding nothing but a cowl, as the thief slipped on her wet stockings and fell to the floor.

He glanced down at her, tossed the cloth aside, and began to reach for her again, only to see her pull her knees up to her chest and lash out with both of her feet. One foot caught him squarely in the pelvis, the other in the abdomen just below the diaphragm. The forceful blow knocked the breath out of him and propelled him into the guard holding the lamp. He landed awkwardly, and he deliberately dropped his short sword to avoid skewering either the guard or himself as he tumbled to the floor.

The young woman turned around and lunged for the stairwell at the other end of the hallway. Demok regained his feet and charged after her in the dim corridor, drawing his long sword. When he reached the stairwell, he vaulted over the railing and dropped to the ground floor, landing in a combat-ready crouch.

Two startled guards stared back at him.

"What's happening?" one asked.

Demok snarled his frustration at having been outmaneuvered.

"Upstairs! Follow me!" he ordered, and lunged back up the staircase, taking three steps at a time.

He reached the third floor just in time to see the thief. She had already run back down the short hallway and entered the room one floor above where they had first encountered each other. He saw her open the shutters, climb through the window, and jump into the alley below. He ran for the window, and as he leaned out he saw the bale of hay on the ground, moved there by the thief herself. He saw no movement otherwise.

He gripped the sill tightly in frustration and stared into the falling snow.

"Grab a lamp," he said. "Follow me outside. Leave those tracks untouched."

CHAPTER NINE

Kehrsyn had always loved the sensation of falling; it reminded her of flying. When she was a kid, she'd spent many hot summer days jumping off a high bridge into the river, trying to capture that evasive feeling. Since she'd become an adult, however, her flying and jumping and falling had all been associated with escaping danger.

Funny, she thought, how much you can think of when you're in serious trouble.

Kehrsyn hit the bale of hay and rolled off to the side that concealed her bag. She snatched the bag's strap and plucked her rapier from the earthenware urn as she ran for the corner of the building. Once around the corner, she flipped the strap over her shoulder, jammed the stolen scepter through her sash in place of her boots (twisting the wand around to create a sort of knot to hold it, for surety's sake), yanked her boots on, and gripped the ties of her scabbard in her teeth. Then, with an unsettling feeling of déjà vu, she climbed up the side of the building across from her. She didn't want to be followed in the streets, but she was also beginning to have uneasy feelings about the name Wing's Reach.

She fled across the snow-covered rooftops as quietly as she could, and dropped back to the streets when she ran out of houses. There she took a deep breath and relaxed her stance. She reversed her cloak so that the lining was on the outside, changing its color to white. At least, it used to be white, but years of use had made it an uneven beige color. She pulled her hair back and secured it in a ponytail, then took her dagger off her forearm and put it back into its hiding place on the bottom of her bag. She carried her bag openly on the outside of her cloak, for no thief would carry such a bulky item. She rested one hand on the hilt of her rapier, so that the end of the scabbard showed clearly through her cloak. That gave her the appearance of being a swordswoman, and everyone would remember that the thief of Wing's Reach had been unarmed.

She moved her pouch of coins to hang over the front of her right thigh, so that it jingled slightly. That would make people think she was either a fool to make her wealth known, or so confident in her abilities that it didn't matter. The wand she moved to the rear of her sash, safely covered by her cloak. All of that together made her look like a person of a flagrant—and not at all a larcenous—bent.

Her disguise in place, Kehrsyn moved through the snowy city streets. Her heart pounded with fear and victory, with trials conquered and trepidations yet to come. Yes, her future was uncertain, but she had penetrated Wing's Reach cleanly, pilfered an item, circumvented several insidious traps, and escaped a chance encounter with a guard. With the staff in her possession, the blackmail of the thieves' guild would be neutralized, and perhaps she might even find herself privy to some permanent lodging with the city walls.

In all, she mused, the benefits of her success were covering over the threats and dangers that had loomed over her life—some old, like her paucity of food, and some new, like the threat of death, or worse. She took some time to watch the falling snow, forgivingly covering up the grime in the streets and providing the overcrowded city with a new garment of pristine white.

Kehrsyn sighed with relief when she finally saw the gates of the Thayan enclave through the falling snow. Though she had just broken a vow that she'd kept for many long years, she couldn't help but feel some tinges of pride at how she'd conducted herself. She'd planned well, allowed for complications, and kept her head when things turned against her. If she could just keep that up for maybe one more day, she'd be all right.

❂

As instructed by the guards, Kehrsyn knocked on the door indicated and pushed it open, letting herself into the room. Her heart pounded. She had never been in a mage's study before.

A large, low wooden table dominated the center. What little of the tabletop could be seen through the clutter of scrolls, tomes, and glassware was covered with scars and stains. A thin silver chain rose from the center of the table and reached two thirds of the way to the ceiling. A greenish phosphorescent flame burned at the end of the chain. It seemed as if the fire's ethereal magic supported the chain against gravity. Kehrsyn could see no other means of support.

A second large table sat against one wall, covered with a humanoid cadaver so thoroughly dissected that Kehrsyn could not even hazard a guess as to its species. Thankfully, a pot burning with heavy incense sat next to the bloody surgical instruments and masked the corpse's dead-meat stink. Bookshelves dominated another wall, filled with thick, leather-bound tomes inscribed with arcane and sinister characters. A sticky pall of incense hung in the air, veiling the misshapen wizard Eileph, who sat on a wide, comfortable chair studying a book that sat propped up on a stand. The book was easily half as large as he was.

Though that was all strange, it was the toad that made Kehrsyn stop in shock. A large toad, closing on a foot in length, sat atop Eileph's nearly hairless head, its paws spread wide across the Thayan's skull to grip his pallid skin in a tight embrace that seemed obscenely intimate. Its color was reminiscent of rotting leaves, and its grotesque and flaccid obesity stretched taut its greasy, warty skin. It had a wide, sagging mouth surmounted by two cold eyes the color of dead fish.

Kehrsyn's lower lip curled in disgust as the toad's head swiveled slowly, just a small adjustment in her direction until it looked squarely at her. Its body pulsed, and its throat filled with an appalling amount of air. It let the air back out in a deep croak that sounded like a glutton's belch. Perhaps, surmised Kehrsyn, it was.

The toad opened and closed its mouth once. Kehrsyn pulled her lip back farther, disgusted.

Eileph sat reading his book and as yet seemed unaware of her presence. Kehrsyn cleared her throat, and the toad responded with an even louder croak.

The hideous thing opened its mouth again, stabbing its tongue into the air in the direction of an empty bench placed against the wall, then staring at her again. When Kehrsyn hesitated, the toad repeated the gesture.

Kehrsyn cringed, closed the door behind her, and edged over to the bench, which sat close to the dissection table. As she put her bag down and sat on the edge of the bench, the toad nodded almost imperceptibly.

As she sat and waited, Kehrsyn took the opportunity to

pull out the magic wand, careful to handle it only through the square of cloth she had cut.

At first glance, Kehrsyn thought that for Eileph to dub it a "necromancer's staff" seemed far too grandiose. It measured less than a cubit, stretching from Kehrsyn's elbow to her wrist, barely even worthy of being called a scepter. At its crown it was no thicker than a flute, tapering to the size of Kehrsyn's finger at the other end. Despite what she'd been told, for some reason Kehrsyn had expected it to be made of some unusual or glowing substance, but instead it was a plain material, almost pure white, perhaps bone or some exotic wood. It looked so clean that one could easily believe it had been forged but the day before.

Still, she thought, the necromancer's staff demanded a name far weightier than "wand." Its polished surface was deeply etched with pictograms of exquisite detail. Tiny stylized birds, eyes, hands, and other images covered the staff from one end to the other, minute and detailed enough to absorb the mind for hours, and with edges sharp enough to provide a satisfying, biting grip in the hands, even through the cloth. The interior portions of the relief work were inlaid with what looked like powdered gold. Viewed at even a short distance, the gold blended with the white to give it a unique color. The bronze band around the top had all of its luster, and was formed into delicate waves of flowing water and studded with smoky quartz. The bronze river whirled up to hold a large piece of black amber at the top, delicately carved. The staff was light and moved easily in the hand, yet it had an indefinable momentum about it that conveyed a sense of consequence.

It was beautiful. Even were it not magical, it would be incomparably valuable, worth far more than anything Kehrsyn had ever seen in her life, let alone held in her delicate hands.

And it belonged to someone else.

The full import of her actions came back to her, washing

away her confidence and exhilaration with the undeniable truth of what she held in her hands. She had stolen a priceless item from someone, selfishly taking their valuables to benefit herself, and she had ruined the cloth during her theft, a thoughtless act of vandalism to further her crime.

Kehrsyn clenched it tightly as the tears began to well up in her eyes. Why did the gods make it so that all her prospects for survival or prosperity could be obtained only by taking that which belonged to others? Why did her benefit have to come at someone else's pain?

Why had the gods conspired to force her to break the only vow she'd ever made?

A loud croak and a rough-edged "*Aha!*" interrupted her painful musings. She looked up through blurry eyes and saw Eileph hobbling over to her with great excitement, the toad still sitting implacably on his head. He let out a long, covetous sigh that sounded like nothing so much as a death rattle. Kehrsyn barely managed to wipe her eyes with the sleeve of her free hand before Eileph reached her.

She drew back as far as she could while sitting against the wall, contained by the corner of the room at one shoulder and the dissected cadaver at the other. Eileph's avaricious eyes bulged out of his head, and his face was blotchy with anticipation. His whole body quaked with excitement, and Kehrsyn could see his trembling fingers flex like a malformed spider. She feared the misshapen Thayan might rupture a blood vessel in his brain just by looking at her ill-gotten treasure.

Instead of falling over dead, however, Eileph moved with a speed Kehrsyn would not have thought possible. He snatched the small scepter from her grip and held it in front of her eyes, shaking his white-knuckled fist.

"*Do you have any idea what you have?*" he shouted, his face and baleful breath mere inches from hers.

Kehrsyn tried not to wince and tried to shrink back even more, both unsuccessfully.

"Neither do I," said the wizard. "Look at this aura, will you? Look at the power throbbing within!"

Eileph held it in front of his face and hers, rotating it in his hand as if he expected she could see the magical auras as well as he could.

"Thissss," he hissed, "is amazing! This is a true relic, an item . . ." His tone changed to a purr as he stepped away from Kehrsyn and limped for his work table, all the while stroking the wand. "Oh, such craftsmanship. It's beautiful. A masterpiece! Such runes, such sigils as I have never seen. And the magic embedded within, wrought within the matrix of these symbols, why . . . why this could be the Staff of the Necromancer!"

"That's what you said last time," offered Kehrsyn.

"Pah! Speak not of things beyond your comprehension, young lady!" bellowed Eileph. "I did not say this was *a* necromancer's staff—well, I did, of course, but that was last time—I said that this might be *the* Staff of *the* Necromancer, a relic forged by the archwizard Hodkamset, favored of the God of Death, of which all other such staves are hackneyed imitations!

"It is said to be carved from the spine bones of a dragon," he continued in a disgruntled voice. "I'd always imagined it would be bigger. Nonetheless, I could spend a lifetime studying this—" He turned back to Kehrsyn, clutching the staff to his barrel chest—"and I will," he said, waggling his eyebrows, "as soon as this war is brought to a successful conclusion. You haven't forgotten that part of the deal, right, wee little thief?"

"Uh, no, of course not," said Kehrsyn, forcing a smile.

Eileph giggled malevolently. "That is wise. It does not do well to anger the Red Wizards." He stopped abruptly and straightened up as much as his misshapen body allowed. "Hmph. Listen to me, I sound just like one of the zulkirs." He sucked in his lips and drummed the fingers of one hand on the table. "Must be the excitement of the moment. Calm, now, old boy, you have work to do."

He closed his eyes, took a deep breath, and exhaled. It would almost have been a sigh, were it not so violent and lustful.

When he opened his eyes again, he was much closer to the almost-personable Eileph that Kehrsyn had met in the plaza.

"Let's see what we have here, shall we?" he said.

He sat at the table and pulled the chain down toward him, links clinking on the tabletop as he drew the light closer. He laid the Staff of the Necromancer down on a cloth, and with his other hand he absently peeled the toad from his head. It tried to hold on, pulling at his skin, but Eileph prevailed and tossed it to the side. The ugly beast landed on the table on its back, and its legs flailed in the air as it tried to roll its bulk over.

"Hmm," said Eileph, as Kehrsyn timidly drew closer.

She noticed that he studied only one side, the side that had not been illustrated in his drawing. Kehrsyn's eyes kept getting pulled back to the periodic flailings of the toad, and eventually she used the scabbard of her dagger to nudge the hapless beast back onto its bloated stomach. Despite its earlier demonstrations of intellect, it did not acknowledge her assistance.

As Kehrsyn used the scrap of cut cloth to wipe the toad's slime from her scabbard, Eileph finally spoke up.

"The color is good," he said, "and the stone I can handle, but I wasn't counting on the gold inlay. Hmph. That'll take some extra time." He drummed his fingers on the table again and smacked his lips. "I can have it for you by noon tomorrow. Shall I deliver it, or will you send someone to pick it up?"

"Um, you'd probably better . . . deliver it," answered Kehrsyn.

"I understand," said Eileph. "If I'd just stolen this, I wouldn't want to carry it around, either. I tell you," he added through gritted teeth, "if someone stole this from me, I'd be testing some creative new ideas I've—"

"I'd just as soon not know," Kehrsyn interrupted.

Eileph laughed, then glanced at Kehrsyn with an intense look and asked, "Still at sixteen 'Wright's?"

"Yes," said Kehrsyn, after a mere heartbeat's pause.

"Begone, then. I have work to do."

Kehrsyn stood, picked up her bag, and headed for the door.

"Be careful," Eileph said as she was closing the door behind her. "It's slippery out there."

"Thanks," said Kehrsyn.

Once the door was shut, she leaned against it for a few moments.

"It's also cold," she whispered to the darkness.

Kehrsyn pulled her cloak around her and paused. Eileph's suite was at the end of a short hallway, and the only guards Kehrsyn had seen were at the gates.

Why not? she thought.

She shrugged off her bag and set it against the wall as a pillow, then she curled up in the shadows at Eileph's doorstep—on her right side, as her left arm was still raw—huddled her cloak around her, and soon fell fast asleep.

CHAPTER TEN

Morning arrived on the butt of a spear as a gruff guardsman jabbed Kehrsyn in the ribs. She mumbled an excuse that she had fallen asleep waiting for Eileph, and if her protestations availed her, she shuddered to think what would have happened to her without them. As it was, the guard merely hauled her out by the collar and ejected her from the Thayan enclave.

The morning was bright, especially after she'd spent the night in an unlit corridor. Sunlight pierced the thin cloud cover and reflected off the newly fallen snow, which was only starting to be plowed into an indistinct gray mush by the day's traffic.

A bracing wind blew steadily from the coast. Kehrsyn took a deep breath of the biting air, clean and free of the strange scents from the wizard's laboratory. Shading her sleepy eyes with her hand, she scanned the streets. Off to her left, she saw a familiar face: the green-hooded and scowling visage of the gritty-looking man who'd been watching her at the Jackal's Courtyard, the one whom she'd been trying to evade when the whole nightmarish venture began.

Obviously, he or his compatriots in the thieves' guild had been watching the Thayan enclave for her arrival, and awaited her departure. A dusting of snow on the man's heavy, hooded cloak attested to how long he'd been standing outside. She drew some small satisfaction that she had made them wait in the cold all night for her reappearance. It was the least she could do to repay them for the difficulties they'd caused her.

She started to understand why his expression at the Jackal's Courtyard had been so studious, so calculating. He'd not been interested in her show, nor in her body. He'd been interested in her skill and technique, scouting her out for the thieves' guild so that the annoying sorceress could "recruit" her.

Kehrsyn set her mouth in a grim half-smile. The man started to move closer, raising one hand to signal her. She turned and headed in his direction, intending to face the guild head-on and demand her full membership. However, she quickly discovered he was not signaling *to* her, but rather signaling to someone else *about* her. As she approached the hooded man, she sensed two large thugs falling in behind her. As she looked over her shoulder at one, the other clamped a heavy hand on her left arm, squarely over the burn. She screamed in surprise and pain and twisted away, the sudden noise and motion startling the thug into releasing his grip.

Kehrsyn felt the other thug grab her billowing cloak. She tried to wriggle out of the garment, but she had slung the strap of her bag over it, and she found herself entangled between the cloak, the strap, and a pair of large, beefy arms. A strong hand seized her chin and turned it up. She found herself face to face with the grim-visaged man. His eyes no longer looked studious, but had grown weighty with judgment.

"Let me go," Kehrsyn said with irritation. "I did what you asked me to do."

"Doubt it," said the man.

"Sure I did," she said. "I got the staff just like you wanted and delivered it where you told me to. Now I want to join."

The man raised one eyebrow and asked, "You got the staff?"

"Yes, I did."

"Glad to hear it."

"Good. Now let me go."

"No," said the man with a smirk.

"Why not?" Kehrsyn asked, deeply affronted.

In answer, the man reached into his vest and pulled out a carefully folded knee-length skirt.

"This is yours," he said.

He draped the skirt around her neck like a cow and untied her rapier from her hip. Her weapon safely in his hands, he tipped his head once, motioning his compatriots to move. The two thugs each grabbed an elbow with the grip of a crocodile and urged her along.

The foursome walked through the streets of Messemprar, their boss following behind. The only sound audible over the street noise was the wheezing of the thug on the right, who apparently had a bad lung.

Kehrsyn's mind was awhirl as she let herself be led along. The man clearly lived or worked at Wing's Reach. Who else but the one who'd snatched her skirt from her neck would think to return it there? He'd caught her, then, thwarting the guild's plans. Yet why had he been watching her perform if he wasn't with the guild? But if he was with the guild, why didn't he just steal the staff himself? And if he wasn't, how had he known she was at the Thayan enclave?

"Where are you taking me?" demanded Kehrsyn, hoping it might shed some light.

None of them answered, and a variety of scenarios ran through her mind, none of which seemed even plausible, let alone likely.

What are they going to do with me?

It all became clear. He *was* a member of the thieves' guild, and had infiltrated Wing's Reach. He had drawn the map of the house. The thieves' guild recruited her, branded her, and used her for its dirty work, then their infiltrator "catches" her after she'd already made the drop to Eileph. Since she's branded, the guild can sell her to someone else as a slave, to be carried off to a distant land on a trade ship. Conveniently, they turn a profit, remove the need to pay her for her services, and excise the chance that their part in the theft might be revealed.

Kehrsyn's jaw dropped in horror and surprise.

No wonder the sorceress never told me her name, she thought. *She figured she'd never deal with me again.*

Her heart began to beat faster. She knew she had to find a way out of her situation. She walked along placidly for a short distance then pulled hard at her captors' grips, trying to escape. She accomplished nothing save perhaps bruising her muscles. Their grips were as iron bands.

"I'm not a slave!" she growled as she continued her futile struggle.

Kehrsyn felt the hand of the leader clamp firmly across her neck at the base of her skull, fingers pressing into the soft spots behind her ears.

"Quiet," he said.

Kehrsyn relented in her struggles but still kept an eye peeled for an opportunity.

Partway across town, she saw a familiar group of faces, three in number. She had just enough time for a desperate gambit before they passed by.

"You!" she called out, straining against her captors.

"Tell these men to unhand me! I have the protection of Tiglath!"

The outburst brought both groups to an immediate halt.

One of the Tiamatans, a man with a bulbous nose and a high forehead topped with pale brown hair, stepped over to Kehrsyn, his eyes narrowed. Kehrsyn couldn't tell if it was distaste for her bluff or a posture of anger to cow those who held her prisoner.

"Morning," said the man from Wing's Reach, his tone indicating that he was not cowed in the least.

"Olaré," replied the Tiamatan. "I am Horat of Tiamat. What is going on here?"

"Justice," said the leader. "She's a thief."

The Tiamatan studied Kehrsyn's face for a moment then asked, "A thief?"

"Almost pinched her red-handed," came the immediate reply, which, Kehrsyn noted, made no mention of her having leveled him with a kick. "Tracked her to the Thayans. Got her just now."

"Do you have others who will stand witness, mister . . . ?"

"Demok of Wing's Reach. Yes, I do."

The Tiamatan's eyebrows went up and he said, "Wing's Reach, you say? Very well. Now we know . . . where to inquire after her welfare." He started to turn away but paused for one last moment. "Tell me, if you would," he asked, without turning back to face Demok, "what was it that she stands accused of stealing?"

"That's private," said the other.

"Really?" said the Tiamatan, with evident interest. "I see. Olaré, thief," he said as he glided away to rejoin his compatriots.

"Make them let me go!" implored Kehrsyn. "Tiglath gave me her protection! Are you going to let them handle me this way?"

The Tiamatan stopped and turned back around slowly. He held up two fingers, as if giving absolution.

"No," he said, waving them side to side, "Tiglath gave you her *sufferance* in a moment of weak whimsy. Having once received mercy, one is unwise to test the bounds of one's fortune again so soon." Kehrsyn started to interrupt, but he cut her off. "However, I shall be certain to communicate your grievance to Tiglath when I return from my errands this evening . . . if she's still awake, of course. I see no need to disturb her rest."

He turned and left, his companions sniggering at Kehrsyn's plight.

Kehrsyn hung her head and walked the rest of the way docilely.

⊛

Despite Kehrsyn's apprehensions, they did not bring her to the slave market, nor did they take her to the Halls of Justice, where, with the tacit approval of the Northern Wizards, judges installed by the god-king Gilgeam still dispensed punishments in accordance with tradition. She breathed a sigh of relief, for she knew that it was a buyer's market for slaves and a seller's market for punishment.

Instead, they brought her back to Wing's Reach, to the center of the third floor, where, she recalled from her map, the master had his rooms. They brought her to a small reception hall paneled in light wood, a fine room of the sort used for an intimate dinner with close friends. A series of pedestals ran along both side walls, each pedestal bearing a single piece of art, be it a sculpture, or a piece of pottery, or an ancient bronze helmet. She had been led in through one side door at the foot of the hall. Another door stood opposite her, and double doors stood in the other two walls, one pair the main guest entrance for the hall, and the other pair leading to the master's study. A very ornate table and chair sat in front of those doors. That, then, would be the location of her interview.

They removed her bag and slung it aside, then took off her cloak and the skirt-turned-cowl, bundled them up beside the bag, and placed her rapier atop the pile. They positioned her in the center of the room facing the far door. A guard opened a small trapdoor at her feet that concealed a set of stout bronze manacles anchored to a ring sunk deep into the flooring.

As her escorts fastened the manacles to her slender wrists, Kehrsyn heard their gruff leader say, "Careful. She's tricky."

They clamped her in well and drew back to stand along the walls. She expected that she would be left there to sweat and dread for a while, but instead the far door creaked open almost at once and a man of average height and trim build entered the room. He took no notice of her as he entered but nodded to the various servants at either side and took his seat. The bald man, Ahegi—apparently a key advisor—followed him in and stood against the wall to one side, his arms folded across his chest.

Once he'd made himself comfortable, the seated man laced his fingers together, rested his weight on his forearms, and regarded Kehrsyn frankly. He sat like that for some time, studying her, and thereby giving Kehrsyn time to study him in turn.

He had curly black hair flecked with gray throughout, short except for a longer lock in the center of his forehead. A thin, closely trimmed beard stretched from ear to ear, though it did not extend far enough down his neck to conceal his pronounced larynx. He had thin hands that had clearly never done much, if any, hard work, though Kehrsyn did see the permanent stain of ink on the fingers of his right hand that indicated he was a man of letters. Piercing blue eyes beneath his high brows likewise gave evidence of his sharp intellect. He had a straight nose, severe without being truly hawkish, and his lips were squared, almost exactly the same thickness from one end to the other.

Kehrsyn could not decide whether that last feature was grotesque or compelling.

For several long minutes, the only sound to be heard was the slight clink of Kehrsyn's chains as she shifted her weight. Despite the weight of scrutiny, she refused to drop her gaze.

The man spoke at last, with a rich, smooth baritone voice. "Here we find, amongst our number at last, the thief," he proclaimed in High Untheric. Kehrsyn raised her eyebrows. The last time she'd heard High Untheric, it had been booming from the sanctuary of the Gilgeamite temple as she'd been sneaking through the back rooms looking for donations to steal. But then, she'd never dealt with merchant princes before. "By which name art thou called, miscreant?" he asked.

"Kehrsyn," she said with far more confidence than she felt.

He inhaled through his nose, his linear lips pressed together.

"Hast thou an idea how I shall dispose of thee?" he asked, his voice and face devoid of emotion.

She narrowed her eyes and tried to cross her arms, but the chain prevented her from doing so. She settled with resting her hands on her hips.

"I suppose you'll be having your way with me," she said, bobbing her head as if trying to duck an invisible hand.

The corner of his mouth twitched, just once, a motion so slight that if she'd blinked she'd have missed it. She didn't know if it was a twitch of lust, a smirk of amusement, or a simple sneer. He blinked and leaned back in his chair, steepling his fingers. He looked carefully down Kehrsyn's body, from her neck to her feet, then back up to her eyes.

"I see before me the vigor of youth, an untamed colt, a bud eager to blossom into full womanhood yet entrapped by hunger and privation. Witness the energy constrained as in a seine, eager to break free anon and swim the seas of life. A year of hunger, and thy petals shall wither, their potential forever lost; a year of plenty, and the flush that even now graces thy body shall turn thy slender form into one of great loveliness. Thou hast height in excess of thy weight, and yet thou hast tamed thy awkward limbs. Thou shalt have a grace that makes even the great cats to weep with envy. The appearance of noble blood graceth thy face and carriage. Verily art thou now at the peak of thy desirability, where the delicate balance of beauty and anticipation, growth and ripening, is at its most precious: tilting, but not yet tilted."

He let his hands slowly drop to the table.

"Yet I see in thy eyes the difference between 'beaten' and 'broken,' and there is a world of difference betwixt. I myself have once explored that terrible wasteland. Were I of the sort to dishonor a woman in thy unfavorable position, I do believe that I would be in risk of my longevity."

He smiled slightly but sincerely. Kehrsyn shifted uncertainly and looked askance at the man.

She asked, "Then what do you want from me?"

"I should think that is self-evident. Thou hast perpetrated a crime upon this house."

"I know," said Kehrsyn bravely. "I figured you'd just either ruin me or kill me. Or both."

He winced ever so slightly.

"Please," he said, holding up one hand, "think thou more broadly. Execution I shall save as a distinct eventuality, but I shall hope to obviate its occurrence."

"What do you mean?" asked Kehrsyn.

"Clearly, thou wert not alone in this misdeed, for this was a masterful, knowledgeable work. Confess thou thy crime, and make thou thy repentance by naming thy fellows. This shall see thee free."

"I—I don't know their names," admitted Kehrsyn, "and I've only ever met one of them, anyway."

Her interrogator blinked several times in surprise.

"It's true," said Kehrsyn, desperation spilling her words out in rapid succession. "They were watching me in the courtyard, and they followed me, and they trapped me in this alley, and they framed me for killing this Zhent that I didn't kill but he thought I'd stolen something only I hadn't because this kid gave it to me, and the woman, she knew I hadn't stolen it, but she made it look like I did, and she gave me this—" Kehrsyn started to point to her slave brand but stopped herself short—"That is, they gave me this map to this building, and told me to steal this staff thing from you or else they'd tell the constables on me and I didn't even kill the guy, so I took it because I had to and maybe if I did it they'd let me join, and I could have a place to stay. See? And—"

She was just about to accuse Demok of allegiance to the thieves' guild, when her interrogator held up one hand for her to stop. He squeezed his eyes shut tight beneath a furrowed brow, and he pinched the bridge of his nose with the other hand. Kehrsyn's hands flipped over and over in her eagerness to spill her story, but she dared not continue until he seemed less annoyed.

"Sir," said Demok, "I can help."

Kehrsyn glanced at him suspiciously.

"Meanest thou that thou canst sort and interpret that singular volley, nay, that tempest of words?" the merchant asked.

"I can start," he replied. "I watched her . . . perform two days ago. Great skill. She left the Jackal's Courtyard. I followed."

Kehrsyn crinkled her nose in confusion. The guild's scout was obviously trying some sort of gambit to cover himself.

"Wherefore?" asked the merchant.

Demok blinked, looked at Kehrsyn, looked back at his employer, and said, "I thought her a good resource. Contractor or employee."

"I see," responded the man, drumming his fingers together.

"Within moments," Demok continued, "the watch raised an alarm. They said a woman had seen this one kill a Zhent."

"That's not true! She killed him and you know it!" blurted Kehrsyn, but she held her tongue when Demok nodded and gestured at her to be silent.

"The accusation was made," he said. "I don't believe it. Don't think she has it in her. Also saw a sorceress shadow her, not to capture, despite the reward."

"That was her," she said, half to Demok and half to the merchant prince. "The sorceress, I mean. She was the woman who got me into that trouble. She killed the Zhent but told the guards I did it, then she followed me to see how well I could get away from them. She said it was a test to see how good I was, but she was also trying to scare me into doing what she wanted. Luckily they didn't check out my hiding spot. Otherwise, I'd probably be a goner by now." Kehrsyn fidgeted with her shackled hands. "After that, she gave me the map and told me what to steal and where they wanted me to bring it, and, if I didn't, they'd either turn me in or just kill me."

"They?" asked the merchant.

"The thieves' guild," answered Kehrsyn.

"There's no thieves' guild in Messemprar," countered one of the guards.

Kehrsyn just shrugged.

"So thou wouldst have me believe that thou wert blackmailed into performing this theft, under threat of being turned over for this murder of which thou art innocent?"

"Murder of a deputized guard," clarified Demok.

Kehrsyn nodded meekly.

"It seemeth a fanciful alibi," grumbled Ahegi. "She shall be tortured for names and discarded."

"Fits what I saw," said Demok. "Zhent was killed. Caught her outside the Thayans'."

The merchant laced his fingers and tapped his thumbs together. He studied Kehrsyn, glanced at Demok, and studied Kehrsyn some more.

"Unchain ye her," he said in a soft voice, "and bring ye her a chair and some mulled wine."

The room burst into motion, and Kehrsyn found herself seated comfortably with a hot mug.

As he held the chair for her, Demok whispered, "Be grateful."

"Let us start of new," said the merchant.

Kehrsyn noticed that his baritone voice had softened. Her heart skipped a beat to hear someone with such power treating her with kindness and speaking so softly. Her experiences with those in power had heretofore always involved raised voices, commands, and threats. She nodded and tried to relax, but she ended up sitting forward in her chair, clutching the warm mug between her hands.

"I am called Massedar," he said. "Wing's Reach is my house, the center of a modestly sizeable mercantile and expeditionary combine. This room is the center of Wing's Reach, wherein agreements are detailed at the onset and consummated at the end. Upon the observations of my servant Demok and my own instincts, we open such an agreement now.

"I deal in the rare, the exotic, and the exquisite. Until recently, I had in my possession an item that not only fit, but dare I say *defined* all three of those categories." He leaned forward. "Until thou, *Kehrsyn*,"—he pronounced the name with added emphasis, causing Kehrsyn to bite her lip—"removed that item at the behest of parties unknown. I trust thou knowest what that item was, for thou removed it with great skill and precision." He paused and looked at her blank eyes. "Knowest thou what that item doth?" he asked.

Kehrsyn shook her head. "I don't really know anything about it other than it's supposed to be some necromancer's staff."

Massedar pursed his lips. "Fascinating," he said. "That is in part correct. The item hath great powers worthy of no small service unto the plight of the army of Unther. We had recently recovered this item upon expedition, which claimed the lives and souls of some twenty of the near thirty who risked the venture. We have since been negotiating a suitable method of granting this item's power unto the army, that it should smite the Mulhorandi forces in one fell battle."

"But the guild said that you were going to sell the staff," said Kehrsyn.

Ahegi snorted. Massedar smiled slightly and said, "And they, a self-styled guild of thieves, hath intent to save Unther? The guild hath reversed the roles, my dear. I shall use the staff to save our people. The guild would fain sell it for profit. They are, after all, thieves, and they care not a whit who ruleth the day, so long as they should rule the night."

"I guess that makes sense," said Kehrsyn, absently running her fingers along the edges of her brand. "They don't trust me, so why should I trust them?"

"That bringeth us to you, my dear," said Massedar, "and thy role in this intrigue."

"Let me guess," Kehrsyn said. She half-smiled, wryly raising one corner of her mouth. "You want me to burglarize the thieves' guild and bring your magic wand back to you."

Massedar winced and leaned back, pressing his fingers to his temples.

"Please," he said, "is it not enough that High Untheric hath been abandoned by the populace? Must we also mangle the vulgar words of the common tongue?" He exhaled. "Please, young gentlewoman, the word is 'burgle,' not 'burglarize.' Thou art a 'burglar,' not a . . . a 'burglarizationator.' " He shuddered. "Thou art a talented young gentlewoman, with grace, intelligence, and beauty. Develop thou thy tongue to be equally attractive."

"Sorry," said Kehrsyn.

"As to thy point, yes, that shall be thy role in this affair. Thou shalt hazard to undo the wrong that thou hast done. Furthermore, the endeavor thou shalt undertake as a retainer of Wing's Reach. Shouldst thou return the aforementioned item, thou shalt be recompensed for thy efforts, with a bounty of, say, one hundred gold shekae for its safe return, plus healing for all wounds incurred."

Kehrsyn's jaw dropped. That was more than she'd made in the last two or three years, and all for what might be a single night's work!

Massedar looked amused. "I take it that this rate is acceptable unto thee?"

Kehrsyn recovered her aplomb—most of it, at least. She'd never seen someone so free with his gold, let alone when it was being spent in her direction. Nor, for that matter, had she ever met someone of wealth and standing who was able to look past her street-urchin veneer and see the woman beneath.

"Uh, yeah," she said, "that would be fine. Then . . . you won't turn me over for stealing?"

"Heavens, no," said Massedar with distaste. "If thou canst do this, why ever would I throw away a work of art such as thee? Perish the thought."

"Good. Well . . . great!" said Kehrsyn. "I'll do my best." She thought about the situation for a moment and smiled. "It'll be good to turn the horns on a certain someone."

"So be it," said Massedar with finality. "Demok shall see to thy needs."

Demok ushered her up and started to guide her out of the room, but at the door Kehrsyn pulled away, just in time to see Massedar open the doors to his quarters.

"I want an advance!" she exclaimed, need overcoming her self-consciousness.

Massedar turned around, a hard look in his handsome blue eyes.

"You want coin?" yelled Ahegi. "Thinkest thou to line thy purse and flee?"

"No," said Kehrsyn, "no gold. I . . . I want a hot bath. Please, sir."

Massedar stared at her for another moment, then chuckled.

"So be it," he said. "See ye her provided with the largest bath in this house, with oils and soaps. Wash her garments whilst she relaxeth, and send unto her whatsoever she desireth to break her fast."

The servants later told him they had never seen someone so thin eat so much.

CHAPTER ELEVEN

By the time Kehrsyn pulled her warm, well-fed body out of the deep bronze tub (she'd insisted on eating while she bathed, for the sensation of being warm was even more delicious than the foods), it was approaching midday. The sky shone bright and clear, and ambient light reflected off the snow that clung on the rooftops. It was altogether a sapphire day.

As she left Wing's Reach, Kehrsyn saw Demok leaning against the wall, watching the crowds walk past, his eyes sharp and attentive, his brows drawn together. He stopped her as she passed.

"Know what you're doing?" he asked seriously.

"I'm burgling unto the knaves whosoever hast maked me unto burgle," she said, her voice flippant but her eyes shining with grim determination.

She started to walk away, and Demok fell into step beside her, his long gait allowing him to keep pace easily.

"Not what I meant," he said as they sloshed their way through the streets, wisps of condensation puffing away from their noses in the breeze. "Can you? Need help?"

Kehrsyn pondered before answering, "Can I trust you?"

He did not answer but held her glance, and she saw his eyes were as cool and solid as granite. About the same color, too, she noted. She pressed her lips together and nodded. Demok had a position of authority with a rich and powerful man, and she doubted anything that passed in through those eyes was ever spoken of again.

Having received an answer to her first question, she asked a second: "You're not, like, a member of the thieves' guild, right?"

"If I were, you'd be dead."

She giggled nervously, then walked along in silence for some time.

"I didn't have a good childhood," she said tentatively. It had been a long time since she'd talked about herself, but so much was new or upside-down that she felt she needed to confide in someone. "I never knew my father, and Mother didn't have a copper wedge to spend. As early as I can remember, I stole food to get enough to eat. I got real good, too, sneaking, stealing, running, hiding . . ." She snorted. "Acting innocent. For a while, I was innocent. It was all a game. But I remember one day my mother was showing me a new trick—I don't remember what it was— and I looked up and there were tears in her eyes. I never asked her about it, but I knew even then that she was crying because she knew it was wrong, but she was teaching me because she wanted me to live. My life was never the same, because, from then on, I knew what I was doing was wrong, but I kept on doing it anyway. As I got older, the memory of those tears made me think about stealing, how I was like a leech, taking food that belonged to other people and leaving my hunger in its place. I tried stealing from different people, but that only spread my own misery around more. I tried stealing only from a few rich people, but that made them poorer, so they had less coin to pay the poor people who worked for them. I was trapped in a life that was crushing my pride, making me hate myself for the pain I caused other people by wanting to eat. It was like I hurt people just by being alive.

"So one spring day I was sitting and watching the buds just starting to sprout out of this lichen-covered plum tree. It was so beautiful, seeing those little nubs shaped like candle flames but colored the brightest green you could ever want to see. On each one you could see the outline of all these little teeny leaves just waiting to unfold and grow. What made it even better was that it was an old, gnarled tree growing wild by the side of a cart track, all twisted and broken and rough, with knotty bark all covered with black and pale lichen. It was like a tree that had been dead for years and shriveled and burned and tossed aside, yet it had all that life inside just bursting to get out, beauty and hope splitting out at the seams all over the place.

"I decided I wanted to be that tree. I wanted a new life. I promised right then and there, swore on the sun god Hokatep that I'd never steal again. I found some work here and there, practiced the tricks you've seen, earned a few egorae that way—at least I did when times were better— and I got by. I had enough to eat most times, but, best of all, I felt good about myself. I found pride in my skills. Sometimes people even wanted me around, when the harvest was in and people had mintweight and they wanted to see someone without the talent play at being a wizard.

"See, here, like this," she said, stopping in the middle of the street. "Hold out your hand."

Demok hesitated, then held out his right hand. She turned his hand palm up and placed a copper in his palm, then turned his hips so his body faced her. Then she struck the heel of his hand with hers, snatching the coin from his palm.

He shrugged, unimpressed.

"The trick is distraction. While you were looking at your palm, I was doing my real trick. Take off your glove."

Instead, he felt the back of his right hand. Through the thin leather of his glove, he felt a coin. He dug in with his fingers and pulled out a silver. He pursed his lips and handed it back to her.

"Thank you," said Kehrsyn. "Since you're giving me my coin back, I guess I can return your dagger."

Demok's hand flew to his hip and found his scabbard empty.

"Impressive," he said, though his tone was one of displeasure.

"Thank you," Kehrsyn said again as she grinned and held out his dagger, concealed behind her left forearm. Her voice grew dim and her eyes dropped as she added, "That's how I've lived for the last seven years, doing tricks like that. I never hurt anybody, and I've never broken that vow. Until yesterday. I had a new life, but now it's gone."

She looked up at Demok, her eyes narrowed with anger and sadness.

"I'm going back to undo a theft that they made me do," she said. "They stole a staff from Massedar, and they stole my vow from me. And here Massedar treats me really good, he's a sweet man, and I've never met such a powerful guy who was so nice.

"So yeah, maybe that's a longer answer than you want, but I know what I'm doing. I'm going to hurt the people who robbed me of my new life."

Demok nodded and chewed on the corner of his mouth.

By silent consent, they began walking again. Kehrsyn scuffed along for a few moments, kicking at higher lumps of slush.

"Sorry," she said finally. "I didn't mean to drop all that on you. It's fine if you didn't want to listen to all that."

"Your father?" Demok asked.

Kehrsyn smiled to herself. He had listened. She was starting to wonder if anything escaped his notice.

She said, "I'd rather not talk about it just now."

Demok remained silent for some time as the two of them walked through the streets of Messemprar.

"Know where you're going?" he asked.

Kehrsyn stopped and said, "No, I guess I don't, but I know the name of the street, so I can find it."

"Ask me."

Kehrsyn laughed, and asked, "Do you know where Right Street is?"

"There isn't one," Demok said.

"There isn't? Maybe Right Avenue? Boulevard?

"No."

"But I know that's what Ei—what I heard him say," she said.

Demok rolled his eyes skyward and thought.

"Wheelwright's Lane," he said. "Near the north wall. Chariot Memorial. Try there."

He turned and started to walk away.

"Hey, thanks," Kehrsyn called after him.

She saw him wave in acknowledgment, a simple, efficient gesture as he moved off into the crowds.

❂

Kehrsyn moved through Messemprar, the heat of her long, languid bath sticking with her as she walked the chilly, slush-filled streets. The slight tang of winter's snow still lingered despite the best efforts of the city's other smells, and Kehrsyn couldn't help but smile. She was warm, well fed, and out for revenge on those who'd wronged her. Best of all, she held the secrets over her so-called employers, and they were none the wiser.

Her brisk, confident gait, billowing cloak, and open sword parted the crowds before her, and she relished the sensation. Her entire life, she had been relegated to skulking in shadows, deferring to others, moving aside when persons of import passed by. She had gone from being the one to bow her head to the one walking down the center of the street.

She owed it all to Massedar, and in her heart, she thanked him for it. It wasn't just that she felt appreciated for a change. True, he'd spoken courteously, looked her in the eyes, indulged her, even promised her payment for services rendered—far more mercy than a thief could expect in Messemprar—but more so, he had set her upon a path of justice, with stakes far higher than the wedges and coppers and egorae she'd performed for.

Most of all Massedar had power and he had extended the aura of his power to her, his chosen agent. He had given a street waif like her a portion of his great stature. She'd never experienced anything like it.

She tried to think of the task ahead, but his piercing sky-blue eyes held her mind's gaze until she saw the unimaginatively named Chariot Memorial looming ahead of her.

The crowds were thick and noisy around the memorial, which suited Kehrsyn fine until she saw the source of the commotion. Some Zhent merchants had set themselves up at the foot of the great statue and were hawking advanced purchases of their forthcoming food shipment. The activity had generated quite a crowd, and Zhent guards and the city watch alike had posted themselves throughout the crowd.

Kehrsyn slid along the edge of the crowd, confident in her anonymity but nonetheless preferring to keep a safe distance.

After a few more tenbreaths' search, she found the building Eileph had inadvertently mentioned. Number sixteen Wheelwright was a two-story building wedged between two convergent streets that intersected some thirty yards away from the plaza of the Chariot Memorial. The building was shaped like a narrow wedge of flatbread, which, Kehrsyn mused, must have made life interesting for the architect.

It was on the verge of becoming dilapidated. The windows on the ground floor had all been securely, if inexpertly, boarded over. Heavy curtains filled the windows on the upper floor. The vertex of the narrow building was blunt, and into the end the main door had been set. In the years since the building had been created, however, it had sunk (or else extra dirt had raised the level of the plaza and surrounding streets), for the outward-opening front door was inoperable and had been boarded over as well. Instead, a ladder of questionable integrity led to a makeshift door roughly cut into the second floor. A sign dangled from one rung, proclaiming "NO ROOM."

Kehrsyn stuck out her lower lip appreciatively. The building looked poor and uncomfortable, declined the interest of the casual passerby, and yet was eminently defensible. In all likelihood, there'd be a hatch to the rear of the roof or a tunnel dug beneath the streets for a quick exit. Maybe both. It looked like a good setup.

Kehrsyn decided that the best tactic would be a straightforward, confident approach. It had worked through the city streets, and it just might work there. Kehrsyn ran her right hand up and down along the edge of her burn. Certainly her experience with the sorceress showed that timidity was asking for trouble.

Without further ado, lest her courage give out, Kehrsyn vaulted up the ladder, keeping a solid grip on the handrails in case one of the rungs should give. She used her dagger to depress the latch of the door and push it open, standing slightly to one side in case the occupants had a crossbow aimed at the entry. She raised her eyebrows in surprise, for whatever her images of a thieves' guild had been, the interior of the building failed to live up to them.

The only light in the room spilled in from the door, the curtained windows, and two other doors that stood slightly ajar on the far side of the vestibule. A variety of packs, large satchels, bags, and water skins hung on pegs along one wall, alongside the cloaks that Kehrsyn had expected to see. The other wall held an assortment of camping gear, ranging from clean frying pans to coils of rope to oiled-canvas rain tarps. At her feet, an old hunting dog lay on a ragged blanket. He opened his eyes and raised his muzzle a bit but declined to raise an alarm in favor of curling up a little tighter. He whined at the sudden influx of light and cold air, so Kehrsyn kneeled down and pulled a corner of the blanket over his haunches.

Kehrsyn heard voices chatting behind one of the doors. Given the ambient noise from the crowds in the street, it was likely that they were unaware someone had entered the building. Kehrsyn put her bag right by the door, paused to think of a suitably casual line of entry, and, when she'd found one, she walked easily across the room, pushed the door open, and leaned against the jamb with her dagger in her right hand, concealed within her folded arms.

"Has Eileph made his delivery yet?" she asked.

"Yeah, this morning," said one of the occupants, his back to Kehrsyn. "He's got it downstairs," he added, gesturing toward an old man seated opposite him.

The others in the room stopped their conversation, the old one holding up his hand to silence his unaware companion.

"And who are you?" he asked Kehrsyn.

"I came to join."

At this, the man who'd answered her turned around. His eyebrows shot up when he saw her, which was the most dramatic reaction any of them had given. He turned back to face his companions.

"Given she found us," he said, bobbing his head, "I for one am inclined to sign her up."

"Well, I guess that settles it," said Kehrsyn. "Will someone kindly fill me in on the bylaws?"

"Gilgeam's gallbladder!" came a female, if not particularly feminine, voice from deeper within the building. "Do I hear the whimpering words of my wayward waif?" Everyone turned to look as the sorceress stormed into the room, her face a mixture of curiosity, disbelief, and shock. "Well, I'll be a horse's hindquarters! You got a whole bushel of stupid rocks in your head, coming here like this," she said. She pointed at Kehrsyn, adding, "Grab her quick, and kill her!"

One of the men shot out a hand and grabbed Kehrsyn's left wrist, but she twisted her arm against the man's thumb and plied her wrist free. She stepped back and drew her rapier with her left hand, subtly concealing her dagger behind her thigh.

She started edging to the front door and said, "I'll scream."

"Like anyone's going to hear you outside, hon?" answered her nemesis. "All they care about are their empty stomachs."

The truth of the statement brought renewed fear to Kehrsyn, and she edged for the door more quickly.

"Stop right there!" came another voice, and Kehrsyn glanced at the other door.

Two figures had entered: a graybeard dwarf with a massive crossbow kneeling in front of a human female with a longbow. Both had arrows pointed directly at Kehrsyn's heart. Kehrsyn stood maybe fifteen feet away. There was no way she'd be able to duck or dodge in time, and neither archer's aim wavered in the slightest.

"Good job, kids," yelled the sorceress. "Now plug the little urchin!"

"You'll do no such thing," ordered the older man, entering the vestibule from the kitchen. "Unless she moves," he added, glaring at Kehrsyn with one murderous eye.

He was on the short side but powerfully built, a man who had clearly lived most of his life fighting and a man for whom command came naturally. Hands on hips, jaw clenched, he looked first at Kehrsyn, then at his followers. He turned on the sorceress, walking up until his nose all but touched hers.

"You know this gal," he said, clenching his fist. "How does she know about Eileph and us? Have you been wagging your tongue over beers? If you have, I swear I'll—"

"No, I ain't, honest, Tharrad," said the sorceress. "Yeah, sure, I got her to steal the staff for us, and I sent her to Eileph, sure, but I have no idea how she found us!"

Kehrsyn saw an opening and took it. "Like you're so hard to track. *Pfft!*"

Tharrad glowered at Kehrsyn, then at the sorceress again. "She—over there, her—you got *her* to steal the staff for us, something we'd been trying to plot for over a tenday, and now you want to just up and kill her?" he asked, his voice raised in spite of the fact that he was standing in her face.

"She knows too much," said the sorceress, standing her ground. "No tongue, no risk, no leak!"

At that, Tharrad lost his composure. He seized the sorceress's collar with both hands and hoisted her off the ground.

"I see only one person responsible for leading this woman to our hideout," he bellowed. "*You* are a risk. Thank the gods she wants to *join*. For that reason and that reason only, I leave you your tongue and your life."

The sorceress gulped. "Thank you, sir," she said.

"Thank me after you heal," he said, setting her down. He turned to the others and jerked his thumb at the sorceress. "Brand her tongue," he ordered. "Maybe then she won't spill our plans outside the group."

Kehrsyn gasped as several of the sorceress's companions seized her and led her away, deeper into the building. To Kehrsyn's surprise, she offered them no resistance. However, as they left the room, she called back over her shoulder, "She doesn't even know who we are!"

Tharrad turned to Kehrsyn. "Is that true?" he asked, one eyebrow raised.

Kehrsyn sheathed her rapier and snorted. She hoped it sounded more confident than it felt. "She lies. The only thing I've heard her say that's accurate is that *I* stole the staff, and I'll bet she didn't even tell you that until just now, did she? I didn't think so. She's afraid I'll upstage her. But yeah, I know who you are, and I have no problems living outside the law and doing what needs to be done."

Tharrad looked at Kehrsyn again, then nodded.

"I'm Tharrad," he said, extending his hand.

Kehrsyn flipped her concealed dagger into the air and caught it with her left hand as she shook Tharrad's with her right.

"Glad to meet you," she said. "I'm Kehrsyn."

Tharrad paused, unnerved at the sudden graceful appearance of a dagger. He watched as Kehrsyn slipped it into her boot.

"Well, this isn't the way I like to do things," he said, "but Ruzzara leaves me with little choice, eh?

"Follow me," he added, gesturing. He walked deeper into the building, to a staircase that descended to the first floor. "So when did you decide you wanted to join up with Furifax?" he asked as he descended the stairs.

Kehrsyn's eyelids fluttered, as did her heart. She was thankful that Tharrad wasn't looking at her at that moment. She'd thought she was joining a simple thieves' guild, not the group of rebels that had plagued the land for nigh on two dozen years. For as long as she could remember, Furifax and his followers had first fought against Gilgeam and his church, then had worked to take the reins of power in Unther.

The Untheric Army, the Northern Wizards, several temples, and many rich merchants had all put generous bounties on the head of Furifax. Even his followers had bounties on them, so it quite surprised Kehrsyn to discover that they were operating in the heart of Messemprar.

"What's the matter, missy?" asked Tharrad. "I didn't brand your tongue, did I?"

"I'm sorry, I'm . . . just a little dazzled to finally be here," said Kehrsyn. "You asked something?"

"Are you eager to join?" he asked.

He stepped off the last stair and opened one of the doors on the first level. He ushered Kehrsyn into what looked like a cross between a trader's office and a general's war room.

"Absolutely," said Kehrsyn. "Something has to be done about this whole situation, and no one else seems to be able to get anything accomplished," she added, hoping Tharrad would read into her vagueness whatever he wanted to hear.

"Quite true," he answered.

Tharrad gestured her to a chair beside a table. She undid her rapier's scabbard, leaned it against the wall, and took a seat. He sat opposite her, leaned back, and crossed his feet on the table.

"Life as a rebel and an outlaw isn't nearly so romantic as the balladeers would have us believe," he said. "It's tough, it's dangerous, and it's full of ugly but necessary actions. Why should we allow you to join?"

"I think I've proven that I have skills, and I'd rather align myself with someone I can follow. And, frankly, if I were going to turn you all in, I would already have done so," embellished Kehrsyn. "I could have gotten mintweight to lead a regiment of soldiers to your doorstep. Instead, I'll add my head to the bounty rolls."

"I can't argue with that logic," said Tharrad. "You'll understand, however, if we refrain from telling you anything of our organization beyond our little group here until you've spent some more time proving your worth and we've gotten to know you better. Our own exposure is no worse off with you present, but infiltration is a grave danger these days and I can't risk the rest of the organization."

"That's fine," said Kehrsyn. "It's just good to know I'm part of something larger. Speaking of infiltration, I understand we have an agent planted inside Wing's Reach?" she asked, deliberately including herself in the pronoun.

"That Ruzzara," Tharrad snorted, shaking his head. "No, we don't, but we have an ally who has a spy planted. More exactly, we have an informant in that group who has given us evidence that we can no longer trust our ally, not really a big surprise, so we've made our own move. We got the map from said informant, in exchange for certain considerations."

"Well, be sure to thank whoever it is for that map of the building; it was really useful."

Tharrad nodded as he unrolled a map of Messemprar.

"Forgive me," he said, "I'm still trying to transfer all of the credit for the heist from Ruzzara to you. Tell you what, tonight I'll pour some brandy and you can tell me how you did it.

"In the meantime, you've given us a good tool, once we figure out exactly how to use it. You'll be doing a lot more of that, because it's far better for us to steal something than it is to kill its owner and take it from them. Makes the targets wonder if they have a turncoat. We can also use you to plant evidence or leave threats that'll make people knuckle under, but we still have quite a puzzle to solve before we can take control of Messemprar and the rest of Unther. The challenge lies in figuring out who can be bought, who can be browbeaten, and who must be fought. Unfortunately, with the pharaoh's army roving just across the river, we find ourselves having to rely on people and factions whom we would not trust, were the times less perilous."

"Believe me," said Kehrsyn, "I understand."

CHAPTER TWELVE

A heavy fist knocked at the door, interrupting Kehrsyn's discussion with Tharrad, much to her dismay. She had found out much more of Messemprar's history and chaotic political situation than she had expected.

"Come in," said Tharrad.

The dwarf archer stuck his head in the door and said, "Someone to see you. The Tiamatans, by the look of them."

Tharrad glanced at the messenger's fingers drumming on the door. "And?" he asked.

"Well, there's kind of a lot of them, and she's not with them."

"Tell them I'll be right up," Tharrad said with a frown.

The archer left, and Tharrad rose and crossed to a small end table.

"Who's not with them?" Kehrsyn asked.

"Tiglath, their high priestess."

"Oh, I know her," said Kehrsyn.

Tharrad's eyes narrowed as he turned back to look at Kehrsyn.

"Do you?" he asked.

Kehrsyn wasn't sure why her acquaintance with Tiglath was cause for concern, though their coincidental appearance half a watch after her arrival might trigger some suspicion. She pinched herself to quell an onrush of nervousness and continued chatting casually, embellishing on the truth.

"Yeah, I ran into her and her thugs on the streets," she said, using choice words to distance herself from them. "I fair angered them, but she managed to keep her rabble in check."

Tharrad laughed as he said, "It's good to see that she still does."

He pulled two long, thin daggers from the end table's drawer and slid them into the leather wrappings that bound his forearms, then pulled a small vial from a padded case and concealed it in the palm of his left hand.

"You look like you're expecting trouble," observed Kehrsyn, by way of broaching a potentially sensitive subject. "I thought you said the Tiamatans were our allies."

"For a long time they have been," he said, grimacing, "and I hope they still are, but as we've drawn closer to power in Unther, they've gotten more . . . testy. More demanding. Furifax and Tiglath always kept things smooth, but since the war began, our relations have become more . . . strained. All the changes, everyone moving into Messemprar . . . the treasure's all in one chest now, and everyone knows it."

"And everyone wants to be the one with the key."

Tharrad winked at her and said, "Let's see what they want, shall we?"

Kehrsyn followed Tharrad up the central staircase but hung back as he approached the Tiamatan delegation arrayed in their distinctive red robes. Concerned that she might be seen and recognized, for she had no idea what complications that might bring, Kehrsyn loitered in the background, keeping her face concealed by shadows and obstructions.

She saw that the Tiamatan speaking for their delegation was the same bulbous-nosed, high-browed, arrogant cleric whom she'd begged for help when Demok and his thugs had first caught her.

She tried to eavesdrop on the conversation, but, as Tharrad faced away from her, his words were swallowed by the muffled roar of the crowds outside. Many of the Tiamatan's words were inaudible, as well. Their body language, however, told Kehrsyn that the meeting was not congenial: clenched fists, narrowed eyes, mouths drawn into snarls, accusing fingers thrust forward like swords.

The Tiamatan raised his voice, cutting through the ambient noise as he said, "How dare you undertake that theft without us! And including the Red Wizards is unthinkable. You have no idea the damage you've caused!"

Kehrsyn, her heart beating rapidly, ducked through a doorway and out of sight. How had the Tiamatans known? How had they found her? And, since they surely knew, would Furifax's gang turn on her?

The Tiamatan yelled, "Give us the staff! Now!"

Kehrsyn twitched toward the dagger in her boot just as one of Furifax's rebels stumbled backward through the doorway, an arrow sticking from his chest. Kehrsyn saw him pull it out. The shaft trailed the oily glint of poison, and the arrowhead remained in the wound.

Kehrsyn hazarded a glance around the door and saw the two groups locked in vicious, hand-to-hand combat. She had seen some of the battles against the pharaoh's army, but that was something different. Kings' battles were filled with crashing, shouts, roaring charges, trumpets, drums, and thundering chariots. The fight was between shadow factions, conducted with brutal silence to avoid the unwanted attention of the city guard. She heard the swipe of steel through flesh, gasps of pain, the twang of bows, and the murmur of spells. The loudest noises were not the sounds of blazing rocks plowing through massed formations, but rather crockery being upset and smashed, chairs buckling under the weight of wrestling bodies, and the cracking of bones.

Kehrsyn ran through the building, raising the alarm first on the top floor, then down the staircase to the rooms below. She remained below, fearful of both sides, for indeed it was likely that in the heat of combat, those who followed Furifax would consider her, a stranger, to be an enemy.

Not knowing what else to do, she remained under the stairs, trembling with fear as the battle developed above her. She feared such combat—mindless savagery in dense groups—where her only advantages, speed and agility, would avail her little when there was no room to escape.

She wondered if there was another exit, a secret underground tunnel, something that might help her escape the danger. She made an effort to locate a trapdoor, quickly poking from room to room, but nothing was easily seen, and the sounds above troubled her. She heard the Tiamatans pressing the advantage, driving the bandits farther back into the building. Their footsteps moved across the wooden floor above her head, the beams creaked with the weight of the assailants, and dust fell from the trembling planks as bodies dropped for the final time. She heard grunts, curses, bottles rolling across the floor, and the strange, whetstone sound of spells being cast. Fear that the Tiamatans might charge downstairs kept drawing her eyes back to the staircase, and she awaited her fate uneasily, wondering whether she could bluff or bargain her way to safety.

A small rivulet of blood began dribbling through a crack in the ceiling, and Kehrsyn recoiled in disgust. She drew back to Tharrad's office, but then thought better of it and moved into one of the other rooms, a bunkroom apparently shared by a pair of Furifax's followers. The room had three beds, but one was covered by assorted pieces of armor and the bare mattress had grease and oil stains all over it. Kehrsyn closed the door most of the way and peered out the gap on the hinge side to keep an eye on the staircase. A few stray shafts of light speared through the boarded-up windows, their occasional fluctuations hinting at the movements of the crowd outside.

After a few long, heart-pounding moments, she saw someone tumble backward down the stairs. She had no idea who it was, though the nondescript attire proved it was not one of Tiamat's people. The unfortunate landed in a heap at the bottom of the stairs, limbs and neck at awkward angles that Kehrsyn had previously seen only at public executions.

A few scant heartbeats later, a Tiamatan stepped down the stairs hefting a pick in his hands, his red-and-black robes tied back for combat. The pick was small enough to be of use in such close quarters, but solidly built, with its head fashioned in the shape of a beaked dragon. Blood dripped from the dragon's vicious, fanged mouth. The pounding in Kehrsyn's ears competed with the crowd noises filtering through the building's walls as she watched the man—cruel-looking, with a pale, sallow face and black hair pulled back into a ponytail—probe his victim for any signs of life. He raised his head and scanned the downstairs for further opponents.

Kehrsyn pulled back from the door and used a trick she'd learned as a child, based on the fact that people almost never look up. She climbed up the corner of the room, using the corner itself as well as the top of the door for her hand- and footholds. She pushed herself into as small a space as possible in the upper corner, hoping that her dark clothes would help her escape notice. Two hands pushed out for support against the ceiling beams, one foot was flat against one wall, and the other foot found a precarious toehold on the hinge of the door for extra balance.

She heard the man stalking around the lower level. Upstairs, it sounded like the Tiamatans were pressing the Furifaxians into the rear portions of the building.

Kehrsyn heard doors creak open and heard the man's footsteps and the swish of his robe as he searched the area. He was breathing hard and occasionally sniffling, recovering his oxygen from the combat he'd just fought. He searched room by room, swinging doors to check for people in hiding.

He glided into the room, pick held high in one hand. He scanned the room, then turned toward the door. Kehrsyn held her breath and tried to think small and invisible thoughts. Following an old Untheric superstition, she stared at a nail in the base of one wall. The man swung the door open, ready for combat, but saw no one hiding behind it. He exhaled sharply, a mix of relief and disappointment, and started to leave the room.

For some reason—to eliminate hiding places, Kehrsyn assumed—the man pushed the door all the way open. The movement caught her by surprise. Though she tried to pull her toe up from the hinge, she was not fast enough. The door pinned her foot between it and the wall for the merest instant before her foot pulled free. The man stopped, then quickly shifted back into the room, pick at the ready. He edged the door open again, squinting into the darkness, until his gaze rose to spot Kehrsyn up in the darkened corner.

"I have protection," blurted Kehrsyn, wracking her brain for the name of the priestess.

"Not from me," the man replied.

"I have the sufferance of Tiglath," blurted Kehrsyn with relief.

"Oh, you're one of Tiglath's, eh?" He hefted his pick with a smile. "Horat will be most interested to know you're here. You'd better hope Tiglath's protection goes a little farther for you in the afterlife."

"You can't harm me!"

"Watch," he replied.

"She's your high priestess! Doesn't her promise mean anything?"

"Not any more," he said.

The Tiamatan started to reach for her with the head of his pick. It looked like he intended to hook Kehrsyn, pull her down, and capture her alive.

Rather than fight it, Kehrsyn leaped. She pushed off with her arms and one foot. The other foot she extended to push the pick's head aside, just a matter of getting her shin inside the man's extended arm. As she leaped, she pulled her one foot back in so that her knee impacted the man's nose. She landed on top of him and heard the cartilage of his nose crunch beneath her weight. As they landed on the floor, Kehrsyn shifted as much of her momentum as possible into a roll. It wasn't enough, and her landing was hard, but judging by the throbbing in her knee, it was better than what her foe suffered. Kehrsyn rolled over and scrambled to her feet, drawing her dagger as she rose.

The man rolled onto his hands and knees and shook his head to clear it. Blood slung in a veritable fan from his injury, his ponytail moving in counterpoint. Kehrsyn jerked back from the spray. The man got one knee in under him and wiped his eyes with his free hand.

Kehrsyn saw her opportunity and stepped on the head of the pick where it lay on the ground. She drew her foot back, flipping the handle into her waiting hand. She hefted the pick and slung it inexpertly but with as much desperate force as she could muster. The cruel dragon's muzzle arced in and cracked the man's shoulder blade, driving him back to the ground. Kehrsyn dropped her dagger and swung again with both hands. The point slid between his ribs and buried itself in his chest. The man's back bent backward reflexively, then he shuddered twice, and save a freakish periodic twitch of one wrist, lay still.

Kehrsyn trembled. She hadn't killed anyone before—hadn't had to, because she'd always had a means of escape. Her heart thundered, and tears clouded her eyes. She felt as if she would be violently ill. Her mind raced with the fact that she had killed one of the cultists and that the others would soon ferret her out and take their revenge. Past the pounding blood in her ears, she could hear that the fighting upstairs had all but stopped. She forced herself to focus, to find a way out of her situation, a means of escaping those who hunted her.

She left the pick in the man's corpse and dragged him by the ankles to the foot of the staircase. There she heaved him on top of the man he had killed, placing him in such a position that, with luck, it would be assumed that he died either just before or during the fall down the stairs. As she stepped back, the heavy pick slid its way out of the man's back and clattered to the ground. Kehrsyn shuddered. Her hands felt greasy and unclean. It unnerved her to have handled—desecrated, her mother might have said—a dead body, still warm with the memory of its lost life.

What to do about herself? Kehrsyn cast about, looking for hope and finding little in the ill-lit lower story. She heard footsteps above, heading in her direction—for the staircase—then she saw the puddle of blood that had dribbled down from above. It had grown to be quite sizeable, even alarming. Kehrsyn lay down at its edge, curling up in a half-fetal position so that it looked like the blood pooling in front of her was hers. She buried her face beneath one arm, clenched her teeth in nausea, and hoped the trembling from her revulsion at the cold blood wouldn't give her away.

She waited. The footsteps of the Tiamat cultists ranged back and forth upstairs for an eternity before they came down.

Kehrsyn's throat convulsed. She wanted to whimper in

fear, wanted to run away as fast as she could. They talked in casual voices, mercifully drowned by the ambient noise of the crowd. Kehrsyn could only presume they were inspecting the bodies at the foot of the stairs.

"Well," said one, more loudly as he walked closer, "at least he took out two of them."

He stopped next to Kehrsyn, his robes rustling.

Kehrsyn tensed as his feet shifted on the dirty floor. Would he stab her to ensure she was dead? The very thought was mortifying. He'd stab her in her back as she lay there. She could see the blade in her mind's eye. It felt like her kidneys were trying to crawl up her spine to hide beneath her ribs. She could feel them crying out as the Tiamatan speared them, time and again, in her imagination. She tried to relax and be limp, but couldn't, and finally she wondered if she was supposed to have rigor mortis.

Why was he standing there for so long? she wondered. Please, go away!

"Pity she got butchered," the Tiamatan said. "That's a nice head of hair."

"So scalp her later," said a companion.

The man standing over her nudged her with a boot, and an involuntary squeak escaped her throat. His feet shifted again, and her heart stopped, knowing her ruse had been betrayed by her surprise.

A voice called down from the top of the stairs, "All clear?"

"All clear," echoed one of the Tiamatans.

"Very well," said the one upstairs. "Tear the place apart. I want it found!"

The man over her stepped away, and he and the others began rummaging through the rooms. They talked and joked, banged drawers and doors, slit mattresses and tapped the walls for false panels, unafraid of being overheard for the noise of the crowds outside. They strode past her time and again as they tore the place apart.

While death stalked around her, she clung to the advice in one of the ancient tales of her people: she never once opened her eyes to see the danger.

☙

After what seemed an eternity, Kehrsyn heard the last of the Tiamatans leave. Just to be safe, she lay there for what seemed another two or three hundred years, hearing nothing but the thudding of her heart. She soon arose, slowly, quietly, looking all around for signs of threat, but every body she saw lay still. Even the twitching of the dead Tiamatan's wrist had subsided.

She removed her cloak, meticulously avoiding the blood as much as possible. In Tharrad's office, she was relieved to find her rapier had been overlooked or ignored, and she retied it to her belt. She recovered her dagger, then sneaked throughout the house, weapons in hand, searching each room for loiterers or survivors. There were none. Even the dog was dead. She found the sorceress in the front room, empty eyes staring at the ceiling, snarling mouth left devoid of threat. Blood soaked her torn jersey, testament to the blows that had killed her. Curiously, her left middle finger had been cut off.

Part of Kehrsyn's mind wanted her to kick the vile woman in the head or spit on her corpse, but her heart could find only relief and some small pity within. No venom remained for the dead.

She brooded as she stared at the slowly cooling corpse. It was frustrating to have her revenge cut short, to be sure, but at the same time she wondered if she weren't better off as a result. She had a job and a place to stay, and she was cleaner and better fed than she had been for months.

The only catch, Kehrsyn thought as she stared at the sorceress, is that if I'm not careful, I'm more likely to end up like you.

Even as she thought that, she heard a creak on the ladder outside the front door. Glancing through the gap in the curtain, Kehrsyn saw the telltale colors of red and black looming to fill the window.

CHAPTER THIRTEEN

The visitor knocked on the door and started to open the latch. Kehrsyn had but a moment to react, so she leaped behind the door, her light frame landing silently and smoothly like a cat on the prowl. The door swung open, sweeping away her elbowroom, yet she concealed her rapier and readied her dagger, making no noise.

A large figure dressed in rich red-and-black robes entered the room and drew up, heavy, wide hands pushing the door closed again.

Kehrsyn heard the intruder gasp at the carnage. Nervous, but confident enough being both behind the newcomer and close to the exit, Kehrsyn stepped forward and placed the tips of her blades firmly into the intruder's back, dagger just behind the left ear and rapier pointed at the right kidney.

The intruder stiffened.

"I see you are a student of anatomy," the woman said in a firm and steady tenor, though the words were spoken softly and inoffensively.

"I discovered many years ago that a good knowledge of anatomy can get you out of a great deal of trouble," said Kehrsyn.

"I came to see Tharrad. Is he . . . ?"

"Don't lie to me," demanded Kehrsyn. "Why did you do this? Answer me, and perhaps I'll spare your life."

She had to hope that her threat carried adequate menace. Kehrsyn knew she couldn't just skewer someone through the back, even if that someone worshiped Tiamat.

"I had nothing to do with this," said the woman, raising her arms to her sides, "though it appears that some of my people were involved." She nodded to a decapitated body dressed in red and black. "I mean no foul play, and I am unarmed. If you please, I prefer to hold discussions face to face. May I turn?"

"Yeah," said Kehrsyn, after some thought, "but keep your arms to your sides, and don't do anything stupid."

Kehrsyn stepped back to ensure she remained out of reach of the woman's long arms.

The newcomer turned around very slowly. With her feet obscured by the long, snow-wet hem of her Tiamatan robe, it was almost reminiscent of seeing a hanged criminal turning on a gibbet.

"Tiglath!" blurted Kehrsyn as she saw the intruder's profile and unique scars.

Tiglath raised her chin and said, "I recognize you."

"Don't play the fool," said Kehrsyn. "You knew I was here, you just didn't expect me to be alive."

"I am never the fool," said Tiglath. A brief pause. "Ah, yes, you were in our narthex, the one who chose to tell the truth. I granted you my sufferance."

"Oh, I remember that," said Kehrsyn. She advanced, dagger held forward and aimed at Tiglath's throat, rapier level behind her, ready for a thrust to the torso. "Is sufferance your code word for 'kill her later'? That's an ugly way to pay someone back for giving you the truth."

Tiglath drew herself up, and though her arms were still spread helplessly wide, her scar-framed eyes blazed with indignation. "How dare you? I would mete out great punishment for such temerity had I not already given you said sufferance."

"Yeah, well, one of your brutes already tried that. Tried to kill me, he did. Your protection isn't worth two grains."

At once Tiglath's eyes blazed even brighter, but the ire turned away from Kehrsyn and focused within as her eyes twitched to the side. Her nostrils flared, and her outstretched hands clenched into fists. At that moment, Kehrsyn decided it would probably be a very wise thing not to push Tiglath's patience too far.

"Really?" growled Tiglath, as slow as rolling thunder.

"Yes'm," said Kehrsyn, taking a step back. "I told him I had your sufferance just like you said, and he was even one of the ones there with you when you gave it." Kehrsyn watched as Tiglath pursed her lips. Her skin started blotching with red, making her scars stand out even more starkly. "You, um, can put your arms down, now," added Kehrsyn, not wishing to stoke the fires any further.

Tiglath fixed Kehrsyn with her gaze again, a look gone from a firestorm to cold steel.

"And where is this disobedient disciple now?" the priestess asked, her lips moving with exaggerated curves across her clenched teeth. Her arms began to drop.

"I, uh . . . well, he's at the bottom of the stairs. Now."

"Show me," Tiglath commanded.

Kehrsyn took a look at Tiglath's eyes and at the tendons standing out on her neck, and decided to obey. She trotted through the house, skipping uneasily over the bodies, with Tiglath's heavy tread close behind. She moved down the staircase, vaulted over the rail to avoid the bodies at the bottom, and moved as far away as she could.

Tiglath stepped over the bodies and grabbed the hair of the Tiamatan that Kehrsyn indicated. She raised his head and stared into his face, swollen and purple with pooling blood.

"You bastard!" Tiglath spat.

It was the quietest yell Kehrsyn had ever heard, yet it packed the anger and malice of an outburst a hundred times as loud. Tiglath's knuckles whitened where they gripped the ponytail, and the extra tension tautened the skin on the dead man's face. She threw the head back down with disgust and, still kneeling beside the corpse, turned to face Kehrsyn. She forced her face into a calm expression, but Kehrsyn could see the fires still blazing behind her eyes.

"If you please," asked the priestess, "would you tell me exactly what happened here?"

Kehrsyn gave a full accounting of what she had seen and heard, carefully skirting her involvement in the issue and especially avoiding any reference to the fact that she had been the one who'd stolen the necromantic wand in the first place. Tiglath nodded throughout the retelling, staring at an empty bit of space off to her left somewhere.

"In short, ma'am," finished Kehrsyn, "I guess maybe it was a raid or something."

"Indeed," replied Tiglath. "That fits the evidence." She stared straight at Kehrsyn. "I note your story neatly omits any reference to your involvement, but as I surmise your involvement was with Furifax and not with this worm, I'll allow your secrets to remain yours. You've been satisfactorily forthcoming with the information I need. Thank you for killing him, though it's a pity he didn't remain alive for interrogation."

"Who was he?" hazarded Kehrsyn, as it appeared Tiglath was in a mood to talk.

"He was one of my inner circle," answered the priestess, "one of my trusted advisors."

"If he was considered trustworthy," observed Kehrsyn, "I'd sure hate to have your advisors."

Tiglath snorted, and with a half-smile, said, "I suppose so. There's a feeling you get when the ground just starts to give way beneath your feet, or when the axle breaks on your wagon, or right after you've drunk too much. It's a feeling that there's something wrong, something imminent and close, but you can't put your finger on it and everything seems normal. I have had that feeling for some time within my church and most especially among my advisors. I dismissed those feelings as worry brought by the war. Now I know the feelings were right. I find that my most trusted people have been operating behind my back."

"You're sure that's what's happening?" asked Kehrsyn.

"I know they have not been pleased with some of my choices. I continued our alliance with Furifax and his people, and refused the aid of other, more aggressive, more ruthless, factions. I did this to ensure that we did not save Unther only to yield our sovereignty to a foreign power. Not everyone sees the wisdom of this choice.

"Further, now that the god-king Gilgeam has been killed, I wish to replace his despotic thearchy with a government modeled after some of the younger nations, a meritocracy where the power resides in the hands of a council that rules for the betterment of the nation, not their own vanity. This decision has also met with resistance. My advisors do not understand that seizing control of Unther for the church of Tiamat only replaces one thearchy with another, and I will not see my life's work perverted in such a manner."

Tiglath sucked in her lips and drummed her fingers.

"It seems," she said, "that those beneath me, some of them at least, have made other plans." She chuckled mirthlessly. "Curious that a high priestess learns more from a street-smart refugee than she does from her own people."

Kehrsyn shrugged.

"I am thankful that I spared you," said Tiglath, rather kindly for a woman of her imposing demeanor.

"Yeah, well, so am I," said Kehrsyn, sheathing her weapons.

An uncomfortable silence hung in the air for a few moments, until Tiglath slapped her knees and heaved her bulk to her feet again.

"Well," she said, "you said they were after something?"

"Yeah, a magical relic that someone told me might be the Staff of the Necromancer. About so long," she added, gesturing.

"Let's see if we can find it, shall we?" asked the priestess.

Tiglath's voice rang with forced cheer, but then, Kehrsyn mused, at least the priestess was trying to be friendly, even if it didn't come naturally to her.

"I really doubt we'll find it, if they didn't," said Kehrsyn. "They were very thorough."

"I have better help than they," said Tiglath. "I'll be right back."

The priestess went upstairs, and Kehrsyn heard her heavy footsteps tromp over to the front door, heard the door open and close again, and heard the stairs creak as Tiglath returned.

On Tiglath's shoulder, Kehrsyn saw the smallest dragon she had ever seen. It peered back at her with two tiny, intelligent, emerald eyes. Its whiskers seemed to float as if underwater, and it bobbed its head as if scenting the air, or perhaps some ethereal breezes that moved beyond mortal senses. It peered closely at Kehrsyn, then stuck its muzzle in Tiglath's ear.

"Really?" said Tiglath, speaking softly to her familiar. She pursed her lips with interest. "Fascinating," she added, as the dragonet withdrew its muzzle.

"What's fascinating?" asked Kehrsyn, rather unnerved that Tiglath was looking at her differently in the wake of the dragonet's message.

"Nothing, dear," answered Tiglath. "We have work to do."

The priestess held her hand up to her shoulder, and the dragonet moved to perch upon it. Tiglath "tsked" and clucked a few times—soft, intimate noises—and the dragon flew away, whizzing from room to room, its wings sounding like giant wasps or paper sheets in a windstorm.

"You sure that'll work?" asked Kehrsyn.

"Absolutely," replied Tiglath. "They are far superior beings and have instinctive sensitivities that we can attain only through years of hard work in magic."

Kehrsyn spread her hands, shrugged, and bowed herself out as the dragonet did its work. Turning on her heel, she began perusing the bunkrooms, looking for a cloak to replace her newly bloodstained rag. With luck, she'd find one that fit her, looked reasonable, and was at least water resistant, if not truly waterproof.

She found one that fit her needs, even if it was too wide and a tad short, and she went back to wait with Tiglath. The dragonet peered out of a different room, looked around, then zipped up the stairwell to the upper floor. Tiglath watched its departure and waited, staring at the stairwell, hands clasped in front of her.

"So, um, priestess?" said Kehrsyn. "Can I ask—"

" 'May I,' dear," corrected Tiglath.

"What exactly is going on in Messemprar these days?" Kehrsyn asked, ignoring Tiglath's interruption. "I mean, Furifax, a bandit who had countless shekae on his head, has spies that know of this staff thing, and they've got all these people, yet they hire someone to steal it, and his allies come in and attack them for it, and their own leader doesn't even know it's going on, and both the bandits and the people they stole it from say they're doing it to help the people, but the Northern Wizards can't even know that it's here, otherwise they would already have bought it or something, but the Red Wizards did know . . . well, it just seems all confusing. You seem to know what's going on—" she paused and looked around—"aside from certain recent events, that is.

So can you tell me . . . something? Anything? I mean, I'm just a juggler."

Tiglath took a deep breath, causing her already ample form to grow, then let the air back out as she framed her answer. She turned to face Kehrsyn, who stood, rolling one toe back and forth on the ground behind her.

"You are far more than just a juggler, my dear," began Tiglath. "For one thing, apparently, you're an accomplished thief."

"I didn't say I stole it," countered Kehrsyn.

"No, you didn't," observed Tiglath, "but neither do you deny it, and who else but someone at the very center of events would know so much about all sides? Oh, don't fret, dear. Your secret is safe, for not only have you my sufferance, but you have provided me with invaluable information." Tiglath moved closer, and despite her passive stance, she still seemed to loom over Kehrsyn's slight build. "Thus, let me repay knowledge for knowledge and answer your question.

"Messemprar is the remnant of one of the oldest empires in Faerûn. Each grain of the sands upon which we stand has been ground from the bones of hundreds of generations of scholars, warriors, artists, and slaves, all of whom died to make Unther a dynasty to endure forever. Yet we find ourselves with a great void in the power structure."

"I thought the Northern Wizards had taken control," protested Kehrsyn.

"That is what they want people to believe," responded Tiglath, "and, for that matter, many others are content to let that illusion remain, for without that false sense of security, the populace would panic. The Northern Wizards do have some power. They have consolidated their hold on the bureaucracy and taken nominal control of the judiciary, which was no small feat, but the rest eludes them."

"But they have the army," suggested Kehrsyn.

"Actually, they don't. Just like a jackal defends her lair

even though vipers have killed all her pups, so the army defends Messemprar and northern Unther. They are too busy fighting to meddle in politics, and frankly, they don't care who pretends to be in power so long as they get their support. So they take what they need, and no one dares stop them, for doing so risks everything we're fighting over."

"But who else is fighting?" asked Kehrsyn.

"The Northern Wizards are opposed by groups like Furifax and his band—Gilgeam called them bandits, but they call themselves revolutionaries—our church of Tiamat (all glory to her name), Mulhorandi sympathizers, the Zhentarim—"

"The Zhentarim?" echoed Kehrsyn with alarm.

"They're a poison in the wine if ever there was. While the rest of us fight at the top, they're undermining the bottom, turning themselves into the heroes of the rabble and many of the minor noble houses, spreading their lies with free bread, extra constables, ploys like that. It wouldn't be so bad if they weren't part of a network that covers most of the continent. The organization is affiliated with the church of Bane, though I'm not clear if the Zhentarim are an arm of the church, or the church is an arm of their network."

"Oh, boy," said Kehrsyn. "I can think of a number of things I'd rather have heard than that."

"I know the feeling," commented Tiglath, and Kehrsyn didn't doubt it. "Then there's the leftover Gilgeamite clergy, two or three so-called royal houses that trace their lineage to Gilgeam's dalliances, the Hegemony of Artisans, and, rumor has it, a subversive group of slaves that wants to turn the power structure upside down. Those are the people vying for power. The Red Wizards and a few other groups are trying to ingratiate themselves with whoever might come out on top by assisting in whatever manner possible."

"I think I get the picture," said Kehrsyn, "and it looks pretty ugly."

Tiglath chuckled and said, "That's the thrust of it. At the center of Unther, there is nothing. That cannot last."

"No wonder you can't trust anybody."

"Almost nobody," Tiglath amended. "The difficulty lies in finding those few who aren't bent by the proximity of so much unwielded power."

The dragonet whizzed back down the stairwell, arced once around the room, circled once again around Tiglath, and alighted on the priestess' shoulder. Once more it thrust its muzzle into her ear, and the speed with which it did so made Kehrsyn cringe. Tiglath hardly appeared to notice.

"It seems our friends were thorough," said Tiglath, after the dragonet had withdrawn its muzzle and curled up in the cowl around her neck. "There is but one enchanted item left in the building. It lies in Tharrad's office. Come, let's see. With luck, it will be the staff of which you spoke.

They walked into the office where, but a watch or so before, Kehrsyn was having a rather enjoyable conversation . . . even if it was with someone she sought to betray. The once-pristine room had been ransacked. Tables had been overturned, drawers pulled out and their contents scattered, even Tharrad's chair was slashed and gutted. The dragonet nosed among some of the detritus and indicated what it had found.

Kehrsyn's heart stopped. There was the coveted wand, broken in two and left behind. Tiglath kneeled, picked up the halves, and looked back over her shoulder at Kehrsyn.

"Is this the item of which you spoke?" she asked.

Kehrsyn could only nod.

Tiglath passed her hand over the object, murmuring an incantation under her breath. After a few moments, she stood up and held the pieces out to Kehrsyn.

"What magic it had has been shattered and is fading

fast," she said. "I'd say that Tharrad or one of his people broke it rather than let it fall into the hands of . . . my people."

Kehrsyn took the pieces and turned them over in her hands, stunned that something that magical could be so readily sundered. She ran her thumb along the smooth surface of the scepter and down the edges of its carvings. She noted with surprise that a hollow tube ran down the center of the wand, empty save for a few motes of alabaster dust from when the item was broken.

"I—I don't know what to say," muttered Kehrsyn. She ran one finger around the smooth, hollow interior. "This is a really old item, lost for a long time, and now it's gone, just like that. I thought this was important to them, important to Unther."

"Regardless, it was a pointless waste," murmured Tiglath. She looked at the bodies at the foot of the stair. "A real waste," she repeated. "I wonder what the cause was?"

"Isn't it obvious?" asked Kehrsyn. "They knew that the Furifaxians had the staff, and they wanted it. That means they had some kind of inside information about its theft."

"What?" responded Tiglath. "How would they know about something being stolen from a merchant house, let alone care?"

"Well, Tharrad . . . you, like, knew him, right? He said that they had allies who had someone on the inside of Wing's Reach. They had a map, and they knew exactly where the staff was being kept."

Kehrsyn stopped prattling and looked askance at Tiglath. The priestess looked blankly at Kehrsyn, then it dawned on her, too.

"Are you saying that I have a spy planted in Wing's Reach? I have no such thing. Why would I give a wedge about a merchant?"

"Because he's got the Staff of the Necromancer," observed Kehrsyn.

She started to step away from Tiglath, resting one hand on the hilt of her rapier. Tiglath folded her arms and sank her head on her chest to think.

"That makes a vile sort of sense, you know," the priestess said, rocking on her heels. "If my people are working behind my back, this is the sort of scheme they might buy in on, but infiltration is not their style—not *our* style, that is. No, the Staff of the Necromancer is supposed to be quite a potent weapon, and that's what they'd be in it for. That makes me wonder if Furifax's people didn't actually doublecross my people."

"How so?"

"Furifax convinces my church to attack Wing's Reach to capture the staff, but the day before they send you in early to steal it. Immediately afterward, my people attack. They take the risk, take the blame, and get nothing to show for it, while Furifax gets the staff and avoids discovery."

"That almost sounds like you're defending your followers, when they're running around behind your back," observed Kehrsyn.

Tiglath snorted and said, "Old habits die hard. And, now that you point that out, that theory doesn't shed any light on how my people found out, now does it?"

"So how are you going to find out the truth?" asked Kehrsyn.

"I don't know," Tiglath said. She paused, her mouth compressed, and blew air out of her nose like an angry bull. "Get used to lies and deceit, Kehrsyn," she said. "These days, nothing in Messemprar is what it seems."

"Does that include you?" Kehrsyn asked, looking at Tiglath from under her brows.

"Well, I certainly hope I'm more than a fat and angry old crone," joked Tiglath. She paused, her eyes turned inward on her own soul. "And I hope, too," she added, her eyes softening to sadness for just a moment, "that I'm not actually as cruel as I probably seem."

Kehrsyn smiled, then her grin faded again as she ran her thumb across the carvings in the halves of the wand.

"Well," said Tiglath, brushing dust off her hands, "I have some undesirable work to do among the faithful. An alliance has been broken, and somehow I doubt those who came here are likely to discuss the matter freely. Good day," she said as she mounted the stairwell. "I do hope we can meet again."

With that, the priestess left Kehrsyn standing at the base of the empty house, amidst broken oaths, broken bodies, and a broken wand.

CHAPTER FOURTEEN

Not knowing what else to do, Kehrsyn shouldered her bag, left the building, climbed down the ladder, and headed for the Thayan enclave to see Eileph.

He wanted to study that thing, she thought, so I guess there's nothing stopping him now. Not that there's anything really left to learn—Tiglath said the magic was fading—but really, I owe him the pieces of the wand.

She worked her way through the crowded streets of Messemprar. The snow had been plowed to slush and pressed away to the margins of the streets, leaving slick cobbles, cold mud, and, in places of greater shade, ice for her to contend with. The wind had picked up again and blew from the southeast in gusts. Kehrsyn pulled her cloak tighter around her face and shoulders and tried to ignore the fact that it smelled of someone else.

When she was most of the way to the enclave, Kehrsyn stopped in her tracks, rolled her eyes, and changed her course for the Mage Bazaar. Of course Eileph would be there, in his tent, selling to a desperate public instead of lounging in his sanctum. She only hoped she would not have to wait long to see him.

At the entrance to the curtain walls that encircled the Red Wizards' pavilion, the guard informed her that Eileph was not selling merchandise that day. He had remained in the enclave engaged in research. Kehrsyn rolled her eyes again and retraced her steps all the way back to the enclave.

She was admitted promptly, and once more found herself entering Eileph's laboratory and erstwhile reception room. As she entered, the deformed wizard was carefully studying a small organ he had cut from the cadaver. The toad sat upon the corpse's flayed face, an image that made Kehrsyn's lower lip quiver with revulsion.

"Um . . . Eileph?" she said.

Eileph hobbled around, leaning on a gnarled cane as misshapen as he was. So did the toad, its amphibian feet slapping on the cold, dead musculature as it rotated its obese bulk in place. Kehrsyn tried very hard to ignore it, but the beast was unavoidably visible in her peripheral vision.

"Oh, mm-hmm, it's you," said Eileph. "I must tell you, it is rare I find myself anticipating anyone's interruption, but you've managed to make yourself an exception, even if you are built like a wee wisp of an elf."

"Thanks," she said.

As she tried to figure out how to break the news, Kehrsyn smiled hollowly.

"Do your people have another commission for me? Hmm?" asked Eileph, waggling his fingers. "More gold for this tired old soul?"

"Well . . . no," said Kehrsyn. "Basically, um, the reason I'm, y'know, here, is that they—well we, that is—*we* agreed that . . . you could sort of . . . study the, uh . . . the staff.

When we were through with it. And . . . I guess we're kind of through with it."

With those words, Kehrsyn placed the broken halves of the wand on a relatively flat pile of papers on the worktable, there being no spot that was actually clear of clutter.

Eileph's jaw dropped, and his skin went deathly pale. One hand clutched at his jersey, just over his heart. He began to hobble over to the remnants of the staff.

The toad began croaking loudly, and Eileph burst into braying laughter. It was a jarring duet. Kehrsyn tried to smile, but her unease made it look like she was going to vomit, which, truth be told, was not entirely out of the question.

Eileph drew in a deep, gasping, rasping breath and slapped the table.

"You shouldn't scare an old man like that, young lady, you really had me going!" He closed his solitary eye and began pounding on his forehead with two stubby fingers. "Oh my, oh, dearie me," he laughed, "I don't think I'll be able to spit for a tenday, you scared me so bad!"

"What?" asked Kehrsyn.

"What? Why, because this is the decoy, youngster!" guffawed Eileph, wiping a tear of laughter from the corner of his empty eye.

"Decoy?" echoed Kehrsyn, trying very hard to catch up with events.

"Well," he said, "I see that it fooled you, eh, young lady? Don't let it stop your wee little heart. This is what I was working on for you lot, a copy of the staff you'd marked for acquisition. Here," he said, as he hobbled over and picked up the halves, "let me show you what I did. Superb carving work, if I do say so myself."

He moved so close that he had to crane his head up to look at Kehrsyn. He held the halves aloft for her inspection, spinning them and pointing to the pieces as he spoke.

"See? First of all, this is stone, not bone like the original.

Didn't have any good bones handy, but it looks much the same as a weathered bone, and anyway that organic stuff is a regular mess to carve properly. But stone is heavier, so I had to hollow it out just like this to match the weight properly. Now this side you already saw in the sketches I showed you, but I didn't know what this side looked like, so I had to wait for your delivery to be able to duplicate it. Hard work, too, but I'd already had practice in the style with this first side here. The river and setting the jeweler made, and laid the black amber and smoky quartz to match the original. Then I cast Mythrellaa's Lust upon it—that's a rather more stylish version of the Fool's Aura, a little trick the zulkir gave me in payment for a small service I'd rendered her. And there it was, all but indistinguishable from the original, except, of course, it wouldn't work."

"That's . . . very impressive," said Kehrsyn, stepping back to get some personal space between her and the sour-smelling magician.

"Hmph," said Eileph, inspecting the pieces. "Of course, that doesn't explain how this came to be broken."

"They don't tell me such things," said Kehrsyn, pleased that she'd come up with such a plausible non-answer off the cuff.

"And who does?" yelled Eileph, flicking a finger at Kehrsyn. "Oh, I know all about such things," he said as he hobbled away, then stopped dead in his tracks. "Or, more accurately, I don't. You see, the zulkirs and tharcions, and all the Red Wizards are very good at not telling things." He hobbled back over to Kehrsyn and stood too close again. "Which makes it very scary," he whispered, "when one considers all that one has been taught by others who thrive on secrets. It makes one wonder how much knowledge they hold back! And that makes all of us hunger for that knowledge, plot for it, scheme for it . . ." Eileph's arm started to tremble, tapping his cane on the floor. "Good thing I'm such a stable person," he said.

Kehrsyn nodded. She didn't trust her voice not to crack were she to lie at that moment.

"Well," said Eileph, as he started back to the cadaver.

He tossed the halves on his table as he passed. Kehrsyn thought maybe the fake one would pass inspection at Wing's Reach, at least until she got the real one. She feared returning empty-handed with Ahegi lurking around.

"Um, Eileph, sir?" asked Kehrsyn. "Can you fix it?"

Eileph whipped around, staggering when his whirl exceeded his balance.

"What?" he bellowed. "First they destroy my art and now they say, 'Jump, Eileph, fix the staff!' What do they think I am, a trained homunculus?"

"Standard rates," said Kehrsyn, raising her voice to be heard over Eileph's tirade. "Double for a rush job."

Eileph's countenance softened in an instant. He picked up the two halves and fitted them together, working his jaw from side to side.

"Hmph," he said. "I can do it, young lady, never you fret. I can have it for you tonight, if you don't mind a bit of a crack, or tomorrow for a job as good as new. If you want one carved afresh, that'll take a while."

"How big a crack are we talking about?"

"Oh, not a very big one," said Eileph. "Fit the halves together and take a look. I can make it a bit better than that."

Kehrsyn fiddled with the broken pieces. The crack would be just a hair wide.

"That'd be great," she said, handing the pieces over.

Eileph limped back over to her and patted her hand gently, almost tenderly.

"Don't you fret your heart, young lady. I'll have it delivered tonight," he said, with a smile that was the picture of warmth despite the malformed frame in which it appeared.

❂

Massedar stood at the window in his study, gazing out at the pale winter sky. Sunshine slanted into the room but did not warm it. He felt the outside chill pouring in through the open window, counterbalanced by the warmth radiating from the roaring fire. The blaze warmed his back and the hands clasped behind, and the reflected flames glinted merrily in his rings.

A knock came at the door—not the door that led to his private bedroom, of course, but the doorway that led to the audience hall in which he had alternately cowed and impressed their young thief.

"Enter thou," he said, not turning his head. His breath misted in the chill draft.

He heard the door open and close again. One pair of footsteps came over to his side.

"Ahegi, faithful servant," said Massedar. "Thou wouldst speak with me in privacy ere the interrogation?"

"Indeed, sir," said Ahegi, likewise in High Untheric.

Massedar turned. Ahegi's head was freshly shaved, and the two circles that adorned his forehead glistened. Ahegi's close-set and piggish eyes, set deep beneath heavy brows, glowered with black irises and blacker thoughts.

"Speak thy heart, then," commanded Massedar.

"My heart ponders, belike we have erred to entrust ourselves unto that maiden," said Ahegi. "Would that we had plied her lips forcibly with red irons and turnspindles, that we might have such knowledge of our trespassers unto ourselves."

Massedar smiled thinly and said, "The spangled sandpiper feigneth grave injury to lure the wolf from its nest, and the butterfly spider feigneth comeliness to lure a mate to its doom. If a simple animal understandeth that nectar draweth the prey willingly whilst the fire repelleth, wherefore dost thou despair of this lesson?"

"Mayhap I find the act of dissimulation cometh less easily unto me than it doth thee," Ahegi replied, his lips pressed together. "By my troth, I find that falsehood taxeth my patience."

"That, old friend, maketh thee an advisor of great worth," said Massedar.

Ahegi bowed and turned back to the door.

He opened it and said, "Demok, thou art granted audience to the Lord of Wing's Reach."

Demok stepped in and nodded slightly but respectfully. He kept his eyes studiously unfocused, looking at a vacant spot in the air to give his peripheral vision the greatest advantage.

"Sir," he said.

"My advisor Ahegi sweareth that thy maiden-thief lieth beyond trust," said Massedar. "What opinion hast thou?"

"Trustworthy," said Demok, nodding. "Sound heart. Looking to impress, find a home."

"Sound heart?" echoed Ahegi with a sneer.

"Good with kids," said Demok. "Cares about people."

"We shall not abide a net of such flimsy braids," said Ahegi. "She hath led us unto the lair of our enemies. Henceforth shall we vanquish them by advantage, striking the vipers in their den."

"Can't," said Demok with a set jaw.

"Thinkest thou not that I possess the power to smite whomever draweth my wrath?" asked Massedar. "Thou hast shadowed her unto the gates of her guild. We strike."

Demok looked at Massedar, then at Ahegi. "She spotted my tail. Got away. Tried to follow; no luck. Don't know where the guild is."

Massedar stepped forward, drawing a breath to say something, but then stopped, closed his eyes, and exhaled bitterly.

"Perforce must we wait," Massedar said eventually. "These are ill tidings, Demok. I pay thee handsomely for better. Leave thou me."

Demok nodded again and left the room in a flickering with his efficient, graceful movements.

Massedar and Ahegi stood silently for some time.

Ahegi said, "He speaketh not the truth unto us," he said.

"I know," Massedar said, nodding, "but we know not yet wherefore. Arrest ye him not before the measure of his deceit hath been revealed in full. Someone within Wing's Reach cleaveth to the Zhentarim. If it be he, must we then proceed with great prudence, lest we alert those who bring our doom."

❂

By the time Kehrsyn left the enclave, the streets had been freshly washed by a squall. The smell and humidity of winter rain hung in the air. Heavy drops of water fell from the eaves and splattered into the sodden drifts of slush.

Kehrsyn had a promise from Eileph that he'd send the repaired decoy staff to her as soon as it was completed. All she had to do was wait for it . . . at "the guild's" head-quarters at sixteen Wheelwright's.

Kehrsyn gathered her cloak around her shoulders and shivered. The chill came not from the weather but from the dread within her breast. She did not want to return to that house. To keep her feet from dragging, Kehrsyn distracted herself by trying to sort out events.

The followers of Tiamat had attacked Furifax's people to seize the Staff of the Necromancer. The Furifaxians had already prepared a decoy, either to fool the Tiamatans or to reinsert in Wing's Reach. That made it seem more likely that the rebels had deliberately double-crossed the dragon cultists . . . or, she mused, that they knew the dragon cultists would double-cross them.

The Tiamatans attacked and slaughtered the defenders. How convenient that the Zhentarim had provided a large, loud crowd of people right there to conceal the noise of the fight. At some point, someone broke the decoy. On top of that, the real staff had been taken. That she knew because someone had said it was "downstairs," which pretty obviously meant Tharrad's office. So either Tharrad had broken the decoy wand, hoping to fool the Tiamatans, or else the Tiamatans had found both wands and broken the false one out of spite. Since all the rebels were dead, it didn't really matter which was the truth. The question remained, where was the Staff of the Necromancer? Did the Tiamatan church have it, which is to say, did Tiglath have it? Or had her followers been working with or for someone else and turned it over to them for safekeeping?

Kehrsyn found herself nearing the lair of the Furifaxians. The crowds around the Chariot Memorial had thinned, and in the buzz that lingered in the wake of the Zhentarim's dealings Kehrsyn went unnoticed. She stood at the foot of the ladder leading to the front door. Her hand flexed on the cold, wet ladder, knuckles alternately turning white from tension and red from chill as she tried to work up the courage to go back inside.

She did, mounting the ladder slowly, heavily, and pausing at the door. She felt compelled to open the door quietly, holding her breath as it swung wide.

She slid inside and closed the door. The atmosphere was morbid, exuding an air of pointlessness. The smell was the bitter, raw odor of the slaughterhouse. The winter sun slanted in through the windows, falling on the cyanotic faces of the dead.

Kehrsyn narrowed her eyes in an attempt to stop her eyelids from trembling. Yes, the Untheri prided themselves on prospering under even extreme hardship, but while she had endured a lifetime of stoic suffering, she was unsure whether she could withstand hours of waiting among the restless souls of betrayers and victims alike.

She stalked into the kitchen, boots making a noise so slight it could be noticed only among those who drew no breath. The lowering fire still burned in the hearth. Though the building was beginning to cool off, she could not bring herself to stoke the fire. Somehow, having a merry blaze burning brightly in the midst of the massacred dead seemed incongruous, perhaps even sacrilegious, and Kehrsyn wanted to do nothing that might attract their spirits back to harry the sole living creature in the building.

She circled the upper floor as gingerly as possible, and finally located a place where she could sit with only marginal discomfort. One of the rooms held only two bodies, and they lay by the doors. She found a tall stool and set it in the center of the room so that she could wait with wide spaces all around and no corpses reposing behind her. Thankfully, her nose seemed already to have become numb to the stink of pierced innards.

She sat on the stool, dropping her shoulder bag next to it. She waited, legs drawn up and back hunched in uncomfortable self-consciousness. She heard the hearth fire popping and hissing as it wound its way down to coals. The light grew dimmer and the air cooler, yet she dared not leave the building for fear of missing the courier. Neither could she bring herself to rebuild the fire or light lamps, for, as the darkness grew, so did the chance of stumbling over a dismembered body, and that was a possibility she wished to avoid.

As she waited, she found her thoughts drifting to her parents. She was surrounded by death, conscious of the lives that had ended so abruptly that cold winter's day. She knew that some of these men and women had left behind families, a legacy of pain and want that they could not ease. Just like her father.

She had never known her mother's husband. He had been killed by Ekur, one of the powerful priests of Gilgeam and ruler of Kehrsyn's hometown of Shussel. Ekur had ruled with a hand that was incompetent in action and potent in reaction, and he had lusted after Kehrsyn's mother Sarae. Loving and devoted, Sarae refused Ekur's obscene propositions, turning down even a wealth of live-stock and spices for the dalliance of a single evening. In the end, Sarae's loyalty turned and bit her as does a trained asp, for Ekur's soldiers brought the hapless woman to him, killing her husband in the process. Ekur didn't take the widow in. He simply took her.

As a child, Kehrsyn had wished that she could have known her father, had someone to love her and protect her in all the ways her mother, desperate just to find enough food, could not. Ever since the pivotal spring day by the plum tree, when she passed out of childhood and into adulthood, Kehrsyn had since wished that her father could have known her, to have had the opportunity to hold his child even once before he'd died. She found it unquench-ably sad that the man had died for Sarae's faithfulness with-out ever getting the chance to see the fruit of their union, and the grief was made all the worse that she, that child, had been an extra mouth to feed, an extra burden on one who unwillingly sacrificed her mate on the altar of love and devotion.

By the time Kehrsyn shook herself from her melan-choly, it was entirely dark outside, and she heard a light winter rain falling, droplets tinkling on the shutters and trickling down the walls. She could see a faint red glow in the kitchen from the dying embers of the hearth, but no other light remained. Assailed by the chill from without and her longing from within, Kehrsyn moved to the corner of the room, gathered a few cushions and pillows by touch, and arranged some of them on top of her to keep her warm and some beneath her for comfort. Her bag did its usual double duty as her pillow. She intended merely to rest, or maybe to catch a catnap, while she waited for the courier.

The pillows soon began to warm to her body. Brooding over memories that never were and lulled by the weeping sky, Kehrsyn let herself slide into a slight doze.

At first, Kehrsyn didn't resister the significance of the fact that she'd heard the floor creak, but then she heard the whispered, bubbly voices of the dead, maddeningly just beyond understanding, like a string of familiar syllables jumbled in a nonsensical pattern.

She heard the corpses rising to their feet, whispering of blood and dark magic. They moved quietly, but in the dead of night every sliding footstep rang like a tolling bell. Their murmuring voices drew closer. Their eyes, glowing like lanterns, scanned the darkness looking for the living. The nearest zombie's neck was broken, and his head lolled around, casting irregular patterns of light and darkness as he looked for her, calling in the gurgling tongue of the deceased.

She heard the door close and latch, sealing her in with the shuffling, hungry dead. She reached for her rapier but found herself naked . . .

Kehrsyn awoke with a start. She glanced around, eyes wide, pupils dilated in fear. She saw that one of the corpses was indeed not where she'd last seen it. Dread gripped her heart, and bile rose in her throat, impelled by her empty stomach. She saw a flicker of light in the kitchen, a dim splash moving in the darkness. It vanished. She heard the sliding sound again, and the feet of a body in the kitchen began to slide out of sight.

Confused, Kehrsyn shrank back into the cushions. She pulled one of the pillows out from behind her and placed it in front. She panned her head back and forth, looking for movement, ears tuned for any noise, mouth open to aid the sharpness of her hearing.

In the kitchen, she saw a silhouette step into her line of sight. It held a bull's-eye lantern in one hand, easily recognized by the telltale red glow of the light behind its slatted louvers. Whoever-it-was opened the slats the tiniest amount and shone the light on the body on the floor.

"Nah," a male voice said, adding some explanation Kehrsyn couldn't quite hear.

He moved on, and two others followed him, passing through Kehrsyn's line of sight one by one. She heard the leader mutter under his breath, and a few moments later the other two passed by again, heading to the door, carrying one of the dead bodies between them, grunting quietly with the dead weight.

Hoping to evade detection, for it seemed they were seeking out the corpses that littered the building, Kehrsyn moved more of the pillows until she lay against the wall, concealed by soft cushions. As far as she knew, only her head was exposed, and that she kept hidden behind a large bolster with her hair veiling her face so that her eyes might not reflect the lantern light.

There she lay as the intruders moved around their grisly task, quietly moving corpse after corpse out of the building. Kehrsyn watched their progress carefully. They cleared her room, they cleared the kitchen, and they began to move deeper within the house.

Knowing they expected no one in the building to move voluntarily, Kehrsyn decided to discover more about the body snatchers. It might shed some light on the events surrounding the troublesome wand. She wriggled out from behind the pillows and worked her way across the room, against the wall where the floorboards were less likely to creak. She avoided the kitchen, in case the group chose to meet—or, worse yet, eat—there when they were finished. Instead, by dint of careful timing, she sidled across the hall and sneaked to the front room, where she hid among the camping baggage.

She watched as shadowy figures shuffled in and out, bearing their dead burdens. She heard the cold rain outside, and, hidden among the sounds of droplets splashing in the darkened streets, the distinctive drumming sound of rain on oiled tarpaulins.

As the activity wound down, the leader of the expedition stood near the front door, sipping brandy from a hip flask. Kehrsyn could smell the potent aroma spreading through the chill air.

One of the workers came in, dripping with rainwater. He wiped his face with a rag, then blew his nose loudly.

"They's all loaded up, sir. It's rather more harder than loading cordwood, if you take my meanin'."

The leader took another swig, recorked his flask with a satisfied sigh, and asked, "How many do we have?"

"I sure'n lost count, sir," came the reply. "But we got 'em all, and we can't do none better nor that, if you take my meanin'."

"Fair enough," said the leader, shrugging.

"So where to, sir?"

"We'll load them aboard *Bow Before Me*."

"What's that, sir?"

The leader waved a hand with some irritation and explained, "The merchant ship that came in the day before yesterday."

"But that's Zhentarim, sir," said the henchman with grave concern. "I don't think we want to be doin' that, if you take my meanin'."

Kehrsyn picked up the slightest pause before the leader answered, "Let's take a look at this carefully now, right? It's clear as a bell why this will be no problem."

He's stalling, thought Kehrsyn.

"What reasons would those be, sir?" asked the concerned lackey.

Another brief pause, then, "First of all, if these bodies get discovered in our possession, we're in serious trouble. Let's let the Zhentarim take the risk of stashing them until we're ready, even if they don't know they're helping. Second, it's a merchant ship. Anyone who sees us loading things up won't think it's out of the ordinary. People load and unload things from merchant ships all the time, day and night. Merchant ships have tight schedules, you know. But if we took them back to the temple, neighbors might see. They might talk."

The lackey scratched the back of his head through the hood of his cloak and asked, "You sure we'll be able to do this without them catching us?"

"The ship's guards don't know any more about what gets loaded than anyone else. They'll be happy to stay inside by the fire on a night like tonight. And if they don't, well, I can talk my way past them, no trouble. Trust me."

"Yes, sir." The lackey took a few steps down the ladder, then stopped to look one last time at the leader. "Glory to Tiamat," he said.

The leader nodded and said, "All glory."

CHAPTER FIFTEEN

Kehrsyn was unsure whether someone might still be guarding the building, watching for any stragglers who might return, so she spent the rest of the night inside. She was, at least, comfortable with the assumption that no one else would enter, there being truly nothing left of interest in the building, so she rearranged the pillows on the floor, scrounged several blankets from downstairs, and settled into a light sleep, fitful with dreams of the dead. Throughout the night, she listened to the rain, which gradually increased from a drizzle to a steady drumming, broken only occasionally by the faint grumble of thunder.

A brisk triple rap at the door roused her from her slumber. She sat up, blinking. A tinge of light told her that morning had finally come. The door rattled with another three raps, and Kehrsyn stood up a little too quickly, lurching to the side as the blood struggled to keep her brain functioning. She staggered over to the door and opened it, to see a stranger wrapped in an oiled overcoat, shifting from one foot to the other, his breath condensing in the air.

Great, thought Kehrsyn. Another cold, wet day. I don't want to face this. Not yet.

"Olaré," said the stranger with forced cheerfulness. "Hope I didn't wake you."

"Wh—what do you want?" asked Kehrsyn.

"Delivery from the wizard Eileph, miss," he replied. "With his compliments."

He fumbled with his coat, eventually producing a small bundle carefully wrapped in waxed paper and bound with twine.

"Oh," said Kehrsyn as she took the bundle. "Thanks. Thanks a lot."

She moved to close the door.

"Miserable weather, eh miss?" he asked, just a bit too loudly, bouncing on his heels and blowing on his hands.

"Hmm? Yeah . . . miserable."

"That's right, a right miserable day," he echoed, forcing a smile.

Understanding wedged its unwelcome way into Kehrsyn's mind. She said something unintelligible (and, truth be told, probably incoherent) as she fished around in her coin pouch. She pulled forth a copper and was about to give it to the messenger, when she reconsidered and gave him a silver instead.

"Thank *you*, miss," he said with honest cheer, touched one finger to his eyebrow, and made his hunch-shouldered way down the ladder again.

Kehrsyn stared at the rain falling in the streets, her view intermittently obscured by the steam of her breath. At least, she thought, the rain has washed away the last of the grimy snow.

She closed the door, blinked, and stretched out the tightness in her back. Noticing that the inside of the building was no warmer than the outside, Kehrsyn wrapped herself up in her cloak and investigated the kitchen. She found a few cold, half-eaten sausages and some stale bread to break her fast, while thinking morosely about the wonderful meal she'd had at Wing's Reach. There was nothing to drink except various alcohol, the very thought of which turned her stomach. Instead, she found a large, clean bowl and placed it on the front stoop to catch some rainwater.

While she waited for it to fill, she unwrapped the bundle to look at the reconstructed wand. It was a beautiful piece and a remarkable forgery. It felt good and solid. The only mark was a crack running around its middle, slightly rough around the edges. It reminded Kehrsyn of a cracked paving stone. She rewrapped the false staff and placed it in her bag, secreting her bag behind some other gear in the front room.

She opened the door, picked up the bowl, and drank her fill of the chill, clean water, then looked at the dark stains of dried blood on the floor. The midnight body snatchers had taken all but three of the residents. Two were the most grotesquely hacked outlaw corpses. The third was the old dog. The others, including all of the Tiamatans who had died during the fight, were gone. The intruders had left behind weapons, gear, and all the rest—everything but what the people had been wearing.

She thought better of leaving the false staff there. She pulled it out and thrust it through her sash at the small of her back, giving her sash an extra twist and using the tension to lock the staff in place. She left her bag. It would be a hindrance where she intended to go, and it wouldn't get wet inside the house.

Her stomach growling as it wrestled with the mean breakfast, Kehrsyn decided to exercise some practicality. While she could no longer get vengeance on the Furifaxians for using her, branding her, and stealing a magic item from the cultured and rather dashing Massedar, at least she could extract some payment for services rendered.

She performed a cursory search for coins and valuables through the building, checking the shelves and occasional footlocker in the bedrooms on the bottom floor. She tried to ignore the personal effects she encountered as they reminded her of the lives that had ended and gave her the uncomfortable feeling that she might, technically, be robbing the grave.

In the end, she found a small collection of silvers and coppers, and one gold piece. She left the building, huddled beneath her cloak against the rain. The small trove weighed heavily in one white-knuckled fist. She could almost feel the blood dripping from her fingers.

She ended up giving it all away to destitute refugees before she'd walked twenty blocks.

❂

Tiglath sat in her study, her quill pen held unheeded in her fingers, the ink long since dry. She'd put the last words down around dawn and hadn't moved much since. She stared blankly out her window at the unending rain. The downpour seemed a gray and misty veil drawn between her cult and the rest of the world, a barrier of mistrust, misunderstanding, and misinformation. The walls of her study were also barriers, which seemed as the walls of a prison cell, dividing her from the rest of her flock.

She had never felt so isolated, so alone. Even when she'd been suffering in the harem of the vain and cruel god-king Gilgeam, the others of the harem had borne the horrors alongside her, and that shared torment had forged them into a self-supporting sorority of suffering.

She had broken those bonds, escaped, and found not only her freedom but a position of power serving a deity of strength and purpose. She had sworn vengeance upon

Gilgeam for the pain he had caused her (and others), and Tiamat had given her the ability to see that vengeance through.

In the fifteen years since Gilgeam's death, the gap between what she had set out to do and what she was doing had grown, until it seemed that her people were on one side of the gap and she was on the other.

She felt as if she were captaining a ship and someone belowdecks had cut the connection between the ship's wheel and its rudder. Were these thoughts simply a reflection of her own self-doubt, or were her survival instincts giving her fair warning? And if she was right, how much longer before the crew mutinied?

She'd spent the night attempting to make some sense of it, to find an underlying order that proved that shadows moved behind her. She'd made a list of all the abnormalities, all the strange little events and unusual reactions that had piqued her curiosity throughout the past few years. The result was maddeningly incomplete. Anomalies, yes— even some events that could be construed as evidence of insubordination—but not enough.

In fairness and hope, she'd also made a list of things that had gone better than expected. Neither did that list provide her with an answer. All it left her with, in fact, was a study table even more cluttered with papers of incomplete stories.

The thief—Kehrsyn, she reminded herself, looking at the heading on one of her papers—had said that members of the cult of Tiamat had attacked Furifax's rebels in their base. Was she right? Had the Tiamatans deliberately slaughtered the rebels or merely defended themselves when the rebels attacked them? The rebels were groomed in underhanded methods of war, and could have invited her followers to a council and deliberately left her out of it. Perhaps the Furifaxians even suggested to the others the possibility of overthrowing Tiglath. They could then have ambushed the Tiamatans and killed many of her followers without having to confront her, the high priestess.

Being double-crossed in a treasonous meeting with the Furifaxians—that would explain why her followers had withheld all mention of the incident. But for a chance observation by her dragonet familiar, Tiglath herself might not know of it at all.

Yet even that theory had several problems. It assumed the Tiamatans were ready to plot an overthrow, and it did not explain why Furifax's people were slaughtered utterly.

No, it was clear that the little thief was right. Her story had the unwelcome ring of truth. Certainly Kehrsyn's narration of events did not paint herself in a good light. She admitted that she had hidden in fear and thus escaped all notice.

Tiglath frowned. So her people had attacked their allies—her allies, truth be told, for the others looked upon them merely as convenient tools—without her knowledge, let alone consent. They did so to seize an item that had just been stolen. Therefore they knew beforehand that the item existed, they knew the item had been stolen, and they knew who had stolen it. Therefore her congregation had already had plans that centered on that item. Plans about which she, the high priestess, knew nothing.

She had to find out, so she would find out straightaway. She would take a roll call, see who was missing, and see who covered for their absence. Once they'd exposed themselves, she would find out what they had intended to take and how they'd known it had been stolen.

She arose and left her study, descending into the main area of the temple. Her followers—no, she corrected herself, Tiamat's worshipers, and there was a difference—rose to their feet as she entered. She noticed that two of them tried to conceal pain and stiffness as they got up. Those two had obviously suffered injuries during the fight. Tiamat only rarely granted her pious servants the ability to heal. In her cruel eyes the strong could bear pain and injury while the weak deserved no mercy. Indeed, Tiamat was far more concerned with her people furthering her goals than with shepherding her flock.

Tiglath paused in inner surprise. The Dragon Queen was much akin to Gilgeam in that manner, using followers like tools. Why had it taken her so long to realize how very alike the two deities were? She was a priestess, privy to every secret! Why had she always persisted in believing that there was a difference between Gilgeam's abuse of power and Tiamat's lust for power?

It all came to Tiglath in that moment, as she looked at the veiled hostility with which some of her people stared back at her. Her need for justice—no, to be honest: revenge—had blinded her to the deal she'd made. Tiamat demanded power. The Dragon Queen wished not only to slay the gods—a goal that had fit nicely with Tiglath's own dreams of retribution upon Gilgeam—but also to rule. And indeed, Tiglath first broke with her goddess years before, when she refused to seize control of Unther. Her dreams of a council-led meritocracy would not satiate the Dragon Queen, and all those there knew it. She had declined the reins of control in Unther, and Tiamat's followers were moving to take those reins themselves.

She looked around the room again, measuring the determination on the faces of those present. She saw arrogance, cockiness, sullen anger, scorn, deference . . . but no loyalty and no defeat. She thought that strange. They had suffered a defeat, launched a raid and seen the item they sought broken before their very eyes. Comrades had fallen. Yet they were not chastised in the least. If she were to push them at once with a personal inquisition, she would force their hand early, and they would rise up against her.

It was not the time.

Instead, she had to decide what to do: uncover the conspiracy and eliminate its leaders, or step in front of the new action and pretend she had been leading in that direction all along?

She had to think. She nodded to her people, if indeed she could still call them her people, and stepped to the cloakroom to grab her cloak. It was raining, but that made it easier to take a long walk by herself and pray to Tiamat for guidance . . . if she dared.

She stepped outside and was adjusting her rain cloak when someone, walking fast yet blinded by a hood pulled too low, stumbled into her, dousing her under one of the miniature waterfalls that streamed from the gargoyles on the building's roof.

It was an inauspicious start to an inauspicious walk, she thought, as she set out, chilled without and within.

☉

What luck, thought Kehrsyn, fingering the keys in her hand. She'd seen the priestess leave her room and hoped it would mean she'd leave the building. Just as she started wondering if Tiglath would make an appearance on the street, the priestess stepped outside and stood on the stoop, her arms raised as she pulled her heavy cloak over her rather large body. One brisk move, one mock stumble over the stone steps, and one mumbled apology later, Kehrsyn had the priestess's keys.

And, since she had the keys, she could discover whether or not Tiglath was truly innocent of the theft of the staff.

As Kehrsyn had suspected, the priestess lodged at a corner of the top floor along the main thoroughfare, where she had a view of something other than the choked alleys that bordered the other three sides of the building. Kehrsyn had watched the priestess staring out the window of her room for a time. She was seated, Kehrsyn assumed, at a desk by the window.

That solved the problem of locating Tiglath's room. The

only problem left was getting in. Climbing into an upper room in the rain posed difficulties in terms of traction, but it did mean there would be fewer people on the streets, and those who were around were unlikely to look up. Otherwise she'd never even make such a daring attempt.

Well, Kehrsyn thought as she glanced around the largely empty street, no time like the present.

She retied her rapier to hang over one shoulder, then gathered the hem of her cloak, wadding the lower half into a sort of thick rope. That she tied around her waist so the cloak wouldn't hang from her shoulders or snag on anything as she climbed. She scaled the building's face on the alley side of the corner, which was concealed from most points on the main street.

Her climb was annoying by any measure. The hood of her cloak blocked her view up, yet if she pulled the hood back, the rain in her eyes had the same effect and cold water dripped down her neck, too. The tied-off cloak was a heavy belt around her middle and hampered her ability to lift her thighs. Halfway up, she realized that her grip through her thin gloves was not adequate in the rain, and she had to pull them off with her teeth, one finger at a time, while hanging. The wet leather tried its best to adhere to her chilled skin, and the procedure took longer than she'd hoped. She ended up holding the gloves in her teeth for the rest of the climb, and the taste of worn leather in her mouth did nothing to improve her mood. With her mouth all but closed, she was forced to breathe through her nose, which started running in the cold air.

In all, by the time she'd reached the top floor and worked open the window to the priestess's room, she was certain that Tiglath was the blackguard behind all her troubles. She no longer felt like she was betraying an acquaintance with the intrusion. She felt she was digging up the evil truth behind a villain. Kehrsyn dropped onto the luxurious rug spread by the window. She glared from beneath a sodden brow bedecked with strands of hair.

Kehrsyn scanned the room. It was a simple affair, almost ascetic in style, yet lavish in appointments. There was a bed, a desk, a chair, a wardrobe, and a small brazier. Each was small and cut with simple lines, but well polished and inlaid with delicate patterns of contrasting woods and metals. The bed looked barely large enough to contain one of Tiglath's girth, and it had no headboard or footboard, but the thick mattress was a far cry from the bags of compressed cotton that Kehrsyn had occasionally used when times had been better, and the sheets looked to be of very fine fabric. There was no pillow.

There was a small rug by the window and a large one beneath the bed. Each was only one solid color—one red and the other black—but plush. There was no art on the walls, and the desk had a single quill of red held in a gold inkwell. In short, it seemed that the priestess allowed herself few amenities, but with those few she indulged herself to the hilt. Somehow the mixture of ascetic and feminine gave Kehrsyn a privileged view into Tiglath's personal life and quenched the displaced anger that she had built up.

Kehrsyn took off her rapier, undid her cloak, and placed them on the chair. The added weight made the chair creak.

The bed rustled, and Kehrsyn froze in place. The cover on the mattress shifted, then the dragonet's head popped out and stared at Kehrsyn. She saw nictitating membranes glide over the emerald eyes, then retract again. Kehrsyn held one hand out defensively.

"I have sufferance," she said to the tiny beast. "Tiglath said so. Don't forget that."

The dragonet growled and emerged fully from beneath the covers. Its whiplike tail lashed back and forth.

Fearing she might have to flee, Kehrsyn held up both hands, showing them to be empty.

"I know what you're thinking," she said, "but I'm not here to steal. I'm here . . . well, I guess I'm here because I hope

I'm wrong. But I have to know. You can watch if you want, to make sure I leave everything where I found it, but I'm not going to harm Tiglath, so you'd better not harm me."

The dragonet growled again, then lay down at the edge of the bed, resting its head on its forepaws. Its tail still lashed, but it made no further move to interfere.

Kehrsyn checked the wardrobe first, her soft steps all but noiseless on the wooden floor. Using the keys she'd picked from Tiglath's pocket, she opened the wardrobe with no problem. It held only a few robes, each of identical cut, and one nightgown, which, in Kehrsyn's opinion, was mercifully modest. She sounded the wardrobe for false panels and found one in the base, though the compartment contained only a diary, which Kehrsyn declined to open. After all, she was investigating; she wasn't there to pry. If she found nothing else, she could look it over later.

She replaced everything exactly as she had found it—an old habit from her thieving days, and one that had always served her well—and turned to the bed.

Her search of the bed turned up nothing. The desk, like the wardrobe, contained a few items—a strongbox with some coins and gems, a collection of what appeared to be personal memorabilia—but nothing resembling a long wand of white bone. She skimmed the papers on top of the desk, since they were clearly new. Kehrsyn was not well lettered, and it was difficult to read the priestess's crabbed handwriting, but the bold titles were unmistakable. One, labeled "Temple," looked to have a roster written on it, with question marks, Ys, or Ns next to each name. Another sheet was labeled "Furifax," and yet others had names that Kehrsyn did not recognize. The sheet that earned the most attention was one labeled "Kairsin." She half-smiled at the misspelling, and she glanced over the unfamiliar writing, but her eyes kept returning to the single word circled at the bottom of the page: "TRUTH."

Satisfied, she then sounded the walls of the room

carefully, tapping only with the pads of her fingertips to avoid attracting any outside attention. She repeated the same process across the floorboards, moving back and forth until her wrists, knees, and ankles ached. The entire time, the dragonet stared at her with its unblinking reptilian eyes, rotating its slender, sinewy neck to stare straight at its young guest wherever she searched.

With a sigh that was half exhaustion, half relief, Kehrsyn abandoned the search.

"There, you see?" she said to the dragonet. "I'm done. And not a thing out of place."

She dragged herself up into the chair, her joints protesting the sudden change. She stretched her arms up over her head and leaned back, popping her spine to loosen it up. Just as she folded her hands into her lap again, someone knocked at the door.

Kehrsyn froze. Her eyes darted over to the dragonet, who still stared at her, unconcerned.

"Kehrsyn?" Tiglath's unmistakable voice sounded muffled through the door. "Open up."

Bewildered, Kehrsyn moved to the door, and, planting one foot firmly to prevent the door from opening too far, unlocked the deadbolt and cracked it open. She peered through the gap and saw the high priestess looming in the hallway.

"Ordinarily, one does not have to request admission to one's own room," observed Tiglath.

Kehrsyn backed away from the door, letting it swing open as she retired to a spot near the window.

"I had rather expected you'd be more, you know, surprised to see me here," Kehrsyn said.

"I was," said Tiglath. "I got over it."

"What do you mean?" asked Kehrsyn, confused.

Tiglath held out her arm, and the dragonet leaped from the bed, buzzing its wings, and alighted nimbly.

Tiglath kissed its muzzle and stroked its scaly little

body, then, as an aside while she petted her creature, said, "Tremor's eyes are my eyes. I see whatever he sees. So while I was surprised to see you enter, I got over it while watching you. Why did you feel compelled to search my room?"

"I had to make sure you weren't behind the attack and the staff and all," said Kehrsyn.

"You don't trust me?" asked Tiglath.

"You yourself said no one is what they seem," parried Kehrsyn. "So because I trust you, by your words I shouldn't. So why did you let me search your room?"

"I wanted to make sure you weren't going to steal anything," said Tiglath as she doted on her pet.

"You don't trust me?" echoed Kehrsyn with a teasing smile.

Tiglath glanced over at her, then turned her attention back to Tremor and said, "I wanted to make sure you weren't going to steal anything."

Kehrsyn's face paled, and her smile vanished in the space between her heartbeats.

"Uh, right," she said as she fished through her sash. "I—I was going to give them back . . . "

Kehrsyn held Tiglath's keys out to her. Tiglath nodded, seemingly to her pet.

"I know," the priestess said.

"You do?"

"You took nothing," replied Tiglath, crossing over to sit at her desk. "You even left me my secrets." She drew a deep breath, then let it out slowly. "If you'd opened that diary, however," she added, "things would be very different right now."

"Right," said Kehrsyn, who didn't know what else to say, yet felt an acknowledgment was necessary.

"So did you find out what you came to discover?" asked Tiglath.

Kehrsyn sucked in her lips and nodded.

"You don't have the staff," she said.

"Of course not," said the priestess. "It's broken."

Kehrsyn hesitated, wondering how much to divulge. She gritted her teeth, hoping she wasn't about to make a big mistake.

"No," Kehrsyn said, "it's not. What we saw was a decoy. The real one—"

"That was a forgery?" gasped Tiglath.

"Uh, yeah," she said, pulling Eileph's forgery from her sash and showing it to the priestess.

"Now, that is truly remarkable," said Tiglath in wonder, reaching for it.

Kehrsyn didn't let her touch the staff, but showed her the crack running around the center.

"See?" she said. "I had it repaired."

"That's a fine job," said Tiglath, squinting at the workmanship.

"So that means that the real staff was really stolen," said Kehrsyn. "I had to make sure it wasn't you."

"I already knew that," said Tiglath, once she had recovered her aplomb. "What convinced you?"

"I saw the way your people acted around you and the way they acted when you weren't around. And I saw the way you are, and how you reacted to the, uh, stuff at . . . on Wheelwright's Street. And here," she added, gesturing vaguely around, "there's the fact that you lock your door and keep your little dragon in your room while you're out, and everything in your room is meticulously arranged, down to the angle of the strongbox so that it lines up against the crack in the bottom of your drawer. All these things show that you don't trust anyone but yourself. And that means that if you arranged for your people to steal the staff, you'd have led them yourself, or else you'd take control of the staff as soon as they got it. And it's not in this room, and, frankly, I don't think you'd keep it anywhere else."

Tiglath considered that and slowly nodded.

"Yes," the priestess said, "I think you're right."

"Plus, you know, your reaction right now, well, that looked pretty genuine," added Kehrsyn, by way of a joke.

Tiglath did not respond. She rose from her chair and crossed to the door, stroking Tremor's tiny serpentine head. She opened the door a crack, and Tremor leaped out, bouncing along like a ferret before launching himself into the air with a buzz. Tiglath nodded once to Kehrsyn as she crossed back over to the chair.

"Give us a moment, will you?" he priestess asked. "I need to know if this staff is under my roof."

She sat in her chair and stared at the desktop for many long minutes, moving nothing but her lips, which framed voiceless words that Kehrsyn did not recognize.

Kehrsyn eventually took a seat on the rug by the window and passed the time by twiddling with a lock of her damp hair.

Finally Tiglath leaned back in her chair and looked in the general direction of the ceiling.

"It is not here," she said with finality. "Tremor found nothing, and I trust his senses. I have him hiding in the main hall, where he will sniff at anyone who enters or leaves. He will not find anything, though. I train my people well."

She grumbled deep within her throat and crossed her arms in frustration.

"That means that whoever here arranged the attack and took the wand has another place to keep it," the priestess continued. "Either they have a hideout, which I doubt, given the lack of living space these days, or else they're working with another group or faction seeking power. That is likely the case. The lure of ruling Unther could create some dubious alliances. The question remains whether this is the work of an ambitious soul seeking to advance within Tiamat's order or a turncoat serving a new master."

"Do you think it might be the Zhentarim?" asked Kehrsyn. "I've been hearing them mentioned a lot lately."

"Those bastards?" spat Tiglath. "The only thing I'd hate to see more than them getting into power is the return of Gilgeam himself! Oh, if one of my people is working with them, they will rue the day they were born."

Tiglath set her chin in her hands, a scowl darkening her features.

Kehrsyn sat for a while longer, then broke the silence. "I should be going," she said as she stood, her voice barely above a whisper. She gestured vaguely with one hand. "I'll just let myself out the, uh, way I came in."

"That," said Tiglath, "would probably be best."

CHAPTER SIXTEEN

Demok stood beneath a faded silk awning and waited for Kehrsyn to reappear. The awning sagged beneath its burden of rainwater, and periodically the level of the water rose to a point where a sudden cataract dumped over one side. The regular purge was as good a marker of time as any.

From his vantage point across the boulevard from the building Kehrsyn had entered, Demok could not make out the seal that hung over the main entrance; the rain was too heavy. Even though the thin pedestrian traffic offered cover, he chose not to move closer and check. Kehrsyn had no idea she'd been shadowed, and he didn't want to give either her or the occupants any chance to discover they were being watched.

Not that Kehrsyn had taken particularly good precautions. To a seasoned stalker like him, her subtlety rang with furtive intent. Still, he rationalized, she was cautious, and that was probably more than enough in weather like that against what he presumed was an unsuspecting target.

He'd watched her study the building, moving in a circumspect circuit around it. She'd seen her study the figure that sat near one window. He'd watched her bump a massively built matron of a resident, presumably to cut her purse or some such. Though the acting was contrived, she had fast hands. He had to give her that—very fast hands, and a light touch. The matron had left, none the wiser.

The front door of the building opened again, and a group of people stepped out. They walked in roughly his direction, hunkered down against the rain. He glided out of his cover along an intercept course, hoping to glimpse a clue to their affiliation as he passed. And, as he asked them for unneeded directions, he did: they were dressed in scarlet and black, and he caught a glimpse of the dragon-heads sigil that marked the bearer as a follower of Tiamat, the Dragon Queen.

Demok touched the brim of his rain-soaked hood in thanks for their assistance and watched them shuffle off into the cold winter rain.

Tiamatans, he thought. How interesting. My masters will be most interested to hear of her escapades here.

Demok crossed back to his watch post and waited for Kehrsyn to reappear.

I only hope she is of the proper temperament to be recruited, he reflected. If not . . . such a weapon cannot be allowed to fall into other hands.

He saw a shadow exit the building from the upstairs window. It was Kehrsyn. His heart skipped a beat as he caught a glimpse of her. The excitement of the hunter when he sees his prey, he told himself.

He watched the lithe, expert fashion in which she climbed back down the building, and one corner of his mouth pulled up appreciatively. She moved away, unrolling her cloak against the rain. She never noticed him slide from the shadows and begin stalking her again.

"Well, fancy meeting you here," said Kehrsyn, her smile a bright oasis in the grim, gray rain that drenched the stalls of the bazaar.

Demok pressed his lips together in an expression that Kehrsyn suspected was as jovial as his scarred face ever got.

"Massedar sent me to look for you," he said.

"Why, Demok," said Kehrsyn with mock astonishment, "I do believe that's the longest sentence I've yet heard you say."

To her surprise, he actually laughed, a single coughing snort that showed teeth.

"I'll work on that," he said.

He stepped aside and gestured chivalrously. Kehrsyn nodded and winked at him, and the two of them walked side by side through the soggy streets of Messemprar, the dense city mud unable to stick to their boots in the face of such a rain.

After several moments of silence, Kehrsyn finally said, "Is there some kind of problem? I mean, I'm surprised that someone as important as Massedar would trouble himself for someone like me."

"Explain."

"I mean, I'm just a juggler who—"

Demok raised his hand so sharply that Kehrsyn thought he was going to strike her.

"No," he said, "you're not."

"Yes, I am," she said. "Call it what you like, but—"

"A juggler you are. You are not a 'just a' juggler," said Demok, glaring at her.

Nervous, Kehrsyn returned his gaze and said, "If you

didn't look so angry, I'd say that was maybe a compliment."

"You have exceptional skills," Demok said, dropping his eyes.

"Well, I don't know if—"

"Good with people, too."

There was a long pause.

"Thanks," said Kehrsyn.

She glanced at Demok, and perhaps he nodded, but that was all the acknowledgment he gave.

They walked a ways farther.

"Does he think that?" she asked, a guilty lilt in her voice.

"Who?" asked Demok.

"Massedar," said Kehrsyn with a smile. "Does he think I have 'exceptional skills'? Is that why he sent you out to find me?"

"In part," said Demok.

"Why else?" asked Kehrsyn.

She glanced at her companion, but she couldn't see his eyes for the hood he wore. All she received for an answer was a resolute set to his jaw.

"Is he . . . ?" she pressed. "Does he think I'm . . . ? That is, I know it's business, but . . . " She couldn't bring herself to say it, so instead she gave up, exasperated. "Oh, you wouldn't know," she sighed. "Just forget about it."

Demok stopped in his tracks and turned to face her.

"I will," he said, "if you will."

"What do you mean?" asked Kehrsyn, but Demok had already turned and was heading on, his long gait even faster than before, and Kehrsyn had to trot to keep pace. "Tell me! What do you mean?"

"Forget about it," said Demok. "Good advice."

Kehrsyn grumbled at his curt behavior but said nothing further for several blocks, though she refused to keep trotting and started to trail behind her escort. Gradually Demok's pace slowed to allow her to catch up.

They walked a while farther in peace, listening to the

rain on their hoods, before Kehrsyn broke the silence again. "I hope I didn't offend him," she said, a little too loudly to be talking to herself.

Demok did not appear to hear her statement.

"Do you think I upset him?"

He glanced at her and said, "You stole his staff."

"No, I mean about saying I expected him to . . . you know, well, have his . . . his way . . ."

Demok slowed just a bit.

"Why did you give that answer?" he asked, his eyes boring into Kehrsyn's.

"Well, because I'm poor, and he's powerful, and my mother was poor, and it happened to her when she attracted the attention of a powerful man. And I've got her good looks, or so people say, so I've always just figured it was a matter of time before it happened to me."

Demok nodded and resumed at his brisk pace.

"You didn't answer my question," Kehrsyn said, but to no avail.

"Well," she puffed under her breath, "if he wants to avoid talking, he should quit asking questions."

❧

"I understand thee not," said Ahegi. "Why dost thou not search the maid straightaway?"

"Dear advisor," replied Massedar, "thou hast the subtlety of a flatulent camel. Heed thou my words, and all shall be reckoned well with the maiden."

"I shall obey thee," said Ahegi, though he bridled speaking the words, especially after such a comparison. "Just rest stalwart that this wench stealeth not thy heart as well as thy treasures."

Massedar narrowed his eyes just a shade and said, "Thinkest thou that I remain not in control of all within this house?"

In response, Ahegi studied his lord. Ahegi knew all about lusts. He had, in fact, spent his whole life indulging his own, and, while he might never admit his own ruled him, he could tell when lust ruled others. He knew Massedar was a man of lust, though he had never quite figured out what its object was.

"Think I that thou dost protest overmuch," answered Ahegi at last, measuring the words evenly.

He bowed and left the audience hall, shutting the door quietly behind him.

◉

A pair of guards met Demok and his quarry at the door. The guards gruffly ordered them to follow, not even allowing them to doff their cloaks. The fluster of movement enhanced the sharp division between the cold weather outside and the warm surroundings inside. Though Demok was used to such abrupt and disruptive arrangements—they being a staple of Massedar's forcible negotiating style—Kehrsyn seemed put out by the aura of urgency. That, of course, was the intent.

The guards ushered them along briskly and blew into the meeting room without preamble. One of the guards shoved Kehrsyn forward so that she stood alone in the center of the room, almost exactly where she had been manacled in the first interview.

As expected, Massedar stood with his back turned. He'd lowered his head almost to his breast, his arms crossed.

Demok counted silently in his head. One . . . two . . . three . . . four.

Massedar whirled, his long robes swirling around him menacingly.

"Where hast thou been?" he shouted, carefully enunciating every syllable of the High Untheric for maximum effect.

Demok nodded appreciatively. It was a good pause, too long to be short, short enough to be surprising.

Kehrsyn stood startled, perhaps even scared. Massedar widened his eyes beneath his placid brows, giving him a murderous aspect. He strode over to Kehrsyn, his lips pressed into a slight frown, his nostrils flaring like those of a frenzied horse.

Kehrsyn's mouth worked, but no sound came out. Massedar didn't break stride but moved right up against her, looking down upon her fair face as he gripped her head in his hands.

"Speak thou an answer unto me," he said, an authoritative tone to his quiet voice, his nose brushing hers, his lips scant inches from her mouth.

Demok could see Kehrsyn trembling ever so slightly.

"I've been trying to find it for you," Kehrsyn wailed, barely keeping her composure from collapsing entirely.

Demok raised one eyebrow. She was trying to find it . . . for *him*. He was right. The young woman was falling for Massedar. Despite demonstrations to the contrary, he doubted the reverse was true. Demok had hardly ever seen the man display an unconditionally honest emotion.

Massedar closed his eyes and drew a deep breath, putting a very slight shudder into it. He released her head gently and stepped backward, letting his fingers delicately trace the curve of her jaw as he disengaged.

He exhaled slowly and opened his eyes, filling them with a pleading look as he locked with Kehrsyn's tear-bedewed gaze.

"Thou must forgive me," he said, softly, sadly, gently, with an almost imperceptible shake of the head. "I have been greatly afflicted by thy absence, and my thoughts have been of thy charge."

"I'll get the staff for you," said Kehrsyn, drying one eye on the cuff of her blouse.

"Of course thou shalt," said Massedar, "but as well must

thou return in safety. Say thou the word and it shall be given to you, even unto the best of my guards to ensure your well-being."

Kehrsyn looked even more confused than she had when he was yelling at her. Before she could say anything, however, Ahegi stepped back into the room.

"My lord," he said, "a moment of thy time."

Massedar glanced at Ahegi, looked back at Kehrsyn, and clenched one fist as if trying to grasp an opportunity slipping away.

"But a moment, lovely one," Massedar said to Kehrsyn with a regretful nod, "and but a moment only, for I must attend to this."

He turned and strode briskly out of the room, all tenderness cast aside for a powerful, martial motion, leaving through the double doors through which Demok and Kehrsyn had entered.

Ahegi cast an eye after Massedar as he left, then shut the doors. He thrust his chin at Kehrsyn.

"Search ye her," he growled.

❧

"What?" asked Kehrsyn, all the more nervous, for Ahegi looked even more familiar with that menacing look upon his face. "Why?"

Ahegi said nothing.

Kehrsyn's thoughts flashed to the counterfeit staff, thrust through her sash at the small of her back. Startled by Massedar's aggressive demeanor, she'd already admitted that she was still looking for the real thing. If the forgery were to be found, she'd have a lot more explaining to do. Under such duress, she had no desire to reveal that she had it to that vile man. She would reveal the decoy on her terms and benefit from it. She wished Massedar hadn't left. Clearly he was far too powerful a man for his advisor to dare such a humiliating search in his presence.

"Fine," said Kehrsyn with a shrug, mustering all the nonchalance she could. "I have nothing to hide. But I'm going to tell him you had me searched."

"No," said Ahegi, raising one eyebrow, "thou shalt not."

Something in the threatening way he said that hit Kehrsyn hard in the heart and ensured that she would remain silent.

The two guards who had escorted her upstairs moved in to inspect her. Kehrsyn undid the clasp of her cloak, let it down over her shoulders, and swung it behind her. As she did so, she pushed the staff out from her sash with one hand and took it into the other, all concealed by the cloak's material. She brought the cloak forward but stepped on the hem, nearly pulling it from her hand and giving her a chance to slide the staff into her right boot. She handed the cloak to a guard, who shook it, checked the inside for pockets, and dropped it to the floor.

Kehrsyn held out her arms as they patted her down, wincing as one guard ran his hand across the burn on the back of her left arm. One guard patted the place between her shoulder blades as well, but thankfully she'd not opted for that hiding place.

Before Ahegi could suggest it, she pulled off her boots. First she pulled off the left one, held it up, shook it, and tossed it to one guard. As she pulled off the right boot, she took the opportunity to glower at Ahegi. It attracted his attention to her eyes and away from her hands. She used her left middle finger to pull open the cuff at her right hand, and her right thumb to keep the staff in place. She raised that boot up, inverting it as she had the last, and the staff slid into her sleeve. She tossed the boot to a guard. Then, with the staff wedged between the heel of her hand and the crook of her elbow, she stood, hands on hips, while the guards patted down her leggings.

Once they finished, she picked up her cloak with her left

hand, shook it, brushed it, and folded it up, sliding the staff out of her sleeve and into the folds before someone noticed the odd shape of her shirt.

She walked over to one wall, tossed the cloak unceremoniously on the floor under a chair, sat down upon it, and said, "Can I have my boots back now, or are you going to stand there and smell them?"

The guards shrugged and handed Kehrsyn her boots. No sooner had she put them back on than Massedar returned. She smiled in relief, stood, and subconsciously moved closer to him, feeling safe once more, perhaps even protected. She looked around the room, and the guards avoided eye contact—everyone except Demok, who studied her, one thumb running back and forth across his lower lip.

"Forgive thou me for that interruption, Mistress Kehrsyn," said Massedar, "as well as for my unseemly outburst earlier. Let us begin afresh, shall we?"

"Sure," she said with a timid smile and a hostile glance at Ahegi.

Massedar clasped his hands together in front of his sternum in a position that was somewhere between martial and supplicating.

"I have been ill pleased that thou hast no further tidings to impart unto me," he said. "Thy absence maketh me to fret for thy sake and as well vexeth me for the fate of the staff which thou hast yielded into the hands of others."

"Well, I think I have an idea where your magic wand might be, but I'm not yet sure who's really behind it all."

"Let my guards be sent to investigate directly."

"I'd rather you didn't," said Kehrsyn. "This situation needs a delicate touch, and I think maybe I can get it back for you without anyone finding out I did it."

"If anyone might succeed, thou, who hast purloined it, shall surely meet with favor," said Massedar with a wry smile. "Tell me, then, who holdeth my goods."

"Well, it's not Furifax and his people, for sure," Kehrsyn said. "The church of Tiamat had a hand in it, but I don't think they have it, either. I think it's someone else, some group working with them."

Massedar looked around the room and asked, "Hath anyone amongst us a suggestion?"

"The Red Wizards stand guilty of all manner of ill-doing," said Ahegi. "Their hunger for magic is boundless. It surely lieth upon their heads."

"No, I know it's not the Red—" began Kehrsyn.

"Submit thou not to their treachery," said Ahegi. "Such a path, though seemly, dealeth hardly with the inexperienced."

Kehrsyn hesitated, wondering if she should reveal her dealings with Eileph.

In that pause, Demok spoke up with a single word: "Zhentarim."

Ahegi scoffed, "Yea, that brotherhood doth weigh with imbalanced scales, but of what use is such a prize to merchants of food?"

"Ties with Bane," said Demok. "The caravans serve the church. God of Death. He'd love the staff."

"Art thou familiar with which Banites do dwell within the city?" pressed Ahegi.

Demok's hands moved to the hilts of his blades.

"Hold!" bellowed Massedar. He turned to Demok. "Thou wouldst have me believe Bane here in Messemprar acting in concert with Tiamat? Such webs are spun only by spiders.

"And Ahegi, thou namest Demok a Banite?" he added lightly, turning to his advisor. "Thou seest the hands of thine enemies raised against thee all about."

Kehrsyn watched the exchange with interest, gauging the voice and expressions of all three. Ahegi and Demok wanted to continue the debate, but clearly Massedar wanted the subject dropped. Did he suspect Bane might have an agent among his people? If so, publicly disregarding such thoughts would put the agent more at ease.

"I think you're both wrong," hazarded Kehrsyn. "Tiamat always opposed Gilgeam, even killed him, right? And no one would willingly let Bane here. I mean, he's a foreign deity, right?" She looked around for support but found only hard eyes upon her, excepting Massedar's gaze, which was much softer. "So I think that whether it's Tiamat or Bane, they're just helping the real enemy: the Pharaoh of Mulhorand. They deliver this to the Mulhorandi army, it helps them take Messemprar, and whoever it was that helped out, they get to rule Unther under the Mulhorandi banner. Doesn't that make sense?"

Silence hung in the room.

"Perfectly," said Massedar. "Kehrsyn," he said, "thou standest against the shadowy hand of the pharaoh. To thy duties: I have retained thee for the recovery of my own property. Thou shalt apprise me of thy progress. At the least, each eve shalt thou return here and thereafter to bed in a room which I shall have prepared for thee." He moved closer to her, reached out, and gripped her upper arms in his hands, saying, "Thy future—"

A flare of heat and pain ripped through Kehrsyn's left arm as his fingers massaged her burn. She cried out and jerked herself out of his hands, dragging the burn through his powerful fingers. Her knees gave way and she crumpled to the floor, her right hand clutching her left arm just below the shoulder, and she scooted away from Massedar.

For a moment, nothing existed but the pain in her arm as it exploded in a surf of fire, but, as her sight returned, she saw Massedar kneel down beside her. She couldn't read his expression through her teary eyes, but his words carried through the ringing in her ears.

"What is the matter? Speak thou!" His voice seemed at once concerned and demanding.

"They burned me." Kehrsyn forced the words out evenly. "The back of my arm, right where you . . ."

She saw Massedar look at his right hand, rub the fingers

together, and smell them. He looked at the back of her left sleeve, then snapped his fingers again.

"Healers!" he ordered, then he leaned closer to Kehrsyn, his voice almost a whisper. "Why didst thou not tell me?"

"It's just a little burn," she answered.

"None of the kind," he replied. "I have but small hopes it is not festered. My best shall attend thee, for I vouchsafe merciful provision on those close unto me. Arise thou," he said, "and be healed within thy room, that nothing shouldst mar thy smile."

He gently helped her to her feet and escorted her from the room. Kehrsyn cast a desperate, sidelong glance at her cloak, wrapped around the counterfeit staff and laid under the chair, but Demok stepped forward and picked it up, tucking it under an arm.

Massedar took her to a private room furnished with a comfortable bed, a nightstand with a few drawers and topped by a candle, and a mirror and washbasin. The stand beside the washbasin held a brush and several scented toiletries. These at once thrilled and mortified Kehrsyn, who had never been able to indulge in such luxuries as perfumes and fine soaps and lotions and balms, and who therefore had no idea which might be which, let alone the proper uses and applications.

Demok tossed her cloak on the floor beneath her bed and left the room without another word, leaving her alone with Massedar for a few nervous heartbeats until the healers came, a craggy old man and a half-elf woman with thin, flat hair.

The men discreetly turned their backs while the half-elf helped Kehrsyn out of her jersey. She then wrapped Kehrsyn's torso in a plush towel for modesty, and the healers inspected the burn.

Massedar sat on the edge of the bed next to Kehrsyn.

"Would that thou mightest abide here after the end of this affair of the staff," he said, an earnest softness in his eyes. After a scant breath, he blinked rapidly and turned his head. "What I mean to say," he said more formally, "is that Wing's Reach re-quireth someone of thy qualities, someone of great skill at infiltration. Thou couldst be of great service to me, a benefit for which I would reward thee greatly."

He turned to meet her gaze once more, adding, "Thou needest only to name thy price and it shall be thine, for thou art indeed a priceless treasure. And if thou wouldst help to secure our house against others of thy skill, I shall give to thee all authority within these walls, to command as you saw fit, save only me."

Kehrsyn shook her head, then tensed as the healers peeled away some dead skin from her burn.

Once the pain had passed, she asked, "Why would you give all that to me? I stole from you, and you've only known me, what, two days?"

"That question affirmeth what I have suspected of thee. Thou hast a true and honest heart, one that remaineth innocent and pure despite thy calling."

"Well, I'm not really a thief. It's not like that's something I really want to do. I mean, they made me, you know," said Kehrsyn.

"These things I know," he said. "Thou art great of heart and frame, and I sense within thy breast the beating of a heart true to Unther and her people, a heart that opposeth the march of Mulhorand and seeketh to thwart the vain-glory of its pharaoh."

Kehrsyn's eyes narrowed and she cursed, "Oath break-ers. Neither empire was ever to cross the River of Swords. They deserve to—"

Massedar held up a hand to silence her and said, "Prithee, no, I would fain not hear curses from thy lips."

The half-elf healer glanced over at Massedar, and he nodded, permitting her to interrupt.

"The flesh is badly burnt, my lord. We can use such

abilities as we have. Full healing will take either time or one of thy ointments."

"She shall suffer not any impairment, for her duties shall be far too important," he said. "Pour thou out what ointments might be needful."

The half-elf took Kehrsyn's arm and turned it so that the burn was easily accessible to her associate. Kehrsyn saw the older healer draw a fine crystal vial from his satchel, finely cut and sealed with a gemlike crystal stopper yet so small that it could hold no more than perhaps a dram in volume. Inside, she saw a pearlescent liquid of bluish hue, thick and milky. She craned her neck to watch as the elder healer unstoppered the vial and raised it to her arm.

He dribbled a few drops out of the vial, aimed so they alighted just at the top edge of her burn. As the thick, gooey drops struck the injured skin, they spread rapidly across the burn like oil on water, coating the entire burn with a faintly luminous layer. The burned flesh began to throb, but it was the healthy sensation of vivacity and youth, a muscle exerting to the fullest.

"I thought it would be an ointment of aloe," Kehrsyn gasped, "but this is magic . . . I don't deserve—"

"Thou deservest not such treatment?" interrupted Massedar. "I protest thou dost. Thou, lovely maiden, art perhaps the most valuable of my house, the sole here who canst my wand recover."

Kehrsyn looked again at the burn, as best as she could. The damage slowly faded as if it was a knitted shawl unraveling before her eyes. Her arm no longer sent her signals of discomfort and injury. The lack of feeling itself felt great, and the vibrant energy that suffused her muscle made her smile.

"I don't understand," she said. "That's so expensive. Why?"

Massedar took a deep breath, and within his eyes Kehrsyn saw a decision slip into place.

"What hast thy former lord said unto thee in regard to the item that thou hast purloined?"

"Well, no one really knows exactly what it is," said Kehrsyn, "but they say it's got . . . necromancy? And some say it's the Necromancer's Staff, made by some powerful wizard a long time ago."

Massedar sighed in relief and said, "It is good that none truly know, else all would be lost. But thou, thou must know that the import of thy task shall press thee onward to success."

He kneeled on the floor in front of her, facing her fully and setting her to wonder, ridiculously, if he was about to propose.

"The truth is far more terrible than thou hast been led to believe," he said. "This work is called the Alabaster Staff. It is an item of legend, tales so old that they are now all but forgotten. The high necromancer Hodkamset didst set to imitate it, in hopes of securing for himself its repute, and created his Staff of the Necromancer, but truly, where his staff is five times as long as this, this work is fifty and five times as powerful.

"The Alabaster Staff is some four thousand years old or more, forged on another world by the ancient gods of our people and imbued with their power. The Alabaster Staff hath within it the authority to command the dead, raising them unto a semblance of life and binding them unto the will of the bearer.

"Make thou not such a face, young mistress. Think thou of Unther! As our army engageth the Mulhorandi army and the enemy is made to fall, those slain shall rise again to serve us, therewith to smite their living brethren and to add again to our ranks. We can drive the Mulhorandi from this ground with their own army!"

Kehrsyn shivered and said, "That sounds horrid, making the dead walk like that."

Massedar nodded and replied, "Truly, it is a dark summoning, but to see their brethren turn and fight against them is a just reward for their betrayal of Unther. Breaking a sacred pact that hath stood since the dawn of our civilizations, they crossed the River of Swords, and all that shall befall them shall lie upon their heads."

"But . . ." began Kehrsyn.

"The foot of Pharaoh Horustep of Mulhorand standeth upon the neck of Unther," interrupted Massedar. "Nothing must be spared to save our empire, for if we fail, the entire nation shall be yoked into slavery."

CHAPTER SEVENTEEN

Once Massedar and the healers had left, Kehrsyn sagged against a wall and slumped to the floor with a heavy sigh. She ran her fingers through her hair and tried to figure out what had happened to the simple life she had once led. So much had changed, she could hardly remember it.

Kehrsyn didn't know what to do in her new-found home. That Massedar had decreed her presence did not change the fact that she was unused to such treatment and felt out of place. She had gone from being an intruder, to being an agent, to being thoroughly searched, to being embraced and healed, all in the space of two days.

She put her shirt back on, tossing her towel on the bed. She pulled her cloak out from under the bed and saw that Demok had placed it there in almost exactly the same position as she had placed it on the floor of the reception room. Such meticulous care struck her as odd, but she was thankful that the false staff was still safely tucked away in its shroud. She pulled it out and ran her finger around the crack in the handle, feeling the slight roughness of the finish. She couldn't help but admire Eileph's craftwork. It must have taken some fine magic to reassemble it so solidly. She tucked it away in her cloak and slid it back under the bed.

Shy and nervous, she left her room and timidly walked to the kitchen and dining area. She asked about meals and ended up with bread and cold, spicy gravy to tide her over until supper. Though the others were polite enough, they looked askance at her when they thought she wasn't looking. Her sharp ears picked up their whispers, many of which insinuated less than honorable activities between her, Massedar, Ahegi, and others. Her ears burning in shame, she retired to her room to stare out the window at the cold rain and sort out her thoughts.

The city guard swept the streets of the excess refugees, breaking her reverie. They moved sullenly about their task in the numbing downpour, rousting the refugees, who were loath to yield up whatever mean shelter they had found under overhanging eaves.

A while later, Kehrsyn heard the jangle of the bell that announced dinner. She got up and went downstairs. That time, however, her footsteps were more confident, for she had a plan. She would prove her value to Massedar that very evening.

She ate dinner by herself, alone at one end of a long table. She watched the exits of the dining room carefully, keeping an eye peeled for Massedar's baldheaded advisor. He did make an appearance, bullying his way into the room, demanding a meal to be delivered to his suite, then shoving his way back out again.

As he left, Kehrsyn rose to follow. She saw that he had turned right, toward the foyer at the main entrance, and guessed that he was heading for one of the corner stairwells. She moved to the opposite exit of the dining room and glided to the foyer herself. Listening carefully, she heard Ahegi's labored breathing as he climbed the stairs. It seemed that his lifestyle had taken its toll on him over the years.

Quiet as a ring-tailed cat, Kehrsyn sauntered across the foyer and ascended the stairwell, keeping a full revolution of the stairs between her and Ahegi. She heard him puff his way up to the third floor, then, immediately afterward, she heard the rattle of keys.

That meant his suite was right off the stairwell, but she had to know which door was his. She quickly ascended the last revolution of stairs, reaching the third floor just as he entered his rooms. His eyes caught the motion behind him, and he glared at her sudden arrival. She waved with a nervous smile and proceeded to walk down the hall.

"Your room," he growled behind her, "is one floor below."

Kehrsyn stopped short.

"Oops," she said, with what she hoped was a convincing giggle. "I guess I've just been up here more often than in the—er, my room. Sorry," she added with a cheesy grin and scooted back down the stairs.

When she heard the door close, she padded back upstairs and paced off the distance from the door Ahegi used to the adjacent doors to either side. Keeping her ears peeled for any approaching footsteps, she peered under each of the doors. She saw lantern light coming from beneath the door Ahegi had entered but not from either of the adjacent ones.

She slipped back downstairs, went to her room, and retrieved her cloak, concealing the false staff in her sash just in case they searched her room while she was out. She wasn't ready to trust anyone yet, especially after the way Ahegi had had her frisked.

She stepped outside and walked around to Ahegi's side of the building. Finding a doorway where she could remain relatively dry, she watched his windows for a long time. She saw the glimmer of light spread from the one window to the window farther down the long side of the building, then back again. She smiled. She knew which direction Ahegi's suite went, at least in part. She walked back inside, returned her cloak to her room, and concealed her staff within it as before.

Wandering affably around the interior of Wing's Reach and asking a few questions, she found the mercantile office, where, using her legerdemain, she helped herself to a few pieces of paper, a pen, and some ink. She took them upstairs, and, lying on the floor to avoid leaving tell-tale marks on the nightstand, she prepared to write a note.

What sort of note would the Zhentarim write? she asked herself. She thought about what she knew of them. Little, she admitted to herself, almost nothing. In fact, all she really knew was that they had a reputation for power that engendered fear and an aura of fear that created power. In that sense, she supposed, they were much like the priesthood of Gilgeam during his reign as god-king of Unther. Gilgeam had set vicious high priests to rule over the various cities, each according to his power, ability, and vice. She'd grown up under such a yoke and knew first-hand how the priests spoke. Such thoughts brought dark clouds of hate and depression—pained memories of her mother, empty longing for her father, and the hated desperation of her childhood—but Kehrsyn willed them away and focused on her idea.

She settled on something brief and demanding, thinking that fewer words would help her avoid sounding out of character, whatever that character might be, and help impart greater urgency. She chose but three words. She had to take several tries before she had a note that looked hastily scrawled yet was still entirely legible. It didn't help that she was not well practiced in letters.

She stood up, regarded her handiwork skeptically, and mentally committed herself to her task.

Kicking off her boots and grabbing her dagger, she glided to her door and cracked it open. No one was in the hall—her room being on the interior side of the short hallway toward the front of the building—so she slid out and shut the door behind her.

The halls were dark but for the guards' lanterns and the light spilling from the odd open door. Silent as a shadow, she ascended the stairs to the third floor. As she reached the top, she heard no footsteps, so she lay low and peered just over the top stair, trusting her dark hair to conceal her. It was early in the shift, and the guard in the hallway was having an amiable conversation with his partner across the middle hall. Glancing to the doors, she saw that the near door, the one that Ahegi had entered earlier, had light pouring out from under it while the next one down looked dark. She rose and moved carefully to the second door, and, though her steps were inaudible, she kept her posture nonchalant in case the guard caught sight of her.

She tried the latch carefully. It moved, but the door was barred shut. She hoped Ahegi's suite had the same dropbar door lock that her room did. Pulling her dagger, she slid it between the door and the jamb, thankful for such a thin blade. Her heart pounded with fear and excitement, so hard that it made her hand tremble. She winced in fear that Ahegi might have some more sinister lock on the door, one that would bring down great noise or fearsome magic. When she lifted the latch, it felt too heavy for a throw bar the size of the one in her room.

Committed to her task and afraid of her ability to restore the door to its former position blindly, she persevered. Once the bar had cleared its mooring, she swung the door open slowly, holding her dagger in place to keep the bar elevated. The hinge creaked ever so slightly, so she stopped. She had just enough room to squeeze through.

Sticking her head through, she saw that her instinct had been right. There was an additional trap: a pair of magically inscribed glass spheres dangled from a piece of twine tossed over the loose end of the throw bar. She wriggled her dagger down the bar, keeping it elevated, until she was able to slip the blade between the strands of twine. Then, in one fluid motion, she thrust the dagger forward until the hilt of her weapon caught the string and pulled the stones off the latch. The twine dropped a few inches and landed safely on the unsharpened base of her blade, just above the hand guard.

She slid into the room and inspected the latch. Unlike the throw bar in her room, that one had been modified to revolve freely around a single bolt. If she had let the bar drop once it had cleared its mooring, it would have swung down and dropped the two rune-inscribed orbs on the floor, and, in all likelihood, Ahegi alone knew what that would have done to her.

Holding the glass balls aloft with her dagger—for she feared that any contact with the floor might activate their magic—she scanned the room. Faint trickles of reflected light from the guard's lantern shone from the door behind her, and light also spilled from beneath the door leading to the other portion of Ahegi's suite. It wasn't much, but it was enough to see the furniture in the room.

She took the note she'd prepared and tossed it on his bed, then undid the latch that held the window secure. She withdrew from the room, replacing the spheres on the bar and using her dagger to lift the bar back into place as she shut the door. She could hardly breathe for fear of jinxing herself, but she was almost finished. She stepped backward to the stairwell, wide eyes glued to the hall guard as he joked coarsely with his compatriot.

Once safely behind the curve of the stairwell, she drew a deep breath of release. Her thudding heart made her diaphragm tremble, and she feared she might cry, but from fear or elation or relief, she couldn't exactly tell.

☻

Kehrsyn spent the next few hours waiting in the stairwell at the far end of the short hallway from Ahegi's suite. After returning to her room, she had availed herself of her chamber pot, and she had purposely drunk very little at dinner so that she would not have to interrupt her vigil. She was fully dressed, with her boots and dagger. Her cloak, her rapier, and the fake staff she had secreted behind the curve of the stairwell on the ground floor, where she could easily don them before departing. If everything went well, she'd need only her cloak and boots. If not, she didn't want to leave anything behind.

Her note had cited "midnight" as an unfortunately inexact rendezvous time, but to be more specific would risk exposing the note for a forgery. She didn't know what the Zhentarim might use for timekeeping. Thus, if Ahegi took the bait, Kehrsyn knew only that he'd leave his suite roughly in the middle of the midnight watch. That left a lot of flexibility, which Kehrsyn's hind end started to pay for as she waited on the narrow stairs.

Ahegi left and reentered his study once, right after Kehrsyn began to wait, but he moved indifferently and was wrapped in a warm woolen housecoat and slippers. Twice she was interrupted when someone climbed her stairwell. To conceal her intent, Kehrsyn broke her vigil to act as if she was moving in the opposite direction. Aside from that, the watch was quite tedious.

Long after Kehrsyn had expected something to happen (but, her intellect objected, still early during the midnight watch), Kehrsyn waited still. She sighed and blew a stray strand of hair from her face.

Funny, she thought, to go from such a dangerous thrill

that seemed to last forever, even if it was a very short while, to such a boring activity that, though not overly long, also seemed to go on forever.

☙

Ahegi marked the page and closed his book, sliding it to the rear of his desk. It was late, and sleep tugged at the corners of his eyes. He rubbed his eyes with his fingers, trying to drive the fatigue back for just a few more moments.

He stood, stretched, and ran his hand over his shaven pate, roughened with stubbly growth. Everything seemed to be proceeding apace despite a few setbacks. The plans were coming together. The young thief, however, had proven disruptive. He hoped her untimely arrival would not undo all they had been trying to accomplish.

He kneeled on the floor and made his obeisance at the darkest hour of the night, whispering the ritual prayers so as not to be overheard. He bowed his head to the floor three times, then arose and gathered his housecoat around him. He blew out all the candles but one, which he carried with him into the next room.

He set his candle on the nightstand, dropped his housecoat to the floor, and sat on the bed. He heard the crinkling of paper as he did so, and felt it buckling through the nightgown covering his posterior. The significance of the sensations trickled into his brain, and he stood up and felt around for the stray paper.

It was folded carefully and creased multiply, though the latter he had done himself. He opened the note and held it close by the candle.

"Midnight. Urgent. —Z."

Ahegi's eyes widened, darting back and forth. How long

had the note lain unattended on his bed? He didn't know, but he was already late.

He quickly put his housecoat back on and gathered it around him, then thrust his feet back into his slippers. Taking his candle, he left his suite, pausing a moment to place a grain of sand on the handle of his door. Should anyone try to penetrate his apartments, they would dislodge the sand and he would know.

He looked around, but the hallways were empty save for the guards at each end of the center hall. He moved toward the light and turned down the center hall, passing the guard without acknowledging his presence.

He rapped on the ornate double doors to Massedar's rooms. No response. He knocked louder. Then a third time, louder still.

He heard a voice, groggy and slurred, ask, "What?"

"Sire, thou ordainest an audience with me?"

He heard Massedar rise out of bed and stumble in the dark, followed by a few moments' fumbling as he attired himself. Feet shuffled over to the doors, and Massedar cracked one open.

"Upon what twaddle blatherest thou?" asked Massedar.

"Thou hast asked for to speak with me," said Ahegi, greatly affronted.

"Art thou mad?" sneered Massedar. "Constrain thou thy dreams to thy own sleep, and leave me be."

He shut the door and threw the bolt once more.

For a moment, Ahegi was confused, then his tired brain put everything together. He moved quickly back to his suite, habitually checking that the piece of sand was still in place. Once inside, he lit a candelabrum and went back into his bedchamber. He looked at his window. It had been left unlatched. They had slipped the note through his window, though whether by magical or cunning means, he was unsure.

He had been late already when he had discovered the

note, and he had wasted even more time since. He threw on his warmest clothes, grabbed his heavy cloak, and left his chambers at a pace so brisk he was almost running. He took the stairs two or three at a time, nearly losing his balance, then strode through the foyer and puffed out the front door and into the night.

The chill air, the sound of rain, and the cold dampness that leaked in through his boots (for, in his haste, he had donned the pair that was not waterproof) reawakened Ahegi. His mood swung from bitter reproach to the gods for the inhospitable weather, to deeply burning ire at being ordered to inconvenience himself with the uncomfortable nocturnal trek, to deep-seated fear at what penalty he might suffer for his tardiness. He hoped he had not been expected to share in the prayer time, for, if so, his absence would prove troublesome.

What chance events would convene a meeting in this manner and on such short notice? Was this a test of loyalty, or had something transpired? Was there an opening, a weakness to be seized and exploited? Or perhaps a bold move was planned, the timetable moved forward behind the concealing cloak of the accursed rain.

He tromped across the city to the docks, his breath puffing out a regular stream of clouds. Every few steps he wiped away the precipitation that tickled the end of his nose. There was very little light, most of it provided by taverns or the occasional street lamp that had not run out of fuel. The poor visibility made it difficult to spot the puddles in the dark. In his anger and apprehension, Ahegi moved as directly as possible, and thus by the time he got to the meeting place, his legs and feet were soaked through and he could not discern between the squishy noises of his stockings and the splashing of the puddles. Yet despite the chill and the rain, beneath his cloak he sweated with prolonged exertion, activity to which his soft lifestyle had not inured him.

Once at the docks, he moved to the farthest end, enduring the easterly breeze that blew the rain, walking all the way to the Long Wharf where it jutted out into the Alamber Sea. He stomped up the gangplank of the only sailing vessel moored at the Long Wharf and crossed the deck to the main cabin. He wiped the droplets from his nose again, then knocked in the appointed pattern: Knock-knock. Knock. Knock-knock-knock.

A small slit opened in the door, and the beam of the bull's-eye lantern shone directly in his eyes.

"Who goes?" asked a harsh voice.

Ahegi blinked rapidly, and, when his eyes adjusted to the glare, he saw a hard pair of eyes glowering out. The lantern illuminated the guard's face starkly from the side.

The password required that the visitor cough before answering, which Ahegi did. It was an easy requirement considering the weather.

"Ahegi, of Wing's Reach," he answered, using the common tongue. "I was summoned for an urgent meeting."

"That's not for two days," grumped the guard.

"No, not that one. The one tonight."

"What are you talking about?" The irritation in the guard's voice was plainly audible.

"An urgent meeting, tonight, at midnight. A note was left on my bed."

"We sent no note."

"It was signed with . . . " And only then did he realize that the Zhentarim would never sign such a note.

"With what?" growled the guard.

Ahegi's eyes narrowed. He glanced quickly back to the dock, and he thought he saw a shadow move, disappearing down an alley. He ran back down the gangplank to the alley and cast wildly around, but he saw nothing, and the pounding rain washed away all sounds. He wondered if the rain and darkness and lingering flare of the guard's lamp had played a trick on his old eyes.

Perhaps it had, but he could not take that chance. Someone had lured him out there, compromising his schemes, and he thought he knew who it was.

With a curse as black as the pits of his heart, Ahegi headed back for Wing's Reach as fast as his aging body would allow.

CHAPTER EIGHTEEN

Though the rain continued to pour hard and chill, it could not repress Kehrsyn's mood. She smiled as she walked back to Wing's Reach, occasionally indulging in an extra skip as she skirted the larger puddles. Everything had paid off. She'd found a place to live, wrangled some coin, garnered the protection of a man who treated her like she dreamed her father would have, pulled off several daring incursions for the betterment of Unther, and tricked Ahegi into revealing himself for the traitor he was.

Arrogant ass, she thought, you're about to reap the tiger. Wait until Massedar finds out what I know. You and your slimy ways will be gone forever.

If only she could figure out whom Ahegi reminded her of, all would be right with the world.

Kehrsyn stepped into the foyer of Wing's Reach, and her irrepressible smile brought smiles to the faces of the two guards on duty. She shook out her hair and tried to dry the rain from her mouth and chin with the equally wet cuff of her blouse. Sniffing with the cold, she pulled off her cloak and shook it out, taking care to keep her back, and therefore the counterfeit wand wrapped in her sash, away from the guards' eyes.

"Need some help warming up, lass?" heckled one of the guards.

"Sure," said Kehrsyn, feeling a little saucy. Then she interrupted herself with a pout. "Ooh, but you're on guard duty. Too bad. Your loss."

"My offer is open," said the guard, with just a hint of desperation.

"Mine's not," she replied with a smile, and the other guard laughed at his companion's expense. "Have a good night, boys," Kehrsyn added, slinging her cloak over her back in such a manner that it looked casual but concealed the wand.

Just as Kehrsyn set her foot upon the first step of the stairs, the front doors burst open and an intruder flew into the room. Startled, Kehrsyn spun around, and the two guards readied weapons at the sudden disturbance.

"Halt!" yelled one guard, before he recognized the predatory snarl on Ahegi's face.

Ahegi panted, air passing almost spasmodically between his bared teeth. He'd abandoned his cloak somewhere and bared his fattened breast to the weather. His clothes sagged beneath the rain and sweat, and the concentric blue circles that adorned his forehead were smeared. Mud covered his legs past his knees and spattered his trousers and robe up to his waist.

"Where," he panted, the cold air pouring in from the open doors and making his breath steam, "is that arrogant, insolent, sanctimonious whore?"

Kehrsyn's heart stopped as Ahegi's words opened a rift in time, and she tumbled back through it to her childhood, to one of her earliest memories. She saw the door to their hut burst open, saw her mother quail in fear before those exact same words, felt the nightmare return. She wanted to run from the pain but couldn't abandon her mother. Kehrsyn wanted to help, but if she interfered, she'd only make it worse for both of them.

All her life those words had lain in her subconscious, words too complex for her young mind but whose meaning was clear by the speaker's tone. She'd never forgotten those words or that voice, and without warning the nightmare had reared its burning, tarry, venomous head from her subconscious and found its way home. Wide-eyed like a child, Kehrsyn stared at Ahegi as her brain grappled with the awful truth.

"Ekur!" she gasped, and her knees began to tremble.

He whipped his shaven head around like a bull to face the young woman. She stared in shock. He'd gained more wrinkles, built himself a sag of pudge beneath his neck and a mantle of fat over his body, and removed the priestly third circle from his forehead, but there was no longer any mistaking the piggish, hateful eyes that burned beneath his brow. He raised one sodden arm and pointed.

"Kill her," he shouted hoarsely. "No quarter—I want her *dead!*"

Kehrsyn didn't have the leeway to make a break for the front door, so she fled up the stairs. Behind her she heard Ekur begin working some magic as the guards gave chase, yelling for help.

As she rounded the stairs, she saw a flash of magical magenta light flare against her trailing hand. She winced from the flare, but felt no ill effects as she ran.

Not knowing any better way to leave the building, she sprinted to the second floor, passed the startled guardsman in the center of the hall before he could figure out what was happening, darted down to and through her room, and leaped out the window to the alley below. She landed poorly on the hard dirt and had to roll to avoid injuring her knee. Soaked through with muddy water, she regained her feet and checked to ensure the wand was still in her sash. Then, just as she was about to put her cloak on, she saw that it was glowing with a bright magenta light, the aura of Ekur's spell.

She put it on anyway and ran off into the rainy night.

❂

Several of the inhabitants of Wing's Reach lounged in the common dining area, enjoying the fire and gambling at dice and sava. Demok sat to one side, whetting his long sword and occasionally offering advice on odds and plays, sipping a goblet of dry wine purchased from some Chessentan mercenaries during the campaign season.

An outcry rang through the building, a pair of voices calling the building to arms. Behind it, Demok heard the unmistakable sound of magic being woven. He leaped to his feet, sheathing his long sword and drawing his short sword, the better tool for indoor work.

He burst into the hall and ran to the foyer, where most of the commotion seemed to originate. Ahegi stood by the open front doors, leaning with one hand against the jamb and panting heavily, soaked through and absent his rain cloak.

Demok ran up to him, a questioning look on his face.

"That whore," panted Ahegi, pointing up the stairs. "The new one. Kill her."

Demok turned to the stairs and heard the heavy clatter of the two guards charging after the lone fugitive, shouting imprecations and calls for assistance. Instead of following them, he sheathed his sword, snagged the lantern that hung over the guards' table, and ran outside, heading for the stables. He kicked open the stable boy's door, which stood to the side of the big barn doors. By the light of his lantern, he saw the stable boy sitting on his bale of hay, bleary eyes wide with surprise. Demok grabbed the loose end of the blanket in which the stable boy was wrapped and gave it a hard pull, spinning the boy out of the blanket and into the cold night's air.

"A bridle, boy!" ordered Demok, raising his voice to help the command cut through the haze of sleep. "Now!"

The boy stumbled to his task, not even yet fully awake or aware of his surroundings.

Demok moved quickly through the stables to his mount's stall. The lantern he hung from a nail that jutted from a post. He opened the paddock's gate, pulled the blanket from the horse's back and spoke gently to it. His hand on the back of the horse's neck, he began to lead it out.

Near the front of the stable, he saw the boy trying to figure out why he was up and around with a bridle in his hand.

"Here, boy!" shouted Demok, and the boy tripped over, one hand offering the reins.

With the skill of a lifelong horseman, Demok strapped the bit and bridle to his horse.

"Open the gate!" he shouted, and leaped atop his horse, bareback.

The boy, sensing that his nightmare would end as soon as he let it out, threw back the bar and pushed one door open. Demok rode out into the night, heading up the alley to find that a group of Wing's Reach guards, each with a lantern, were already spilling out to pursue Kehrsyn in the downpour.

"There she is!" shouted one, and there, distant but yet visible in the downpour, he saw a cloak, glowing with a bright phosphorescent light and bobbing with a runner's pace.

The group pursued, and Demok went with them. Ahegi wanted Kehrsyn killed, not captured, which meant that whatever she might say was forbidden, knowledge far too dangerous for anyone to hear. He knew he could not let any of them reach her before he did. They wouldn't understand the urgency.

Fingering the hilt of his short sword, he vowed that his superiors' mission would not be thwarted. The group followed the glow, which led in a straight line, until, of a sudden, it dropped to the ground.

"Damn! She tossed her cloak," cursed one guard.

As the group reached the abandoned cloth with its unwelcome enchantment, the officer of the guards looked around at the alleys that lurked in the darkness.

"You five," the officer barked, gesturing to a cluster of guards, "keep pursuing in this direction, all the way to the docks. She hasn't turned once since we left. Maybe she's panicked or hopes she can hire passage. The rest of you, split into groups of three and search these alleys carefully. She might have been playing dumb, hoping we'd pass her by as she hid in the dark. Move!"

As the guards dispersed, Demok paused. He was certain she was neither panicked nor hiding. From everything she'd told him, Kehrsyn had been through many such dragnets before, and, since she still possessed both hands, evidence implied that she'd always escaped clean. Instead, he figured she would move to a safe place to lair. She had no other home, and after all the time he'd shadowed her through Messemprar he knew of only two places she might go. One was the Thayan enclave, to seek the protection of whomever she'd spent the night with after the theft. The other was the hideout of the thieves' guild, or whatever organization it truly was, where the occupants had been killed and carted away like cordwood.

Fortunately for him, she was on foot and had to avoid being spotted. He had neither of those handicaps. He lashed his horse and rode hard to the enclave, the sound of his horse's hooves lost beneath the heavy rain.

As he approached the enclave, Demok saw a guard-house with a single desultory guard leaning against one wall, wrapped in his cloak and feebly warmed by the red glow of a magical fire that hovered in the rear corner.

Demok rode up and reined in his horse as the guard stood to challenge him.

"Miserable night to stand guard," said Demok.

"Worse for riding about," responded the guard, and Demok caught the definite edge of a veteran soldier in his voice. "What ails you?"

"A young woman may come. So tall, slender, pretty."

"Dark hair?" asked the guard. "Big smile? Moves like a cat?"

Demok nodded and said, "Came here two nights ago."

"I know her," said the guard.

"Excellent. If she comes, give her shelter. Keep her safe. And keep her here. I'll be back for her, personally." Demok fished in his purse and produced ten gold coins. "For any expenses incurred while under Thayan protection."

"Understood," said the guard, placing the coins in a leather pouch at his belt. "You have a night ride, now." He raised one eyebrow and worked his tongue. "Bleah. Listen to me. I'm not sure whether I was going to say 'nice ride' or 'nice night.' Well, whichever it was, have it."

With a nod, Demok swung around and rode for Wheelwright's Street. He hoped he would beat her to it, and he hoped it would be otherwise unoccupied.

His job would be much more difficult if the body snatchers returned.

CHAPTER NINETEEN

Shivering with cold, Kehrsyn looked around at the open plaza surrounding the Chariot Memorial. The entire area, as she'd expected at such a late hour on such a wretched night, was deserted. She moved quickly over to Wheelwright's, down to the wedge-shaped building, and climbed the ladder. She wondered how long it would be before people figured out it was abandoned.

Maybe, she thought, I could set myself up as landlord and charge people rent to stay here. But first I'd have to clean it up. And get rid of the dog and those last two mangled bodies.

She opened the door and stepped in, eager to get out of the frigid rain and put anything solid between herself and the legions of guards she envisioned chasing her throughout the streets of Messemprar.

The door slammed shut. Someone behind her wrapped one arm around her arms and clamped a hand over her mouth.

A rough voice hissed, "Quiet!"

A man's voice. Kehrsyn kicked upward with her heel, looking to discommode whomever it was, but she felt him twist slightly and her heel struck his thigh. The man dropped onto his back, pulling them down together, then he rolled over, pinning her body beneath him. Doing so, he'd freed up the arm that had pinned her hands, and just as she thought to grab his hair or claw his eyes, she felt the tip of a blade at her throat. She considered biting the fingers that stifled her mouth but decided that the blade's tip was too great a threat. Instead, she slowly held her hands out to the side and tapped the floor in surrender.

The man kept one knee on her back as he rose. She heard him mumble something in an arcane tongue, and a small glowing orb, not much larger than a firefly but much brighter, appeared in the middle of the room. Once the room was lit, he rose to his feet, backing away so that she could sit up. She did so and turned to see who had captured her.

"Demok!" she gasped, seeing his short sword bared and leveled. "Please don't kill me. Please, I have important news for Massedar. You have to take me back, but don't let Ahegi see me, or he'll kill me."

Demok raised one hand and leveled it at Kehrsyn, pointing it in a commanding manner.

"Quiet," he said.

"But—"

"Quiet!"

Keeping one eye on Kehrsyn, Demok used his free hand to move a few packs and bags in front of the door, blocking it. The makeshift barricade wouldn't stop someone determined to pass, but it would slow someone— someone like her—for a few precious seconds. Kehrsyn grew more and more nervous, for what would one more body in the building be?

It crossed her mind to wonder how Demok knew where

the building was. No one in Wing's Reach knew about the place. She'd been very careful . . .

"Oh no," said Kehrsyn, "you're one of them. You're with the Dragon Queen! I won't tell anyone . . . please. I promise."

Demok did not acknowledge her outburst. Rising, he circled around Kehrsyn to put himself between her and the other two exits from the room.

"I watched you perform at the Jackal's Courtyard," he said.

"Yeah, I know," replied Kehrsyn, on the verge of tears. "I saw you."

"I let you," he said. "I'd watched three days."

"You did?" asked Kehrsyn, eager to perpetuate the conversation, as the longer they talked, the longer she stayed alive.

"Studied your skills," he said. "You're good."

"Thanks," said Kehrsyn.

"When the woman framed you, you escaped. Saw me. Ran. Guards gave chase. We fell, entering the alley."

"Yeah, I remember," said Kehrsyn.

"Deliberate."

"What do you mean? You mean you—"

"Later, you hid in an alley," interrupted Demok. "Two Zhents closing in. Then a whistle. They chased after someone else. False lead."

"Yeah, that's what happened," said Kehrsyn. "The sorceress said that Mask, the God of Thieves, favored me."

"That was me, too."

"What?"

"I tripped so you'd get away," he said. "I led them away so you'd live." He paused, studying Kehrsyn's reaction, then added, "Had a reason. Still do. So I'm not going to kill you now."

Kehrsyn closed her eyes, sagged to the floor in relief, and started to cry.

"I'll build a fire," said Demok.

A short while later, Demok had a bright fire going. He'd lit a lamp and placed candles burning at key points throughout the building to burn away the growing stink of death.

Kehrsyn's clothes lay spread before the fire, slowly drying. Her bag, dagger, and rapier stood nearby. The decoy staff lay buried at the bottom of the bag, placed there when Demok had left the room to allow her to change in privacy. She sat wrapped in several warm blankets staring at the fire.

"Can't go back tonight," Demok said. "Too dark. Dangerous. We'll go in the morning."

"That's probably best," said Kehrsyn.

"Important news?"

Kehrsyn looked up at Demok's face, illuminated by the fire.

She hesitated, then said, "I know I can trust you, but I mean can I really trust you? This is big. I mean, you have to keep it secret. Really, really secret."

In answer, Demok clenched his fist and held it in the flames. Kehrsyn gasped. She saw the hairs on his arm ignite and flare into nonexistence. The smell of burned hair quickly spread.

"A'right a'right a'right, I can trust you," she said. "Please just take your hand out!"

He did so, flexed his hand, and blew on it.

"Right back," he said, took a dishcloth, and stepped outside.

When he returned, the cloth was soaked with chilly rainwater and wrapped around his hand.

"I hope you didn't hurt yourself," said Kehrsyn. "We may need your sword."

"I'm always ready to fight," said Demok. "Tell me."

Kehrsyn took a deep breath and said, "Well, first of all, Ahegi is actually Ekur."

"I grew up in Sespech," said Demok. "That name means nothing."

"Oh, right . . ." said Kehrsyn. "Ekur used to be a high priest of Gilgeam."

"Gilgeam I know," said Demok.

"Ekur was in charge of Shussel, which was the town where I grew up. I knew I knew him when I first saw him, but last time I saw him was over twelve years ago, and it took me until now to figure out who he was. I'm glad I finally recognized him. Anyway, I found out that he's working with the Zhentarim, and I think he was behind me stea—uh, behind the theft of the Alabaster Staff, and I think either the Tiamatans have hidden it somewhere or, more likely, the Zhents have it."

Demok looked genuinely surprised.

"He's a Zhent?" he asked, leaning forward. "How?"

"Well, the, uh, people who made me . . . you know . . . they had this map of Wing's Reach. They said they got it from the city archives, but it had all the recent additions, so it was a new map. And it had the location of the Alabaster Staff marked on it. That meant someone was a traitor. And they said as much, but they didn't know who it was, because it was this 'friend of a friend' sort of thing."

Kehrsyn bit her lip as she considered what to say next.

"I figured it was the Zhentarim," she continued. "From everything I've been hearing, they're working hard to worm their way into Unther, and despite what I said back in Wing's Reach I can't see anyone selling out to the pharaoh. The question was, who? I figured it was someone high, because they knew about the staff's hiding place. That meant it was you or Ahegi, most likely. I chose to try Ahegi first, because I figured it'd be harder to get something past you. And to be honest, I wanted it to be Ahegi, because he'd been giving me butterflies every time I saw him.

"So I find out. I write this note like I think maybe the Zhentarim would write it, and I sneak in and leave it on his bed. And for some reason he goes to talk to Massedar first, maybe to tell him he's leaving the building or something, and he goes all the way across town in a real hurry to a ship."

"A ship," echoed Demok, unable to follow Kehrsyn's train of thought.

"Don't you see? When the people came here and took all the bodies away—oh, wait, you weren't here. See, this used to be where the thieves' guild was, and—never mind, it's not important right now. But these Tiamat guys came in the middle of the night, and they took away all these dead bodies, and the guy in charge said they were going to leave them on the Zhentish ship. So these guys gave the Zhents all kinds of dead bodies! So that's why I think either Tiamat is helping them or the Zhents are using them, too."

Demok narrowed his eyes and asked, "Did they say which ship?"

"They said it was called the *Bow Before Me*."

Demok nodded again, running a thumb across his lower lip, and said, "It's in port, all right. It's tied up at the Long Wharf."

"Yes!" said Kehrsyn. "That's where Ekur went when he read the note. He went to the ship on the Long Wharf."

"When he got back, he ordered you killed," concluded Demok. "Makes sense."

"Yeah, maybe he spotted me shadowing him. I'm not as good as you are."

Demok ignored the comment, causing Kehrsyn to wonder if he thought anyone was as good as he was.

"So Ekur," said Demok, "an ex-Gilgeamite, has embraced Bane, Lord of Darkness."

"That sounds bad," said Kehrsyn.

"Worse," said Demok. "Devoted my life to fighting them. Had a hunch they were holing up here. Wondered if they were in Wing's Reach, the way the house rose to prominence."

"Is Massedar in danger?" asked Kehrsyn.

"Only if Ahegi finds out we know. I'll speak with Massedar directly." He rose and grabbed his swords. "You wait here."

"Please be careful," said Kehrsyn. "And tell him I'm fine."

Demok left, heading into the rain without acknowledging her request.

☙

Demok recovered his horse and rode back to Wing's Reach, taking a circuitous route in hopes of avoiding the house guards. The horse balked at galloping in such dim light, but Demok's continued prodding kept its pace high. He was concerned that Ekur, thinking his cover blown, might try to assassinate Massedar.

He reached Wing's Reach, left his horse in the stable, and struck the stable boy to awaken him.

"Saddle," he barked, and strode into Wing's Reach.

He vaulted up the stairs three at a time to the third floor, where he went directly to Massedar's quarters. He pounded loudly on the doors.

"Whatever it is, it shall await the morning," came a sleepy and very irritated voice. "I have had my fill of interruptions."

"Demok, sir," said he. "Important!" he added, then pounded again.

Massedar muttered as he arose, the emotion, if not the exact words, clearly audible through the doors. At last the door creaked open and Massedar's face, at least a vertical quarter of it, appeared at the door.

"Speak thou thy tidings," he commanded.

"Ahegi, sir," said Demok, in a low, urgent voice. "Kehrsyn has proof he's a Zhent. The traitor we've suspected."

Massedar's sleepy eyes awoke at once, burning with fires of indignation. He pulled the door open wider and looked as if he was going to shout but fought back the impulse. Instead, he closed his eyes, clenched his fist, and drew in a deep breath through his nose.

"Ahegi . . ." he said, in a voice of resignation.

"Kehrsyn says he's Ekur of Shussel. Ex-Gilgeamite overlord."

"Truly is she more . . . more valuable than pearls."

"Where there's one priest, could be others."

"No," Massedar said, "there are no others."

"Certain?"

Massedar nodded and said, "Ahegi hath been in my employ these . . . thirteen, fourteen years . . . from the beginning. The others have I myself recruited, and none be so lettered as he."

"Best to keep quiet, anyway," said Demok.

"Well spoken, for perhaps he hath adherents of his own." Massedar shook his head, clenching and unclenching his fist. "He, a traitor. That provideth how the thief so well knew where to uncover the Alabaster Staff. Surely the black hand holdeth it now. Would that I knew what other poison and slander he hath spread amidst this house. He hath betrayed everything. The memory of his deity incarnate, the future of his people, and the trust of his benefactor. All these hath he yielded up to the hunger of a foreign god. Such bitter news must I endure. Where is Ahegi at this hour?"

"Hunting Kehrsyn."

"Seeketh he to still her tongue ere it can uncover his treason. Thus hath he pronounced his own doom," said Massedar, and though his voice was calm Demok noticed that his body trembled. "Find thou him, Demok. Do thou whatsoever thou must, to slay this wayward kin-seller who playeth the harlot to foreign gods in our ancient empire. Slay thou him ere his tongue might wag, seeking to poison thee against this house, even me. Only ensure thou that the head remaineth attached to the body, and the mouth and brain save thou undamaged. The fate of the rest I leave in thy hands and whims, if they be fast and sure. When thou hast finished, then shalt thou bring the body unto me. Thence shall we divine where his cabal hath placed my Alabaster Staff. Go thou now, to the kill."

"Pleasure, sir," said Demok, bowing ever so slightly as he turned away.

⊙

Kehrsyn huddled by the fire, wrapped in her blankets. Occasionally she turned her clothes over or rotated them around to expose fresh portions to the fire. She smiled as she saw them slowly drying. They would feel good to put on, nice and warm and dry.

A knocking at the front door sent her scrambling for her rapier before she realized that, of everyone she'd seen come and go, only Demok would have the consideration to knock. She chuckled in relief and embarrassment, quickly gathering her blankets around herself as he entered.

"Hi," she said. "I didn't expect you back so soon. Is everything all right?"

"Yes," said Demok with a dangerous smile. Though his cloak hung limp and dripped rainwater, his eyes had a satisfied gleam like that of a cat. "I am to kill Ekur."

Beside the fire, Kehrsyn closed her eyes in thanksgiving. Massedar had heard her story, and her life had been spared.

"Well," she sighed, "I for one won't shed any tears when he dies."

"Need your help."

Kehrsyn's eyes popped back open. "You need my help?" She laughed nervously. "I've never killed anyone. Well . . . one, but I didn't have a choice and I didn't want to and I can hardly remember any of it anyway, it was so fast. I don't see how I can be much help to a warrior like you."

"Ekur has guards," Demok said.

He looked Kehrsyn in the eye and waited.

"You want me to draw the guards away from Ekur so you can kill him?"

Demok nodded once.

Kehrsyn looked back into Demok's eyes, steely and penetrating above the determined set of his craggy face.

"I can do that," she said, for his confident demeanor bolstered her courage against the fear that clawed at her heart.

"Good," said Demok. He stood and started to walk out of the room. "Get ready. We'll catch him while he's still out."

Kehrsyn grimaced as she turned back to the fire.

"And my stuff was almost dry," she grumbled, reaching for her clothes.

❧

Demok waited outside for Kehrsyn to prepare, speaking gently to his horse beneath the slim shelter of an overhanging roof. He saw Kehrsyn open the door, her figure silhouetted by the reflected light of the fire. He mounted up and rode over to the base of the ladder. He held his hand out to help her up behind him.

She took his hand and paused.

"So what do I do?" she asked.

"Mount up. Talk as we ride."

"No, I mean, how do I get up there?"

"Never ridden?"

Kehrsyn shook her head with an embarrassed look.

Nimbly sliding off the horse, Demok stepped behind Kehrsyn, gripped her by her slender waist, and lifted her onto the horse with one mighty heave. Kehrsyn squealed in mixed fear and delight. Once she was up, Demok mounted behind her and took the reins.

Through the rain-washed city streets they moved, Kehrsyn riding in front of Demok, gripping his arms to stabilize herself. She seemed glad to hold onto the rock-steady soldier, and, for his part, he did his level best to ignore it.

They discussed the plan as they rode, Demok constantly alert for the sights or sounds of any of the Wing's Reach guards.

"Can't I have the horse?" asked Kehrsyn. "That way I'd be sure to get away."

"No," said Demok. "Can't change. Left with a horse, have to ride back on one."

"You could say I took it from you," said Kehrsyn, turning over her shoulder to look at Demok. In answer, all she got was a wry smile.

They continued to search, crisscrossing the city streets and gradually moving closer to Wing's Reach.

"That's them," said Demok. "Lie down."

Kehrsyn lay low against the horse's back, one arm reaching forward to grip the front of the horse's harness, the other arm held close to her body with the hand tightly gripping the horse's mane. She hid her head to one side of the horse's large neck. Demok slung his cloak over her to conceal her form as well as he could. For the rest, he would rely on the poor visibility and his cleverness.

He rode up to a pair of guards carrying a lantern.

"Ho there," said one. The other sneezed.

"Ahegi?" asked Demok, casually steering away from the two, so that Kehrsyn's head and reaching arm remained on the far side of the horse. He kept his mount pacing forward, both to imply urgency and to help keep Kehrsyn concealed behind the motion.

"Yonder, two blocks out," said the guard in answer, pointing. "He's a slave-driver. The gal's long gone, but he'll have us out here searching every nook and rat hole, block by block, until dawn comes or we catch our death of the flux."

"Whichever comes second," added the other guard.

Demok waved and continued forward. He circled around to the far side of Ekur, to place Kehrsyn and himself between the former priest and Wing's Reach, then he turned his horse back toward where the guard had indicated Ekur would be found.

"Ready?" he asked.

"I guess," she replied, and he helped her dismount. "Ooh, this is cold," she grumbled as she moved away.

Demok watched as she glided down the side street in front of him, reached the end, and looked around.

She slid back and said, "This'll do. Just be sure you pass me first."

Demok nodded, and she moved off again. He waited until she was in position at the head of the side street, where it connected to the main thoroughfare. He walked his horse down the side street as well. As he approached Kehrsyn's position, he could hear her teeth chattering.

The horse passed her hiding place and trotted out into the street.

Ekur and a few aides and senior guards stood forty yards away, well lit by a cluster of lanterns. Demok noted with scorn that one fawning aide held a parasol over Ekur's head, despite the fact that the latter had a rain cloak and wore his hood up.

"Ahegi!" bellowed Demok, cupping his hands to his mouth to be heard over the heavy rain.

Three bull's-eye lanterns swung around to illuminate the horse and rider. A mere heartbeat after Demok became fully illuminated, Kehrsyn bolted from her hiding place nearby, knocking over a barrel and shovel. She fled down the street. The sudden racket drew the bull's-eye lanterns' glare.

As soon as their beams alighted on Kehrsyn's fleeing back, Ekur's shriek carried through the night: "She's heading back to Wing's Reach. Stop her! Catch her and kill her."

The portly old priest gesticulated wildly in the rain, his sheer hysteria whipping his followers to immediate action. With a clatter of steel weapons and cleated boots, everyone around, even the bearer of the parasol, rushed after the fleet young woman, their lanterns jostling in the rain like fireflies caught in a waterfall.

Within the span of a tenbreath, the street was vacant except for Demok and Ekur, the latter bearing a staff that glowed with a powerful, magical light.

"I thank thee for flushing the quarry," said Ekur as Demok rode up to him.

"She is not the problem," said Demok as he dismounted.

"She is more than trouble enough," said Ekur.

Demok stepped closer, reaching beneath his cloak to pull a small item from his vest.

"I have a clue to the turncoat in Wing's Reach," the warrior said.

Ekur drew back slightly and assumed a more commanding stance.

"Hast thou?" asked Ekur.

Demok nodded, held out one hand, and said, "This was in the quarters of one of our people."

He placed a small silver brooch in Ekur's palm, and the aged former priest brought his lighted staff closer to inspect the item. He gasped when he recognized the intricate design worked into the brooch. It was a gasp that, Demok noted, was at once both relief and alarm, as when one dodges an asp only to step upon the tail of a lion. Ekur turned the brooch over in his pudgy hand, his breath quickening in fear.

"This—these—those who follow this path are the most vile of conspirators," he blustered. "And we have one such assassin in our very midst? Why, nothing is safe! Knowest thou the name of this perfidious rebel?"

"Me," said Demok, stepping in close so that his nose touched that of the former priest.

Ekur's eyes went wide in surprise, but Demok couldn't tell it if was from hearing the sudden confession of his true allegiance or from feeling the cold short sword that pierced upward through his diaphragm and into his black heart.

Truth be told, Demok didn't care.

☉

Kehrsyn huddled in a recessed doorway in a dark, narrow alley a few blocks from Wing's Reach, precisely where Demok had ordered. She'd easily escaped the guards. In the end, she'd followed the guards themselves as they chased her phantom feet back to their home at Wing's Reach.

Once there, she'd circled around them as they made their follow-up plan, and watched with no small relief as they departed back in the direction of Ekur and Demok. Spotting the landmarks that Demok had drilled into her, she'd found their rendezvous per his instructions. Despite her confidence, however, the cold weather teamed up with her exhaustion, both mental and physical, to make her a sodden, unhappy wretch.

She abandoned all intent of subterfuge. She stamped her feet on the paving stones, relatively dry beneath the arch. She let her teeth chatter fully, and the noise overcame even the heavy rain, at least to her ears. She wrapped her arms as tightly as she could around her and shivered uncontrollably.

She stared out at the rain, feeling entirely alone. No one was stupid enough to be out in such bad weather, and certainly no one was stupid enough to be out without a cloak. No one except her. She found herself missing the relative dryness of the crawl space beneath the back stairs of the Tiamatan temple, but she dared not move anywhere, because Demok had told her to meet him exactly there.

She was too cold to be mad. She just wanted to stop

waiting, hoping her torment would end before she surrendered herself to the tears dammed up behind her eyes. How long could it take a veteran like him to kill a fat old priest, anyway?

At length, she heard the clop-clop of approaching horseshoes. Demok loomed out of the rain, leading his horse by the reins.

Kehrsyn forced a single word past her numb lips and chattering teeth, "Ekur?"

In answer, Demok walked up close to her, filling the doorway's arch.

"You realize," he said as he drew his short sword, "that you cannot enter Wing's Reach alive."

CHAPTER TWENTY

Demok rode up to the front door of Wing's Reach, the splash of the collected rainwater in the streets almost drowning the clop of his horse's hooves. He had one arm wrapped around Ekur, who sagged in the saddle in front of him. Behind his saddle, Kehrsyn's lifeless body dangled across the horse's back, her dark hair swaying with the horse's stride. A slight curtain of excess rainwater dripped from her fingertips with every step.

"Ho the house!" Demok shouted.

Four guards burst out of the front door, wet and tense and tired. The sergeant looked up at Demok, while the other guards scanned the rainy darkness.

"Ahegi's hurt," Demok said. "Bad. Massedar's room. Now."

"What happened?" gasped the sergeant.

Demok gestured over his shoulder with a thumb and said, "She got him. I got her."

"Good job," said the sergeant, casting a bitter

glance at Kehrsyn's body. He grunted as Ekur's limp body slid into his arms. "Gimme a hand, boys," he mumbled through clenched teeth. "He's a hefter."

Demok watched the four of them struggle with Ekur. Between the chill, the rain-slicked steps, and Ekur's porcine build, he knew it would take them time to get the body up the spiraling staircase. He dismounted and held the front door for the foursome. Then he cast a glance in and motioned to another guard who stood by, chatting quietly with a few comrades.

"Stable my horse," he said in a tone that demanded immediate compliance.

He trotted back down the stairs, walked over to his demoralized mount, and unceremoniously heaved Kehrsyn's inert body over his shoulder. He walked back inside Wing's Reach and ascended the stairwell across the foyer from the one the guards were using to port Ekur.

He reached the third floor, his breath heavy from the exertion of carrying an extra hundred-odd pounds of meat over his shoulder. He moved down the hall, Kehrsyn's hand batting against his legs. He reached Massedar's room and pounded on the door. Massedar opened it after but a moment's pause.

"Here's one," said Demok, stepping in and lowering Kehrsyn's body to the floor, face down. Massedar started to say something, but Demok cut him off. "Other's coming."

After a moment, a foursome of guards shuffled in, panting and puffing, and dropped Ekur.

"Here y'are, sir," wheezed the sergeant.

Massedar stepped closer to the old priest and stared at his lifeless face. He kneeled and pressed his fingers into the fleshy neck, looking for a pulse he knew he wouldn't find.

"I fear the hours of his life are spent," he said with measured sadness. "Nothing remaineth to be done, save only the final rites of passage. These shall I do for my old friend, alone. Let the doors be closed and the news be borne to the others of the house that Ahegi hath fallen."

The guards nodded and backed out, closing the doors behind them.

Massedar rose, stepped over, and kneeled down beside Kehrsyn. He took her cold hand in his, and a curious, chuckling sigh of longing escaped his lips.

He turned to Demok and asked, "What hath come to pass here?"

☙

Kehrsyn awoke with a groan.

"What happened?" she slurred.

She tried to sit up, but her vision swam. It seemed like a huge, heavy stone was rolling around inside her skull, whipping her head back and forth on her weak, noodle neck. She started to cry out in pain and despair, but a hand clamped over her mouth. Fortunately, whoever it was also cradled her head and shoulders in one arm and lowered her gently back down.

"Rest easy," said a terse, rough voice.

"Demok?"

"Sshh, quietly," he answered, pressing a flask of warm liquid to her lips. "Drink this."

She took a few sips of the bitter, musky tea, then drank several heavy swallows once she got used to the flavor. She sighed and sank back, only then realizing that she lay on a comfortable mattress with a pillow beneath her head and warm woolen blankets tucked around. She heard a fire crackling and the incessant drumming of the winter's rain on the roof over her head.

"Where am I?"

"Massedar's suite."

"But—" she began, and memory returned to her. "What did you do?" she asked, suspicious, but too weak to do anything about it.

She turned her head toward his voice and stared with bleary eyes.

He sat beside her, cross-legged on the floor. He ran one knuckle back and forth across his lower lip, his palm facing Kehrsyn so that his hand partially shielded his face. He looked back at her from beneath his brows, not an intimidating expression, but rather one of discomfort and shame.

"I . . . struck you. Base of the neck. Pommel of my sword. . . . I'm sorry."

"Why?" she asked, and the pain of betrayal leaked into her voice.

Demok's eyes flickered, almost a wince, and he said, "Ahegi's order still stood. Kill you on sight. No questions. You couldn't enter Wing's Reach alive."

"So you knocked me out?" she asked.

He nodded.

"Why not change Ekur's order?"

"Might be accomplices. They must think you're dead."

"I could have snuck in," she said.

He drew his mouth into a grim line and replied, "Couldn't take the chance. The guards are alert. Besides, it helps for them to see your corpse."

"Well, why hit me like that? I could have pretended I was dead."

"Would have shivered. Or twitched."

"You could have at least asked before you did it," she groused.

"Would have been harder," replied Demok. "For both of us," he added, more quietly.

"Well, I still think there must have been a better way."

Demok turned the cold compress over and brushed a lock of hair from her forehead.

"I know," he said.

He rose and stepped over to the fire. Kehrsyn heard some clinking, as of coins, and after a few moments he came back holding a burlap bag that looked like it had something the size of a cat in it. He shook it. It jingled.

"Silvers, warmed by the fire," he said. "They'll help."

He sat back down beside her, pulled back the blanket from her shoulder, and gently placed the bag of heated coins at the base of her neck, tucking some behind her and draping the others across to her collarbone. The burlap was scratchy, but the warmth radiating from the coins suffused her neck with a welcome ease.

"Do you have some more of that tea stuff?" Kehrsyn asked.

Demok held the flask and she drank some more. The aftertaste was an unusual bitter flavor, and left her mouth dry.

"I think it's helping," she said, smacking her lips.

Demok smiled, though only for a second, and said, "Herbs from Sespech. Potent."

Kehrsyn lay back, closed her eyes, and listened to the fire for a while, drifting in and out of sleep. She felt the pain slowly recede, vanquished between the warm tea within and the warm coins without.

"Where's Massedar?" she asked, her voice dreamy and slurred.

"Waiting next door. When you're ready."

"Thank you for taking care of me."

Demok laughed, nothing more than a tiny snort through his nose, and said, "Least I could do."

"It's almost worth it to get hit like that just to relax in a bed like this."

"Kehrsyn, I'm—" began Demok.

"Don't worry about it," Kehrsyn interrupted. "It just kind of scared me that you'd . . . you know . . . nah, just forget about it."

Another long pause filled the room, broken only by the occasional pop from the fire. Eventually, Kehrsyn started flexing her fingers and toes to get her circulation going again. She stretched her arms and legs, exhaled wearily, and lay still again.

"If you're ready," Demok said, "he's waiting."

Ekur's body sagged on the tabletop. He had been thoroughly searched. His clothes were undone and his pockets turned out, revealing rather more of his pallid, cyanotic flesh than Kehrsyn would ever have cared to see. The bulbous way the flesh oozed over the wooden tabletop reminded Kehrsyn of the toad squatting atop Eileph's bald head.

A cone of clove incense smoked on Ekur's forehead, planted in the precise center of the two concentric rings that marked him as a man of letters. A shiny copper covered each eye. A deep stabbing wound in Ekur's belly lay open like a rancid mouth, the skin around the cut pulled akimbo by the inert weight of his bulk. Massedar moved carefully around the corpse, inspecting it. Kehrsyn winced and turned her head.

"Why are you keeping him here?" she whispered.

"Soon shall his secrets be mine," said Massedar. "I wished your presence—both of ye—that ye might witness the gravity herein and as well catch any nuance that lieth outside my ken. Silence, now, and attend ye."

Kehrsyn stepped back. She held her arms across her chest, with one hand on her cheek as if it might shield her. She chewed on the inside of her lip. Demok stood to one side, hands crossed placidly in front of him.

Massedar crossed over to a large cupboard rather like a wardrobe, but when he opened it Kehrsyn saw it was a vast apothecary filled with alchemical preparations, raw materials, and unknown magical mixtures. His hand swayed like a cobra as he searched his supplies, then snatched an earthenware jar the size and shape of a soup bowl.

He pushed his fingers through the wax sealing the top of the bowl as he walked over to Ekur. Kehrsyn saw that the bowl was filled with a balm of a pale, disquieting shade of green. Massedar scooped the balm out by the fingersful and smeared swaths of it on the inside of Ekur's forearms, at the hollows of his knees, at the base of the breastbone, and across the bottom of his jaw. The scent of myrrh flooded the room, overpowering the incense, and tendrils of green started to spread beneath Ekur's skin, following the veins like blood poisoning. It was hideous to watch but also fascinating.

Massedar set the salve casually on the table and stalked back to his library of concoctions. He pulled out two flasks, one small and made of dark glass, the other large and formed of cut crystal. He slid the smaller flask into a pocket and removed the stopper from the larger, crystal flagon. He drizzled the contents over Ekur's body, starting at the head and working his way down, until almost the entire corpse had been wetted. The liquid smoked and fumed with the smell of sulfur as it struck the skin, but Ekur's body appeared unchanged by whatever magical reaction was taking place. Finally, Massedar tilted Ekur's head back and poured some of the concoction into his nostrils. That done, he set the bottle down on the table next to the balm and elevated Ekur's shoulders a little bit, letting his head sag backward. Kehrsyn figured that would help some of the strange potion to drain down Ekur's throat without being blocked by his dead tongue.

Massedar returned the corpse to its original position. Then, his outstretched hands gripping the edge of the table, he leaned low to Ekur's ear.

"Ekur," he said.

The body did not move.

"Ekur of Shussel, answer thou me," he commanded.

Kehrsyn shuddered and closed her eyes as she saw the corpse's mouth move. It made no noise other than the wet, sucking sound of an unattended tongue flopping around in a dead mouth. She realized that, after the nightmare of two days past, she couldn't bear to keep her eyes closed. Instead, she opened them and stared at the ground, shielding her eyes from the abomination taking place on the table.

"Thou must inhale," said Massedar.

There followed a guttural, empty, choking sound of air being pulled past dead flesh.

"What is thy wish, my lord?" asked Ekur, in a sighing, falling, monotonous voice, his diction listless and slurred.

The remaining air exited the fat, dead lungs like a death rattle.

Kehrsyn heard a cork pop. She cast a quick glance up and saw that Massedar was pouring some of the contents of the small glass bottle into Ekur's slack jaw.

"Swallow thou that," said Massedar, "that thou mayest speak only the truth."

The body swallowed it noisily, open-mouthed. Kehrsyn looked away, gooseflesh crawling over her like a million scarab beetles.

"Thou hast conspired to betray me, Ekur of Shussel. What is thy goal?"

The body inhaled again, a horrid sound that made Kehrsyn wince and curl her lip in disgust.

Again, the slurred voice came in a hollow, even-paced decrescendo, saying, "Thou art weak in the face of Bane . . . Bane shall take this land from the dead hand of Gilgeam and drive the—" the body inhaled again, slowly, noisily— "Mulhorandi back to the River of Swords . . . Unther shall rise, and I shall lead them to glory against the pharaoh."

Again the lungs rattled their way to emptiness.

"With whom hast thou conspired? Speak!" said Massedar, the anger in his voice was palpable.

"We schemed with Tiamat and Furifax to steal the Alabaster Staff . . . " said the airy, dead voice, "then we turned one pawn against the other . . . I—" another hideous snoring inhalation—"will use the staff to raise an army of undead and defeat the Mulhorandi forces . . . their own dead shall rise to—" the wet noise of flaccid inhalation sounded yet again—"serve me . . . and I shall rule this empire for our new lord god Bane . . . thy devotion to—"

"Enough!" barked Massedar.

His explanation aborted, Ekur let the rest of his air escape his cold lungs.

Massedar scowled at Ekur's body, drumming his fingers on the side of the table and thinking. Kehrsyn realized that she was unconsciously holding her breath, waiting for Ekur to breathe again. The silence was unnerving. She glanced up, freakishly hoping to see Ekur's chest rising and falling, so that she'd feel less awkward about breathing herself. Instead, she saw the green striations beneath his skin starting to fade and suspected that Massedar had little time left for his grisly interrogation.

"Where lieth the Alabaster Staff?"

With a fleshy, wet breath, Ekur said, "It was brought to the *Bow Before Me* . . . they sent it to a lair I know not of."

Massedar twisted his lips in frustration. He clapped a hand over Ekur's nose and mouth so that he couldn't exhale. With a grimace, Kehrsyn turned her head away. She realized she was holding her breath again, in sympathy for the image of Ekur being suffocated, and she forced herself to breathe.

"How shall I find the Alabaster Staff and recover it?" Massedar asked, pulling his hand off Ekur's face.

"Two days hence at midnight the—" he inhaled—"ritual begins, in the Deep Hall beneath the Temple of Gilgeam . . . it shall be there."

"With all the Zhents," muttered Demok.

❧

The city of Messemprar was starting to stir in the predawn darkness when Demok and Kehrsyn finally entered the empty building on Wheelwright's. They had slipped Kehrsyn out of Wing's Reach without incident, and the former guildhouse seemed the best place for the young woman to hole up until the appointed time.

Demok started a fire in the kitchen and unwrapped a stock of provisions. Kehrsyn tossed her cloak on the floor of the foyer, sat in a chair, and stared at the growing flames.

Once the food was heating, Demok opened up some windows to vent some of the smell that had accumulated in the building. The weather had eased off, loitering somewhere between a rain and a drizzle, though the air was no less cold.

They ate in silence as the first glimmers of the winter sun's light filtered through the cloud cover. The heat from the fire fought the cold air from outside, but their breath and the food both steamed. Demok ate his food mechanically. Kehrsyn poked at hers and didn't really eat until Demok leaned close and ordered her to.

Once it was clear that Kehrsyn was finished, Demok took her plate and flipped the food out the window. The extravagant waste would ensure that people thought the building was fully occupied.

He set the dishes aside and sat down next to Kehrsyn. He looked at her face as she stared into the fire.

"You all right?" he asked.

After a pause, Kehrsyn nodded.

"Hard to watch?"

Kehrsyn nodded again, exactly as she had a moment before.

"Thought you hated Ekur," he pressed.

Kehrsyn bit her lip and drew in a trembling breath. "I do," she said, her voice barely above a whisper.

Demok leaned in closer to hear her over the fire.

"He killed my father," she continued, "he tormented my mother, used her for pleasure. I've always hated him and I always will."

A long pause.

"Go on," said Demok.

Kehrsyn drew in another deep breath through her nose, and Demok noted that her trembling was diminishing.

"He's an evil man," she said, "and I'm glad he's dead. I don't mind that Massedar used his . . . used him like that. But it was an ugly thing to hear, and . . . I'm . . . I guess I'm just . . . put off that Massedar could do such horrid things with such a casual air."

"Sometimes we must do tasteless things," said Demok.

She glanced over at him. He dropped his eyes.

"I guess he did what he had to," continued Kehrsyn after a moment's reflection. "And now we know what's been going on."

Demok nodded. They sat in silence for a while, and Demok tended to the fire. Finally, he stood up and leaned against the wall, facing Kehrsyn.

"Ever know your father?" he asked.

Kehrsyn shook her head, regret and longing marring her features.

"No," she said, "I didn't. Ekur killed him about a year before I was born. All I've ever seen of him is the rock that marks his grave. It's just a rock. Doesn't even have his name on it. Just the pollen stains of countless wildflowers."

"Come again?" said Demok.

"A rock," said Kehrsyn, measuring with her hands. "About this wide around or so, pretty heavy, really, so I figure Momma had some friends help her."

"No, about your father."

"Never knew him, I said."

"Died a year before you were born."

"Yeah, Momma told me that once when she was drunk."

"Pregnancy takes nine months," said Demok.

Kehrsyn's face went pale, and she raised her hands to her open mouth.

"Oh my word," she gasped, "I never thought of it that way. . . ."

Demok regretted his rashness, letting surprise guide his tongue instead of his intellect. He reached for Kehrsyn, but she rose and walked over to the window, her blanched face unmoving. She looked alarmingly like the walking dead.

"I don't believe it," she murmured as she stared, unseeing, at the falling rain.

As the sun rose somewhere to the east, Kehrsyn leaned her hands on the windowsill and began to cry. She tried to hold back her sobs but failed, whining in pain as she exhaled, and inhaling trembling, reluctant breaths.

Demok could do nothing but sit and wait as the city awakened and the air filled with the sounds of pedestrians. Periodically, he stoked the fire. He wished he could help her, but she was lost somewhere in the past, experiencing pain he knew nothing of.

Kehrsyn raised her head to the sky, wiped her eyes with the heels of her hands, and turned back around to face Demok.

"I don't believe it," she said. "After all this time, he didn't kill my father." She sniffled and ran the heel of her hand across her eyes again. "I love my father!" she sobbed, her voice crescendoing as she struggled to maintain control. "What am I supposed to do now?"

She buried her face in her hands and began weeping openly. Full-force grief wracked her body, waves of anguish pounding against her throat. Demok hemmed for a moment, then awkwardly reached out to hold her. She ended up resting her head against his breast, but he wasn't sure she was aware of it.

He held her to the best of his ability, his jaw set in a grim line as he stared out at the city, a cold, gray world beset by warfare and hunger with little room for a hopeful, compassionate juggler. He could only see it as an allegory for her entire life.

The tide of her grief eventually receded, leaving her

spent and quiet, her arms still pulled close and her head leaning on his breastbone.

"Kehrsyn," he said.

"Yes," she answered, her voice like a little girl.

"Your father is still your father."

"No, he's not," she said.

"He's done more to raise you and guide your steps than Ekur ever did. Even after his death, he was your mother's helper and your companion. He's far more your parent than the one who sired you."

"But—" began Kehrsyn.

"Nothing Ekur can do can change that," interrupted Demok. "Don't you give it away. Hold onto it. Protect it. Your father makes you who you are."

A long pause.

"All right," said Kehrsyn.

Demok took a deep breath. While these personal talks were curiously rewarding, they still made him nervous, scared. He preferred to deal with threats that could be stabbed through the heart or beheaded. It was so much easier, so much clearer.

"And you can thank the gods that you look like your mother," he said, looking to end the moment before he foundered somewhere beyond his understanding.

Kehrsyn snorted.

"Yeah," she said, pulling away from him to sit by the fire once more.

☙

The day was a quiet one. Kehrsyn kept her own council, while Demok cleaned out the corpses downstairs and disposed of them. Periodically he'd stoke the fire, and usually he found Kehrsyn sitting in a chair by the hearth, staring out the open shutters at the continuous drizzle.

Later that evening, Kehrsyn and Demok sat at the table,

quietly eating the supper he had prepared. Kehrsyn set down her knife and fork and leaned her cheek on one fist.

She looked over at her companion with vulnerable eyes and asked, "Am I a bad person, Demok?"

He blinked twice, then replied, "Why do you ask?"

"I'm a thief. I steal things. It's against the law, and it's wrong. I'm sure my father wouldn't have liked it, either. I just take things from people. Sort of like my actual father."

Demok took a deep breath and looked at the ceiling.

"You just want me to talk," he said.

Kehrsyn giggled in spite of her serious mood.

Demok crossed one arm across his chest to support the elbow of the other. He ran his thumb across his lip between sentences as he spoke, a professorial tone to his voice.

"Every creature does what is required to survive. You grew up hungry. You stole food. When you could eat without stealing, you stopped. I see no fault."

"Yeah, but I promised myself that I would never steal again," confessed Kehrsyn. "Then, when that sorceress pushed me, I fell right back into it."

"You were cornered. Theft or death. You did what was required to survive."

Kehrsyn sat back in her chair, folding her arms. The chair creaked with age, making a sound of wood snapping.

"But we're supposed to know better," she said. "We're supposed to have values and ideals."

"You do," replied Demok. "You never steal for gain. You steal for survival. Given the chance to make amends, you did."

"But it's still theft, and I still broke my promise," protested Kehrsyn.

Demok considered that, and said, "If you're asking whether you should have died rather than steal, that's between you and your gods. I couldn't fault that choice, either. I don't have *the* answer to that question. I only have *my* answer."

"What's your answer?" asked Kehrsyn.

Demok's thumb froze in place.

"I'm a killer," he said, no trace of pride or shame in his voice. "It's my skill. People kill rabid dogs. I kill people. Because it needs to be done."

"That's hardly reassuring," mumbled Kehrsyn.

"If someone were about to use something to cause widespread plague," he asked, "and you had the chance to steal it, would you?"

"Yes," said Kehrsyn.

"Thus you'd use your skills to save a hundred lives," said Demok with finality.

"That doesn't make it any less wrong."

"Doesn't make it any less right," said Demok. He shrugged. "I don't have the answer. Only mine. You find yours."

"Fine," said Kehrsyn, a leaden tone to her voice.

Demok studied her.

"Something still bothers you," he observed.

Kehrsyn looked at him, then looked away, then tried to look at him again but failed.

Demok waited.

"I'm . . ." Kehrsyn said. "I know it's wrong and stuff, but I just can't help it. Especially these last few times. It's . . . I don't know, it's, like, exciting or something, breaking in and stuff," she confessed. "I think I'm starting to really enjoy it."

Demok smiled, a grim motion that didn't touch his eyes.

"I know what you mean," he said. "Like an addiction."

The two sat in silence for a long time, lost in their own thoughts as darkness once more descended upon the city.

CHAPTER TWENTY-ONE

The waiting was over. In contrast, the bitter winter weather was far from finished. A fresh, gusty wind blew in from the north, whipping people's cloaks and bringing repeated hard showers to rake the land.

It was a miserable day. For most people, it was a miserable night. Massedar, however, was happy to be out. The storms suited his mood, the dark temper that roiled beneath his calm and disciplined demeanor. It was time for revenge.

Massedar rode in a wagon, thoroughly furled in his great, warm cloak. A trusted servant drove the unwilling horses through the darkened streets, quietly and calmly. Midnight was approaching on its own time; best not to attract attention with reckless speed.

The only other passengers in the wagon were a pair of corpses in the rear, each carefully swaddled in oilskin tarpaulins. Rain drummed on the hard fabric, a pleasing sound to the aging merchant prince. He matched the sound and rhythm, drumming his fingers impatiently on the inner folds of his heavy cloak. The lower lid of one eye twitched in barely contained fury.

After all those years, he brooded, all those long years. After I took him in, made him an advisor, a confidante, even a friend, Ekur betrayed me. Sacrilege! He sold himself unto a foreign god and used me, used my house, used my wealth. How many years had it taken for me to recover the Alabaster Staff? And for how much of that time hath he, the traitor, been working behind the scenes, playing upon my faith, my trust, my mistaken impressions of the man?

Massedar worked his jaw back and forth. If he truly were to have his way, he would storm the gathering of Bane-worshiping heathen Zhents with every guard at his disposal, as well as a platoon of Chessentan mercenaries. That way he could ensure that no one left the area alive (or, at the least, that no one survived the painful interrogations).

Unfortunately, he did not have that luxury. The Zhents held the Alabaster Staff, and he had to recover it. That was crucial. He would not let the Zhentarim and their backstabbing servant wrest the staff away from him, not after all that time. But, more significantly, Ekur had been working for Bane, and therefore it was quite possible that one or more other people in Wing's Reach were also Zhent agents. The way the Zhentarim worked, Ekur might not even have known. Thus, Massedar could not trust his own people. Even if he could hire any mercenaries in the midst of the war, it would attract attention. In the end, Massedar was forced to work with Demok and Kehrsyn, the only people in on the secret of Ekur's adopted identity. They would have to be enough. They . . . and his other friend.

Ahead, he saw that the wagon was approaching the

Chariot Memorial. His eyes narrowed. If Demok and Kehrsyn kept him waiting, he would be quite upset.

"Time," said Demok, as he leaned in the front door of the former Furifaxian quarters.

Kehrsyn stopped her pacing, blew out her breath, and said, "Right, let's go."

"Got everything?" Demok asked.

"Yeah, I think so. I don't really need much, do I? I have my rapier and dagger, I'm wearing my armor . . . and," she added with a smile, "I've got this."

She pulled out a slender, bone-colored wand and twirled it expertly. For the first time, she saw Demok startled.

"What's that?" he asked, genuinely curious.

"It's a replica of the staff," she answered. "I thought I'd better bring it along, so if I get a chance to . . . reclaim the original, I can leave a double in its place, and maybe we can just sneak out of there without getting into a fight."

"Worth a shot," he said. "Where'd you get it?"

"You probably don't really want to know," said Kehrsyn with an uncomfortable smile.

Demok nodded and led the way outside to where his horse waited. The two mounted up, Kehrsyn sitting behind Demok, and the grim guard reined the horse around to head back to the Chariot Memorial.

As they approached the great statue, they saw a wagon waiting in the lee of the huge pedestal. Demok steered the horse for it.

"Art thou ready?" came a familiar voice.

"Always," Demok replied. He halted the horse next to the wagon. "More bodies for the Zhents?" he asked.

"It seemeth to me that none should question one bearing more fodder," Massedar explained. "Ensure thou that such a fate befalleth not me."

"Lead on," said Demok.

The wagon lurched forward in the rain, the horses eager to finish their task and return home. Demok and Kehrsyn fell in behind.

Kehrsyn leaned close to Demok's ear and said, "Good thing you like to kill."

"I don't," said Demok.

"But—"

"It's what I do, and I'm good at it, but killing I do not enjoy," he said over his shoulder. "Killing is wasteful. *Combat* I love. Pitting my skill and wits against another with the ultimate stakes. There is no purer test." He turned his head to face forward again, nodding to himself. "I'd wager that's what you find addictive about theft," he added. "Not stealing, but testing your skills in dangerous situations."

Kehrsyn cocked her head and furrowed her eyes as she considered that

"Got incredible skills," Demok continued after a moment, interrupting her thoughts. "Good heart, too. Question is, can you find a way to use those skills that doesn't break your heart? If you can, you've got it made."

A gust of wind ripped through the street, whipping their cloaks. Kehrsyn pulled hers back around her and tried to huddle down as small as possible behind the shield of Demok's shoulders.

"You did that," said Kehrsyn, finally understanding the source of Demok's quiet self-assurance. "So how did you answer the question?" she asked.

"Killing is a by-product. Didn't want it to be a waste, so I dedicated my life to the destruction of the Zhentarim and the church of Bane. If I found someone else who needed killing in the meantime, I didn't have a problem with that, either." He reached for something beneath his cloak, and after a moment's fumbling reached over his shoulder to hand something to his companion. "Know what this is?" he asked.

Kehrsyn took the item and studied it, holding it very close to her eyes in the dim light.

"It looks like a pin in the shape of a harp," she answered. "What does it mean?"

"I'm a Harper."

"So what does *that* mean?"

Demok paused a moment, then explained, "We protect civilization. Fight the tyrant gods and their followers, strike down those who need it. I came here when I heard Bane was moving on Messemprar. Wing's Reach seemed a likely target. Other Harpers are elsewhere in the city."

"What, right now?"

Demok nodded and said, "We need them. Dark times are coming."

"So why'd you join the Harpers in particular?"

"May not be a home, but it's a family," he said.

Kehrsyn handed the pin back to him. He took it and replaced it somewhere inside his cloak.

After a pause, he spoke one last time. "Consider that an offer," he said.

❦

Massedar's wagon led them to the Temple of Gilgeam. During the rule of the god-king, who had taken the throne in the stead of his father Enlil some two millennia before, it had been the centerpiece of all life in Messemprar, where the god-king basked in the worship of the lesser beings of his empire. Everything had changed when Tiamat slew Gilgeam, and even after fifteen years the pillars and capitals of the temple still showed some of the blackened smears from the oily fires that had devoured the lives of so many priests. Ever since the excitement of those first heady days had waned, the occasional new graffito still gouged its way into the pillars and walls.

The great pedestal out front was, of course, still empty.

"I hope we never see Bane's likeness erected on Gilgeam's pedestal," Kehrsyn murmured.

"One way or another," replied Demok, "we won't."

After Gilgeam fell, no one really knew what to do with the massive building. No one remotely associated with the priesthood wanted it. The army used it for a while, hoping the tradition of power that emanated from the building would help them maintain control, but even the soldiers didn't want to be there. As the Northern Wizards consolidated their power, they avoided the issue. In the end, the edifice ended up being used for two purposes: barracking foreign mercenaries, as their very presence would further despoil Gilgeam's memory, and executing criminals, as that activity remained very much in line with the building's original purpose.

The foreigners were left to argue among themselves how best to divide the space, so it was easy to understand how the Zhentarim could appropriate some of the subterranean levels for their own nefarious activities.

The wagon rolled around the great, empty pedestal and pulled up at the base of the grand staircase. The massive marble steps stretched almost the entire width of the building and were carved both tall and deep, specifically designed to make even the tallest visitor walk up the steps in the manner of a child.

At the top of the steps, a group of three or four figures stirred. Kehrsyn could see the telltale glow of a shuttered lantern in their hands.

Massedar got down from the wagon and directed Demok to pick up the larger of the bodies. That he did, working the corpse over his shoulders. The other corpse remained in the wagon as Massedar led Demok and Kehrsyn up the steps. Though clouds were scudding in, no rain was falling at the moment. Massedar removed his heavy cloak just as a gust of fierce wind blew through, and the sheer drama of the movement made Kehrsyn's heart thrill.

At the sudden motion, the figures at the head of the stairs flicked one of their lanterns open and shone it fully on Massedar. Kehrsyn saw that Massedar was dressed in priestly Banite raiment, no doubt the robe worn by Ekur himself. The long gown was full and black, with green rays and mystic sigils showing in the lantern light. Massedar had thrown the hooded cowl over his head, and he held his rain cloak out in one arm for Kehrsyn to take. As she stepped up to take it, she saw that he had shaved his beard to better match Ekur's clean-shaven face, and, thanks to the wind, she saw that Massedar had padded out his normally trim form beneath the garment, the better to emulate Ekur's bulky build.

As Kehrsyn took the proffered cloak in her arms, the light flicked off, shuttered once more within the glassy confines of the lantern.

As they reached the top of the stairs, Demok jerked his head back toward the wagon below.

"One more," he grunted.

Two of the sentries moved quickly down the steps to unload the other corpse as Massedar, Demok, and Kehrsyn entered the Temple of Gilgeam.

Kehrsyn's heart fluttered with fear. She had not set foot inside so much as a Gilgeamite shrine since the day Ekur had killed her mother. Even in the high holy days, when the troops searched the city for stragglers and the impenitent, she had risked her life rather than bow a knee to the despotic thearchy that had taken her parents from her. In a bizarre way, she almost felt that trying to stop the Banites in their plot would be defending Gilgeam's memory, but that thought made her so angry that she shelved it far away, to be dealt with later.

Massedar led the way through the temple, his accursed Banite gown billowing as he walked. Demok moved behind, carrying the heavy corpse over one shoulder. Despite the bulk of the body, and despite the sweat that trickled down his temples and the breath that labored in his lungs, Demok's face was calm and placid. Kehrsyn trailed, holding Massedar's rain cloak. As she passed a convenient lantern alcove, she quickly stuffed it in the nook. She needed her hands free to do her job, and if they were to pass that way again, they'd either have time to search for the cloak or they'd have concerns far more urgent than getting wet.

In the distance, the reflected light of fires danced along the walls like will-o'-wisps. They heard the sounds of a bawdy Chessentan song reverberating though the temple. The regiment was trying to liven up the dreary evening, but the hollow way the tune echoed among the huge walls of slab marble twisted their cheerful lark into a mournful, ghostlike sound.

Near the center of the great structure, Massedar quickly located the ramps that serviced the lower levels of the temple. One level down was the actual Chessentan base camp, a solemn, military place. Massedar led them lower still. On the next level, the Chessentan officers made their encampment next to a platoon of Thayans. Kehrsyn mused the Thayans had been called in to help ensure the safety of the enclave should Messemprar fall to the pharaoh's forces.

They continued down, past a prison level left empty by the foreigners, save only for a few rowdies held under guard for infractions. A desultory guard stood watch, in all likelihood a punishment in itself, doubly so for the whispers of the cloying stink of death that skulked around the still air at that level.

Two soldiers in full armor and Zhentish tabards stood at the top of the ramp that continued down.

One of them saluted as the group filed past, saying simply, "Ahegi," in respectful greeting.

As they descended, the butcher's smell of the dead grew with every step. They debouched into the bottom level, and Kehrsyn saw that it was dedicated wholly to torture. She realized also that the wide, open ramps would help convey the sounds of the damned to the heart of the temple itself, warping and twisting the screams to provide a macabre backdrop to the worship ceremonies.

The room was very large and open, and lit by a matrix of blood-red candles suspended in black iron chandeliers. The whole of it was filled with a bewildering array of devices of every sort imaginable, and many others of which the operation was so invasive, so cruel, that Kehrsyn's innocent mind could not in the slightest imagine what they actually did.

Between these instruments of torture, the floor of the room was stacked with bodies neatly arranged like firewood. They seemed incongruously peaceful when contrasted with the sinister mechanical shapes of the devices. Two aides staggered at the edge of the stacked remains, carefully placing another corpse.

The torture floor itself was sunken some three feet. A walkway circumnavigated the room, eight feet wide and without a rail. From the walkway the priests of Gilgeam could oversee the torture without having to step in the fluids of the maimed. Steps periodically descended from the walkway to the floor itself, in case a priest saw fit to intervene personally. At the time, though, a large number of Banite priests occupied the walkway, their black-and-green robes whispering and hissing across the stones. None stepped down the stairs, leaving the few workers to finish the arrangement of the bodies.

Behind the walkways on each side were galleries, outfitted with ornate stone seats for those witnesses who grew weary of the victims' resistance. Those stood empty at the moment.

Kehrsyn roused herself. Massedar and Demok were already moving onto the walkway. Kehrsyn marveled at Massedar's ability to disguise himself so thoroughly. Even his gait had become Ekur's. Demok followed behind with perfect ease, apparently unconcerned to be carrying a corpse among a cabal of those he said he'd sworn his life to destroy. Unbidden, Tiglath's words came back to her: *no one is what they seem.* Kehrsyn wondered how far she could trust the self-proclaimed Harper. Unfortunately, in her current situation, she had no choice.

No choice. It was becoming all too common a theme in her life. She hurried after her two companions, doing her best not to look awkward or rushed as she did so.

Massedar stopped toward the far corner of the room, while Demok continued around to where, judging by the ornate design of the robes, the senior cleric stood talking with his subordinates. Demok stepped down onto the torture floor, unwrapped his burden, and lay it on top of a stack in front of the chief priest. With a deft move, he draped a cloth over the corpse's face. Two guards entered with the other body.

Massedar whispered to her, "Tell thou the guards to place that body here before me."

She passed his message along, and, with as much of a shrug as could be managed while hefting a corpse, they placed the body where she indicated. When they unwrapped the oilcloth from the corpse, they saw that the body had been carefully wrapped head to toe in a mummy's bindings. A smell of dust and mildew graced the already inhospitable odors of the room.

"Whoa, been keeping that one for a while, have you, Ahegi?" said one of the bearers with a leer. "Must be someone special. If you need an onyx, just tell one of them," he added, pointing to the several workers who moved among the bodies placing black stones into the mouths of the deceased.

Demok moved back to stand close to Massedar, out of the way in the corner of the gallery.

Kehrsyn joined him there and whispered, "How on

Toril did they get so many bodies? Wouldn't they rot?"

"Embalming," whispered Demok. "Or a prayer that keeps them fresh. Simple work for priests. They've been stockpiling."

Kehrsyn grimaced.

"Zhents are patient," added Demok.

"And . . . tolerant. I don't think I could handle having a dead guy in my—"

"Sshh!"

Kehrsyn looked over and saw that the high priest had stepped to the very edge of the walkway. Everyone in the room ceased their conversations and waited attentively. Silence ruled the room for a long tenbreath, broken only by the sound of a cough heard faintly from the ramp.

The high priest's hood was huge, draping over his shoulders so that only the lower part of his jaw could be seen. Kehrsyn assumed that the material of his black hood was thin enough, at least in places, to allow him to see. His sleeves trailed along the floor, and his gown washed behind him for several feet. Every inch of his robe was stitched with fine sigils and formulae in bright green thread. At a distance it appeared the black material had a green opalescence. Upon his chest he wore a circular ephod emblazoned with Bane's sigil, a clenched fist emitting green rays of power, and in his right hand he bore a long, ornate staff topped with a fist carved in obsidian.

"My servants," began the high priest, and his voice was low, seductive, reasonable, "it is time. No longer shall Unther wallow without a ruler. No longer shall the Untherites, in fear of the pharaoh, turn to other, weaker gods for help. Tonight we shall place Unther under the outstretched arm of Bane. Tonight the army will have a cause to fight for, and a cause greater than mere survival, for no one is willing to die for survival, but all will be willing to die for the glory of Bane. Tonight the Northern Wizards, who stand atop the chaos and proclaim themselves lords, shall have their weakness revealed to all. They shall be torn down and dragged through the streets, to be spat upon by the widows and stoned by the children. Tonight shall the army grow greatly in strength and continue to grow as it smites the forces of the Pharaoh of Mulhorand. Tonight marks the return of the new Empire of Unther, under a new god with a new king!"

Kehrsyn almost moved to applaud at the pause, expecting it to be done, but held herself when she saw that no one else moved.

"We have just spoken with the Chessentans, and they understand that their services have been contracted by Unther, not by any particular faction within Unther. They will not interfere as we move. In fact, I rather fancy they'll be relieved to see a stable government paying their wages."

A chuckle rippled through the assembled priests.

"Let us then begin. Let those who have fallen by the weakness of their government"—he gestured to the carnage at his feet—"be the first to strike a blow for a new power!"

He reached with his free hand into the voluminous sleeve of his other arm and pulled out the familiar thin lines of the Alabaster Staff. Violet swirls of energy began to coalesce as he held it out over the bodies.

CHAPTER TWENTY-TWO

The assembled priests stepped forward to the edge of the walkway with a great rustle of fabric on stone. One cleric, a woman who stood at the right hand of the high priest, intoned a liturgy to lead the others. While the high priest held the Alabaster Staff high, the other priests joined the canter and began to weave their magic.

As they moved through the gestures of the incantation, their hands seemed to draw energy forth from the wand, and the luminescent purplish smoke reached outward in a web of energy until the wisps drifted in the wakes of their hands and the power of the staff covered all the room.

The words and gestures looked like a spell, but whereas most spell invocations lasted a short while, that one continued on and on, the priests droning and moving in unison.

"What kind of ritual is this?" Kehrsyn whispered to Demok.

He gestured with one finger for her to be quiet,

then started to slide stealthily along the wall toward the high priest.

A body in the far corner of the torture floor moved and started to rise, lurching upward from the waist as if a drunkard abruptly awakened. Kehrsyn watched in horror as its limbs flailed around before it found its feet and stood, swaying slightly. A hellish light shone from its open mouth, and a purplish haze wafted from its nostrils like smoke and merged with the web of energy emanating from the Alabaster Staff.

Kehrsyn cast her eyes around the floor in shock and saw several other bodies twitching as the priests' ritual took hold. She glanced over at Massedar and saw that, while he was going through the same motions and appeared to be chanting in unison with all of the others, no magical traceries graced his gestures. She was at once alarmed that he knew the choreography of the ritual and relieved that he was not actually participating.

Other bodies rose up in no apparent order, other than that they were, of course, the ones on top of the hideously quaking pile. One near at hand staggered to her feet, and Kehrsyn saw that it was a geriatric woman, apparently dead of malnutrition, her slack mouth showing her few remaining teeth. She stood like all the others, facing the high priest with the same vile glow shining from her gullet. Somehow the fact that she might have been someone's grandmother made her animation all the more heinous.

Others rose, singly or in pairs, until about four dozen zombies had risen to their feet. The frequency with which they rose was increasing.

Then the body that Demok had carried in began to rise. It shuffled to its feet, the cloth laid across its face sliding off as it stood. It stared at the high priest with dull but undivided attention. Kehrsyn scrunched her face in wary disbelief as she saw its profile.

The high priest started in surprise, his body shuddering

as he saw who stood at his feet. He used the thumb of the hand holding his long Banite staff to jerk back his hood and stared at the zombie with bulging eyes.

"Ahegi!" he gasped. He cast around the room, then found Massedar, dressed in the dead man's garb. He turned toward him, still holding the Alabaster Staff high in his left hand and gesturing with the Banite staff in his right.

"Then who are—"

At that moment, Demok stepped forward and, with a powerful thrust, speared his short sword through the ribs of the high priest. With his left hand, the Harper seized the Alabaster Staff, tearing it from the strands of energy it had woven, and tossed it to Massedar, who caught it with both hands.

The canter at the high priest's right spun toward the attacker, but Demok flipped his short sword high into the air, drew his long sword and beheaded her with one arcing motion, then caught the handle of the spinning short sword in his left hand, blade down. He thrust back with his short sword, skewering the bowels of the priest behind him, then leaped forward and cleaved the priest next to the canter from collarbone to sternum. He yanked the sword from the man's body as the blood began to gush from the mortal wound. All that took place in the space of less than ten of Kehrsyn's frantic heartbeats.

Demok's flurry of mayhem spurred Kehrsyn into action. She drew her dagger and rapier, and, stepping up behind Massedar, placed the point of each blade into the necks of the priests on either side of her employer. They didn't know she didn't have the courage to stab them, and it gave her an excuse not to look at the blood that Demok had just shed.

There was a brief moment of hesitation, and in that empty space Massedar's voice rang out, "Cease ye this folly!"

He held the Alabaster Staff aloft in his right hand, and all the zombies in the room turned to face him, illuminating him with the hellish green glow that shone from their mouths. Silence held the room, save only the feeble, dying groans of the priest.

With a pause in the bloodshed, several of Bane's followers decided to improve their position. To Kehrsyn's left, the priests, threatened by her blade above and the zombies below, pulled back in uncertainty until they better understood their new foes. To her right, the three remaining priests trapped between her and Demok pulled away and tried to slink along the walls past Demok's wary eye to safety. The Harper waited until they were all close, and, with another flurry of bloody blade work, they too, slumped, dead. Kehrsyn glared at Demok.

The priests surged forward, angered by the brutal killings.

"My servants," Massedar crooned to the dead, and his voice carried through the dark murmurs of the Danites, "see ye that none of these children of Bane moves against thy master or his people; whosoever moveth, rend ye his limbs from his body."

As one, the zombies turned to face the Banite priests and moved closer, their dead eyes watching, unblinking.

Kehrsyn glided up to Massedar's right side, the better to gauge the mood of the priests. She flipped her dagger around, catching it by the blade in case she had to throw it.

Massedar spread his arms wide and surveyed the Banite assembly.

"Who am I? thy leader hath asked with his last breath. I am Massedar, even the man whom Ahegi hath betrayed, even the man from whom ye have stolen this very staff. Ye have engendered treason within my house, and ye shall pay for Ahegi's transgression."

He reached up with his free hand and pulled his hood back. He had shaved his head; even his eyebrows were gone. His strong features seemed even more grotesque and alien, free of the concealment of his hair and beard. But most striking was that his forehead bore three circles of blue.

Kehrsyn cast a quick glance over at Demok. She could see he was concerned about the way events had developed, as well.

"Behold!" Massedar cried as he reached into his robe and held aloft a flask filled with a glowing oil. He poured it upon the tightly wrapped mummy that had been laid at his feet.

"Great Bane!" yelled one of the assembled priests. "It's Zimrilim! The High Priest of Gilgeam!"

Massedar—Zimrilim—laughed loudly and nodded to his accuser.

"Certain that is, thou Chemikkassar, formerly of the Northern Wizards," he bellowed. "And wherefore so surprised? Did 'Ahegi' never inform ye that he was named Ekur, second only to me in the cult of Gilgeam? Nay, I perceive that with that omission he left unto himself a way to betray all of ye unto me!"

Kehrsyn edged toward Demok. She stared at Zimrilim and saw no vestige left of his compassionate merchant-prince persona. Its usefulness had ended, and he had cast it aside. She wondered if that would be her fate, as well.

"Ahegi hath seen his treason unmasked," said Zimrilim, "and now shall ye see the same. This plan is but a mewling kitten before my intent. Ye wished to bring your god in to rule over Unther. I say unto ye that Unther needeth no new gods!"

He aimed the Alabaster Staff down at the corpse at his feet. A massive weave of supernatural energy reached forth and caressed the wrapped body.

"Arise!"

The oil-soaked bindings that wrapped the corpse burst asunder in a brilliant flare of light, flying apart with such force that shreds of the canvas flew across the room. Kehrsyn blinked several times to clear her eyes, and she saw the former corpse standing at Zimrilim's feet, shreds of oiled grave wraps still clinging to his skin.

He was tall, well over six feet, with a powerful, military build. Long, flaxen hair, limp and gray with dirt, hung in damp clusters over his shoulders, and a matted beard covered his chest. His skin was the pale blue of the dead and had a wrinkled, desiccated appearance.

His eyes were white and dead, yet even as Kehrsyn looked they began to glow with an evil inner light. Something akin to intelligence began to show through, even though the surface of the glassy eyes remained dull. As she watched, the animate corpse flexed his arms, and huge muscles rippled beneath the dead skin. A sound like creaking leather came as the large muscles strained against the skin, then the flesh covering the muscles split asunder and the undead thing—for he was clearly far more than a zombie—finished his flexing with a grimace that looked part pleasure, part pain.

He bowed his head and flexed his shoulders, and the skin split down his spine. Wherever the skin pulled apart, the layer beneath showed golden, glowing with a soft radiance. The thing groaned—there could be no other word for the deep, burbling utterance that came from his dead lungs—and as he straightened up, he seemed to have grown a foot taller and expanded to twice his original size.

The dirty, matted hair began to wave in an ethereal wind.

Kehrsyn stared in frank amazement at the creature's naked body. The powerful muscles rippled with crisp definition. The lines of the face, jaw, and brow were handsome, even beautiful, without a trace of femininity. Each move was executed with the grace of a dancer. He would have struck her down with desire, had it not been for the dead eyes and the slack, hanging mouth.

"Gilgeam!" hissed a dozen voices in the room, as the priests shrank back in fear.

The animate corpse of the slain god turned to face them, head swaying back and forth like a scenting tiger.

CHAPTER TWENTY-THREE

The moment for which he'd waited so patiently had, at long, long last, arrived.

Zimrilim felt better than he had in years, if not his entire life. No more need he mince his words and actions as the compassionate and sociable Massedar, merchant prince of Wing's Reach. Gone also was his need to imitate the treacherous Ekur, lurching around his conspiracy. The burden of his aliases was vanished. Better yet, the weight of patriotic duty and personal ambition had been taken from his shoulders. He felt light, even giddy, soaring upon his success. With the theft of the Alabaster Staff just days before, it had seemed that his very heart had been ripped from him forever, but, within just a few days, not only had he managed to retrieve the priceless Alabaster Staff, he had the added privilege of grinding his enemies' faces in hopeless defeat. Such a fine extravagance during his moment of victory.

Zimrilim looked at the assembled priests,

held back by the zombies and staring in horror at the return of Gilgeam. A smirk crossed his features. He usually didn't like to show genuine emotion—he considered it a sign of weakness—but that day, of all days, he would indulge himself.

"Now ye ken why thy plans are paltry kittens," he said. "Unther needeth not Bane. Unther hath its devoted lord Gilgeam! And as the people make obeisance unto him, they shall be worshiping me, who maketh the god to dance at my whim."

To prove his point, he aimed the staff at Gilgeam and bent his will to force the dead god to dance.

"As the Empire of Unther drapeth the mantle of its faith upon Gilgeam, he shall yield it unto me, placing it at my feet, and I shall ascend to the divine, with Gilgeam— my avatar—at my right hand! And lo! the powers I shall unleash upon the Pharaoh of Mulhorand and upon the followers of Bane who darken the thresholds of the Untherites' doors shall be utterly without mercy!

"Gilgeam!" he shouted. He focused his energy on directing the powerful beast, and even with the ancient necromantic artifact, it was difficult. "Smite the heretics!"

Gilgeam raised his hands, fingers spread with thumbs touching, and launched a bolt of raw divine power at the thickest congregation of priests. The sound of a thunderclap drowned out the screams of Bane's devoted as they perished. The other priests stampeded for the ramp, their flight harried by the zombies that reached up and gripped at their ankles with a strength only attainable by the dead.

Let them flee, thought Zimrilim. They can flee neither far enough nor fast enough to escape my wrath.

He redirected the staff's energies toward the priests that Gilgeam had just slain, and they, too, rose up. Gilgeam paused in his destruction, but Zimrilim cared not. He chuckled as he watched his new servants rise.

Why, he thought, I shall send those who know the

Zhents best to kill them, and therewith gain more to serve me.

He paused to survey the room. In the corners of the walkway, clusters of zombies struck and tore at groups of trapped priests. Several other priests, rather more brave than those who'd fled, called down the wrath of Bane upon Gilgeam, but the god-animate seemed only enraged by their efforts. He strode over and struck one of the priests with his bare fist, punching his sternum so hard that the breaking of a score of ribs resounded in the torture chamber.

The god-thing was acting without direction, but Zimrilim cared not. For a few moments—ages to the Banites, but less to him—Zimrilim let Gilgeam run unfettered by his authority. The priest swirled the staff to drag more corpses to a semblance of life and aim their directionless hunger toward the Banite priests. But then he felt the wrath of Gilgeam rising, threatening to erupt, and he felt the dead mind of the deity slowly turning his fury on him, the master. He applied his willpower against Gilgeam's, using the Alabaster Staff as a fulcrum. It was difficult, tasking work, but the outcome for one such as him was unavoidable, and Gilgeam was brought back to heel.

At that moment, Kehrsyn flung herself at him, wrapping her arms around him, grinding her pelvis into his hip.

"O my lord!" she cried. "Make me thy queen! I shall see to the safety of everything that is thine for as long as I shall live."

"What?" sneered Zimrilim. "Thinkest thou I have need of thy petty skills, when my apotheosis is at hand?"

Kehrsyn's eyes widened, and tears started to form at the corners of her eyes.

"But . . . but my lord, I thought you loved me—or at least found me attractive . . ."

Zimrilim snorted. "Prefer I my women cold and obedient," he said.

Kehrsyn quailed in shock and horror, but in the blink of an eye she abandoned her ruse, and, prying his middle finger back, she wrested the Alabaster Staff from his grasp with a move that was as fast and sure as an owl's strike. She turned to flee, but he seized hold of her thick hair and wrenched her around to face him again, yanking her head back to expose her jugular.

"Return thou the staff, whelp," he hissed, pulling her head farther back, "lest I raise thee to serve me more *personally*."

Kehrsyn whimpered in pain and offered the staff back to him with a trembling hand.

Taking the thin wand back, he threw Kehrsyn to the torture floor, where she landed on a pile of twitching, squirming, almost-animate bodies. He turned to look at Gilgeam, once again threatening to run amok.

He raised the Alabaster Staff to bring the boastful deity back under his thrall. He glanced at the staff itself.

That's odd, he thought, *I don't remember it having a crack . . .*

Though it bridled him not to fall upon the high priest of Gilgeam with a whirlwind of steel, Demok held himself back as she had bidden. It was all but impossible not to attack, though it would mean his death, and instead watch a lovely young girl put herself in grave danger.

She moved in, pleading and cajoling, and though Demok could not hear a word, her actions communicated her tack clearly, worming into Zimrilim's weakness through offering her beauty and praising his power.

He scowled. If she'd had the time to tell him her plan, he would have told her not to try. He knew Zimrilim far better than she did. Even though his true identity was a surprise to the Harper, the fundamentals of his brutal personality had leaked out over the years.

Demok moved closer, scanning the room. It was clear that Zimrilim no longer cared who was killed and when. The zombies were acting indiscriminately. He smote first one, and another that reached its pallid, dead arms toward him.

He glanced up and saw Kehrsyn make a grab for the Alabaster Staff. She pried it out of the priest's grip and turned to dash away. Demok moved to cover her escape, bulling his way through the zombies that occupied the walkway. Then, from the corner of his eye, he saw Zimrilim hurl Kehrsyn from his presence. The young thief tumbled in midair and landed on her back atop a soft cushion of twitching, squirming corpses.

Zimrilim had taken back the staff.

With a curse, Demok leaped toward her. She rolled over to her hands and knees, shaken but not hurt. Thank the gods, he thought.

He moved next to her, his swords drawn and ready.

"Nice try," he said, speaking loudly to be heard over the din.

It was not false praise. She'd come within a hair's breadth of disarming the most dangerous villain Demok had ever seen. There remained no options left but the sword. He rose up and began to advance, his short sword ready to parry, his long sword held behind him, swaying gently.

"No!" shouted Kehrsyn, grabbing his leg. "Don't!"

Demok turned and snarled down at her, "Let go!"

"I succeeded!" hissed Kehrsyn, trying to make herself heard above the sounds of slaughter but not speaking so loudly that Zimrilim might hear.

"What?"

She grabbed the front of his vest and yanked him down.

"I got it!" she said, flashing just a bit of the bone-colored wand that protruded from her sleeve.

How? thought Demok.

Then he remembered how she'd palmed not only a coin into his glove but a dagger out of his scabbard, and hidden all before he could see.

He glanced up at Zimrilim. The Gilgeamite priest held the Alabaster Staff—at least, it looked like he did—but he was inspecting a portion of its handle. He raised it again and pointed it at Gilgeam, but the undead god-animate did not obey. Instead, he bellowed some war cry, ancient words turned inarticulate by a dead tongue, and advanced on Zimrilim.

"Right," said Demok. "Follow me. Now!"

He charged toward the torture room's exit, working his twin blades to clear as wide a path for Kehrsyn as possible. He focused on disarming the zombies in a very literal sense. He trusted Kehrsyn's agility and balance to see her safely through the press of dead flesh, so long as they couldn't grasp and overpower her.

It was grisly work, maiming that which was already dead, and the smell was doubly unpleasant, but the virtue of his task gave him strength.

The efforts of the last remaining cluster of Zhents helped him win a way through, for as he neared the ramp several zombies were caught between his blades and the Zhents' maces and spells.

With a glance of thanks, the Zhents began to run up the ramp. Demok checked to ensure that nothing had waylaid Kehrsyn, then followed, the young woman close on his heels.

As they ran, he switched his swords from one hand to the other, and, as the Zhents ahead approached a corner of the ramp, he hurled his short sword at the rearmost. The blade plunged into the man's kidney as he reached the corner, felling him. Demok snatched up the blade as he ran past, giving it an extra twist to ensure the Zhent never rose again.

Kehrsyn shrieked in disgust and empathic pain.

At the next corner, another of the Zhents glanced back and noticed that their companion wasn't following. He paused and called out to him, then abruptly ceased as Demok's long sword took off his head. Too late the Zhent's hand raised to block the attack; then the body toppled.

Demok heard Kehrsyn cry out in shock.

"Will you quit that?" she yelled from behind.

"No," growled Demok.

As they approached the level of the Chessentan encampment, one of the Zhents paused for just a moment, yelling, "To arms! To arms!"

Demok and Kehrsyn caught up with her, and, as they did so, Demok speared his short sword up through the woman's ribs and into her heart.

He threw her body to the floor and yelled, "Fall back! Get help! Now!"

An explosion rocked the foundation of the temple, and a tremendous gout of flame licked up the ramps, spending the last of its energy trying to turn the corner below them. There followed a long, ululating howl, a hollow cry mixed of agony and triumph.

Demok looked at Kehrsyn and said, "He's coming. We need help. Lots of help."

Kehrsyn looked at him, at the body at his feet, back down the ramp, then at Demok again.

"I know where to get help," said Kehrsyn, shivering. "At least I hope I do. Come on."

She led him out of the temple at a run.

They fled outside as another tremor rocked the temple, but despite the trembling foundation Kehrsyn drew up short, staring at the sky. Demok looked up. Gone were the gusty winds that had blown their cloaks around when they'd ridden over. The air was absolutely still. Straight above them the moon and stars shone brightly in a clear sky, but farther away Demok saw the clouds thick and bunched, lightning arcing between them. It was as if a drop of oil had fallen upon the sky, clearing the air as it spread and pushing the angry clouds back. Even as he watched, he saw the clouds being pressed farther away, roiling intensely.

It reminded him of the eye of the storm in the one hurricane he'd experienced.

"The world is making room for the return of a god," Kehrsyn said, awe-struck.

"I'd just as soon it didn't," swore Demok, and he charged down the steps for the wagon, whose driver was staring at the sky, ignoring the skittish horses.

Demok leaped up into the driver's seat, his body slamming the hired help off the far side. Kehrsyn hopped into the wagon behind him.

"I hope your help is good," Demok yelled, as he whipped the horses into motion.

☉

Demok yanked hard on the reins, pulling the horses up short and causing the wagon to slew to a stop. Kehrsyn hopped from the rear, frankly thankful that she—they—had arrived in one piece. She bounded up the steps and pounded on the door, though her slender hands and none-too-brawny arms made no more than a small noise on the thick wood.

With a growl, Demok leaped from the driver's seat and bounded up.

He slammed the door open wide, stepped in, and yelled, "Hey! High priestess! C'mere! Now!"

Three Tiamatans inside rose at the sudden disturbance and came glowering over to Demok. One brandished a cudgel, and another drew a wide dagger, serrated like a dragon's teeth.

"Mudsucker," said one as they closed in, "you just got a whole heap of—"

Before he could finish the sentence, Demok lunged into action. He drew his weapons as he kicked the leader in the groin, cracked the pommel of his long sword against the back of the man's skull as he doubled over, and charged in on the other two, jamming one against the wall of the cloak-room with his short sword held across the man's neck, while the other found the point of a long sword probing the skin of his solar plexus.

"No," hissed Demok, "I am a whole heap of trouble!"

"Announce Kehrsyn and Demok here to see Tiglath," said Kehrsyn, showing a poise that surprised even her, given the situation. "I have her sufferance, and you will not harm this man."

"I can see that," said the Tiamatan pressed against the wall.

The third man sheathed his dagger and gently pushed the point of Demok's long sword away from his stomach.

"I'll get her," he said.

"Tell them they're here on urgent business," added the man against the wall.

"While we wait, why don't you put down your club and help your friend here?" asked Kehrsyn.

The man nodded and dropped his weapon, then care-fully moved to his fallen comrade and helped him to the rel-ative safety of one corner of the cloakroom.

That done, Kehrsyn leaned over to Demok and said, "Please put your weapons away. Tiglath won't take the sight of them very well."

"Tough," grunted Demok.

"She'll take it as poorly as you would," elaborated Kehrsyn.

Demok considered that, then sheathed his weapons qui-etly and efficiently. Kehrsyn noticed, however, that he rested his hand on the pommel of the quick-drawing short sword. Just in case.

In just a few moments, Tiglath came bustling along,

wrapped in a thick robe. Her little dragonet sat on her shoulder, flexing its wings to keep its balance as she walked.

"My dear," she said, "I'm coming to think that you're a storm crow."

"You don't know the half of it," said Kehrsyn. Tiglath cocked her head. "The guy I work for, it turns out he's Zimrilim, and he brought back Gilgeam."

"Gods, no . . ." Tiglath gasped. "You—you're jesting!"

"He must have kept the body hidden all these years, and he used this ancient magical wand and these potions and—"

"Zimrilim," echoed Tiglath, still with a tinge of disbelief, "resurrected Gilgeam?"

Demok shook his head and replied, "No, not resurrected. More like . . . animated. Mummy, perhaps."

"Yeah, like that," said Kehrsyn. "He was all wrapped up and stuff, and he just ripped his way out of the wrappings and grew in size and—"

"Fiery hells," swore Tiglath, "he . . . *animated . . . a god?* To be his *pawn?*"

"Yep," said Demok.

Tiglath put her hands to her head as if to keep it from exploding under the pressure of that new revelation.

"He must be mad . . . " the priestess said, speaking primarily to herself.

"Well, yeah," said Kehrsyn.

"To even think of forcing a dead god back into its corpse is . . . is unconscionable. Only the very highest undead would be capable of holding Gilgeam's intellect. Such an act . . . even creating a greater undead being . . . it would excise the higher levels of the corpse's mind, leaving only the basest and most violent processes in place." She looked up at Kehrsyn and Demok, as if remembering their existence. "That's the basis of animation, you know. You take a human and stimulate only the basest, most animalistic desires, their simplest instincts of hate and hunger. It makes them easier to control and ensures their hostility if they are encountered out of one's control. Doing that to a divine being like Gilgeam would be insane. Think of all of the heinous acts he committed in his life, when he had some semblance of self-control! How much more, then, when his higher brain is wiped away, leaving only a vague sense that nothing is right within his own mind!"

"Well, that would pretty much fit with what we saw," observed Kehrsyn.

"Didn't like having a master," observed Demok.

"And Zimrilim, after all these years! I knew we should have searched harder for his body!"

"Don't bother," said Demok.

Tiglath rocked back on her heels, looking up to the ceiling. "So if what you said is true, Zimrilim made him some sort of greater undead, which means he'll have all of his instincts and many of his mental faculties. He won't have much of a sense of identity, which means we won't be able to reason with him. He is almost certainly mad . . . not that he wasn't mad enough already when he was alive."

Tiglath turned to her followers and said, "Full combat regalia, people, move!" She looked back at her visitors and shook her head slowly. "There will be a lot of blood tonight. We have to do our best for Unther, but even if we succeed there may not be enough left of Messemprar to interest the pharaoh anymore. Last time we fought Gilgeam, we had the Dragon Queen Tiamat herself at our side. Now all we have is a city full of tired, hungry refugees and defeated soldiers."

"And we have this," said Kehrsyn, pulling out the Alabaster Staff. "You seem the best bet to carry it. I just hope you can figure out how to use it."

Tiglath took the long, slender wand and turned it over in her hands, whistling through her teeth. She glanced askance at Kehrsyn, a glint in her eye.

"Would this happen to be the 'ancient mystical wand' that you mentioned earlier, young one?"

Kehrsyn grinned, but her pride in her accomplishment shone through in her eyes.

"Yeah," she said from the corner of her mouth.

Tiglath rocked back on her heels with a self-satisfied smile and said, "I'm greatly pleased to find that my trust in you was not misplaced, young one." She handed the staff back. "Come with me, and tell me everything you know about it while I don my armor. You," she added, turning to Demok. She paused, then fluttered a hand at the two Tiamatans in the corner of the cloakroom. "Make sure those two get their armor on right away."

Demok laughed between his teeth and said, "Armor. Right."

CHAPTER TWENTY-FOUR

The still night's air echoed with the sounds Messemprar had dreaded for over a year: screams of pain and anguish, the whip-crack of fires burning out of control, the ring of martial horns, the shouts and imprecations of soldiers fighting a determined last stand. The scents of smoke, blood, and fear filtered their way through the city.

It was cold consolation that the sounds were not caused by the pharaoh's army. Many in the city would choose defeat over the return of Gilgeam.

Kehrsyn and Demok walked with Tiglath at the head of the Tiamatan cultists, marching in formation and arrayed for war. Their heavy scale (was there any armor better suited to dragon worshipers? thought Kehrsyn) clanked as they strode forward. Most carried war picks or maces with the heads shaped into dragon's heads. A few others had wide-bladed swords with fanciful dragon's head hand guards shaped to make the serrated blades look like fire emitting from the mouths. In the center of the squad, five fighters carried arbalests, crossbows so powerful that they required winches to be cocked. Kehrsyn's keen eyes caught the sheen of silver coating the quarrels they carried in open cases at their hips.

Every Tiamatan in the group carried a large, pentagonal shield embossed and painted with the symbol of a five-headed dragon, each head in a different color.

Throughout the city, fearful citizens peered out of windows to see what was happening. They watched as the Tiamatan force moved through the streets, then withdrew again to bar the doors and windows and whisper among themselves.

Tiglath moved in Demok's shadow, trusting the experienced swordsman to keep her safe. She kept her head bowed over the Alabaster Staff, working spells of revelation to better understand the artifact she held in her hand. Tremor, her dragonet, clutched her armor and craned his neck forward as well, sniffing at the artifact. Under the coaxing of her magic, the powerful glow of the wand's aura provided more than enough light for everyone to see. Tiglath had to squint even to look at the staff.

The sounds of sporadic battle grew louder, until Demok held up one hand and clenched it into a fist.

"Hold," he said. He turned to Tiglath, shielding his eyes from the bright glow of the staff. "Time," he said.

Tiglath set her jaw and nodded. She turned to her people, clasping her hands behind her back. The staff silhouetted her body, giving her a sort of bright halo.

"This will be hard," she said. "We are going up against our enemy of old, as we did fifteen years ago. We do not have our goddess at our side, only each other and whatever other soldiers have gathered together to oppose Gilgeam's return. Of course, more people won't do much good. We are fighting a single being, after all. Fortunately, Gilgeam probably does not have his full faculties. Also fortunately, we will receive his undivided attention when he sees the blazons on our shields. This puts him right where we want him, which is enraged and unthinking, within reach of our weapons."

She raised her hand, spreading her fingers and curling them slightly. Kehrsyn noticed that she did not spread her thumb wide, but held it fairly close, so that her hand as a whole looked somewhat like five serpentine necks bending forward to strike.

"Bear your shields proudly, followers of the dragon, and trust to our goddess, whose face taunts our foe, to guide your strikes."

As Tiglath lowered her hand again, Kehrsyn leaned in toward her and asked, "Why don't you pray for protection?"

One of the cultists overheard her and answered, "Only the weak need protection. The strong can withstand great pain and punishment."

Well, I guess that means only the weak need to wear heavy armor, now doesn't it? thought Kehrsyn, but she wisely held her tongue.

Tiglath formed her people up into two lines, shoulder to shoulder. She held the center of the front line, and the five with arbalests took the center of the second line. Working the cranks, they cocked their weapons. The wood groaned as it bent, seemingly in anticipation of launching a deadly projectile. They loaded their quarrels into the slots.

"Wow," murmured Kehrsyn, "I've seen silver-tipped arrows but not ones covered completely in silver."

"They're solid," said Tiglath. "No sense being cheap with plated bolts. I'd rather save my life than save a few coins."

"Makes sense," said Kehrsyn.

"Stand aside, young one," said Tiglath. "You weren't made for this kind of fight."

"What?" blurted Kehrsyn. "You expect me to just—"

Demok grabbed Kehrsyn's arm and pulled her to the side.

"Good luck," he said to the priestess as he ushered Kehrsyn off the street. "We'll look for an opening."

Reluctantly, Kehrsyn followed Demok away from the Tiamatans.

Tiglath raised the Alabaster Staff over her head and shouted, "Shields front! Forward!" The double line moved down the street, less rapidly than before but with a ponderous martial sedateness that was at once fearsome and enthralling. They held their shields in front, creating a solid wall of steel, crenellated at the top edge due to the varying heights of the warriors and saw-toothed at the bottom from the dropping points of each shield that protected the bearers' knees. With grim and deadly eyes they advanced, their path illuminated by the interaction of the staff with the divinatory spells that Tiglath had cast upon it.

Demok led Kehrsyn along the edge of the street just ahead of the Tiamatans. As they closed on Gilgeam's position, it became apparent that the magical light would be unnecessary. The dead god stood in the center of a small square, raising his arms and bellowing to the heavens. Bodies littered the courtyard, and a large resting house and tavern across from them was engulfed in flames, lighting the quad and silhouetting Gilgeam's rippling body and lank locks in an eerie glow. The flames reflected across the cobbles and the armor of the slain as well and made it impossible to tell what was rainwater and what was blood.

A barrage of arrows struck Gilgeam in the back. The beast—for it was hard to think of him as either human or deity—roared in defiance and turned to face his attackers. A squad of archers occupied the roof of one of the buildings, a tall, thin residential building situated on the corner formed by the court and one of the streets that led into it. The archers fired another volley, the arrows striking Gilgeam in the chest. If anything, the missiles served only to enrage him further. He moved over in a peculiar, looming gait and slid between the building and its neighbor, then began to growl with exertion.

The archers moved to the narrow gap between the buildings, aimed their bows straight down, and fired a volley at Gilgeam's head.

They fired another.

As they nocked their arrows for a third volley, the building shuddered and the archers panicked. They started to run, but Gilgeam's strength prevailed, and the building cracked and began to lean. Then, slowly, gracefully, the building pirouetted and fell to the ground like a dancer bowing before her judges.

As that happened and fresh screams of pain and fear rang through the court, the detachment of Tiamatans drew to a halt. They stood just inside the small courtyard, blocking the street and preventing Gilgeam from attacking them anywhere but from the front. Demok led Kehrsyn to the dubious shelter of a recessed doorway that faced the square.

"Wait for it," he said.

Tiglath looked around, appraising the damage. Her eyes alighted on a group of Untherites to the left of her troops, all kneeling in prayer.

"Great Mother," shouted Tiglath, "they're praying to that thing! Gibbur, smite those cowards!"

"Aye," grunted the leftmost soldier in the front row.

He was a big chap, and burly, and he gripped his serrated sword in clear anticipation as he paced over to those who lent Gilgeam their support and worship in exchange for a chance to receive his dubious mercy.

By the light of the fires, Kehrsyn saw that Gibbur's work was brutally fast. He stood in front of the kneeling lines of worshipers and hewed heads with rhythmic, almost mechanical efficiency. Grotesquely, his butchery only redoubled the fervent prayers of those still alive.

Perhaps it was chance, perhaps it was the smell of fresh blood or the cries of the slaughtered, or perhaps somehow the desperate prayers of the faithful wormed their way into the decayed brain of the undead deity, but after Gibbur began executing the worshipers, the god-king turned around and faced him with a feral snarl.

"Gibbur!" snapped Tiglath.

The Tiamatan turned to his priestess, then glanced over at Gilgeam. The god-king started to trot over, and, seeing that, Gibbur broke into a run for his comrades. Gilgeam howled, picked up a large stone from the wreckage of the building, and hurled it at Gibbur with great force. Its trajectory looked almost flat. Several people called warnings, but just as Gibbur turned to look, the missile struck him in the ribs with a crunch that was both metallic and all too organic. He was knocked sideways off his feet, dead before his helmet clanged to the pavement.

Kehrsyn drew in her breath between her teeth.

"Yep," said Demok, beside her in the shadows. "This'll be tough."

Gilgeam moved toward Tiglath's troops, eyeing the row of armored warriors arrayed against him.

"Tiamat says you have no place in Faerûn," called Tiglath, stressing the name of her goddess, "and we will ensure you obey!"

So saying, she brandished the Alabaster Staff and focused her mind upon it.

The words caused a visible reaction in the once-dead god-king. He stiffened and flexed his muscles so hard Kehrsyn could hear the tendons creaking and popping. Gilgeam wagged his jaw as if to say something, but he looked more like an animal trying to work something free from its craw. He continued his approach, slipping back and forth between an upright, martial posture and somewhat sideways, animal posture. Both gaits were still suffused with the shuffling, inelegant motions of the animate dead. But most striking were his eyes, which shone with fierce hatred and cunning, a look all the more horrid for the pale, magical glow that shone from them.

"Looks like he's beginning to reclaim himself," warned Tiglath.

"What?" asked Kehrsyn.

"Getting his mind back," clarified Demok.

"He's got the hunger and will of a god in there some-where," said Tiglath. "If we let him go, he may recover everything, and we'll lose all our work. Look alive, people, and stay alive."

Tiglath drew a deep, focusing breath and let it back out slowly through rounded lips. She inclined the Alabaster Staff toward Gilgeam. She set her jaw and narrowed her eyes with concentration.

Gilgeam hissed through his spasming mouth, a noise far juicier than anyone had expected. He approached Tiglath, his arms outstretched and his fingers hooked like claws, yet, for as much as his powerful legs strained, the pace of his approach slowed dramatically. Even though she wasn't entirely familiar with the artifact, Tiglath's willpower, channeled through the Alabaster Staff, held the creature at bay.

From the shadows to the side of the Tiamatan line, Kehrsyn watched the confrontation. Tiglath showed strain. The side of her mouth pulled back into a rictus snarl, her eyes narrowed further, and sweat began to trickle down her face. Gilgeam leaned farther forward toward the priest-ess, his bare feet scrabbling on the slick cobbles. His muscles tensed and flexed beneath his golden skin, and his toes pried up a cobble from the sheer power of his body pushing forward against the magical resistance. He stumbled, but then his feet found extra hold, planted in the empty socket left by the paving stone. He inched closer to Tiglath and strained his arms to reach her.

"Strike him," growled Tiglath through clenched teeth.

"This is your chance to prove you have the strength to lead us," responded the high-browed, bulbous-nosed cultist to Tiglath's right. "You're doing well so far. Don't throw it away by crying for help."

Kehrsyn blanched.

With an irritated growl, Demok stalked out from the shadows beside Kehrsyn and moved behind Gilgeam.

For just an instant, Tiglath glanced at the man who had spoken.

With a victorious howl from the grave, Gilgeam leaped.

⊙

Gilgeam's leap seemed slow, as if seen in a dream, and Tiglath wasn't sure if it was because she was in such a state of excitement or if the magical effects of the staff actually slowed Gilgeam's flight through the air.

He landed on the priestess, driving her to her knees. His eyes, inches from hers, had a strange look to them, like he saw nothing but sensed everything. Just as she recovered her balance, his right hand clubbed at her, a horse's kick smashing her shield back against her chest. The shield buckled with the impact, and her entire arm went mercifully numb. His left hand grabbed her right forearm, squeezed, and twisted. She fought to hold onto the Alabaster Staff, but she felt the bones in her arm snap. Pain shot up her arm, and the staff tumbled from her nerveless hand and clattered on the rain-washed cobbles, its magical glow showing strangely blue in the firelit night.

Gilgeam howled—a grotesque, burbling noise from a slack mouth that smelled of myrrh and mold—and used Tiglath's broken arm to drive her to the ground.

So this is it, she thought. After all this time, he finally kills me.

She spat in the god-king's lifeless face.

Then she saw Demok loom over him, his sword raised

high. He struck Gilgeam in the shoulder with a mighty blow of his long sword, but the edge hardly bit the flesh. Gilgeam wildly swung one arm backward, catching Demok in the ribs and sending him tumbling away.

❂

Finally seeing his opportunity to supplant Tiglath as the leader of the Tiamatans, Horat snatched up the Alabaster Staff from where it lay. He felt the raw power of the wand, the weight of its age, and the surge of potential.

"Kill him!" he cried to the others, gesturing at Gilgeam.

The assembled Tiamatans obeyed his command. They encircled Gilgeam and lay into him with picks and swords and maces. It was a peculiar sound, more like a mining crew than a battle. A battle had a lot of screams and yelling, but here one side only rarely made noise, and the mortal soldiers, when struck by Gilgeam, often had no voice left.

With the others doing his bidding, Horat stepped back and aimed the slender wand at the body of Gibbur where he had been felled. Magical streams of energy curled from the carved runes and Gibbur began to twitch. He climbed back to his feet and stared at Horat with vacant, obedient eyes.

Horat laughed, a loud, glorious peal—he knew the power of the staff, a far greater power than he had imagined, and it felt good to let it channel through his soul. He'd been aide to a sodden cow of a priestess long enough. No more gutless decisions. He ruled the Tiamatans. And with this staff, come morning, the Tiamatans would rule Unther!

❂

Kehrsyn, hoping the Tiamatan assault could bring the god-king down, scuttled over to Demok's side.

"That's not meat," he grunted as he staggered to his feet. "Feels like clay."

"He's made of clay?" gasped Kehrsyn.

Demok gave her a wearying look and said, "He's made of god!"

Kehrsyn looked over at the melee and saw one of the Tiamatans surge upward two feet in the air, his head thrown way back on his broken neck. There was another animal roar and a metal impact, and Kehrsyn saw several of the Tiamatans along one side stagger back from the force of Gilgeam's strength.

The man with the wand aimed it in the direction of Gilgeam and began chanting a prayer to Tiamat. Beyond him, Kehrsyn saw Gibbur, gripping his sword inexpertly and shuffling toward the melee.

"In the name of Tiamat, the all-powerful Dragon Queen," Tiglath's rebellious lieutenant shouted, "I command you, Gilgeam, to cease your resistance and obey your new master!"

Gilgeam roared his displeasure and struck one of the Tiamatans so forcibly that his fellows behind were knocked off their feet, creating a breach in the circle of armored warriors, a breach that led straight to the one with the Alabaster Staff. Gilgeam stepped out of that gap, stomping one foot upon the throat of a fallen cultist, killing him.

As Gilgeam stepped forward, the circle of Tiamatans moved with him, though for the moment they did not engage. They left behind a number of mangled bodies, most of which did not move. Demok and Kehrsyn ran over to where Tiglath had fallen.

☙

Tiglath cursed the usurper Horat for a fool, dividing their forces at that crucial moment against an enemy far more important than his own designs for power. She cursed herself, as well, for letting his ill-timed ploy distract her from her true duty.

She lay on the ground, holding her shield up with her numb left arm while using her feet and her right elbow to try to crawl out of the melee. She felt Gilgeam strike her shield again, but then a veritable stampede of metal-shod feet surrounded them both. She winced, her eyes almost closed, as the cleated boots scrabbled for traction a hair's breadth from her face.

She heard scuffling, impacts, and a non-stop stream of grunts and curses as her people—if indeed she could call them that anymore—battled the monster. The sounds were punctuated by fierce impacts as Gilgeam claimed victim after victim. One of the unfortunates fell across her legs. His angry face landed nose-first on the pavement beside her, bouncing none too gently. Drool and blood flowed slowly from his open mouth.

With one arm numb and encumbered by a shield in the midst of a tight melee and the other broken outright, she could not shove the armored corpse off her, so she resorted to keeping as small as possible and using her shield to protect her head from being stepped upon or struck by an errant blow.

After what seemed an eternity of stomping feet and meaty blows, the melee moved away from Tiglath, leaving her gasping in pain on the cold, wet cobbles. Her tiny dragonet alighted on her helmet and began licking her face.

Through the flaring haze of pain, she saw two silhouettes kneel beside her.

"Are you all right?" asked Kehrsyn.

Tiglath nodded. She knew it was not convincing.

Demok kicked the corpse off her, and she rolled onto her back with a sigh of relief and exhaustion. He kneeled by her head.

"My blade," he ordered. "Enchant it!"

Enchant his blade? thought Tiglath. That would take a

season or more . . . No, she corrected herself, he means *bless* it. Confer upon it the divine prowess of Tiamat, Queen of Dragons, that, imbued with her divine wrath, his bare steel might cleave the useless flesh of the god-king. There was just one problem . . .

"You don't serve Tiamat," gasped Tiglath.

"I don't care," said Demok.

Tiglath tried to ponder whether it might work, whether it might be sacrilege for her to do that, but her pain was too great.

"Good enough," she muttered.

She shucked the shield from her left arm with a few careless flailings and reached for the chain around her neck. She felt along the length of the chain for the holy symbol that dangled there. She held it forth and touched Demok's blade.

"May Tiamat," she slurred, trying to keep her voice steady, "as well as whichever deity you follow, guide thy blade that we might smite our mutual foe. May the strength of the dragon be yours."

❂

As Tiglath prayed, Kehrsyn looked over to where the remaining Tiamatans fought against Gilgeam. She saw the god-king grab the one with the Alabaster Staff by the hips. The Tiamatan screamed in terror as he looked into Gilgeam's undead face. Gilgeam lifted him up and slung him down, crushing him headfirst onto the cobbles, abruptly ending his scream. She closed her eyes, glad that the sound of crunching metal drowned out the other, more visceral noises.

The Tiamatan closest to Gilgeam took a step back. His show of fear spread quickly, and the other Tiamatans who still had their feet all began giving ground. Gilgeam grinned at them, and, though his flesh was pockmarked by numerous dents and gashes from the Tiamatan weapons, he seemed to have no discomfort.

"We're running out of time and allies," said Kehrsyn, deeply worried.

Even as she spoke, Demok moved forward, waving his sword, gripping it with both hands for extra power. As the blade moved, Kehrsyn saw tracers of divine energy glittering in its wake.

Gilgeam moved toward the Tiamatans, who fell back before him. Demok circled in behind and delivered a heavy, double-handed blow, striking the god-king in the side, just below the floating rib. The blade bit deep, though by no means as deep as it would have any ordinary man.

Thus wounded, Gilgeam screamed, a noise that sounded more alive than any utterance he had yet made, and Demok jerked the blade free of the undead creature's body, trailing a strand of viscous black blood behind it.

Gilgeam turned to face Demok, a new anger on his face, and to Kehrsyn it looked like Demok had succeeded in finally awakening the intellect within the undead casing. Her heart caved in fear for Demok's life.

Demok circled around Gilgeam, while the god-king turned in place, one hand over the oozing wound in his side.

The swordsman moved easily, swinging the glistening blade back and forth in easy arcs. He launched himself at Gilgeam again, striking a pair of vicious blows, one of which struck Gilgeam's knee and the other of which the undead god-king blocked with his bare arm. The momentum of Demok's attack had brought him in close to Gilgeam, too close, in Kehrsyn's opinion, for him to fight effectively with his sword.

But that wasn't his intent. With a nimble flick of his foot, he flipped the Alabaster Staff from the dead lieutenant's hand over toward Tiglath. Though he executed the maneuver almost perfectly, he paid for the shift in his attention as

Gilgeam punched him hard, one arm striking his ribs from the right, the other striking his stomach from the left. The impact flipped Demok completely over, and he fell to the ground, his sword clattering away.

Kehrsyn, kneeling by Tiglath's head, tried to pull the heavy priestess up to a sitting position.

"The staff!" she yelled. "Use it!"

"I can't," gasped Tiglath through clenched teeth, her eyelids fluttering. "Too . . . run, Kehrsyn," she added, panting. "Don't let him wreck your life . . . like he wrecked mine."

Kehrsyn glanced up. The few remaining Tiamatans were fleeing the area. A company of guards had appeared at some point during the fight and had taken up position across the courtyard. They seemed to be awaiting Gilgeam's victory. Demok was moving slowly on his hands and knees, trying to recover his breath. Gilgeam stalked over, roaring in his ghastly, flat voice, balling his fists for the final strike.

Desperate, Kehrsyn let Tiglath go and lunged for the Alabaster Staff. She dived and tumbled, snatching up the slender wand in one hand without losing her momentum, and ran toward Gilgeam. She knew she could not wield the wand, not without years of arcane discipline. Her only hope was more direct action. All she had to do was cross fifteen yards. Gilgeam raised his fists, and she saw that she would be about five yards too late.

A small shadow darted past her with the sound of fluttering parchment. Tremor swept in on its tiny wings and fired a gout of bright flame across Gilgeam's eyes just as he was flexing his arms to kill Demok. Gilgeam roared again, stumbling with surprise, yielding to Kehrsyn the extra sliver of time she needed.

She ran up behind the god-king as he stared down at Demok. She plunged the Alabaster Staff into Gilgeam, narrow end first, driving it upward between the ribs, aiming for the heart. It slid in much more easily than she had expected, every bit as easily as if it had been her rapier and he no more than a straw man. She had put everything she had into the blow, and it plunged the staff almost entirely into Gilgeam's body, leaving only the carved top still in her grip.

The undead thing roared and arched his back. Kehrsyn, in fear and surprise, tried to pull the wand back out, but between her haste and his motion, the wand caught between his ribs. She panicked, yanked, and felt the wand bend, levered against Gilgeam's bones.

There was the sound of a small crack.

There was a flash so bright the whole world seemed white.

Then there was nothing.

Demok walked stiffly, trying not to strain his rib cage. Despite the bandages that tightly bound his broken ribs together, the freedom of motion he needed to breathe was motion enough to cause himself pain. The magic of the healers had helped knit the bones back together—in all likelihood they had saved his life—but he was still an injured man.

It was closing on high noon, and the sun shone weakly in the winter sky. It was nice to see it again, to know that indeed it had been lurking behind the clouds the past few tendays. His skin felt warm where the sun hit it, if only for a moment before the chilly breeze swept the sensation away again.

He walked outside Messemprar, his boots making small squishing noises in the muddy cart track that led from the city to the Hill of the River. The hill's name did not refer to the River of Metals, which flowed behind him, slowly and gracefully heading toward the Alamber Sea, heedless of the small, short, squabbling lives of the mortals who encamped by its shores. The name instead spoke of the river that was said to separate life from afterlife.

To his mind, the only such river the Untherites ought to believe in was the river of blood that had marked Gilgeam's rule for the past two and a half millennia.

The Hill of the River was far enough from the city that it had no strategic value. It had been chosen so that the dead could see their beloved city and also so that the tombs and graves would not be too close, which in summer could be problematic. A fence encompassed the lower slopes of the hill, a thin line of sticks and reed work that kept only the most incurious or overfed vermin out. The cats that lived and hunted on those grounds were far more effective at maintaining the sanctity of the place.

The top of the hill was also surrounded by a fence, a well-built wall of stone. Behind those walls stood the tombs of the city's wealthy and important. The lower slopes were for the rest of the city.

Demok passed through the gate in the lower fence and turned, circling the hill toward the back, where the unmarked graves were.

After a long, quiet walk through the tall, brown stalks of grass, he stepped up to the side of a familiar, if bulky, figure.

"Knew you'd find me here, did you?" asked Tiglath.

Demok said nothing.

"Such a waste," said Tiglath, looking over the graves covered with freshly turned dirt. "So many good people fell. So many more lives ruined and sacrificed to Gilgeam even after he was dead."

"You?" Demok asked .

"I still have nightmares," she said. Then she chuckled. "Smelling fifteen-year-old morning breath is not something you get over easily."

"Your arm?" he asked.

Tiglath looked down at the sling and wrappings that held her arm across her chest and said, "It'll heal with time, but I don't think I'll ever have full use of it again. The chirurgeon set it as well as he could, but I can feel the broken chips in there. Gilgeam didn't just break my arm; he crushed it like a shell."

"I know some healers," he said. "They can help."

Tiglath snorted, "Tiamat takes a dim view of those who resort to magical healing."

Demok considered that, then said, "So?"

Tiglath cast a sideways look at him, then chuckled.

"Yeah," she said, "I guess you're right. I accept your offer."

"Let's go."

"Hold on," said Tiglath. "I'm not quite finished."

Her eyes passed back and forth over the graves one more time, trying to sense the magnitude of loss.

"Any idea where Kehrsyn is?" she asked.

"Jackal's Courtyard," said Demok. "Her favorite."

Tiglath smiled, thinking of the young woman's penchant for performance, and said, "Good for her."

The two turned and left the graves behind, walking side by side, each lost in their own thoughts. As they exited the gate, Tiglath looked up at the sun, squinting against its pale light.

"Spring will be here soon," she said.

Demok nodded and said, "For the kids in the courtyard, it's already here."

The richness of Sembia yields stories within its bounds...and beyond.

LORD OF STORMWEATHER
Sembia
Dave Gross

Thamalon Uskevren II thinks he has a long time before he'll inherit Stormweather Towers and the responsibility such inheritance brings. When not only his father, but also his mother and mysterious servant Erevis Cale disappear, Tamlin will have to grow up fast. To save his family, he'll have to make peace with his brother and sister and face a truth about himself that he imagined only in his wildest dreams.

TWILIGHT FALLING
The Erevis Cale Trilogy, Book I
Paul S. Kemp

Erevis Cale has come to a fork in the road where he feels the pull of the god Mask and the weight of a life in the shadows. To find his own path, he must leave the city of Selgaunt. To save the world, he must sacrifice his own soul.

July 2003

FORGOTTEN REALMS

The foremost tales of the FORGOTTEN REALMS® series, brought together in these two great collections!

LEGACY OF THE DROW COLLECTOR'S EDITION
R.A. Salvatore

Here are the four books that solidified both the reputation of *New York Times* best-selling author R.A. Salvatore as a master of fantasy, and his greatest creation Drizzt as one of the genre's most beloved characters. Spanning the depths of the Underdark and the sweeping vistas of Icewind Dale, Legacy of the Drow is epic fantasy at its best.

THE BEST OF THE REALMS
A FORGOTTEN REALMS *anthology*

Chosen from the pages of nine FORGOTTEN REALMS anthologies by readers like you, *The Best of the Realms* collects your favorite stories from the past decade. *New York Times* best-selling author R.A. Salvatore leads off the collection with an all-new story that will surely be among the best of the Realms!

November 2003

The Hunter's Blades Trilogy

New York Times best-selling author
R.A. SALVATORE
takes fans behind enemy lines in this
new trilogy about one of the most popular
fantasy characters ever created.

THE LONE DROW
Book II

Chaos reigns in the Spine of the World. The city of Mirabar
braces for invasion from without and civil war within. An orc king
tests the limits of his power. And *The Lone Drow* fights
for his life as this epic trilogy continues.

October 2003

Now available in paperback!

THE THOUSAND ORCS
Book I

A horde of savage orcs, led by a mysterious cabal of power-hungry
warlords, floods across the North. When Drizzt Do'Urden and
his companions are caught in the bloody tide, the dark elf ranger
finds himself standing alone against *The Thousand Orcs*.

July 2003

FORGOTTEN REALMS

R.A. Salvatore's
War of the Spider Queen

Chaos has come to the Underdark
like never before.

New in hardcover!

CONDEMNATION, Book III
Richard Baker

The search for answers to Lolth's silence uncovers only more complex
questions. Doubt and frustration test the boundaries of already tenuous
relationships as members of the drow expedition begin to turn on each other.
Sensing the holes in the armor of Menzoberranzan, a new, dangerous threat
steps in to test the resolve of the Jewel of the Underdark, and finds it lacking.

May 2003

Now in paperback!

DISSOLUTION, Book I
Richard Lee Byers

When the Queen of the Demonweb Pits stops answering the prayers of her
faithful, the delicate balance of power that sustains drow civilization crumbles. As
the great Houses scramble for answers, Menzoberranzan herself begins to burn.

August 2003

INSURRECTION, Book II
Thomas M. Reid

The effects of Lolth's silence ripple through the Underdark and shake the drow
city of Ched Nasad to its very foundations. Trapped in a city on the edge of
oblivion, a small group of drow finds unlikely allies and a thousand new enemies.

October 2003

Starlight & Shadows

New York Times best-selling author Elaine
Cunningham finally completes this stirring trilogy
of dark elf Liriel Baenre's travels across Faerûn!
All three titles feature stunning art from award-
winning fantasy artist Todd Lockwood.

New paperback editions!
DAUGHTER OF THE DROW
Book 1

Liriel Baenre, a free-spirited drow princess, ventures beyond the dark halls
of Menzoberranzan into the upper world. There, in the world of light, she
finds friendship, magic, and battles that will test her body and soul.

February 2003

TANGLED WEBS
Book 2

Liriel and Fyodor, her barbarian companion, walk the twisting streets of
Skullport in search of adventure. But the dark hands of Liriel's past still
reach out to clutch her and drag her back to the Underdark.

March 2003

New in hardcover – the long-awaited finale!
WINDWALKER
Book 3

Their quest complete, Liriel and Fyodor set out for the barbarian's homeland
to return the magical Windwalker amulet. Amid the witches of Rashemen,
Liriel learns of new magic and love and finds danger everywhere.

April 2003